RANDOM HOUSE
LARGE
PRINT

POWER PLAY

Also by Danielle Steel
Available from Random House Large Print

DANIELLE STEEL

POWER PLAY

A Novel

RANDOM HOUSE
LARGE PRINT

Copyright © 2014 by Danielle Steel

All rights reserved.
Published in the United States of America by
Random House Large Print in association with
Delacorte Press, New York.
Distributed by Random House LLC, New York,
a Penguin Random House Company.

Cover design: Scott Biel
Cover images: © Claudio Marinesco (couple);
Alan Ayers (background)

The Library of Congress has established a
cataloging-in-publication record for this title.

ISBN: 978-0-8041-2112-5

www.randomhouse.com/largeprint

FIRST LARGE PRINT EDITION

Printed in the United States of America

10 9 8 7 6 5 4 3 2 1

This Large Print Edition published in
accord with the standards of the N.A.V.H.

To my beloved children,
Beatrix, Trevor, Todd, Nick, Sam,
Victoria, Vanessa, Maxx, and Zara,

May the surprises in your lives always be good ones.
And may the people in your lives treat you kindly and fairly.
Any may the choices and sacrifices you make in your
lives be the right ones for you.

May you be blessed in every way, and happy in your lives.

I love you with all my heart,
Mommy/d.s.

POWER PLAY

Chapter 1

Fiona Carson left her office with the perfect amount of time to get to the boardroom for an important meeting. She was wearing a businesslike suit, her blond hair pulled back, almost no makeup. She was the CEO of one of the largest and most successful corporations in the country. She hated being late and almost never was. To anyone who didn't know her, and many who did, she appeared to be in total control, and one could easily imagine her handling any situation. And whatever personal problems or issues she had, it was inconceivable that she would let them interfere with her work. A woman like Fiona would never let that happen.

As she approached the boardroom, her Black-

Berry rang. She was about to let it go to voice mail, and then decided to check who it was, just to be sure. She pulled it out of her pocket. It was Alyssa, her daughter, who was currently a sopho- more at Stanford. She hesitated, and then de- cided to answer it. She had time. The board meeting wouldn't start for a few minutes, and as a single parent, it always made her uneasy not to answer calls from her children. What if it was the one time that something was seriously wrong? Alyssa had always been an easy child, and han- dled her life responsibly as a young adult, but still . . . what if she'd had an accident . . . was sick . . . was in an emergency room some- where . . . had a crisis at school . . . her dog got run over by a car (which had happened once and Alyssa had been heartbroken for months). Fiona could never just let the phone ring and ignore it if it was one of her kids. She had always felt that part of being a parent was being on call at all times. And she felt that way about being CEO too. If there was an emergency, she expected someone to call her, at any hour, wherever she was. Fiona was accessible, to the corporation and her kids. She answered on the second ring.

"Mom?" Alyssa used the voice she only used for important events. A fantastic grade, or a disastrous one, something seriously wrong at the doctor, like a positive test for mono. Fiona could tell that whatever this was, it was important, so she was glad she had taken the call. She hoped it was nothing serious and sounded concerned.

"Yes. What's up?" she answered in a subdued voice, so no one would hear her on a personal call as she walked down the hall. "Are you okay?"

"Yes, of course." Alyssa sounded annoyed. "Why would you say that?" It never dawned on her what it was like being a mother, and the kind of things you worried about, or imagined, or how many things could go wrong, really bad ones. It was Fiona's job to be aware of all those things, and be ready to spring into action when necessary, like the Red Cross or the fire department. Being a mother was like working for the office of emergency services, with a lifetime commitment. "Where are you? Why are you talking like that?" Alyssa could hardly hear her. She hated it when her mother whispered into the phone.

"I'm on my way to a board meeting," Fiona answered, still speaking in a stage whisper. "What do you need?"

"I don't 'need' anything. I just wanted to ask

you something." Alyssa sounded mildly insulted at the way her mother phrased it. They weren't off to a good start, and Fiona wondered why her daughter hadn't just sent her a text, as she often did. She knew how busy her mother was all day. But Fiona had always made it clear to her children that they were a major priority for her, so they weren't shy about reaching out to her, even during her business day. So Fiona assumed that Alyssa needed to tell her something important. They knew the rules. "Don't call unless you really need to, while I'm at work." The exception to that had been when they were younger, and called to tell her they'd gotten hurt, or really missed her. She had never scolded them for those calls, neither Alyssa, nor her son Mark.

"So ask me," Fiona said, trying not to sound impatient. "I've got to go to the meeting in two seconds. I'm almost there."

"I need a favor." It better be a good one, Fiona thought, given the timing, the edge in her voice, and the introduction.

"What favor?"

"Can I borrow your black Givenchy skirt with the slit up the side? I have a big date this Saturday night." She said it as though it were a crisis, and to her it was.

"You called me for that? It couldn't wait till tonight?" Now she was annoyed. "I haven't even worn it yet." She rarely got to wear anything first. Alyssa either borrowed it, or it vanished forever and became only a dim memory in her closet. It was happening more and more often. They were the same size, and Alyssa was starting to like more sophisticated clothes.

"I'm not going to wear it to a track meet. I'll give it back to you on Sunday." **Which year?** Alyssa's notion on the timing of returns was a little vague.

Fiona was going to argue the point with her, but she didn't have time. "All right, fine. We can talk about it tonight, when I get home."

"I needed to know, otherwise I have to go shopping. I have nothing to wear." That was too long a conversation to get into now.

"Fine. Take it. Talk to you tonight."

"No, Mom, wait . . . I have to talk to you about my econ paper. It's due Monday, and the professor hated my topic, I wanted to . . ."

"Alyssa, I can't talk about it now. Later. I'm busy. That's too big a subject to discuss in two seconds." She was starting to sound exasperated, and Alyssa immediately sounded hurt.

"Okay. Fine, I get it. But you always complain that I don't discuss my papers with you, and the professor said . . ."

"Not in the middle of my workday, before a board meeting. I'm very glad you want to discuss it with me. I just can't do it now." She was at the door to the boardroom and she needed to end the call.

"Then when can you?" Alyssa sounded mildly huffy, as though implying that her mother never had time, which wasn't fair since Fiona did her best to be accessible to them, and Alyssa knew it.

"Tonight. We'll talk tonight. I'll call you."

"I can't. I'm going to a movie with my French class, and dinner at a French restaurant before that. It's part of the class."

"Call me after," Fiona said, desperate to get off the phone.

"I'll pick up the skirt on Saturday. Thanks, Mom."

"Anytime," Fiona said with a wry smile. They always did it to her, especially Alyssa. It was almost as if she had to prove that her mother was paying attention. Fiona always did. Alyssa didn't need to test it, but she did anyway sometimes. She just had. **Yes, I am paying attention,** Fiona thought, and hoped Alyssa wouldn't call again to ask for the black sweater that went with the skirt. "I love you. Have fun tonight."

"Yeah, me too. Have fun at the board meeting. Sorry I bothered you, Mom," Alyssa said, and hung up. Fiona turned the phone on vibrate then and slipped it back in her jacket pocket. She had work to do now. No more lend-lease program calls for the latest brand-new, as-yet-unworn skirt. But this was real life in the life of a modern-day CEO and single mother.

She adjusted her face to a serious expression, and walked into the boardroom of NTA, National Technology Advancement, and smiled at the board members gathered around the long oval table, waiting for the others to arrive. There were ten members on the board, eight men and two women, most of them heads of other corporations, many of them smaller and some of equal size. Half of the group was already gathered, and they had been waiting for Fiona, the chairman of the board, and four other members before the meeting could begin. At forty-nine, Fiona had been the CEO of NTA for six years, and had done a remarkable job. She had come in on the heels of a predecessor who had stayed too long and had clung to old-fashioned, minimal-risk positions that had caused a dip in their stock in his final years. Fiona had been carefully selected by a search committee, and lured away from an important job.

She had taken over in her quiet, thoughtful way, had been incisive in her assessments, and bold and courageous in her plans. She took no undue chances, and everything she did was well thought out, her long- and short-term goals for the company had been brilliant and right on the mark. Within months, their stock had soared and continued to climb ever since, despite the tough economy. Both management and stockholders loved her, and she was respected by her peers and employees. Their profits continued to increase. She was merciless when she had to be, but everything she did was meticulously researched and carefully executed, and with their bottom line in mind. Fiona Carson was a star, and had been for her entire career. She was an intelligent woman, with a flawless mind for business. She was one of the most successful women in the country, at the helm of one of the largest corporations in American business, and responsible for a hundred thousand employees.

She chatted quietly with the board members as they filed in. It was still ten minutes before the board meeting was due to start. She usually arrived a few minutes early, so she could talk with them. The chairman, Harding Williams, always arrived just as the meeting was about to begin. He had had a distinguished career in business, though not as illustrious as Fiona's. He had been head of a large corporation for most of his career, though not quite as big as NTA, and he had run it like a dictatorship, which had been the accepted style in his early days. Things were different now, as Fiona tried to point out to him when he made some rebellious move, based on his own opinions and whims. Fiona adhered strictly to the rules of corporate governance, the boundaries corporations and the people who ran them were supposed to respect. And Fiona expected the board to do the same. It caused disagreements between Harding and Fiona almost every time the board met. Fiona very charitably said that they were like two parents, who had the best interests of the child at heart, and that their widely divergent opposing points of view frequently benefited NTA, when they arrived at compromise positions. But getting there gave Fiona severe headaches, and brought out the worst in them both. She respected Harding

Williams as a chairman, and his long experience, but it was obvious to everyone that she loathed him as a person, and he hated her even more. He made no secret of it, frequently making uncalled-for derogatory personal comments about her, or rolling his eyes at her suggestions, while she was unfailingly diplomatic, respectful, and discreet, no matter what it cost her to do so. He hurt Fiona's feelings with the cutting things he said, both to her face and behind her back, but she never let it show. She would never have given him the satisfaction of letting him see how much he upset her. She was a professional to her core. Her assistant always had two Advils and a glass of water waiting on Fiona's desk when she got back to her office after a board meeting, and today would be no different. Fiona had called the emergency meeting, to attempt to solve a problem with the board.

Harding thought the meeting ridiculous and had complained about coming in. He had been retired from his own job for the past five years, but was still a powerful chairman, and on several other boards. He was going to be obliged to retire as chairman of NTA's board by the end of the year, when he would turn seventy, unless they voted to overturn the rule about mandatory retirement age for a board member, but no one had done so so far. She was looking forward to his leaving at the end of the year, in seven months. And she had to deal with him constructively until then. It was an effort she always made, and had for the past six years, since she had come to NTA as CEO.

And she had known for the past six years, since she took the job, that Harding Williams said she was a woman of loose morals and a bitch. He had been at NTA, on the board, long before she got there, and they had crossed paths before, in her youth, at Harvard Business School, where he taught a class during her first year. He had formed his opinion of her then and never changed it since.

Fiona would have been a beautiful woman with very little effort, which she chose not to make. She didn't spend time worrying about being attractive to the men she met through her work. Her only interest was in guiding the company and its hundred thousand employees to ever greater heights. She had long since adopted the style of women in the corporate world. She was tall and thin, with a good figure, she wore her long blond hair in a neat bun, and she had big green eyes. She wore no jewelry, no frills. Her nails were always impeccably manicured, with colorless polish. She was the epitome of a successful, powerful female executive. She was the iron hand in the velvet glove. A strong woman, she did not abuse her power but was willing to make all the tough decisions that came with the job, and she accepted the criticism and problems that came with it. No one could ever see her own concerns about her decisions, her fear that things might go wrong, her regrets when they had to close a plant that eliminated thousands of jobs. She lay awake thinking about it on many nights. But at work she always seemed calm, cool, fearless, intelligent, compassionate, and polite. Her gentler side, and there was one, never showed at work. She couldn't afford to express it here; it would have been dangerous to do so in her job. She had to be their fearless leader, and she was aware of it at all times.

Fiona waited until all the board members were seated, and Harding Williams called the meeting to order, and then he turned to her with a sarcastic look, which she ignored.

"You wanted this meeting, Fiona. Tell us what you want, and I hope it was worth getting everyone to drop what they were doing and show up for a meeting that wasn't planned. I don't see why you couldn't send us all a memo. I have better things to do than run in here every time you get a new idea, and I'm sure my fellow board members do too." So did she, but she refrained from pointing it out to him. And she'd had good reason to bring them together, and she knew that Harding knew it too. He was just giving her a bad time, as he always did. He never missed a chance to put her down. She always felt like a student with him, and one who was failing the course, which was certainly not the case. But nothing showed.

Harding had let slip more than once over the years that he didn't think women should run major corporations, nor were capable of it, and he was convinced that Fiona was no exception. He hated the powerful positions women had today, and it always irked him. He had been married himself for forty-four years to a woman who had gone to Vassar, had a master's in art history from Radcliffe, and never worked. They had no children, and Marjorie Williams lived entirely in his shadow, waiting to do as she was told. It suited Harding to perfection, and he always bragged about the length of their marriage, particularly when he heard about other marriages that had failed. There was nothing modest or humble about Harding, and his arrogance made him disliked by many. Fiona was top of that list.

"I called the meeting today," Fiona said quietly, sitting up straight in her chair. Despite her calm voice, she had a delivery style that people listened to, and she could electrify every person in the room, when she shared some of her more innovative ideas. "Because I want to discuss the recent leak in the press." They all knew about it, and every member of the board was concerned. "I think we all agree that it puts us in an awkward position. The closing of the Larksberry plant is going to impact thousands of our employees, who will be laid off. It's an announcement that will need to be made with extreme caution. How we deliver that message, and how we handle it thereafter, if managed badly, could have a very serious negative effect on our stock, and could even cause panic in the market. And there's no question, even though we voted on it in our last meeting, that announcing it to the public, our stockholders, or our employees is still premature. Now we need time to put damage control measures in place, and I've been working on that full time since we last met. I think we have some very good plans to take at least some of the sting out of it. We **have** to close that plant, for the health of the company, but the last thing any of us wanted was for that to be leaked to the press before we had the details settled. And as you all know, it came out two weeks ago in **The Wall Street Journal** and then **The New York Times**. I've been doing nothing but clean-up ever since. And I think we're all in agreement that the most disturbing thing about this is not just the timing, but that clearly, it was leaked by someone on the board. The information that appeared in the press is only known by us, in this room. Some of it has never been in writing, and there is just no way for the press to know any of it, unless someone in this room talked."

There was a heavy silence, as Fiona looked from one to the other with an intense and serious gaze. Her expression let no one off the hook. "It's unthinkable that that should happen here. It's the first time in my six years at NTA, and I have never had a leak from the boardroom in my entire career. I know it happens, but this is a first for me, and probably for some of you too." She looked at each of them again, and they all nodded. None of them looked guilty to her, and Harding looked seriously annoyed, as though she were wasting their time, which they all knew she wasn't. Clearly someone on the board was leaking information, and Fiona intended to find out who it was. She wanted to know as soon as possible, and to get the errant member off the board. It was far too serious an offense to take lightly or ignore.

"I think we all deserve to know who violated the confidentiality of the board, and so far you all deny responsibility for it. That's not good enough," she said severely with fire flashing in her green eyes. "There's too much at stake here, the health of our company, the stability of our stock. We have a responsibility to our stockholders, and our employees. I want to know who talked to the press, and so should you." Everyone nodded, and Harding looked bored.

"Get to the point, Fiona," Harding Williams cut in rudely. "What are you suggesting? Lie detector tests for the board? Fine, you can start with me. Let's get this over with, without a ridiculous amount of fuss. There was a leak, we seem to have survived it, and maybe it gives the employees we're laying off and the public a little warning. I'm not excusing what happened, but maybe it was not an entirely bad thing."

"I don't agree with you. And I think it's important that we know who did it, and see to it that it doesn't happen again."

"Fine. You can have your witch hunt, but I'm warning you that I won't agree to any illegal methods to determine that. We all know what happened at Hewlett-Packard a few years ago, over the same kind of issue. It nearly tore the company apart, made a spectacle of the board in the press, and its members had no idea illegal methods were being used to investigate them, and the chairman nearly wound up in prison when it was discovered. I'm warning you, Fiona. I don't intend to go to prison for you or your witch hunt. You can conduct some kind of investigation, but every single procedure had better be legal and aboveboard."

"I can assure you it will be," she said coolly. "I share your concerns. I don't want a replay of the HP problems either. I contacted several investigative firms, and will submit their names to all of you today. I want a straightforward, entirely legal investigation of all our board members, and myself as well, to discover who is responsible for the leak, since no one is willing to admit to it."

"Does it really matter?" he asked, looking

bored again. "The word is out, you said you're doing damage control. It's not going to change anything if you find out who talked. It might even have been a very clever reporter who figured it out some other way."

"That's not possible, and you know it. And I want to be absolutely certain it won't happen again. What occurred is completely counter to all our rules of governance, how we run this company and this board," Fiona said, and the chairman rolled his eyes as soon as she did.

"For God's sake, Fiona, it takes more than 'governance' to run a board. We all know what the rules are. We waste half our time discussing procedures and inventing new ones to slow us down. I'm amazed you find time to run the company at all. I never wasted all that time during my entire career. We made good decisions and followed through on them. We didn't fritter away our time making up new rules about how to do it."

"You can't run a corporation like a dictatorship anymore," she said firmly. "Those days are over. And our stockholders wouldn't put up with it, as well they shouldn't. We all have to live by the rules, and stockholders are much better informed and far more demanding than they were twenty or thirty years ago," she said, and he knew it was true. Fiona was a modern CEO, and lived by all those rules that Harding thought were a waste of time. He criticized Fiona often for it.

"I'd like a vote on an investigation to find out who the source of the leak was, using legal methods only to get that information." Fiona turned to the board with her request, and Harding was the first to vote the motion in, just to get it over with, although he made it obvious that he thought it was foolish and a waste of NTA's money, but he made no opposition to her request. Everyone voted for the investigation of the leak.

"Satisfied?" he asked her as they left the boardroom together.

"Yes, thank you, Harding."

"And what are you going to do when you find out who it was?" he asked with a mocking look. "Spank them? We have better things to do with our time."

"I'll ask them to resign from the board," she said in a firm voice and looked him in the eye, and what she saw there was the same contempt she had seen in his eyes for twenty-five years, since Harvard Business School. She knew that in her entire lifetime she would never win his respect and didn't care. Her career had been phenomenal, no matter what he thought of her.

The root of Harding's dislike for her was an old story. She thought of it again after she left him and hurried back to her office, for an afternoon of meetings, that she had to rush for now. The emergency board meeting had taken longer than planned, with their discussions of the investigation, and Harding's interruptions and caustic comments.

In Fiona's first year of Harvard Business School, she had felt inadequate and in over her head, and thought about dropping out many times. She felt less capable than almost all her classmates, most of whom were men, and seemed a great deal more sure of themselves. All she'd had was ambition, and a love of business, which didn't seem like enough to her, particularly that first year. It had been a hard time for her. Both of her parents had died in a car accident the year before, and she felt completely lost and devastated without them. Her father had encouraged her to do anything she wanted, and she had followed through on her plans to get an MBA even after he and her mother died. Her only support system had been her older sister, who was doing her residency in psychiatry at Stanford, three thousand miles away. Fiona had been frightened and alone at school in Cambridge, and many of her male classmates had been aggressive and hostile to her. And her professors had been indifferent to her.

Harding had taken a sabbatical from his career that year, and had been talked into teaching at the business school by a classmate of his from Princeton, and Harding had given Fiona a nearly failing grade. Her only reassurance had come from Harding's old friend Jed Ivory, who had a reputation for doing all he could to help and mentor his students. And he had been incredibly kind to her, and had become her only friend.

Jed had been separated from his wife then, in a stormy marriage. She had originally been one of his students, and both had been cheating and having affairs for years. He had been quietly negotiating a divorce with her, while separated, when he began helping Fiona, and within a month, they were sleeping with each other, and Fiona fell madly in love with him. She wasn't aware of it, but it wasn't unfamiliar ground to him. But it caused talk around the business school nonetheless. And Fiona was re-

motely aware that Harding strongly disapproved. Later, he blamed her for the end of Jed's
marriage, which she had very little if anything
to do with. And her affair with Jed ended
abruptly at the end of her first year when he was
forced to admit to her that he had been involved
with another graduate student, in another field,
had gotten her pregnant, and had agreed to
marry her in June. Fiona was devastated, and
spent the summer crying over him.

In September, when she went back to school,
she met David, the man she would eventually
marry. And somewhat on the rebound, they got
engaged at Christmas, and married when they
graduated, and she moved to San Francisco
with him, where he was from. It seemed like
the right thing to do at the time. But the affair
with Jed Ivory had left her bruised.

It had been awkward running into Jed during
her second year at Harvard. He tried to rekin-
dle their relationship several times, although he
was married and had an infant son by then, and
Fiona managed to avoid him, and never took a
class from him again. By then, she knew that
his affairs with his students were business school
legend, and he had taken advantage of her youth
and vulnerability. She had never seen or heard

from him again after she graduated, but she knew from others that he had married twice since, always to much younger women. In spite of that, Harding seemed to think he walked on water, and chose to disregard his reputation for having affairs with his students. Harding's view of Fiona as seductress had never wavered, although she had been the victim and not the culprit. In his old boy mentality, always partial to men, he still believed that she had broken up Jed's marriage, and had treated her like a slut ever since. He never hesitated to hint darkly at her previously "racy" reputation while at Harvard, and Fiona offered no explanation. She didn't feel she owed anyone that, and had long since come to view her affair with Jed Ivory as an unfortunate accident that happened during her student days, in the ghastly year after her parents died, which he had taken full advantage of as well.

Fiona had nothing to apologize for, but Harding was still blaming her for the affair twenty-five years later, despite her astounding career, seventeen-year marriage and consummately respectable life. If anything, it seemed ridiculous to her, and she couldn't be bothered explaining it or defending it to him. She had been dismayed to find that Harding was the chairman of the board when she took the job as CEO of NTA in Palo Alto, and he hadn't been pleased either, but there was no denying her remarkable skills, impressive work history, and sheer talent, so he voted her in. He would have looked like a fool if he didn't. The entire board said they were lucky to get her, and he didn't want to admit to his personal grudge against her. And Fiona had felt she could overlook his unpleasant style with her. She had, except for the headaches she got after every board meeting. She tossed back the two Advils and took a sip of water as soon as she got back to her desk. She had a thousand things to attend to that afternoon, and gave the green light for the investigation of the board. The firm they hired to handle it hoped to have the information about the source of the leak in six or eight weeks.

By the time Fiona walked to her car in the parking lot at six o'clock, she had had a full day. She stopped at the white Mercedes station wagon she drove, unlocked it, took off her suit jacket and laid it on the backseat, and rolled up the sleeves of her white silk shirt. Without thinking, her actions were the same as her male colleagues before they got in their cars to drive home. She was thinking about everything she'd done that afternoon, and the board meeting, as she drove out of the parking lot and headed home. It was a beautiful May afternoon, the sun was still warm, and she could hardly wait to get home to Portola Valley, where she swam in the pool every day when she got home. She could have had a car and driver, and no one would have criticized her for it, but she preferred to drive herself. She had never been enamored with the superficial perks of the job. She used the corporate jet when she traveled around the country for meetings or to visit plants. But she had never wanted a chauffeur, and enjoyed the time to unwind on the way home. The time between office and home had been particularly useful to her while the kids were still at home. Now, for the past year, she came back to an empty house every night, which was painful, but she brought work with her, and more often than not, she was so exhausted by the time she finished her nightly reading that she fell asleep on her bed with the lights on, fully dressed. She worked hard, but she had always been there for her children, despite her demanding career.

She had always believed that you could have

a family and career if you were willing to put in the time, and she had done it to her children's satisfaction, even if not her husband's, who had resented her career from the time she took her first serious job when her son Mark was three. The three years she spent at home with him had been her gift to her son, and she had worked full time, at important jobs, ever since. Both children had never seemed to suffer from it, and her relationship with them was strong even now. As witnessed by her call before the board meeting, Alyssa called her mother frequently, on any subject, for advice or just to chat. Fiona cherished the warm, open relationship she had with her, and her son Mark. Her dedication to family **and** her career had paid off. She had managed to go to school plays, her son's lacrosse and soccer games, had done Cub Scouts with him, had gone to Alyssa's ballet recitals, helped with homework, and made Halloween costumes for them at two in the morning.

Alyssa was now a sophomore at Stanford, and wanted to go to Harvard Business School after she graduated, like her parents. Mark was in graduate school at the Columbia School of Social Work in New York. Unlike his sister and mother, who both had a passion for business,

Fiona referred to her son as the family saint. All
he wanted was to right the wrongs of the world.
And as soon as he finished at Columbia, he
wanted to spend time working in an underde-
veloped country. He had no interest in business
whatsoever. His girlfriend was a medical student, who had spent the previous summer
working for Doctors Without Borders in Libya
and Kenya, and shared his dreams and altruis-
tic points of view. Fiona loved him for it and
was proud of his goals, and Alyssa's too.

Fiona considered her career as a mother to be
as rewarding, important, and successful as her
professional career. And the one area where she
felt like a failure was in her marriage to David.
Very early on, it had become obvious that it
was a disaster, and she had stuck with it for
seventeen years nonetheless. She had always
wanted to make it work, but David wouldn't
let that happen. He had inherited a modest
family business, and was a small-scale entrepreneur. Fiona's interests had been in major
corporations and the business world on a much
broader scale. He had wanted her to help him
run the family business with him part time
once she wanted to go to work, and she had
refused, convinced that it would be fertile

ground for them to get into bitter battles, with each other and his family, and she was wise enough not to try. And she didn't say it to him, but she didn't find his business interesting enough. She much preferred the harder challenges of big corporations and their impact on the world, and the problems they faced, and their far more engaging pursuits. And already with her first job, she had become aware of David's acute resentment of her success. She came to be the epitome of everything he hated. Not unlike Harding Williams, David used her as an example of everything that was wrong with women in business, and often criticized her for not being at home with their kids, when in fact she was far more present with them than he had ever been. He spent every weekend and two days during the week playing golf with his friends, while she rushed home from meetings to be with her children.

Fiona had covered all the bases, and tried to be a good wife to David, and he criticized her nonetheless. And the final showdown had come when she was offered the job as CEO of NTA. She had been stunned when he demanded that she turn down the job or he would leave her. Alyssa had been thirteen and Mark sixteen then, and she realized that it had nothing to do with them, despite what David claimed. It was all about his ego, and a chance to deprive her of the realization of her ultimate dream. After lengthy debate and careful consideration, Fiona had taken the job and David moved out that week in a rage. She was sad about it at first, but in the six years since, she realized that it was the best thing that had happened to her. No one was criticizing her, battering her emotionally, putting her down, telling her what was wrong with her and what a bad wife and mother she was, or making her feel guilty for her success in the corporate world. She had never made a secret of her ambitions to him right from the beginning, but she had just gotten too big for him. Or maybe he was too small for her.

In the end, although she felt guilty about it, and didn't say it to her children, it had been a relief when he left her. And it was lonely at times, especially now that the children were gone, although Alyssa dropped in often from Stanford, and Mark came home for school vacations, but she loved how peaceful her life had been for the last six years. Sometimes she thought it would be nice to have a man in her life, but so far that hadn't happened, and she was happy with her work and her kids, happier than she'd ever been with David. She realized now how bitter he had been, and how angry, and how much he had resented her for most of their marriage. It was a comfort and refreshing not to be the target of his envy and rages anymore.

He had remarried two years after the divorce, to a very nice woman who suited him much better, but in spite of it, he was still furious with Fiona, and expressed it every chance he got, particularly to their children. David's anger at her appeared to be an eternal flame. And his wife Jenny had the same negative feelings about the corporate world that he did. Her first husband had committed suicide when his career fell apart and he lost his job over an accounting scandal that could have been easily resolved. She married David within the year, made him a good home, had never worked, and hung on his every word. And although he was only four years older than Fiona, he had retired at fifty, a year after he remarried, and he and Jenny spent most of their time traveling the world, while Fiona continued working, loved what she was doing, and maintained her position in the stratosphere of the corporate world. As far as she could see, she and David were both happy now, which seemed like a vast improvement to her, and she was surprised and disappointed that he continued to refuse to forgive her for her failings, and be friends. He just didn't have it in him. And their children were disappointed about it too. It was almost impossible to have both their parents in one room, without their father making barbed comments about their mother, and saying something overtly nasty to her. Fiona refused to stoop to his level and get into his games, and usually chatted with Jenny instead about her latest creative project or their most recent trip. She thought Jenny was a good woman and perfect for him.

And Fiona's own life was simple the way it was. She saw her kids whenever she could, worked hard at NTA, enjoyed friends occasionally when she had time, traveled for business though usually only on short trips, and had long since given up on blind dates arranged by her friends. She didn't have the time or the inclination, and the people they chose for her were always laughable mismatches. She was also well aware that women with careers like hers were not in high demand on the dating market. They were much too scary to most men, and the assumption was always that if she was the CEO of a major corporation, she had to be a ballbuster or a bitch. She wasn't, but few men were willing to find out. She didn't have the energy for dating anyway. By the time she came home from work, she was exhausted, she brought too much work home with her, and it was hard to feel sexy and interested after running a major corporation all day, which had been one of David's many complaints. He had accused her of no longer being a woman. He told her she dressed like a man, thought like one, and worked like one, and if she wasn't reading quarterly reports, she was helping Mark with his science projects, which left too little time for sex or romance. His new wife Jenny had no children, which suited him just fine. He was the only focus of her world.

Fiona still felt guilty over some of the things he'd said. She knew he was right that she hadn't made enough time for romance between them, but bringing up two kids, while fighting her way through the minefields of corporate America, hadn't left time for much else. And with the kids grown up and in college, it was no better now. She had no partner or distractions, worked even harder than before, and filled all her spare time with work. It was something she knew she did well, which was a lot more rewarding than being told what a failure she was as a wife. And she had no desire to repeat the experience again. She was sticking to what she was good at now, working and seeing her kids whenever she could. It worked for her.

She drove up the driveway of the large handsome home in Portola Valley, where they had lived for the past dozen years, and she smiled as she got out of the car. She missed seeing the kids when she got home at night, and having dinner with them, but it still felt good to come home to the house she loved at the end of the day.

She set her briefcase down in the front hall, and went to her dressing room to change. She had long since taken over all the closets. She couldn't even imagine living there with a man anymore, and it was hard to remember when David was there with her. She lived a solitary life now, but one that suited her. In some ways, she had almost forgotten what it was like to be a woman, with a man she loved in her bed. But she had stopped loving David years before he left, just as he had stopped loving her. They had stayed together for the last years of their marriage out of habit and duty, and supposedly for the kids. And then she realized how much happier they all were when he left. Their life together as a couple had been bleak and stressful for years. And now her life was a familiar place, where she was comfortable and in control of her world.

She slid open the door to the patio, and walked out to the pool in a black bikini that showed off her figure. She was long and lean and in good shape, and didn't look her age, and feeling the last of the spring sunshine on her back at the end of the day, she walked down the steps and took off with long, clean strokes down the length of the pool. It felt wonderful after her long day, and suddenly her battles with Harding Williams, her concerns about the employees of the Larksberry plant, and all the big and little aggravations of the day seemed to fade, as she sliced through the cool water. She didn't have everything she had once dreamed of when she married David and had high hopes for their future, but she had what she wanted and needed now: a career she loved, two kids she adored, and a peaceful house to come home to. To Fiona, it was a perfect life.

Chapter 2

Marshall Weston drove home to Marin County a little too quickly from Palo Alto, as he always did, in the Aston Mar-tin that was his favorite toy. He worked in Silicon Valley, and was the CEO of UPI, United Paper International, the second-largest corporation in the country, and he and his wife Liz loved living in Ross. It was beautiful, and they had built their home there ten years before, when their kids were younger. The schools were great, and he liked living a little farther from his office. It allowed him to clear his head on the drive home at night, and he liked Marin County better than the peninsula. It was worth the commute to him.

Marshall was fifty-one years old, and had

worked for UPI for fifteen years, and come up through the ranks in stellar fashion. He had run the company as CEO for ten years now, and made a fortune with them, in UPI stock, and his other investments had done well. UPI had been good to him, and he loved everything about his job. If anyone had asked him, he would have said he had a perfect life. His career was all-important to him, and Liz was the ideal wife for his needs. They had been married for twenty-seven years, and she had turned fifty in March and was still beautiful. She took good care of herself, played a lot of tennis, and exercised every day. She took Pilates classes, and swam in their pool, and she loved their life as much as he did. They had three wonderful children, and Marshall had provided for them beyond her wildest dreams. She had never expected him to make the fortune he had at UPI. She thought he would do well when they married, he had been hardworking and ambitious, even in college, but his success had been exceptional for several years. All their dreams had come true.

Liz had a law degree, which she had never used, and a good head for business. But she had opted to stay home for their entire marriage, and their three kids kept her busy. Their older son Tom had been born on their first anniversary, and he was in law school at Boalt now, and doing well. He was a good boy and got on well with his mother, although he had always been competitive with his father, and more so now with age. He had rivaled his father for Liz's affections when he was little, and had always competed with his father in athletics and every other kind of game. The two men acted like stags in the forest, crashing antlers, confronting each other at every opportunity, which was stressful for all concerned. And as he got older, Tom had been critical of his father and accused him of trying to control everyone. And he was quick to accuse him of dishonesty that Marshall denied and Liz didn't see. She thought Tom was unreasonably tough on him. And as a result, at twenty-six, Tom came home less often now. He was busy with law school, and whenever he came home, he argued with his father about business, politics, and everything his father stood for. Liz was always trying to calm them down, and explaining each to the other. She had been caught in the middle of their macho rivalry since Tom had been old enough to talk and challenge his father on every sub-

ject. She still thought it would calm down in
time, but it hadn't yet. And she knew that Marshall was proud of his firstborn, but disappointed that Tom's criticism of him was so
vocal.

She heard Marshall bragging about Tom to
friends at times, his outstanding grades and
achievements, and wished he would express it
to their son more often. It was almost a point of
pride to Marshall not to say it to Tom, only to
others, as though Tom's academic success enhanced his own achievements, which was something Tom pointed out and complained about
to his mother too. He accused his father of
being narcissistic, and seeing everyone in his
world as an accessory to himself, which Liz denied. But there was no question that the relationship between father and oldest son was not
easy. And in some ways they were a lot alike.
They were bullheaded and stubborn and un-
forgiving. What she didn't like about it was that
the tension between them kept Tom from coming home more often. He showed up for dinner
sometimes midweek when he knew his father
was in L.A. He was tired of arguing with him.
He had great respect and admiration for his
mother, who he thought was better, smarter,

kinder, and more patient than his father deserved. Liz did everything to make Marshall's
life easier for him, in gratitude for all he did for
her, and simply because she loved him deeply.
Liz had been the perfect wife for twenty-seven
years in every possible way. And her oldest son
thought too much so and his father didn't deserve her.

Marshall's relationship with his second son
was infinitely easier. John was the son he had
always dreamed of, star athlete, star student,
model son. At twenty, John was a junior at
Stanford, was on the football team, was getting
almost straight A's, and came home frequently
to see his parents. The strife between his father
and older brother was a source of tension between the two brothers as well. John thought
his father was a hero, and admired everything
he did, and raved about him to his friends. John
thought Tom was too hard on their father.
Where Tom saw him as a sinner, John viewed
him as a saint. The two boys couldn't have been
more different, and John was the light of his
father's life. Marshall took him to football,
baseball, and basketball games, and on hunting
trips, for male bonding. He offered the same
opportunities to Tom, who rarely took him up

on them once he was older. Marshall and John had some wonderful times together, which always warmed Liz's heart. She just wished that her older son would relax and be more open to spending time with his father too, and appreciate him more. She still hoped they would grow closer, and tried to encourage both of them in that direction. But it was clearly easier for Marshall to spend time with his younger son, who adored him unconditionally, and they had a good time together.

The real challenge for both Marshall and Liz at the moment was Lindsay, their sixteen-year-old daughter. She shared none of their ideas, and was constantly at war with both her parents, and she was difficult for Liz too, who had infinite patience with her. Lindsay's current battle was for a piercing and several tattoos she wanted. She had six piercings in each ear, had gotten a nose ring, which her father had forced her to remove, under threat of restriction for the rest of the year. She had recently become a vegan, and refused to eat with her parents, and said that what they ate disgusted her, and she felt sick to watch them eat it. She had a boyfriend who looked like he'd been shipwrecked and had worn his hair in dreads for the last year.

And when she wasn't seeing him, there were others just like him or worse. Lindsay was nothing Marshall had expected of his daughter, and Liz constantly reassured him that she'd grow out of it, and he hoped that was true. It was a lot easier for him to go to baseball games with John, or even argue with Tom about politics, than to deal with Lindsay's constantly rebellious behavior and ideas. She was barely scraping through school, and had been on academic probation for most of the year. She did everything she could to annoy her parents, and argued with her mother every chance she got. Liz was used to it, and tried not to let it upset her, but Marshall admitted to her privately that it drove him crazy and wore him out. Reasoning with her seemed hopeless. She was the most strident dissident note in their otherwise peaceful home life, and it was almost a relief to Marshall when he arrived after work, if he found that Lindsay was out with her friends. The only thing about her that reassured him was that she was not into drugs, but she was incredibly difficult anyway. That would have been the last straw for him. She was hard enough to get along with as it was. The sound of her bedroom door slamming punctuated almost every conversation they had with her. He was used to it by now, but dreaded seeing her at all.

In Marshall's opinion, Liz was not only the ideal mate and corporate spouse, but an extraordinary mother, and had spent untold hours helping and bringing up their three kids. She never complained about what she had to do alone while he was working, the parent-teacher conferences or school events he didn't have time for, the social engagements he couldn't attend because he was at their L.A. office two days a week, or the weekends she had to spend helping him entertain clients from foreign countries, or the parties she had to host to further his career. Liz had signed on wholeheartedly for the role of corporate wife, and he knew he probably told her more than he should have, about upcoming deals or internal secrets, but she gave him excellent advice and he trusted her opinions completely, and she frequently gave him good ideas that he hadn't thought of himself. And in the midst of what she did for him and their children, she did volunteer work at a homeless shelter, and served on several committees. She was tireless in her efforts for the community, and had served on the Ross school board, and participated in their children's activities as well. He couldn't have had a better wife to help him in his career. Both of them were busy, he with his all-consuming career, and she with their children, the things she did to help him, and the volunteer work that was meaningful to her.

Marshall felt as though they were partners in the life they had built together. It was comfortable, warm, and successful. Liz wasn't a passionate woman, but she was dedicated, honest, reliable, trustworthy, and intelligent, and everything she committed herself to, she did well. She served as the role model for every corporate wife he knew. And he was proud to have her at his side when he entertained clients or members of the board of UPI. They ran their marriage like a well-run ship, and she had always been content to let him be at the helm. She had no desire to compete with him or have a career of her own. She never regretted the fact that she hadn't practiced as a lawyer, she just used the knowledge to better understand what Marshall was dealing with every day, while she drove carpool, took the boys to soccer, and Lindsay to art classes and ballet.

Marshall drove into the driveway, parked the Aston Martin in the garage, and let himself into the house through the back door. It was a beautifully designed house with tall ceilings, lovely skylights, a handsome staircase, and antique hardwood floors they'd had brought over from Europe. And the kitchen where he knew he'd find Liz was state of the art, with long black granite counters and all the appliances that Liz had wanted built in, and a glass atrium where they ate their meals most of the time. They only used the dining room when they entertained.

When Marshall walked into the kitchen, Lindsay was arguing with her mother, as Liz got dinner ready for him, and he could smell something delicious being prepared. The subject of their current battle appeared to be a concert at the Russian River that Lindsay wanted to go to that weekend with friends. Liz had already said no several times, and was sticking to her guns.

"Why not? Everyone else is going!" Lindsay said with a look of outrage, as Marshall walked in and greeted both of them. Lindsay ignored her father, and Liz smiled and leaned toward him for a kiss, and then handed him a glass of white wine, and pushed some raw vegetables and dip in his direction, while Lindsay didn't miss a beat.

"I already told you," Liz said calmly. "That's a

heavy drug scene. A lot of unsavory people go there. I don't want you to go." Liz appeared perfectly calm, as Marshall sipped his wine and took in the familiar scene.

"We go for the music, Mom, not the drugs." In her case, that was true.

"I'm happy to hear it. You still can't go. Figure out something else to do this weekend. Besides, you have SATs next week, and you need to study for them this weekend. They really count this year, for your college applications in the fall."

"You know I'm taking a gap year when I graduate," Lindsay said in a dismissive tone, and Marshall looked surprised.

"Since when?"

"I've been saying that all year. You never listen," Lindsay said with a disgusted look, as Liz took a roast out of the oven, and Lindsay made a face.

"I listen, but I haven't agreed to a gap year. I think that's a bad idea." With a kid like Lindsay, who hated school anyway, he was afraid she'd never go back for college. And academic achievement was important in their family. Both her brothers had done well in school, and still were, at Stanford and Boalt.

Lindsay looked at him with total disgust then, and flounced out of the room. The familiar sound of her door slamming was heard a moment later, as Liz carved the roast beef, which looked like a page in a gourmet magazine. Lindsay had already eaten and couldn't stand the sight of red meat.

"I don't know how you deal with her all day," Marshall said with an irritated look.

"She'll outgrow it. It's all pretty typical stuff at her age." Liz looked undisturbed by the exchange with Lindsay, and smiled at him. "How was your day?"

"Interesting," he said, happy to see her. She was like coming home to an old friend, his best friend for twenty-seven years. "The market was up, which always helps."

"I saw that." She mentioned a business scandal in the news then, and a CEO they both knew who had been accused of insider trading by the SEC. Liz was up on all the business news as soon as it happened, and it was interesting to talk about with her.

As usual, she had set the table herself with fresh linens, and he could see from her still-damp hair that she had just taken a shower, and she had put on an immaculate white shirt and perfectly pressed jeans. She still had the fresh girl-next-door looks that she'd had when he married her. She had straight blond shoulder-length hair, she very seldom wore makeup, except when they went out, and her graceful hands had short, trimmed nails. Her one indulgence was manicures and pedicures every week, and she wore bright red polish on her toes.

The meat was cooked exactly the way he liked it, with fresh steamed vegetables. She was careful to feed him a healthy diet and make sure he didn't put on weight, and it was like coming home to a restaurant every night, with all his favorite foods. He hardly even noticed it anymore, but he loved the way she cooked. She had learned that for him too, along with conversational French and Spanish so she could talk to his foreign clients. They were always impressed by how proficient she was, as was he. She even knew a few phrases of Japanese and Chinese. Whatever Liz undertook, she did with an eye to helping him.

They were halfway through dinner when Liz mentioned the film festival she wanted to go to the next day. She knew that cultural events weren't his favorite activity, but once in a while she could convince him to go with her. Marshall preferred business-related events. He was all about his work, and usually so was she, but she enjoyed other things too, with a broader scope.

"I have tickets for tomorrow, in the city. What do you think?" she asked with a hopeful look, and he was quick to shake his head.

"I'm going to L.A. tomorrow. I need an extra day down there this week. We've had some problems in the office, and I think they need the big guns to help resolve them, so I'm going down a day early. Why don't you take a friend?" he suggested, looking relieved. He spent every Wednesday and Thursday in their L.A. office, and had for the past ten years. When they were younger, it gave her time to do things with the kids, and they were used to it by now. He left on Wednesday mornings and came back on Friday nights, in time to do whatever they had planned for the weekend, although he was always tired after his two days in L.A., and liked staying home on Friday nights. "By the way," he added, "I've got Japanese clients coming in this weekend. I'll play golf with them on Saturday and Sunday, and I thought we could take them to dinner on Saturday night."

"Do you want to entertain them here?" She

had a good caterer she used for important evenings, so she could pay full attention to their
guests.

"The Japanese like fancy restaurants, and
they're bringing their wives. I thought maybe
Gary Danko, or the Ritz. Besides, that's less
work for you." He smiled at her as she cleared
the table, and served him fresh fruit for dessert.
"Sorry about the film festival," he said with a
slightly guilty look and she laughed. She knew
him well.

"No, you're not. You hate that kind of thing.
I just figured I'd ask. I'll take a friend." She
had a number of friends she did volunteer
work with, or knew through their kids, whom
she invited to events like that. She could seldom convince Marshall to go. It was the price
she paid for being married to a successful
man, and part of the normal landscape for
her. She was used to Marshall being busy, at
meetings, traveling around the country, or in
L.A., or exhausted and just not in the mood
to go. He made the effort if he knew it was
something important to her. He knew this
wasn't, but it would be fun for her. She was
good about keeping herself entertained when
he was away.

Marshall went upstairs and showered after dinner, and then read a stack of reports he had brought home, while Liz curled up in bed with a book. She had gone to say goodnight to Lindsay, who was talking to friends on the phone about the concert she had to miss, and she had given her mother a dark look but kissed her goodnight anyway. Evenings were always peaceful and quiet in their home, especially now with only Lindsay at home. It had been a lot livelier when all three kids were still there, and Liz missed the boys. She was grateful that they had both gone to school in the West, close to home. At least she had the chance to see them now and then. And she knew it would be much too quiet when Lindsay finally left. She was threatening to go to college in the East, after her gap year, which she wanted to spend traveling abroad with friends. So Liz only had one year left before she had to face an empty nest, and she knew it would be hard for her. She thought that maybe then she'd start spending a day or two with Marshall in L.A. He had an apartment he used there. Liz just never had time to go with him, and he was constantly busy working anyway. And she didn't want to leave Lindsay, at sixteen, alone; the temptation for her to get up to mischief with no supervision would be too great. As a result, Liz hadn't been to L.A. with Marshall in years. She saved herself for his more important trips, like Europe, the Far East, and New York. And with some advance planning, she loved going with him. It was one of the many perks of their life.

It was after eleven when Marshall finally put his work away and came to bed with Liz. She was ready to go to sleep by then too. It had been a busy day for both of them, and he had to get up early the next morning to go to L.A. on the company plane. It was a lot easier for him than flying commercial, and eliminated waiting, delays, and long security lines. He drove up to the plane, boarded, and they took off for L.A. It was a terrific way to travel, and Marshall was never shy about using the company jet. It was one of the many benefits of his job that he enjoyed. And Liz had been on the plane with him many times in the past ten years, and she loved it too. It spoiled you for any other kind of travel.

"I'm beat," Marshall said as he slid into bed with her, which was their code for his letting her know that he didn't want to make love with her that night. He never did the night before he went to L.A., he had to get up too early and knew he'd be tired the next day if they stayed up late. And they never made love the night he came home either. He was exhausted after long days there. Most of the time they made love on the weekend, usually on Saturday or Sunday, if he wasn't too worn out after eighteen holes of golf. And now and then they missed a weekend entirely. But sex three or four times a month seemed about right to Liz after twenty-seven years.

He was sound asleep in less than five minutes, and as she looked at him, in their bed, Liz smiled. He still seemed like a kid to her. He was in great shape, and looked hardly any different than he had when they met almost thirty years before. Since then, he had become her partner, her best friend, the father of her children, and the husband she had always dreamed of. The life they shared was to be envied. Marshall was everything she had ever wanted and hoped for, and more. Even if their relationship was no longer hot and steamy, and they didn't climb in and out of bed three times a day, no one's life stayed that sexual after twenty-seven years. She was realistic.

She had a fabulous life and a husband she still loved, and who loved her. After twenty-seven years, as far as Liz was concerned, that was pretty damn good, and more than enough for her.

Chapter 3

Fiona Carson was swamped on Tuesday morning. She had interviews scheduled with both **The Washington Post** and the **L.A. Times,** to do damage control about the leak that had appeared two weeks before in **The Wall Street Journal.** She was careful not to outright lie about the closing of the Larksberry plant so as not to lose her credibility, and she admitted that it could happen someday, but she said that for the moment, the matter was still under discussion, and at the appropriate time, the board's decision would be announced. She tried to steer the interviewers off the subject after that and stress the progress they were making in other areas, and the positive decisions the board had made on many issues. Given the circumstances, in the aftermath of the leak, it was all she could say. Because of the interviews, which were a minefield, her day had gotten off to a stressful start. But handling delicate situations was part of her job, and she did it well.

She was halfway through her first meeting after the interviews, when Marshall Weston boarded UPI's company jet for L.A., calmly and in style.

He called Liz when he got settled on the plane, right before they took off.

"I'll call you later," he promised, as he always did. He had forgotten she would be going to the film festival that night.

"I won't be home till late," she reminded him. "I'll send you a text when I get home. You'll probably be asleep. I don't want to wake you up."

"I'm having dinner with some of the guys in the office after our last meeting, but I doubt it will go late. I'll text you when I go to bed." It had become a convenient way of communicating with each other when he was traveling, or even sometimes when he was in town. They had picked up the habit of texting from their kids, particularly Lindsay, who texted constantly, and had had a BlackBerry since she was

fourteen. It was her main means of communi-
cation with the world, and Liz found it convenient now too.

The plane took off a few minutes later. There
were twelve seats in the corporate jet, and Marshall was traveling alone. The flight attendant
brought him coffee after takeoff, and had **The
New York Times** and **The Wall Street Journal**
neatly folded on the table next to his seat, although Marshall preferred reading them elec-
tronically. But he spent most of the time reading
earnings reports, and as soon as the plane
landed, a car was waiting to pick him up and
take him to the office. He walked into their
L.A. offices at a quarter to ten, and was in a
meeting twenty minutes later and didn't stop
for the rest of the day. He left at six o'clock, and
had the driver drop him off at home. He had an
apartment in a building on Wilshire Boulevard
in Beverly Hills, and as soon as he got out, he
let the driver go. Once he was in L.A., he preferred driving himself. The driver was useful to
and from the airport, but Marshall kept a car in
L.A., it was an old Jaguar he had bought several
years before. It was perfect for L.A.

He texted Liz and told her to have a good
time at the film festival, showered, and at

seven-fifteen he took the elevator to the garage in the building, got in the Jaguar, and took off toward the ocean. When he got there, he took a right onto Pacific Coast Highway, and headed toward Malibu. The traffic was as bad as it usually was at that hour, but he was in a good mood as he turned on the radio. There was always a holiday feeling to his two-day stays in L.A., and it felt good to be down there, in the warm weather. The city had a more festive feeling than life up north.

It took him half an hour to get to the familiar address. It was a mildly run-down house with white shutters and a slightly crooked picket fence. It looked like a cozy cottage, but Marshall knew it was bigger than it appeared. He drove into the driveway, and turned off his car just outside the garage. There were two pink bikes lying on the ground side by side, and he walked in through the back door, which he knew would be unlocked. It led him past a large, slightly disorderly kitchen, and he opened a door into a huge sunny room, set up as an artist's studio, where there was a beautiful young woman working on a large canvas with a look of intense concentration. Her mane of blond curls was half pinned to the top of her head.

She was wearing a man's undershirt that was well worn and splattered with paint, and she had nothing under it. She had on cut-off jeans that were very short shorts, and she had paint on her long shapely legs too, and rubber flip-flops on her feet.

She looked surprised to see him, and then sat back on her stool with a slow smile. "You're here?" She looked pleased.

"I told you I was coming on Tuesday this week," he reminded her as he walked toward her with a look that drank her in.

"I forgot," she said, but she didn't look unhappy about it. On the contrary, her whole face melted into a broad smile as he approached her, and she put down her paintbrush and wiped her hands on a towel. He was wearing jeans and an open blue shirt, and he didn't care if she got paint on him. It had happened before. She reached out her arms to him, and he put his arms around her, nestled his face in her mane of curly hair for a minute, and then kissed her longingly on the mouth. It was a searing kiss that went right through them both.

"I miss you so much when I'm not here," he said hoarsely as he nuzzled her neck, and she kissed him again.

"You know what the solution to that is," she said softly, but without malice. They both knew that solution, but it had been impossible for him for eight years. "I missed you too," she said, and then kissed him again. There was an over-whelming sensual quality to her that he had found irresistible since the day he met her, and she felt the same way about him.

"Where are the girls?" he asked in a whisper. He lived five days out of every week for these moments with her.

"At the gym with the sitter. They'll be back soon," she said, lost in his arms, as he wrapped himself around her like a snake, and she could feel how much he wanted her, as much as she wanted him.

"How soon?" he asked, and she giggled. She had a wonderful girlish quality to her. She was entirely female, and every inch of her excited him.

"Maybe half an hour," she answered, and with that he picked her up in his arms, and carried her up to her bedroom. She was reason-ably tall, but thin and as light as a feather. And a moment later, he set her down on her bed, tore his clothes off, as she peeled off her an-cient paint-splattered undershirt and dropped

the cut-off jeans and the thong she was wearing underneath. Less than a minute later, they
were both naked and wrapped in each other's
arms, overwhelmed by the passion that had
consumed them for eight years. It had been a
white-hot union from the moment they met.
She had been a temporary receptionist in his
L.A. office, and by the time she left a month
later, they were having an affair, and he hadn't
been able to tear himself away from her ever
since. He could never get enough of her, he was
obsessed with her and always had been. And
he came with a roaring sound that was always
music to her ears. They were both more careful
whenever the girls were home, but now they
didn't have to be and could abandon themselves to each other.

He lay in bed with her afterward, and looked
at her. He didn't know how it could get any
better, but it always did. Just the few days he
spent away from her every week made him fall
in love with her all over again.

"I missed you so much this week," he said,
and meant it.

"Me too." She never asked him how his week
had been, how work was, or about his life in San
Francisco. She didn't want to know. They lived

in the present moment, with no past and no future. Ashley Briggs had become the woman of his dreams.

She was a talented artist, and he had bought the house in Malibu seven years before. She had lived there ever since. They heard the front door slam then, and voices below, and both Marshall and Ashley leaped out of bed and back into their clothes, and then followed each other downstairs with a guilty look. There were two identically beautiful little girls at the foot of the stairs, in gym clothes, with the same lush curls as their mother, and they looked at Marshall with delight and ran halfway up the stairs and threw themselves at him and almost knocked him down, but he was laughing, as he pulled them each toward him with one arm. He was an entirely different man here and had been for all of the years with her.

"Daddy! You're home!" Kendall squealed in delight while Marshall tickled her, and Kezia just clung to him with a happy smile. Kendall was the older of the identical twins by four minutes, and she never let Kezia live it down. She claimed priority in everything by virtue of age, but Marshall loved them both. They were like two angels who had fallen into his life, and

Ashley was the guardian angel who had brought them to him. He had never felt love in his life as he did for her and their girls. What he shared with Liz was entirely different. That was reason. This was love, as he had never experienced it before.

"How was the gym?" he asked them as though he had seen them that morning. The girls were used to his schedule and the fact that he was only with them for two days a week. It had been that way all their lives, and they no longer questioned it. Their mother had told them that Daddy had to work in San Francisco for five days a week, and then he came home to be with them. And the rest of the time, Ashley was alone with the girls. It wasn't always perfect for either of the adults, but it seemed to work. The years had sped by.

The babies had been an accident, but a fortuitous one. Ashley had been twenty-three when they were born, twenty-two when Marshall met her and was bowled over by her. And now at thirty, this was the life she led, with a man who couldn't bring himself to leave his primary family nor his wife. After promising to marry her initially, when she got pregnant, he had decided his kids were too young for him to leave them.

There had been other reasons since. And Ashley was hoping he would finally make a move when Lindsay left for college. It wasn't much longer, and then he would have no excuse. He had also been afraid of the potential for scandal, if people found out about her and how they had met, and the impact it could have on his career. Major corporations didn't always take kindly to their CEOs having flagrant affairs with young women, and fathering children out of wedlock. And the stock market might not like it either, which would be worse. It had been hard to explain that to Ashley, especially when she was carrying his babies. She had cried herself to sleep every night when he wouldn't get divorced. But now, after all this time, his children in San Francisco were finally older, and she knew he couldn't live without her. She was praying that sooner or later, he would leave Liz, and move to L.A.

He had bought her the house to reassure her right before the twins were born, and he paid all the bills for Ashley and the girls. He would have bought her a bigger house, but this was the one she had wanted, and she and the girls were happy there. It suited Ashley to perfection, and he loved staying there himself. It was the coziest place on earth, and even more so when he was in her arms in their big comfortable bed. And yet when he was in Ross, that felt right to him too. He loved Liz and the life they had shared for so many years. In truth, he loved both women and both lives. They were the perfect complement to each other, and he couldn't have said it to anyone, and never had, but he needed both of them, in different ways.

"Do you want to go out to dinner?" Marshall offered, and Ashley hesitated. There was always a slight party atmosphere when he was in Malibu with them, and she let him indulge the girls, since they only had their father two days a week.

"Yes! Yes! Yes!" the girls shouted happily in answer to the question, and they went to a Chinese restaurant nearby that they all loved. And well after the girls' bedtime, they all came home, and Ashley put them to bed. They shared a room on the main floor, below her own. And Marshall went to tuck them in and kiss them goodnight.

"They love it when you're here," Ashley said softly, when he came back to her room, where she was lying on the bed, sated after dinner, and their lovemaking earlier. Marshall had just texted Liz before coming back upstairs, to wish her goodnight, and so she didn't call him when she came out of the theater.

"So do I," Marshall said about how much he loved being there, and Ashley knew he meant it. And then he lay on the bed next to her, looking up at the familiar ceiling. He knew all the cracks in it, and the shadows, and had lain here a thousand times, thinking about her and how much he loved her. He couldn't imagine his life without her now. But when he went back to Ross, he couldn't imagine a life without Liz either. It was the single greatest agony in his life, and he had put off the decision for eight years.

Ashley knew all about Liz, and Liz knew nothing about her. And Marshall did everything he could to keep it that way. For now. He didn't want to hurt Liz, or destroy the love and respect they had shared. But the ramshackle house in Malibu was where he really lived and where he came alive, with Ashley and their girls, who had been a gift to him since the moment they'd been born. He had flown down from San Francisco the moment Ashley went into labor, spent hours at the hospital with her, and was there when they were born, and cut both cords. He had spent two weeks in L.A. then and told Liz they had two weeks of intense meetings that he couldn't get out of. He had stayed with Ashley to help her get settled with the twins, and hired a baby nurse to help her when he wasn't there. And Ashley had cried but been forgiving when he left. She had been very emotional then, during and after the pregnancy, but she had never considered not having his babies once they were conceived. She wanted them. And no one at the office knew what had happened, only Ashley's close friends, who didn't think much of Marshall. He was a man with a double life, which seemed dishonest to all of them. Only Ashley understood and forgave him, no one else she knew did. Her friends knew better than he did how often she cried when he wasn't there, and she kept it from the girls, and portrayed him as a hero, so they wouldn't blame him for their mother's tears.

They made love again before they went to sleep that night. He lay spent in her arms afterward, and drifted off to sleep as she lay naked beside him, in all her glory, grateful for every moment she was with him. She had lived the agony of their situation for eight long years, while he lived out all his fantasies with her. She knew it wasn't fair to her or the girls, but she loved him, and all she could hope was that one day she would win a real life with him, no longer hidden. And for now, she was exquisitely happy and complete for two precious days a week.

Chapter 4

Ashley always felt as though they were a normal family, leading a regular life, when Marshall was with them in Malibu. He had breakfast with her and the girls, and dropped them off at school afterward. They loved it when he did that, and chattered happily in the car with him. He put them both in the tiny backseat space of the Jaguar XKE E-type, and drove them the few blocks to their school, teasing them and telling them funny stories. His relationship with the twins was entirely different than it had been with his other children. The boys had been rougher and sturdier and related to him through sports. And Lindsay had always been difficult, even when she was small. She had been argumentative and often oppositional, and a tomboy because of her brothers, who had always been her heroes. Kezia and Kendall were cuddly, feminine, flirtatious, and totally girls, and as beautiful and bewitching as their mother. Marshall's love for them was an extension of what he felt for her. And he loved how pretty they were and how enamored they were of him. People noticed them and Ashley wherever they went. They were a striking-looking group.

Liz also ran their family so efficiently that there had been little time for whimsy and idle play. Ashley was so whimsical and creative that everything she did with him and the girls seemed enchanting. He couldn't have run his life that way every day, but for two days a week, he felt as though he were in a fairyland with her, and she and their twin daughters were the fairies, and he was the king. It was impossible for him to resist.

He was always in a good mood when he got to work, and rarely stayed late at the office when he was in L.A. He was anxious to get home to her. They usually went out for dinner, or brought in Chinese or prepared food from the grocery store. Ashley was the most exciting woman he had ever known, but definitely not a homemaker or a cook. There was gentle artistic chaos everywhere. And Marshall felt like a boy again when he was with her. All his problems and worries seemed to disappear, and he just wanted to play with the girls and lie in bed with Ashley. It was magical being in her world. And she felt that way too when he was there. He was the heart and soul of all her dreams. In the past eight years, her entire life had come to revolve around him, to the exclusion of all else, except their twins.

Hardest of all was when he left them after breakfast on Friday mornings. He dropped the girls off at school, and usually came back to the house to be with Ashley for a little while longer. More often than not, they made love again, sometimes in haste, before he would go to the office, and then he liked to fly back to San Francisco around lunchtime, so he could spend the last few hours of the day in his office there before the weekend. It was perfectly orchestrated and well organized, but it tore his heart out every time, as the plane took off in L.A. and he knew he wouldn't see her again for five days, four if he could find an excuse to go back to L.A. early, and he felt numb afterward all weekend, which was why he disappeared to the golf course for two days. He had withdrawals from Ashley each time he left her.

By Friday afternoon, every week, Ashley was deeply depressed. She couldn't even send him a text. She had agreed to his ground rules early on, and lived by them. She had to wait to hear from him, and could not contact him in San Francisco or even at the office in L.A. It made her feel breathless and panicked sometimes after he left, knowing he was out of reach and she had to wait to hear from him. What if something happened to one of them? She knew she could call him then, which somehow made it even worse. She couldn't just call him to hear his voice. He always called her before he left the office on Friday afternoon, and from the golf course on the weekend. But the only time she had full access to him was when he was in Malibu with her. The rest of the time, he was like a phantom in her life, and the reality of it hit her every week with greater force as time went by. It was hard for her to believe now that she had lived that way for so long. And at thirty, with two children, she wanted more.

She was sitting staring into space in her studio, with a bereft expression, when her friend Bonnie wandered in on Friday afternoon. She had seen Ashley look like that a thousand times, and knew what caused it. Bonnie hated Marshall for what he had done to her friend, worse yet, with Ashley's full consent. Because of her love for him, and then the twins, she had tacitly agreed to be the hidden woman in his life, and she was no longer the same woman she had been eight years before. She lived for him, and the dream of the future life Bonnie felt certain he would never share with her. No matter what he said to Ashley, Bonnie no longer believed he would leave Liz.

"Hi," Ashley said, looking despondent when Bonnie walked in. She was wearing the same shorts and T-shirt she had worn the day before, because they smelled of him and his cologne. Marshall did exactly the opposite, and changed his clothes before he left L.A., so nothing he wore home would smell of her. Marshall had thought of everything to protect his double life for the past eight years, and he had it down to a science. Ashley had no concept of how careful he was.

"I know that look," Bonnie said with a disapproving glance at Ashley's face and drooping shoulders when she walked in. Ashley had been sitting in the studio in front of a blank canvas, staring into space.

Bonnie was her oldest friend, they had known each other since childhood. Bonnie was a production assistant on feature films. She worked sporadically and was currently between film assignments. She was always ten or fifteen pounds overweight, and hadn't had a boyfriend for a year. It gave her lots of time to hang out with Ashley and the girls. And it broke her heart to see her pining for Marshall, still hoping he'd leave his wife, and giving up her life for him. Bonnie thought he was the worst thing that had ever happened to Ashley, in spite of the enchanting twins.

"What are we doing this weekend?" Bonnie asked, helping herself to a Diet Coke from the studio fridge. She was always on a diet, which rarely worked.

"I don't know," Ashley said, looking vague. It took her two days sometimes to get over his leaving. She never got used to it. And sometimes she didn't get out of the pit till he returned. Bonnie hoped it wasn't going to be one of those weeks. "Maybe it'll rain," Ashley said with a look of gloom.

"Maybe it won't, and if it does, we can take the girls to a movie." She sat watching Ashley for a few minutes, as she tried to gather her thoughts and still couldn't. She was missing him too much. Seeing her that way was more than Bonnie could stand. "How long are you going to let him do this to you?" Bonnie asked in a strangled voice, full of desperation and concern for her friend. "He's been doing this for eight years. You know, he's never going to leave her, as long as he can have you both. And she doesn't know about you, so if someone is going to take a stand, it will have to be you. He'll never make a move until you do." She wanted Ashley to stand up for herself, but she never did. She was too afraid to lose him.

"I can't," Ashley said miserably. "What if he chooses her?"

"He already has," Bonnie reminded her, "by not leaving her till now. He chose a double life. And it's killing you," Bonnie said, looking angry. She was furious at both of them, at Marshall for what he was doing, and Ashley for letting him. She was participating in her own destruction. It was an old story, and drove her insane to watch.

"What if he gives me up?" Ashley looked panicked as she said it.

"Painful as that would be, you might finally find a decent guy, who's actually willing to share his whole life with you, not just two days a week," Bonnie said with a sour look. She always told Ashley what she thought, as a friend.

"His daughter is going to college in a year. I think that's what he's been waiting for. He didn't want to upset her. She's a very difficult child," she said, parroting his excuses. Bonnie had heard it all before, and so had Ashley.

"She's not a child, Ash. As I recall, she's sixteen. And he always has some excuse. The boys, his wife, his career. Do you realize that he hasn't made a single move in eight years? How long are you going to let him dick you around?" Bonnie looked at her in despair. "You're the most beautiful woman I know. You're better looking than most of the movie stars I work with, but you're thirty years old. I've been watching you go through this since you were twenty-two. One of these days, you're going to wake up and be forty, or fifty, and you'll have wasted your whole life with a guy who sees you two days a week, is still with his wife, and keeps you in the closet. Ash, you deserve so much better than that."

Ashley nodded, trying to believe what her friend was saying, about deserving more. But being with him was like playing the slot machines in Vegas. She kept thinking that if she put in a little more time, another month, another year, he'd come around in the end. And instead, even she was beginning to suspect that he was comfortable the way things were. It was easier for him to have them both. And what he really didn't want was to cause a scandal that would jeopardize his career. That was the most important factor of all to him, more than hurting her or his wife.

"I keep hoping some fabulous guy will come along who will sweep you off your feet. But you're never going to meet anyone, holed up here, waiting for Marshall to show up." They both knew that Ashley was emotionally unavailable. She was totally in love with Marshall, even more than she had been eight years before. She had still had her own life then. Now she no longer did. She was soldered to him. She felt completely married to him, and he was married to Liz. Bonnie didn't want to say it, but her worst fear was that to Marshall, all Ashley was was a gorgeous piece of ass. Bonnie didn't trust him farther than she could throw him.

"Why don't we take the girls to a movie tonight?" She was willing to do almost anything to distract her friend and cheer her up.

"Yeah, maybe," Ashley said halfheartedly, but she was too depressed to want to go anywhere and Bonnie could see it. They went through it every week, and usually by Sunday night she felt better and more like herself again. Monday and Tuesday were decent days, and on Wednesday he would arrive and sweep her off her feet again, they would live their fantasy for two days, and on Friday night, Ashley was at the bottom of the pit again. And Bonnie was afraid that one of these days, she wouldn't be able to climb out of it anymore. Marshall was killing her by inches.

They went for a walk on the beach that afternoon, before Ashley picked the girls up from school, and they talked of other things. Bonnie made her laugh, and told her funny stories from the last movie she had worked on, and for a minute or two Ashley looked like the girl she had been before she met Marshall, carefree and beautiful and happy. All Bonnie hoped for her was that she would find that girl in herself again and reclaim her, before it was too late.

When Marshall got back to Palo Alto on Friday afternoon, he went straight to his office. He had two important appointments set up, and his Japanese clients were coming in that night. His secretary had made dinner reservations at Gary Danko for both men and their wives and him and Liz on Saturday, and he had already promised them two days of golf at Lagunitas Country Club, and they were looking forward to it. He was completely focused on his visitors from Japan, and the deal he was trying to make with them. It was an important one for UPI, which was all he could think of as he got to the office. He sent a quick text to Ashley to tell her how much he missed her and to give his love to the girls, and another text to Liz to say he was back, and would see her in a few hours. And after that he went to work.

He didn't think of Ashley again until he was driving home that night. He tried to call her from the car, but she had texted him that she and the girls were going to the movies with Bonnie. Marshall didn't like Bonnie, and knew that she was one of his harshest critics. And he didn't want her influencing Ashley against him. But he also knew that his relationship with Ashley was sound, and she was as in love with him as he was with her. They were linked to each other by the pleasures of the flesh, the passion they had shared for eight years, and their twins who were the fruit of it. And what bound them was stronger than anything Bonnie could say to her. But he didn't like her troublemaking anyway.

And as he crossed the Golden Gate Bridge, he began to think about Liz and the weekend they had planned with his Japanese clients. He knew she would handle it perfectly. She always did. And her finesse in handling his clients and being the wife of a CEO was something he knew that Ashley couldn't handle. She was far too flighty and vague. She was an artist, and a gorgeous, sensual woman. But Liz handled her role as a corporate wife like a profession, with genius and precision. Ashley kept his soul alive, and his body screaming for more. Liz impressed his clients and colleagues. He needed them both, one for his heart, and the other for his career. And he respected Liz in a way that he never had Ashley, and knew he probably never would. Ashley had different talents than Liz, but Liz's skills were essential to the smooth running of his professional life and career. It would have been nearly impossible to choose between them, so he never had, although Ashley had begged him a thousand times to divorce Liz.

But so far he just couldn't. He had to think of more than his romantic life. He was, after all, a CEO. And of the second-biggest corporation in the country. He couldn't ignore that.

When he got home, Marshall was as tired as he always was on Friday nights, after his two days in L.A. Liz expected it, and had cooked a simple dinner. Lindsay was out with friends, and the house was quiet. She knew he was planning to get up early to meet his Japanese clients for a breakfast meeting, followed by a day of golf and a fancy dinner, and he wanted to get some rest that night.

"I think I'll go to bed," Marshall said, with a kiss that grazed the top of her head after he thanked her for dinner.

"I figured you would. You look tired." She smiled at him. "Tough week in L.A.?" He nodded.

"We had a lot of meetings. But everything seemed fine when I left." Liz nodded and watched him go upstairs while she cleaned up the kitchen after dinner. She had been reviewing her Japanese phrasebook that afternoon, so she could greet their guests properly when they met them for dinner. She knew she would have to keep the wives entertained, while the men talked business. It was second nature to her, and she was looking forward to it. She loved being part of his business life, and doing whatever she could to help him. In the end, it had provided her a more interesting and rewarding life than if she'd become a lawyer. At least she thought so, and she knew how grateful Marshall always was for her help.

And as he lay down on the bed, before Liz came upstairs, Marshall sent a quick text to Ashley, just to tell her he loved her, and as soon as he had sent it, he erased it. She knew not to respond, while he was at the house in Ross. And by the time Liz came upstairs twenty minutes later, he was fast asleep. Ashley had totally worn him out the night before. Liz smiled as she got into bed beside him, happy he was home.

Chapter 5

Fiona met her sister, Jillian, for tennis on Saturday morning. They tried to play as regularly as possible, but at least half the time, one of them was busy. Fiona loved seeing Jillian, and they were both strong tennis players and enjoyed the exercise and the time together. Jillian was six feet tall, and as dark as Fiona was fair. Fiona looked like their mother, and Jillian was the image of their father. Jillian was six years older, lived in Palo Alto, and still saw patients at Stanford, as she had since she did her residency there twenty-five years before. She had had a solid and satisfying career and was successful and respected in the psychiatric community. She had published two books for laymen on psychiatric issues, one on the perils of

marriage and how to avoid most of them and
maintain a relationship that worked for both
parties, and the other on navigating the shoals
of depression in the modern world. And she
was currently working on her third book, on
the effects of power and success on both men
and women, and how differently it affected
them.

When they took a break, Jillian chatted with
her sister.

"You realize that you're my model for the female side of the book, don't you? Or one of
them anyway. I've been using you as a guinea
pig for years," Jillian said about her new book.

Jillian had never married and had never
wanted children. She had several long-term relationships, and many short ones, and was
rarely without an interesting man in her life.
She loved men, but it had never even remotely
appealed to her to turn any of her relationships
into marriage. And usually, after a few years,
she moved on, to someone even more interesting and better, after auditioning several new
ones. The men in her life adored her, and she
stayed friends with them long after they broke
up. She had always said that her niece and
nephew, Fiona's children, were enough of a

"kid fix" for her, and she was close to both, and called them regularly to see how they were. She was a terrific aunt, but had always been convinced she'd be a terrible mother. "I'm too self-involved," she admitted readily. "I could never stop what I'm doing long enough to give a child enough attention. Or a man." She had a busy, extremely independent life. And no matter how intelligent they were, she treated the men in her life as sex objects more than equal partners. They were so startled by it, they loved it. She was unashamedly sexual, even at fifty-five.

"Power acts as an aphrodisiac for powerful, successful men," Jillian informed her sister, and then went back to the game, as she sent a crushing serve in her direction, which Fiona missed, intrigued by what she said. "And an anesthetic for women," she concluded, as Fiona listened with interest. "Like you," Jillian continued. "How long has it been since you got laid?"

"You expect me to answer that?" Fiona looked shocked.

"If you can't answer that question," Jillian said smugly, "my guess is you can't even remember the last time."

"Of course I can. It was two years ago," Fiona

said, looking momentarily miffed as they continued to play.

"That's ridiculous, for a woman your age. And you don't look anywhere near your age, by the way. If you weren't successful, you could have any guy you want. The problem is that you're a successful CEO, which scares the shit out of any guy. A man in your same position would have women ten deep lined up at his gate, and be screwing everything that moves. Men in power feel sexy and are driven by sex. Women in the same jobs go underground and forget they're women. Success is very isolating," she said, as the game came to an end, and they met at the net. Jillian had beaten Fiona. She almost always did, except if she was exceptionally tired or sick.

"I'm not sure I agree with the anesthetic part, but it is isolating," Fiona said, looking thoughtful as they both cracked open bottles of water when they left the court, and took a long drink. They always played hard. It was relaxing for them both.

"I don't think women in your position feel sexy, because men don't pay attention to them. They're too threatened by successful women so they ignore them, and treat them like men, which is devastating for any woman's self-image, to be overlooked as a woman."

"Maybe," Fiona said pensively. "I never think about it."

"That's my point. I'll bet you never even think about guys, most of the time. You're too busy working. The male CEOs I know are having affairs, usually with unsuitable women. When was the last time you heard about a female CEO having an affair with a guy she picked up at a massage parlor?" Fiona laughed at the idea, and Jillian looked serious about her theories. "Look at you. When was the last time you went on a date, or a guy asked you out for dinner?" Fiona thought about it, and honestly couldn't remember.

"I don't know, it's been a while . . . a long while . . . but in my case, loss of memory is a blessing. I've had some of the worst blind dates in history."

"So has every female CEO I've interviewed. The good guys are too afraid of them to ask them out, and those women wind up with the dregs who go after them for all the wrong reasons, or some terrible blind dates set up by friends."

"That sounds about right. Why do you suppose my male counterparts have more fun?"

"Probably because they go after it. And a successful man is a hero, particularly one with power. A woman in a powerful position is automatically presumed to be a bitch." It was true, but the theory sounded depressing to Fiona, who had encountered the results of that stereotype too. Most of the men she had met had been afraid of her, and didn't want to get involved. And now she didn't either. She'd given up. "Everybody wants to date a successful guy, they're in high demand. No one wants to date a successful woman, or damn few men anyway. They're too scared. Powerful, successful women get a bad rap. Not every female CEO is a bitch," Jillian said, thinking about it, and Fiona laughed nervously.

"That's reassuring. I was beginning to worry. Am I one of the good ones or the bad ones?" She looked concerned for a minute, as they sat down on a bench with their water.

"What do you think?" Jillian asked with a wry smile, sounding like a shrink.

"I don't know. Maybe a little of both."

"Welcome to the human race. I'm not so charming every day either, and I'm not a CEO," Jillian said as they put their rackets in their cases.

"I try to be strong but fair at the office, otherwise they'd walk all over me, especially the chairman of the board." She thought of Harding Williams as she said it. "But I tried to leave the gladiator stuff at the office and be a woman at home when I was married. According to David, I failed abysmally."

"Look what he married. Would you want to be her? She's a nice woman, but her greatest accomplishment is making three-dimensional snowflakes and Easter bunnies from Martha Stewart's book. Come on, Fiona, you don't want to be that. You never did." She would have been disappointed in her sister if she had. Jillian had enormous respect for her. Fiona was capable of so much more than that, which David had never appreciated. Fiona had always wanted more for herself too, much to Jillian's relief. The two sisters were very different in their lifestyle choices, but they were similar in some ways. Both were high achievers and perfectionists, and harder on themselves than on anyone else, and successful in their fields. And Fiona was powerful as well. Jillian thought it was their way of living up to their parents' expectations for them, even after they were dead. And Fiona didn't disagree. They had both been terrific students in school. Fiona was a gentler person. Jillian was tougher and more direct. And Fiona liked the commitment of marriage. Jillian never had.

Fiona was still thinking about what Jillian had said about David's wife. "No, I don't want to be like Jenny. But I'm not so sure I want to be me either. You'll notice there's no one in my bed at night, or knocking on my door. So something isn't working right. Snowflakes and Easter bunnies are a hell of a lot less scary than a woman who runs a major corporation." Fiona didn't look distressed as she said it, and knew it was the truth, and Jillian didn't disagree.

"That's my point. If you were a guy, everyone would want you. As a woman, it's **much** harder to find a good man. Particularly one who likes you for who you are, and isn't angry about it."

"So what am I supposed to do? Get a sex change to get a date, if I ever want one again?" Fiona was laughing by then. She wasn't desperate by any means, or even interested, but once in a while she thought it would be nice to have someone to talk to at night, after work, or wake up next to on the weekends. It had been a long time. And at other times, she was convinced that she was happier now alone.

"No, you've got to find a guy with guts, who's not scared of you, or your job, who's not jealous of you, and has the brains to look beyond the title on the door." Jillian was serious about it. She thought Fiona should have a partner, a good one, which was easier said than done.

"I don't think that man's been born," Fiona responded. "Maybe I'm too old," she said quietly, and Jillian looked enraged.

"At forty-nine? That's ridiculous. You could live another fifty years. Seventy-five-year-olds date and fall in love. One of my patients got married last year at eighty-nine, and he's still going strong."

"They're retired and not CEOs anymore. I don't have a hell of a lot of free time. And I have a feeling that as long as I'm working, in this job anyway, no guy is going to come near me. I'm not sure I care, in fact I don't, but I think it may just be the way things are. And I'm not giving up my job for a date. My dating life hasn't exactly been stellar since the divorce, which happens to be when I started this job, six years ago."

"You haven't been trying," Jillian said with a disapproving look again.

"I don't have time," Fiona said honestly. "I work my ass off all day. I try to keep up with my kids, and see them when I can. And by the time I read the papers I bring home every night, I'm too exhausted to get up and take my clothes off. How am I supposed to date? And if I have a date, some kind of crisis comes up, and I get fourteen phone calls at dinner. No guy is going to put up with that." And none had in six years. And David had hated it before that, and her as a result.

The men who had gone out with Jillian had been much more tolerant of her and less threatened by her, although she was more outspoken than Fiona.

"The right one will deal with it," Jillian said confidently. "Maybe a guy in the same boat you are." She had thought about it for Fiona before, because she hated how alone she was, particularly with the kids gone now.

"Two CEOs?" Fiona said with a look of horror. "What a nightmare. Besides, my counterparts are dating twenty-two-year-olds. I'm out of the running. And they're mostly go-go dancers and porn stars. I don't qualify. Successful men don't go out with serious, successful women. They know better, or something."

"You just haven't met the right guys," Jillian said firmly.

"Maybe there are no right guys. The good ones are all married," Fiona said simply.

"And cheating on their wives," Jillian said knowingly.

"I don't want one of those," Fiona said matter-of-factly.

"You need to get out more and meet more people," Jillian said honestly. "Just to have some fun."

"Yeah. Maybe," Fiona said, looking unconvinced. "Maybe when I retire." Jillian gave her a dark look, and then she asked about the leak she'd read about in the press. Fiona explained the situation to her and the implications, and told her about the investigation to find the source. She mentioned what a hard time Harding Williams had been giving her, as usual, which infuriated Jillian.

"What the hell is he so pissed about?"

"You forget, he was Jed Ivory's friend at Harvard. He blamed me for getting involved with him, and the divorce, and has treated me like pond scum ever since." Fiona smiled as she said it, although he upset her at times.

"You were a kid, for chrissake. Jed was already separated when you met him, and has he forgotten that Jed knocked up someone else, while you were believing his bullshit to you about it being true love? Please!"

"Harding doesn't believe that and never will. He thought Jed was a saint because they went to Princeton together. Old boys' club and all that crap. Besides, I think Harding hates women, except for the saintly wife he talks about all the time."

"She probably has a mustache and a beard," Jillian said, and Fiona laughed out loud.

"I'll admit, she's not too pretty. But he seems to think she is. So, good for him. I just wish he'd get off my back and stop punishing me for causing a minor scandal twenty-five years ago. It's gotten a little old. I'd practically forgotten Jed until I ran into Harding again. It's such ancient history, it's hard to believe he still cares." But he did, and still blamed her, unfairly.

They chatted a few more minutes, about Mark and Alyssa, and what they were up to, and Jillian put an arm around her sister as they walked back to their cars. Fiona always loved their time together, and valued Jillian's wise advice.

"I really think you're on to something with your new book. I never really think about how different men and women are, in the same position, but I like your aphrodisiac theory about men. I think you're right." She liked less her assessment that power and success anesthetized women and dulled their sexuality, even if for lack of opportunity, but she suspected she was accurate about that too. Jillian certainly seemed to understand the differences of how power affected men and women.

"It's not good news for you, but I think I'm on to something too. I've been noticing it among my patients for years. I can't believe the messes my male patients get themselves into, if they're in the power game. They pull stunts no sane man should ever try, but a lot of them do, and then it blows up in their faces and everyone acts surprised. I no longer am. I wish there were a little more of that in your life," she said, giving her younger sister a hug. She was a good woman and Jillian thought she deserved a good man. It had always been easier for Jillian to meet men, and she was more open to it than Fiona, who was more willing to give up on romance in her life, and be satisfied with just kids and work. "You need to make more effort to meet a guy," she said gently, and Fiona looked surprised.

"Why? I'm happy the way I am. Besides, I don't have time for a relationship."

"Yes, you do. You just don't want to make the effort, or risk getting hurt again." Jillian always told it like it was.

"Probably," Fiona admitted. The last years of her marriage had been so bitter that she had been gun-shy about relationships ever since, and had put more effort into avoiding one than finding one now. And the kind of men who approached her or she got fixed up with were a good excuse.

"There are some good men out there," Jillian assured her. "You just need better luck next time. David was never right for you. It just got more apparent over time. He was always jealous of you and your career. He wanted to be you, he just didn't want to put the time in to do it, and he wasn't smart enough to pull it off so he beat you up for it instead. It's a pretty typical tactic when a woman is more successful than her husband, but it's a cheap shot." He had accused and blamed Fiona for years, as they both knew.

"I think it cured me from marriage forever," Fiona said simply.

"Hopefully not from relationships. I still keep hoping you'll meet the right guy," Jillian said honestly and Fiona shrugged.

"Why? You don't have one at the moment," Fiona said.

Although usually she did. She had taken a breather for the past few months, after her last lover had died suddenly of a heart attack at fifty-nine, and she had been sad about it. They had gotten along well for two years, which was about how long Jillian's relationships lasted. She got bored with them after that and moved on.

"We're different. You're better suited to long-term relationships than I am. I would have killed David after a year for his antiquated ideas and opinions." And she knew that Fiona had endured untold amounts of emotional abuse from him, and still did, for her children's sake. He always had something nasty to say about her, which Jillian thought was pathetic and Fiona agreed. But he was the father of her children so she had to see him from time to time, mostly at events that were important to them, like graduations. He was poisonous every time. It no longer hurt her, but it was petty and annoying, and upset the kids, who couldn't get him to stop either, and they had tried. And even though he was happy with Jenny now supposedly, he was still miserable to Fiona, and resentful of the past. "You got great kids out of it, that's something," Jillian said as Fiona unlocked her car.

"Next Saturday?" she asked Jillian hopefully. They always had a good time. "You can tell me more about your book about men and women and power. It sounds good to me."

"I don't need to tell you. You're living it. I should interview you officially one of these days."

"Anytime," Fiona said, and hugged her, and then slid into her car.

The two women went their separate ways, and Fiona was in a good mood all the way home, and even happier when she found Alyssa at the house when she got back. She was picking up clean clothes and doing a load of laundry while she waited for her mother. And she'd already helped herself to the skirt she wanted for that night. She had texted her mother and knew she was playing tennis with her aunt.

"How's Aunt Jill?" Alyssa asked after she kissed her mother. Fiona was delighted to see her at the house.

"Fine. She's working on a new book about men and women and power. She thinks it turns men into sex maniacs and women into nuns," she summed up, and they both laughed. And it sounded intriguing to Alyssa too, whose dream was to have a career like her mother's, despite the pitfalls and the problems she knew it caused. She thought her parents' marriage had failed because of it, and Fiona wouldn't have disagreed. And neither of them was surprised that Alyssa's brother had opted out of the corporate world completely. It looked like too high a risk to him, and an unhappy life. He had seen the price his mother had paid for her success, and thought his sister was crazy to want that too.

"Can you stay for lunch?" Fiona invited her, and Alyssa nodded. She looked a great deal like her mother, and she was a very pretty girl. Fiona made them a salad, and they sat down to eat at the table by the pool. It was a beautiful day, and Alyssa told her mother that she was dating someone new.

"What's he like?" Fiona asked with interest. She was delighted that Alyssa shared all her secrets with her. She loved being part of her life, and was always happy to make time for her.

"He's nice, he's a junior, he's on the football team. His name is John Weston. And his dad runs UPI."

"Marshall Weston's son?" Fiona looked surprised. She had met Marshall Weston several times at Senate subcommittee hearings in Washington, although she didn't know him well. "His father is the poster boy of what CEOs are supposed to look like, the perfect all-American guy. I think he played football in college too, or looks like he should have."

"I met his dad last weekend," Alyssa said casually. "He says he's a big fan of yours."

"He's just being polite." Fiona brushed off the compliment and searched her daughter's eyes. "Is this serious?"

Alyssa shrugged noncommittally. She hadn't had a serious boyfriend since high school, but something in the way she looked told Fiona that this could be.

"Maybe. It's too soon to know, but I like him a lot. We're going slow. His mom seems really nice, and I liked his dad. He and Johnny are really close. He has an older brother at Boalt, and a younger sister who drives them all nuts. She's cute, just kind of a pain." Fiona laughed at the description. They sounded like a normal family to her. "Maybe I'll bring him by next weekend."

"I'd like that a lot," Fiona said warmly, and they continued to chat for a while. Alyssa was trying to decide on summer plans with friends, and she said Mark was talking about going to Africa with his girlfriend in August, but he hadn't made up his mind yet. And Fiona had invited both of them to Malibu in July. She had rented a house for three weeks, and they were all looking forward to it. They did it every year. Alyssa said Johnny might come for a weekend, which sounded good to Fiona too. She wanted to get to know him.

Alyssa left when her laundry was ready and promised to drop by sometime that week. Fiona loved that she still came by the house often to see her mother. Her life would have been empty without her children. And as she stretched out that afternoon by the pool with some of the work she'd brought home to read, she thought of her sister and what she'd said to her that morning, about making an effort to find the right man to share her life with. It was hard to imagine finding such a man, and being willing to let him into her life if she did. Her life was so much simpler like this, and she had all the closets. No one was torturing her or blaming her for anything. No one was angry about her career or telling her what she was doing wrong. Fiona couldn't imagine dealing with any of it again. For the past six years since her divorce, her life had been lonely at times, but it was so peaceful. She realized that she was perfectly content just as she was, and the last thing she wanted at this point in her life was a man, to complicate her life. She was much happier alone, which proved Jillian's theory. Fiona had been anesthetized by her success. The part of her heart that used to want a man in her life had gone totally, completely numb, or died. And Fiona didn't mind a bit.

Chapter 6

Marshall and Liz's dinner for his Japanese clients at Gary Danko went off without a hitch, and their guests loved it. The food was exquisite as always, and the men talked business all night, while Liz engaged their wives in conversation, and used the Japanese phrases she'd learned. Marshall was very pleased with the results of the evening, when they drove back to Marin that night after dinner. And he filled Liz in on what the men had discussed. She had listened with half an ear but couldn't follow the conversation closely while talking to the two wives.

"I think we cemented the deal tonight," Marshall said, looking pleased as they got to Ross. And Liz had been perfect, charming, respectful, discreet. She had handled it flawlessly, just as she always did, and he was grateful to her. And when they went to bed that night, he made love to her, as much out of gratitude and a sense of duty, as out of love. He felt he owed her a lot for the evening. She was the perfect wife for his career, and she made him happy in many ways. And he wanted to make love to her to thank her, but as soon as he had, he felt a pang of missing Ashley so severe that it nearly choked him. All he could think of as he held Liz was the woman he had loved in L.A. for the past eight years. He knew every inch of her body, and every ounce of her soul, and she filled him with such desire and longing that he could hardly keep himself from calling her late that night, just to hear her voice.

Everything he felt for Liz was so different. He was grateful for all the things she did for him, to make his life run smoothly, but Ashley was the enchantress who put excitement and spice in his life, and her loving was so tender. After nearly thirty years, his lovemaking with Liz was familiar and mechanical. With Ashley it was fire, and she was twenty years younger than Liz. Being with her made him feel young too, with their little girls close by, who were so thrilled to see him whenever he came home. When he was with Liz, he felt old. But he was constantly aware that he needed them both, in different ways. Neither of them would have been enough on her own.

He lay awake late into the night after they made love, and he finally sent Ashley a text from his bathroom. It was full of all the steamy desire he was feeling for her, and he could hardly wait to see her on Wednesday and make love to her again.

And on Sunday morning he played golf with the two Japanese men for the second time. And when he left them on Sunday afternoon, they confirmed to him that the deal had been made. It had been a very successful weekend, and he told Liz when he got home. She was pleased and proud of him. She always was.

John came home for dinner that night and brought Alyssa with him, and both his parents liked her very much as they got to know her better. And even Lindsay the Terrible pronounced her "cool." She and Alyssa had a long talk about rap music, and Lindsay was impressed by how much she knew. And on the way back to Stanford with John, Alyssa laughed about it and told him his sister was a sweet kid.

They sat in his car talking and kissing for a long time when they got back to the campus, before Alyssa went back to her dorm and he to his apartment. Their relationship was going well. And she liked his family a lot. It made her miss having parents who liked each other and got along, which was something she'd never had. The Westons seemed like the perfect couple, and it made her sad for what she didn't have and never would. She thought John was blessed to have parents who were so loving to each other.

Alyssa called her mother to tell her about it on Monday at the office, and Fiona was having an insane day. She had a run-in with Harding Williams when she called him to report on the investigation, and he referred to it as her witch hunt again. She lost her temper with him, and was then furious at herself for doing so. She was so tired of his arrogance and pompous attitude with her. She had almost called him an old fool, but had restrained herself. And she was aggravated with herself for letting him get to her. In the end, with one thing and another, it was a stressful day. A typical one for a CEO. Not every day was fun. But she enjoyed hearing from her daughter, even in the midst of it, and took the time to listen to her about her date with John the day before. And it confirmed her good opinion of Marshall Weston if he had such a solid family and nice kids. He was obviously a good guy, which was nice to know, and she was looking forward to meeting his son.

Marshall's day hadn't been nearly as stressful as Fiona's. He was pleased with the Japanese deal he had sealed over the weekend. It was an important one for UPI, and he knew the board and stockholders would be pleased. It had been difficult to consummate for months, and was a major coup for him. He had just finished dictating a report about it to the chairman of the board when Simon Stern, their chief in-house counsel, called and asked him if he could come up to Marshall's office to see him. Marshall told him that he could, and had just finished for the day when Simon walked in, and chatted with him for a few minutes before discreetly closing Marshall's office door. Marshall couldn't imagine why he'd come, or why he appeared so secretive about it.

As soon as he had closed the door, Simon gazed at Marshall across his desk with grave concern.

"We have a problem," he said, looking Marshall in the eye. He seemed nervous about what he was about to say, as Marshall waited to hear. What he heard next had been the furthest thing from his mind and took him by surprise.

"We got a call from an attorney today," Simon explained cautiously, not wanting to anger the CEO. He had no idea what his reaction would be, and he didn't like being the bearer of bad news. "And apparently, a former employee, a woman named Megan Wheeler, is going to sue you for sexual harassment and wrongful termination. She claims she had an affair with you two years ago, and she says you got her the job and then she believes you had her fired when she ended the affair." Simon Stern sat looking at him, and waited for Marshall's reaction. Marshall looked like someone had just exploded an atom bomb in his lap. He stared at the attorney in total disbelief.

"Are you serious? Is she insane?" He looked horrified by what the attorney had said, and completely shocked.

"She may be," Simon said, looking hopeful,

still praying it would all go away, but suits like
that rarely did. Even if you didn't believe the
"where there's smoke there's fire" theory, in his
experience women who brought sexual harassment suits were very determined about it, and
didn't just disappear. They were usually scorned
women who wanted to get even for something,
either a badly handled affair or advances that
had not been returned. Either way, they were
zealous about it most of the time and always
wanted vengeance and big money. "Do you
know who she is?"

"I vaguely remember the name," Marshall admitted. "I think we hired her to do some client
events, but I certainly never had an affair with
her. I don't even remember what she looks like.
I think she is some kind of party or event planner. We may have put her on staff for a while
after the events, and then I lost track of her."

"She says you had an affair with her for eight
months, and met her at a hotel repeatedly. And
when she wanted to break it off, you got her
fired. And yes, she's a corporate event planner. I
don't know why we would have put her on staff
instead of keeping her as an independent con-
tractor. She said you suggested the job to her.
She got a damn nice salary for it too. I checked

with HR, and she was on the payroll for seven months, and then we let her go. Her story matches up with her employment dates, as far as the timing goes."

"I can promise you, I never slept with her," Marshall said with a look of desperation. He could see his whole career flashing before his eyes, and about to end in disgrace.

"She says she has documentation to prove your involvement with her, e-mails and letters from you, I think, where she claims you made sexual references and offers to her." He couldn't imagine that Marshall would have been that stupid, even if he had slept with her, but he had to report to him what her attorney claimed. "It gets more complicated than that. Apparently, she's a breast cancer survivor, which she says you knew, and the laws about firing cancer survivors are even tougher than sexual harassment. If that's true, she has us over a barrel, and this won't look good in the press." Their house counsel was obviously worried, and Marshall looked sick.

"The woman is lying. I've never written letters to anyone, making sexual offers. Why would I do something like that?"

"It didn't sound right to me either. We'll see

what she's got. She may have written them herself. If so, hopefully we can prove it and scare
her off. But for now, they're being aggressive in
the initial attack. Her lawyer sounds like a
nasty piece of work. He's probably a contin-
gency lawyer, and figures that we'll settle. And
if there's any truth to this, we will, with the
board's approval, of course. They're not going
to want something like this surfacing in the
press. Her attorney says they're serving us next
week. I think we need to talk to Connie about
this as soon as possible." Connie Feinberg was
the chairman of UPI's board. She was a reasonable woman and Marshall liked her, but he
had no idea how she would react, and neither
did Simon Stern. They had never faced a suit
like this at a CEO level before. It was new to
them, and to Marshall, whose reputation had
been squeaky clean till then. Simon knew he
was married, a family man, and devoted to his
wife and kids. This was going to be hard on
them.

"What does she want?" Marshall asked in a
choked voice. This was not what he wanted
happening in a thus-far-flawless career. He had
visions of being fired, and his career and reputation destroyed. He was on the verge of tears,

particularly when he thought of the impact on Liz and his kids.

"She wants a million dollars. Her attorney says they're suing us for five, but he was pretty clear that she'll settle for one. Something tells me she's not going to let it go. And he insists it's a valid claim," Simon said unhappily.

"I can tell you that it's not. I never slept with this woman. There was no affair. I remember who she was now. She looked like a cheap floozy, but she did several good events for us. I had no idea we even hired her. And I never saw her after the events."

"I'm sure you didn't, Marshall," the attorney reassured him. "I'm sorry this has come up. Unfortunately, it's part of the modern world, and there are some very dishonest people out there. We're all targets for it, particularly in your position." Marshall nodded, feeling sick. And as well as Connie, he would have to warn Liz, in case it appeared in the press. And eventually he'd have to tell Ashley too. And his children. It was a nightmare waiting to happen, and all he wanted to do was wake up.

"I'll give Connie a call. What do we do now?" Marshall asked in a tense voice.

"If there is any truth to it, negotiate like crazy.

And if not, just wait and see what she does. Her lawyer said he'd send over copies of the correspondence she claims to have from you, and apparently there are some photographs too. It's probably all bogus. You're not the first CEO this has happened to, and you won't be the last. We're not going to negotiate with her if it's not true, unless the board thinks we should. We need some guidelines from them." Marshall nodded, and a moment later the attorney left his office and promised to keep him informed.

Marshall sat for a long moment at his desk, with tears in his eyes, and then he called Connie Feinberg at home. She had run a large, respected family-owned corporation for many years. She was a smart woman and an excellent chairman of the board. She was surprised to hear from Marshall, and even more so when he told her what was happening. She sounded upset, but not shocked. She had known of situations like this before. Her own brother had been sued for sexual harassment, so this wasn't entirely unfamiliar to her. And he had won. His accuser had been discredited and withdrawn the suit.

"I can promise you it's not true," Marshall said in an anguished tone.

"I appreciate your calling me, Marshall," she said kindly. "And I'm very sorry to hear about this. At least she's not claiming you raped her, and bringing criminal charges against you. I've heard of that happening too. With luck, she'll go away without making too much fuss. And even if there's no truth to it, it may be smarter for us to negotiate with her and settle for some reasonable amount, just to make her go away. If we do, it's giving in to extortion, but sometimes it's smarter to just pay up to protect your reputation, and ours, rather than getting into a swearing contest with some greedy nutcase who may try to take it all the way in court. I'll arrange a conference call with the board, and let you know how they feel about it. My recommendation would be to pay her off and shut her up before this goes any further."

"But wouldn't that imply that it's true?" Marshall asked. "I don't want to admit guilt for something I didn't do. I have my family to think of too. And UPI, of course. It breaks my heart to cause a problem like this, and it makes me sick to think of costing the company blood money this woman doesn't deserve."

"Sometimes that's the way our legal system works," Connie Feinberg said practically. They both knew that settling lawsuits, whether legitimate or not, was commonplace. She was a sensible woman and not easily shocked. "You've been a wonderful asset to this company for fifteen years, ten of them as CEO, and we have an obligation to protect you from people like this. We don't want your reputation hurt any more than ours. And I'm sure this is very distressing to you, your family, and your wife."

"I haven't told her yet. I just found out ten minutes ago. I called you first," Marshall said, and Connie thanked him for calling her so quickly.

"Let's just see where this goes, but I think Simon should be prepared to negotiate whatever deal he can, if you'll agree to that."

"I'll do whatever is best for UPI," he said in a somber tone, and she thanked him again for letting her know, and promised to call him after her conference call with the board.

He felt dazed as he drove home to Marin County, and wondered what he should tell Liz. Mercifully, Lindsay was out, having dinner at her boyfriend's house, and Liz took one look at him when he walked in and knew something terrible had occurred. He was fighting back tears, and broke down in sobs at the kitchen table when he explained the situation to her.

"I don't understand how something like this can happen. I never even spoke to the woman, and now she's claiming we had an affair and I had her fired. She even said I got her hired by UPI. I barely remember who she is. And the last thing I'd ever want to do is hurt UPI, and you, and our kids." He was completely unglued by the accusation, and Liz held him in her arms while he cried. It took him half an hour to regain his composure, and Liz assured him that she didn't believe a word of the woman's claim.

"We'll see it through, Marsh, whatever it takes. You know you didn't do it." She had total faith in him, and he could see it, which was comforting for him. They were sitting at the kitchen table holding hands when Connie Feinberg called him, after talking to the other members of the board.

"I just want to assure you, Marshall, that the board will back you one hundred percent. You're too important to us to let you down on something like this. We'll do whatever it takes. I'll speak to Simon myself tomorrow. And we're all in agreement, we want to negotiate with this woman as soon as possible, and buy out of this mess as quickly and as quietly as we can. We don't want to get aggressive with her, and have her go to the press."

"I can't thank you enough," Marshall said in a voice filled with gratitude and emotion.

He and Liz talked about it quietly until Lindsay came home, and then they went upstairs to bed. They didn't say anything to her, and agreed that it was too soon to say anything to the children, and there was no point upsetting them if the matter could be handled internally without the public ever finding out.

It was the worst thing that had ever happened to him, and he was terrified that his career was about to go down the tubes and everything he had built for UPI, and personally, would be destroyed. He was horrified by his accuser's claims and badly shaken. He hardly slept that night and was awake before dawn. He lay there for a long time, not wanting to disturb Liz, and then got out of bed and stood and watched the sun come up.

"You're up?" Liz asked when she saw him and he nodded.

"I'm scared," he said softly.

"You'll be okay," she said, coming to stand with him, and put her arms around him.

"I don't deserve you," he said humbly.

"Yes, you do," she insisted, and believed it with her whole heart.

Liz held him in her arms again for a long moment before he left for work that day, and assured him of how much she loved him, and that he had her full support. She never wavered for an instant, and he thanked her again. And on the way to work that morning, in the Aston Martin, Marshall took comfort in knowing that the board was behind him, and trusted him. He knew that despite what had happened, he was a lucky man. And all he wanted to do now was get this over with and put it behind him as fast as he could.

Chapter 7

Marshall didn't leave for L.A. on Wednesday that week. Instead, two days after he learned of Megan Wheeler's accusation, she and her attorney came to a conference room at UPI in the morning, to meet with Marshall and Simon Stern. She sat across the table from Marshall and her eyes bored into his. Her attorney repeated her accusation, and stuck to her story about their affair. She didn't hesitate or even appear nervous as she listened to what he said and nodded confirmation. She did not try to avoid Marshall's eyes, and she wore a tight black dress and stiletto heels to the meeting. She had made no attempt to look demure, and had done everything possible to show off her spectacular figure. She looked racy and overdressed for an early-morning business meeting, but she was also very attractive. She was a good-looking woman, somewhere in her late thirties. And halfway through the meeting, her attorney handed a manila envelope to Simon Stern, after reiterating the damages his client had sustained from being fired from her job. He claimed that she had closed her own party-planning business after being hired by UPI, and had been unable to get it going again, after she was let go. And he spoke of her emotional distress from their affair, as the muscles tensed in Marshall's jaw.

Simon carefully opened the envelope and took two letters out of it, and copies of several e-mails, all allegedly written to her by Marshall. He read them expressionlessly, and then handed them to Marshall for him to read as well. The letters were written on a computer, and none of the missives were personally signed.

"How do we know Ms. Wheeler didn't write these herself, to falsely incriminate Mr. Weston?" The letters were full of sexual references to nights they had spent together, and the sexual acts they had engaged in. They were painfully explicit. And then her attorney handed Simon the pièce de résistance, a smaller envelope that contained two photographs of Marshall's accuser stark naked in suggestive positions, taken by a man you could see clearly in a mirror. It appeared to be Marshall, equally naked, and another one of him alone, also naked, and apparently asleep on a bed. It was undeniable evidence that they had been together in a sexual way. Simon handed the photographs to Marshall without a word. And nothing about the photographs appeared to have been doctored. They were taken with a proper camera, not her cell phone, and the man in the photographs was Marshall.

Marshall's face was pale as he sat across the table from her with no sign of acknowledgment or recognition. And she met his eyes without flinching. This was business to her and nothing else. There was no talk of broken promises, broken hearts, or unrequited love. This was blackmail, pure and simple. They had had sex with each other, he had hired and then fired her, and she was seeking revenge. Her anger had a price, a big one.

Simon reacted immediately, as he put the photographs back in the envelope. They were only copies, and it was obvious that she had kept the negatives. They were the best bargaining chip she had.

"We are prepared to offer Ms. Wheeler a million dollars for her time and trouble, in exchange for complete confidentiality about this affair and a retraction of her accusations against Mr. Weston," Simon said to her attorney. The board had given their permission to go as high as two million. Marshall was worth it to them, as the most competent CEO they'd ever had. He was the best thing that had ever happened to UPI. They didn't care if he was innocent or guilty, all they wanted was for Megan Wheeler to disappear, preferably before she went to the press. She had waited just over a year to come forward after the affair ended and she'd been fired. And the attorney she had consulted had convinced her to threaten a suit, and shoot for a handsome settlement. Her attorney looked unimpressed by Simon's offer, and then gave them another piece of stunning news.

"I think we should tell you that we issued a statement to the press this morning, that Mr. Weston had an affair with my client and caused her to be fired from UPI after she ended it, and we are suing for sexual harassment and damages." It was a simple factual statement of their intentions, devoid of emotion. The attorney looked sleazy but was smart, and so was Megan Wheeler.

Marshall looked instantly ill, and Simon tried not to react and didn't glance at his client.

"That seems like an extremely unwise thing to have done, and premature, while we are trying to negotiate with you in good faith."

"There is no good faith here," her attorney said bluntly. "Your client had sex with mine, as CEO of this company. He used his influence and power to get her hired, possibly to induce her to have sex with him, and then to get her fired when she stopped. And she had had chemotherapy and radiation for breast cancer six months before, which she told him. It seems pretty clear cut to me. She is a cancer survivor, and he took gross advantage of her."

"What seems clear cut to me is that Ms. Wheeler wants to be paid a great deal of money for having had sex with my client. There's a name for that. Extortion, or worse," Simon said with a steely look at the opposing attorney. "And giving a statement to the press about it is only going to make this harder. You've already damaged my client's reputation. Why should we pay you anything now?" He had a point. "If we agree to pay your client anything, we will expect her to recant what she said, and admit publicly that her claims against Mr. Weston were false. We will want the negatives of those photographs and the original letters. And we will offer her two million, and that's our final offer." Simon Stern seemed as though he meant it and gave Marshall a look that told him to remain silent. And Marshall could see pleasure register in Megan Wheeler's eyes. She saw pure hatred in his. They never exchanged a word.

"Your CEO's reputation should be worth a lot more," the lawyer said, trying to figure out how far he could go, but he hit a wall with his tactic. Simon had run out of patience. He wasn't happy with the situation Marshall had put them in, but it was his job to get him out of it, not to pass judgment, which was also the wish of the board, which had vowed to support Marshall against the claim.

"We don't pay blackmail," Simon said quietly. "We negotiate. We just did. Two million, and that's it, or we'll go to trial on this, and win." With the photographs he knew they wouldn't. Simon was bluffing, but he wouldn't budge an inch. And Megan Wheeler didn't want to take the chance of losing the money, nor did her lawyer.

"As a breast cancer survivor, I think Ms. Wheeler deserves at least three."

"He didn't give her cancer," Simon said as he stood up and signaled to Marshall to do the same. The meeting was over. They started to leave the conference table, and the other lawyer looked at his client and she nodded. She wanted the money. Two million was enough for her.

"We accept your offer," her lawyer said quickly.

"I assume the story is all over the press and the Internet by now. I expect a full retraction from your client by end of business today," Simon said coldly. "With a signed confidentiality agreement," he added.

"As soon as we have the check," the attorney said, and stood up too.

"I'll take care of it right away," Simon said, and left the room with Marshall just behind him. They rode up in the elevator in silence, and didn't speak until they got to Marshall's office.

"I'm sorry," Marshall said in a choked voice to the attorney. "I had no idea she had those pictures. I must have been drunk out of my mind. Maybe she drugged me," he said weakly, and Simon didn't comment. She hadn't drugged him for eight months, or forced him to give her a job. It was a nasty situation and had just cost UPI two million dollars for his little fling. Personally, he didn't like what had happened, nor Marshall lying to him about it, but it was not his place to judge him, just to solve the problem. "I'll call Connie right away," Marshall said quietly as Simon nodded and left his office. He had to draw up the agreement for Megan Wheeler to sign. He had promised to messenger it to her attorney's office by that afternoon.

Calling Connie Feinberg to tell her what had happened was one of the worst calls Marshall had ever made. He had no choice now but to tell her the truth, and he offered to pay the two million dollars himself.

"If you do, it will eventually come out that you did, and that will implicate you further and cause a bigger scandal. I think our only recourse here is to pay her the money, and have her retract her accusations publicly. It makes more sense for UPI to settle with her than for you to do it. Corporations settle legal claims to avoid lawsuits, whether bogus or not. If you pay her, it sounds like blackmail. If we pay her, you won't look as guilty, it's just another lawsuit.

We can take it out of your bonus at the end of the year, if that's what the board decides and you're amenable to it." It was a rap on the knuckles, instead of something far worse, and sounded reasonable to him, and he was more than willing to lose two million of his annual bonus to save his neck and career, and grateful for it. "I think, more than likely," she said quietly, "the board will decide that this episode is the price to pay for an exceptionally competent CEO. These things have happened at other companies, and everyone survives. People will forget it in the end." Her voice was cool and calm. It was obvious that she wasn't happy with the situation, but the board had agreed to support him unconditionally, and she was relieved it hadn't cost them more, which it easily could have, if the Wheeler woman and her attorney had been even greedier.

"I don't know how to tell you how grateful I am, and how sorry. I promise you that nothing like it will ever happen again."

"I'm sure it won't," she said kindly. "I know that these things happen. But let's hope it never does again. It was an expensive mistake. I'm going to have Simon write the statement for her to give to the press, retracting her accusations."

"I think he's working on it now."

"We'll have to let the stockholders know that we paid her a settlement to avoid the time, expense, and bad publicity of a lawsuit. And she retracted her false claims, and we're considering the expense an early installment of your bonus, from what you'd get at the end of the year anyway." It was far less than his projected bonus, so it shouldn't upset anyone unduly. What he wanted to be sure of now was that Liz would never know his accuser's claims had been true. He could tell Liz that they had been forced to settle with her to avoid further scandal and a lengthy lawsuit. But he would say nothing about the photographs and letters. There was no reason Liz would ever know, and his reputation would be salvaged. All they had to live through now was the scandal in the press for a few hours until she made her statement, hopefully by the end of the day.

He called Liz after he spoke to Connie, and warned her that there would be some ugly stories in the press that day, as part of the pressure Wheeler was putting on him to settle, but they would be recanted by tonight or tomorrow, and the threatened suit had been settled, and she had gotten honest and was retracting her claim.

"Is everything okay?" Liz asked, sounding panicked.

"It will be soon. She wouldn't back down unless we paid her a settlement. It's extortion, but the board doesn't want to deal with a lawsuit, even if we won. It will all be over soon. And you'd better warn the kids about what will be on the news today. You can tell them it was all a lie." What mattered most to him was that Liz believed him and would never know the truth. Of that he was now sure. And after he spoke to Liz, he called Ashley from his office. He warned her of what would be on the news that day, and he said it was all posturing over a threatened lawsuit, based on a false claim of sexual harassment, made by a disgruntled employee who had been fired, and tried to take revenge on him for it. It sounded sensible to him and was a plausible explanation for what had happened.

"What the hell is that about?" Ashley said, instantly suspicious. But Marshall was calm now. The nightmare was almost over. And he sounded quiet and confident when he answered. He was no longer frightened or panicked, now that he knew his career wasn't at stake.

"It's just an employee who tried to extort money from us. It happens. We were forced to settle with her, to get rid of her, and she's going to admit later today that her claims were false."

"Were they? Or did you have to buy her off because she was telling the truth?" Ashley asked the right questions, but Marshall had ready answers.

"If she were telling the truth, she wouldn't have settled and would have won the suit. We would have won in court, but the board didn't want to go through it," Marshall said matter-of-factly. "I never had an affair with her, Ashley. Her accusations were false. Liz believes me. And so does the board. I hope you do too." He sounded faintly hurt that she was doubting him at all, and she hesitated for a long moment before she answered.

"I know you better than Liz does. I know you're capable of having an affair and lying to her about it." Her argument was hard to refute, and he didn't try.

"I don't consider us an affair," Marshall said, sounding offended. "We've lasted longer than most marriages. We have two children, and hopefully a future. This woman came out of left field, and is nothing more than a bimbo with a sleazy lawyer trying to extort money. Women like her do that."

"I hope you're telling me the truth," Ashley said sadly.

"I don't need to sleep with anyone but you," he said in a voice filled with emotion. "I'll be in L.A. tomorrow. We can talk about it then. I just wanted to let you know what would be on the news today, and not to worry about it." He sounded innocent and reassuring, and very loving.

"Thank you," she said, but her tone was as confused as she felt. And when she saw it on the noon news an hour later, despite his warnings, she felt sick. The story had the ring of truth to her. And Bonnie called her five minutes later. She had just seen it on the Internet.

"What the hell is going on with Marshall?" Bonnie was stunned.

"Marshall says the woman is crazy, and tried to extort money from him. She's an employee they fired and she's pissed about it, so she drummed up a sexual harassment suit to shake the company down for money," Ashley explained, as Marshall had to her earlier. "They just made a settlement with her, and she's going to admit her claims were false by the end of the day. I guess it's what people do to large corporations. They sue, so they can settle and get money."

"I wonder what that cost them," Bonnie said cynically, and Ashley didn't want to concede to her that she didn't know what to believe and had her doubts about it too. He seemed like he was telling her the truth when he said he had never had an affair with her, but she no longer knew what to believe, or who. Hearing about it on TV had shaken Ashley's faith in him.

By two o'clock the check had been drawn up and delivered to Megan Wheeler's attorney, and she had signed the agreement, of both confidentiality and retraction. And her statement clearing Marshall was released in time to make the five o'clock news. The story had come and gone in a single day. And everyone knew that claims like that were occasionally made against the heads of major corporations, or men in power generally, and were often false. And sometimes true.

The board had asked Marshall to hold a press conference at the end of the day, after her announcement, which he did, with a pained look, wearing a well-cut dark suit, a white shirt, and a sober tie, with Liz standing beside him. He issued a brief statement, expressing his gratitude for the support of UPI, the board, to Ms. Wheeler for ultimately telling the truth and admitting his innocence, and thanking his wife for her support. He smiled at Liz as he said it, and she looked dignified and loving. The camera zoomed in on their clasped hands then, and as Ashley watched them in L.A., she started to cry. Liz looked so peaceful and proud next to him, as though she had no cause for concern whatsoever. He smiled at her as they left the stage, and she followed him off camera. She looked like a confident, respectable woman who was standing by her husband. And as Ashley watched them, she knew what Bonnie would say, and maybe she was right, that he would never leave his wife. It certainly looked that way to her, and she could see the profound respect between them. She sat gulping air as she choked on sobs with a feeling of panic, and suddenly she knew instinctively that he had probably had the affair, UPI had more than likely paid to buy him out of the scandal, and he was far more married to Liz than he had ever admitted to her. She felt as though her whole world were crashing in on her. It all sounded like a lie to her now that she had seen him holding hands with Liz and the proud, assured look in her eyes. It was obvious that Liz believed her husband, but Ashley no longer did. She knew that in one brief moment, watching Liz stand next to Marshall on TV, her world had come to an end. She would never fully believe him again, or trust what he said about his allegedly dead marriage. It didn't look dead to her.

Marshall spoke to all of their children on the phone that night and explained the situation to them about the threatened lawsuit, the settlement to avoid it, at UPI's request, and Megan Wheeler's admission that her claims against him had been false. Lindsay said it was embarrassing, John offered his sympathy and support, and Tom didn't believe him, but didn't want to upset his mother by challenging them and accusing his father of being a liar and a cheat. Marshall could hear it in his tone and curt responses on the phone.

It was all over by seven o'clock that night. Marshall called Connie again to thank her and the board for supporting him, and Connie said that it had been worth it to avoid a scandal for UPI. They had done what they felt was best.

And everyone was relieved that it had been resolved so quickly, despite the price.

Marshall went to bed that night, thinking of
Ashley, and knowing that he would have to
deal with her in L.A. the next day. But the
worst was over. And most important, he hadn't
lost his job or been publicly disgraced. He had
been vindicated. And Liz lay in bed next to
him, looking tired but reassured. She had
never wavered for a moment and trusted him
completely.

"It has certainly been an insane couple of
days," he said as they lay in the dark, thinking
about it again.

"Things like this happen," Liz said quietly,
grateful that it was over and the woman had
finally told the truth. It would have been a lot
worse for all of them if she hadn't. But at no
time had Liz doubted him. She was absolutely
certain that Marshall was telling her the truth
the entire time, and all she had felt was com-
passion that he had to go through it, and total
faith in him.

Marshall felt like he'd had a near-death experience, and knew just how narrowly he had escaped. He closed his eyes then, and with an
overwhelming sense of relief, he fell asleep. The

nightmare was over, and all he wanted to do now was get back to Ashley, see their babies, and put his arms around her. It had been an agonizing three days. But all was well, and he was safe.

Chapter 8

Marshall boarded the UPI jet for the flight to L.A., a day later than usual, still shaken by everything that had happened. He had brought a briefcase full of paperwork with him on the plane, but never touched it. He just sat staring out the window, thinking of Ashley, and trying to force the vision of Megan Wheeler from his mind. It was frightening to realize how easily she could have brought him down, how close she had come to doing so. His name had been cleared, thanks to UPI's support. He was a chastened man, and was well aware that his brief fling with Megan Wheeler had been a huge mistake. It had all started one night when they both had too much to drink at a client event, met for another drink afterward, and it had snowballed from there. Thank God she had recanted. She could have brought about the end of his career, and his marriage.

When the plane landed in L.A., he didn't go to his office, and had the car and driver drop him off at his apartment instead. He didn't bother to change, but picked up the Jaguar and headed for Malibu on Pacific Coast Highway. It was a hot, sunny day, and he had taken off his coat and tie, and put the top down, and as always drove too fast. He was anxious to see Ashley now, and calm her down, after their unsettling conversation the day before. He had sent her two text messages late that night, and again this morning, and she hadn't answered.

He parked in front of the garage at the house in Malibu and saw that her car was there. He was relieved that she was home and the kids were at camp. He hadn't wanted to wait until that night to talk to her. The only thing he was afraid of now was her reaction to the affair he had been accused of. He could tell that she hadn't believed him, when he said he was innocent of the Wheeler woman's claims. And the only ones who knew the truth now were Megan herself, Simon Stern, and the board of UPI, and no one would ever mention it again.

They had all signed confidentiality agreements, binding them to silence, and she had turned over the negatives of the photographs.

He found Ashley in the studio in a white T-shirt and pink denim shorts. She was holding a mug of tea, and staring blindly out the window, and didn't hear him come in. She felt his hand on her arm, and knew who it was, but she didn't turn to see him. She didn't want to. All she could think of was seeing him with Liz on TV, holding hands. And then slowly, she looked at him, and he could see her beautiful, ravaged face, that showed all the agony she felt.

"Why aren't you in the office?" she asked in a broken voice. She felt as though her heart had been shattered in a million pieces the day before, first by the affair he'd been accused of, and then by the sight of his holding hands with Liz at the press conference, as she stood staunchly beside him, the loving wife who Ashley always tried to pretend didn't exist. But she did, and Ashley had seen clearly how much Liz cared about him, and Marshall's hand on hers had spoken volumes.

"I wanted to see you," he said quietly, and pulled up a stool to sit beside her. "I'm sorry I had to call and tell you about the threatened

lawsuit yesterday. It upset me too. It's all over."
His voice was warm and reassuring.

"I know," she said, as she set the mug of tea
down and looked at him. She didn't know if
she was seeing him, or a stranger. Suddenly, he
looked different to her. "I saw your press conference last night. How much did they have to
pay her to withdraw the suit?"

"Two million dollars," he said honestly. "It's
an advance on my end-of-the-year bonus. We
would have won the suit, but they didn't want
the bad publicity. It was just easier to settle.
That's how those things work. Sometimes you
have to settle even false claims. That was what
she wanted. I hate giving her a penny for lying
about me, but at least it's over. It would have
been a nightmare fighting it in court." Ashley
nodded and said nothing. He didn't ask her if
she believed him. He could see she didn't.

"So when did you have the affair with her?"
Ashley dragged her eyes to his, and they burned
into him like hot coals.

"I told you. I didn't. She got fired, and she
was angry about it. She decided to take it out
on me. It was a cheap shot, but it worked."

"I don't believe you," Ashley said quietly in a
voice he had never heard before. It frightened

him to look at her—she looked as though she were a million miles away. He wanted to put his arms around her to bring her back again, but he didn't dare. She looked like she might bolt, or scream.

"I know you don't, Ash," he said just as quietly. "But I didn't sleep with her. I don't even know her." His mind shut out the letters and the photographs. All he could think of now was Ashley, and the relationship he was trying to save, just as he had fought to save his job the day before, and his marriage, whatever it took.

"You lied to me about Liz too," she said with heartbroken eyes. "You said your marriage is over, and has been for years."

"I was telling you the truth about that too. It still is. Our marriage has been dead for years."

"You were holding her hand on TV. I saw it," Ashley said as tears rolled down her cheeks, and he gently brushed one away. She didn't move toward him, nor pull away. She looked like a beautiful statue with soft curly hair. And he didn't try to explain why he was holding his wife's hand the day before.

"This was hard on her too. It was public humiliation for all of us. The company, my family, Liz, me, you. That woman hit us all where we live." He looked angry as he said it. "And I hate that it hurt you too," he said sympathetically.

"It hurt just as much watching you hold hands with Liz. Your marriage isn't dead. She looked like all those politicians' wives who stand next to their husbands while they deny having affairs, or confess publicly and cry about it. And the wife forgives him publicly to make him look good. She loves you. I realized that for the first time yesterday. And you love her. I saw it in your eyes when you looked at her. You're still totally married to her. That's why you've never left her. You lied to me. It's not about your kids. It's about you and her. There's no room in your life for me."

"I wouldn't be here now, Ash, if there weren't," he said gently. "I love you and our girls more than anything in the world. And when Lindsay leaves next year, I'll be ready. And so will Liz. I think she knows it's coming. My heart hasn't been there for years. This was different. It was a highly publicized assault on all of us. We had to make it look good."

"Your holding hands with Liz looked real to me," she said, as she got up and walked away and stood staring out the window. Marshall came up behind her and put his arms around her, and she didn't move.

"It wasn't real," he assured her in a whisper. "It was for TV. **This** is real. You and I are real, and we always will be."

"What about the other woman?" she asked, as he stood behind her with his arms around her waist. Her fluff of curly hair was brushing his chin, and he could smell her shampoo, and the fresh clean smell he loved about her, a combination of soap and faint perfume.

"What about her?" Marshall said, debating what to tell her. There was suddenly a lot at stake here, and he knew it.

"Tell me the truth. Don't lie to me. I know you slept with her. I can feel it." She turned and looked him in the eye, and her gaze didn't waver.

He hesitated for a long moment, and then decided to tell her the truth, a version of it. She didn't have to know about the photographs, or how long it had lasted. He didn't want to hurt her any more than he already had, which in his mind justified modifying the truth for her. It was more than he was willing to tell Liz. But the circumstances here were different. Ashley was aware of things Liz didn't know, that he was unfaithful and didn't always tell the truth.

"It was a one-night stand, and I was drunk out of my mind. It happened two years ago, when you and I were fighting, and I was upset. That's all it was, Ash, a one-time fling, and I never saw her again." There had been a time two years before when Ashley had threatened to leave him if he wouldn't get divorced. Then Lindsay had had a crisis, Liz had gotten sick, which turned out to be less serious than they thought, the twins had started school, and Ashley had calmed down. Until now. But by reminding her of the timing, Marshall thought it might make sense to her.

"How do I know you're telling me the truth?" she said suspiciously, but she remembered the time, and it was conceivable to her that he had slipped, although she never would have done that herself.

"You don't," he said candidly. "But you know I love you. That's why I'm here."

"Yeah," she said, as tears rolled down her cheeks again, "and you love Liz too. I could see it." She started to sob then and buried her face in his chest as he held her. She loved him so much, and now she was afraid they would never be together as she had hoped. He was married to a real woman and Ashley had seen that she loved him too.

"I respect Liz," Marshall said as he held Ashley. "We have a lot of history together, nearly thirty years, and three kids."

"We have eight, and two kids. That counts for something too," Ashley said, feeling pathetic for even saying it to him. And as she did, he tipped her face up to his and kissed her.

"We have a lot more than that. We have something very special, Ash, that I've never had with anyone else." It hadn't stopped him from sleeping with Megan Wheeler, Ashley knew now, but at least he had been honest with her about it, or so she thought. "And one of these days, we'll be together. I just want to get Lindsay through high school and out of the house. Then it will be our turn." But she wondered now if it ever would be, and now she was questioning if Liz would really let him go. She had been so staunch beside him at the press conference. It had been obvious that for Liz their marriage wasn't dead, and Marshall was still her man. But he was Ashley's too.

Ashley didn't answer him, and he kissed her then, and the next thing she knew he was holding her so tight she could hardly breathe, their clothes were off, and they couldn't get enough of each other. It happened as it always did, and this time they never made it to her bedroom, they made love on the small battered couch in her studio. And whenever they made love, she forgot everything she was afraid of in their relationship, all the times he had disappointed her. She forgot everything in his arms, and afterward they lay together, and it all came back to her. She couldn't get the image of his wife out of her head now, and the realization that she was nothing to him, just the woman he made love to in L.A. and slept with two days a week. Nothing else about their life was real, except the twins.

He showered and dressed for the office after he made love to her, and he had to rush. He had a luncheon appointment, and he had put everything aside while he was with her. He could see that she felt better, but when he looked at her closely, he was aware of a worried look when he kissed her goodbye.

"I love you. That's all you need to know." She nodded, feeling dazed by everything he'd said and their lovemaking. She couldn't think clearly when she was around him, and he kissed her again. "See you tonight." He was only going to be able to spend one night in Malibu that week, because he had been busy dealing with the sexual harassment suit. She would have liked him to spend Friday night with them, to make up for it. But she knew he never could. He always went home for the weekends, which frightened her now too. He said he played golf on Saturdays with clients, but now she wondered what else he did with Liz. The vision of their clasped hands at the press conference was still haunting her, and maybe always would. She had gotten a glimpse into his married life that she had never had before.

She heard the old Jaguar drive off, and went upstairs to shower. She was just coming downstairs in her T-shirt and shorts again when Bonnie showed up. She had gotten hired to work on another movie, but she wasn't starting for two more weeks.

"Is Prince Charming in town?" Bonnie asked as she looked at her, and helped herself to a Coke from the fridge.

"He got here today," Ashley said quietly. She didn't want to get in an argument with Bonnie over him. And recent events in his life were hard to defend, especially now that she knew the truth, that he had cheated on her, even if it was a one-night stand. "He's leaving tomorrow."

"I saw his press conference last night," Bonnie said, as they went to sit outside on the deck. It was a hot day, and both women looked like kids as they lay on deck chairs in the sun.

"Yeah, me too." Neither of them commented on his wife standing with him, but Bonnie knew Ashley must have seen it too, and their holding hands.

"It sounds like he got out of it pretty cleanly. They must have paid her a bundle to take back what she said," Bonnie said.

"Maybe so." Ashley didn't want to discuss it with her, but as she lay on the deck near her friend, Ashley's heart sank, at the realization of what had really happened. Marshall had cheated on her, and he had a wife who was willing to stand by him through thick and thin, and he had just told her that morning that he couldn't leave his wife for another year, until their daughter graduated. He had said as much to Ashley before, but it was different now that she had seen how Liz looked at him, and how Marshall looked at her. It was a much stronger bond between them than Ashley had realized, and one which she felt no power to interfere with. And it was a tie that had not yet been severed and maybe never would be. She wasn't angry about it anymore, just sad.

"You okay, Ash?" Bonnie asked her friend gently, and Ashley shrugged.

"More or less." Bonnie suspected what was troubling her. She had seen the same connection between Liz and Marshall that Ashley had the day before. It didn't surprise Bonnie, and had confirmed her worst fears, and now she was even sadder for her friend.

"Why don't we do something with the girls this weekend? Maybe take them to Venice, or go to Disneyland or something. You look like you need a break." More than that, she needed to have some fun, instead of sitting at home obsessing over Marshall, crying about him, or waiting for him to come to L.A. for a day or two. Ashley needed a lot more in her life.

"Yeah, maybe," Ashley said without enthusiasm. The last two days had left her feeling depressed. It was hard to rev up her motors again. All her tires were flat.

"You have a choice, you know," Bonnie said softly. She always tried to be the voice of reason for Ashley, out of friendship, but she never got

anywhere. "You don't have to stand by him forever if it's killing you. You can get out of it, or
even go to a shrink to help you do it, if you
can't do it alone."

"I know," Ashley said as she started to cry
again. She felt as though she had done nothing
but cry for the past two days. Seeing him on TV
with Liz had been too hard, and a revelation she
had never wanted to face. She had never even
seen a photograph of her till then, in eight years.
She was twenty years older than Ashley, but she
was still a pretty woman, in a suburban-soccer-
mom kind of way. And in her simple black dress,
she had looked like the perfect corporate wife
that she was, something Ashley knew she could
never be. She wondered now if that was why he
stayed with her too, not just for the kids. "I don't
really have a choice," Ashley said to Bonnie then.
And maybe Liz didn't either. Ashley wondered
about that now too.

"Why not?" Bonnie looked puzzled and hoped
she wasn't pregnant again. It would just tie her
to him even more.

"I love him too much," Ashley said, as she
brushed away her tears, and the wind blew her
curls and framed her face with them. She looked
like an exquisite angelic child, and not just the

vulnerable woman that she was. "I can't leave him. I would die."

"He may destroy you if you stay," Bonnie said seriously.

"I know," Ashley said, looking straight at her, and the worst of it was that she seemed as though she did know, and was completely lucid about how dangerous he was for her.

"Don't let him wreck your life," Bonnie begged her, and Ashley nodded, and for a long time they lay on the deck, soaking up the sun and saying nothing at all. Bonnie was even more frightened for her now than she had been before. And she knew, looking at Ashley, that Marshall Weston owned her, body and soul. He was a man of extraordinary powers. And Ashley was like a feather on the wind, and no match for him at all.

Chapter 9

Fiona was still waiting for answers from the investigation service that was analyzing the board and checking on its members, when she got a call from a well-known investigative business reporter the day after Marshall Weston's press conference about the sexual harassment suit. The reporter's name was Logan Smith, and she knew his name and had read his pieces for years, which were frequently in **The Wall Street Journal, The New York Times,** and business and financial magazines. He was best known for his incisive points of view, sometimes unpopular ones. He had fearlessly exposed money-laundering operations and corruption, and he wrote best about controversial issues. And she vaguely remembered that he had won a Pulitzer, although she didn't know exactly what for. She had no idea why he'd be calling her, and hoped it wasn't about the leak. At first she wasn't inclined to take the call, she didn't like talking to the press. And then she decided that avoiding him might be even more dangerous. So she picked up the receiver, and answered with a slightly harassed voice. She was even more so than her tone indicated.

"Fiona Carson," she said, sounding curt. But she was the CEO and could afford to be prickly at times. She had a huge amount of responsibility to contend with.

"Hello, Ms. Carson, my name is Logan Smith." She smiled to herself. His name was as well known in the business community as her own. She wasn't sure if he was being modest or showing off. It could have been either one. He had a deep, pleasant voice, and sounded young. She had no idea how old he was. All she knew about him was the Pulitzer and the articles she'd read, some of which could be acutely hostile to big business. He left no stone unturned in the course of his in-depth reporting, no matter how uncomfortable it made his subject. He was a seeker of the truth, and often acted as though he was on a holy mission.

"Yes, I know who you are," she said, with a look of amusement. "That's why I took the call. What can I do for you, Mr. Smith?"

"I wondered if you have any comment about the recent sexual harassment charges made against Marshall Weston by a former employee. I'm writing a piece about the sexual habits, liberties, and sometimes perversities of men in power. Any thoughts?" She almost winced at his words. The last thing she wanted to do was comment about another CEO's sexual habits, and she didn't know the man.

"I thought the former employee retracted her claim against him yesterday. Isn't that old news today?"

"Not really. And yes, she did recant, although we'll never know exactly why. A lot of behind-the-scenes fancy footwork goes on, cleaning up those claims, as we both know. He may have paid her off. They said there was a 'settlement' to avoid litigation. But you know what that means."

"Fortunately, I don't. I've never had sexual harassment charges brought against me in the workplace or anywhere else."

"Actually, that's one of my theories," he said, sounding pleasant and warming to the subject, "that women never engage in those activities. When was the last time you heard about a female CEO involved in a sex scandal, or sleeping with a male bimbo? What about Weston? Do you think her claim against him was valid, or just a ploy for money and she withdrew because she didn't have a case?" It was anyone's guess, and they'd never know. Fiona felt herself instantly on thin ice with his questions, a place where she did not want to be. But she was much too smart for that.

"I have absolutely no idea," she said innocently. "I don't even know the man."

"You've never met him?" Logan sounded surprised. "Don't CEOs go out and play together occasionally, or have a secret handshake or a clubhouse somewhere where they hang out?" She laughed. He was funny, and bright. But that also made him more dangerous, and she didn't plan to enter his game.

"I wish we did. That would be fun. Actually, I've met Marshall Weston a few times, at Senate subcommittee hearings in Washington where we both appeared. We shook hands on the way in, and that was it. I have no idea what his habits are, and no interest in them. Nor if the allegations against him were true or not."

"How disappointing," Logan Smith said honestly. "I was hoping I could lull you into a little loose-lipped indiscretion about him. Some nice friendly gossip among rivals."

"We're not rivals," she corrected him. "We have similar jobs for two very different companies. And I hear he does an excellent job."

"And you're not loose-lipped either. My efforts to pry inappropriate information from you have been a total bust." She laughed aloud at that. "What do you think about my theory, about the difference between male and female CEOs and their sexual habits?" She wasn't going to give him a quote on that either. In fact, she wasn't going to give him anything, except two minutes of her time on the phone, no comment, and then send him on his way and wish him well.

"You should talk to my sister," Fiona said pleasantly, "Jillian Hamilton. She's a psychiatrist at Stanford. She's writing a book on the subject. She's as fascinated by it as you are, and said pretty much the same thing to me."

"In what context? About anyone we know?" He was looking to hang his hat on something, and Fiona had given him nothing so far, although he liked talking to her. She sounded

easygoing and very intelligent. Her sister probably was too.

"About men and women in general. And she
claims that she uses me as a guinea pig for her
research, about female CEOs."

"And what's her conclusion?" he asked with
interest.

"That we work just as hard, don't have nearly
as much fun as our male counterparts, and are
better behaved."

"That's my point," he said, sounding excited.
"I think your sister and I are really on to something. Guys in power seem to go berserk, and
it becomes sexual for them. For women it becomes like some sort of vow of chastity and
dedication. They don't do anything but work."
And then he came right back to his topic. "So
you've got nothing to say about Marshall
Weston?" he tried again, and she didn't volunteer that her daughter was dating his son. It
was none of his business anyway, and might
make him think she knew him better than she
did, which was not at all. All she actually knew
about him was that he had a nice kid, according to Alyssa.

"I wouldn't presume to comment about a
man I don't know," she said wisely.

"That never stops anyone else," he said, laughing.

"Would you like to talk to my sister about her book? Maybe the two of you can share ideas."

"Not yet," Smith said honestly, "although I might like to interview her eventually, about her book, and how she arrived at her theories. Mine come from careful observation and writing about the heads of corporations for many years. Actually, there is something else I want to ask you." She hoped it wouldn't be about her sex life. If so, she wasn't going to answer him. "What about letting me do an in-depth profile of you? I've wanted to for years." She was startled by what he said, although she had had numerous requests. There had been one piece about her in **Time** magazine when she first took the job, in the business section, but usually she declined interviews. She didn't want the spotlight on her. It was unnecessary and she didn't like it.

"That's very flattering, Mr. Smith," she responded, "but I don't think so. I'm not much for publicity. I prefer to stay behind the scenes and do the work. That works better for me."

"That's why you're so interesting," he explained. "I've been watching you for years. I never hear about you, one rarely reads of you. You just run the corporation with incredible efficiency, and go about your business. And the value of the NTA stock goes up every five minutes. As a matter of fact, the only money I've ever made in the stock market was thanks to you."

"I'm happy to hear it." She smiled at the compliment, which was the only kind she was interested in, about her skill in business. "But that's really all the public needs to know. If I'm doing my job right, that's all anyone needs to hear about. Where I went to school, what I eat for breakfast, and whether or not I get my hair done is all irrelevant." He had heard the theory before, but if enough people felt as she did, he would have been out of a job, so it wasn't a philosophy he loved.

"You went to Harvard, right?" He was just checking, but remembered that about her. He had always been intrigued by her, and how quiet she was. The public knew a lot more about Marshall Weston, particularly now. He made a lot more noise, as most of the male CEOs did.

"Yes, I did," she confirmed, "but there are a lot of other good schools in the country, and business schools, that turn out fine young people who wind up in important jobs and have great careers." Like her own daughter at Stanford, and several of her friends. But she didn't say that to him. It was more personal information than she wanted to share.

"You don't give away anything about yourself, do you?" he complained. "That's why I want to interview you. People deserve to know more about you, especially your stockholders. You're a hero in the business world, and you refuse to act like one. That's because you're a woman. If you were a man, you'd be blowing your own horn, and out chasing bimbos," he added. "And you'd make a lot more noise."

"That's one of my sister's theories too. You two really should get together. You have a lot in common."

"We'd probably bore each other to death, or argue about who thought of what first. Similarities don't usually attract."

"I wasn't suggesting you go out with her." She thought it was a good idea, but she wouldn't admit it to him. "Just talk."

"I'll call you for her number sometime. Now I'm going to go to the sleazy bar across the street from my office and cry in my beer, because you told me absolutely nothing I can use about

Marshall Weston for the article I'm working on, with a deadline, I might add. And you won't give me an interview. You win. I must be losing my touch." He wasn't, but she was relentlessly discreet, which was what he had suspected about her too. But she was also pleasant to talk to, which had surprised him, and she sounded like a real human being. Just one who didn't talk to the press, or divulge anything private about herself. And he admired that about her. Some of his male interview subjects had such big egos, he could barely fit them on the page. She was the opposite of that, although he was sure she had one too. She was just a hell of a lot more modest.

"Thank you for calling," she said sincerely. "It was nice talking to you." She dismissed him politely. And after they hung up, Smith looked up Jillian Hamilton on the Internet. He was curious about her sister too, and wondered if he had read anything she'd written. Her credentials were impressive, the list of books and articles she'd written was long. He figured out that she was about ten years older than he was—he had just turned forty-five. From a photograph he could see that she was an attractive woman, but looked about ten feet tall.

Clearly not a date, but possibly an interesting source, and he jotted down her name. But he wanted to interview Fiona, not her sister, and he had no idea how to convince her that she should agree to it. He decided to try again in a few weeks. Meanwhile he had to dig up whatever he could on Marshall Weston, and whoever was willing to comment on him. But he would have loved to have Fiona's female point of view, and clearly that wasn't going to happen. He just hoped he could talk her into an interview one day. He was sure that he'd enjoy it, and he'd been honest with her, and not pandering, when he told her he was a fan.

After Fiona and Jillian played tennis, they went out for coffee and Jillian brought up Marshall Weston as an example of her theories. She had followed him in the news, and had seen his press conference, with Liz standing at his side.

"He looked guilty as hell to me," Jillian commented over cappuccino.

"What makes you think that?" Fiona was intrigued. "He looked innocent to me. Shows what I know."

"He looked much too virtuous, and his apology to everyone and gratitude for the woman's retraction made me retch. And the business of holding his wife's hand spells guilty to me. He probably cheats on her all the time and she doesn't know it. That's usually how it works."

"What made you so cynical?" Fiona asked her, startled by her refusal to believe Marshall Weston innocent. She sounded almost bitter about it, but Fiona knew she wasn't, and her experiences with men had almost always been pleasant.

"I have a lot of male patients who are the CEOs of companies. They all cheat, and tell me about it. It really makes you realize how badly behaved most of those guys are, and emotionally dishonest. I'd never date one of them after what I hear every day. Marshall looks like one of the boys to me."

"He seemed like a nice guy when I met him. And Alyssa is crazy about his son. She says they're a nice family."

"That's what it looks like. Then women come out of the woodwork like this one, and the next thing you know, they're at the center of a sex scandal, and their wives are in shock, and everybody's crying. I have a couple of them who even have second families they keep hidden. Their wives help them in their careers, but they're in love with the other woman who is usually younger and better looking, while the real wife is dedicated to them. And one day they all find out about each other, and the guy finds himself in a huge mess and is stunned that his original wife and kids are pissed off at him and think he's a dishonest prick, which of course he is. They're too chicken to get divorced, and too self-serving, so they want to have their cake and eat it too."

"That must get pretty dicey." Fiona was impressed. It would never have occurred to her to do that, or cheat on David while they were married. She never had, although they'd been unhappy for years, and she didn't think David had cheated on her either. But with what Jillian was saying, she wondered. Maybe he had seen women on the side who had been less threatening to him, and less busy than Fiona. But if he had fooled around on her, at least he'd been discreet.

"It definitely gets dicey," Jillian said with a grin. "I think they get off on it, having a secret, a double life, two women who serve different purposes for them, one for sex, and the other for business. It's all about them and their needs."

"Why do you suppose the second woman puts up with it? I'm assuming she knows the guy is married, even if the real wife doesn't know about the other woman."

"Most of the time the second woman loves him. And it's all about the power thing again. The excitement of having a man in your life who runs the world. Most women find that exciting. I sure as hell don't," Jillian commented. "I'd rather have a guy who's smaller scale and more human. But powerful men are exciting to a lot of women."

"How's your book coming?" Fiona asked her then.

"It's coming. Slowly but surely. I use a lot of my patients for research to support my theories."

"By the way, I talked to a guy this week who thinks like you do on this subject. He called me to comment on Marshall Weston's sexual harassment accusation, and I refused to. We got on the subject and I told him about you and your book. He's an investigative reporter, specializing in business, and he's come to a lot of the same conclusions you have about powerful men, and the difference between how men and women react to power, and how others view them. Smart guy, maybe you'd like him."

"What does he look like?" Jillian sounded intrigued.

"I don't know. I talked to him on the phone and I've read some of his pieces. He writes well, and his articles are good. His name is Logan Smith. He sounds young though." That had never stopped Jillian before, but he had sounded even younger than he was when Fiona spoke to him.

"I've read him before too," Jillian said, and knew instantly who he was. "He won a Pulitzer for a series of interviews he did with Nelson Mandela. Fantastic stuff. I think he went to Harvard too." He hadn't said so to Fiona. He had told her very little about himself, in fact nothing, and was more interested in her, and writing an article about her.

"He wanted to do an article about me. I turned it down. I hate that stuff." Jillian knew she did, but thought she had missed an opportunity to meet an interesting person.

"You should meet him anyway. And I don't think he's all that young, from what I remember. He's somewhere around your age."

"He didn't ask me out on a date." Fiona laughed

at her sister, who was always willing to meet new men. But Fiona wasn't, and too busy to date. "He just wanted to interview me."

"Well, tell him to call me. I'll check him out for you," Jillian teased her.

Then they finished their coffee and talked about their summer plans. Jillian was going to Europe with friends who had rented a house in Tuscany, and she knew Fiona rented the same house in Malibu every year. She and the children loved it, and it was so easy to get there.

"You should do something different for a change," Jillian suggested, but she also knew that her younger sister was a creature of habit, and too busy to plan a real vacation. And the house in Malibu was relaxing for her. It belonged to a Hollywood producer and was a beautiful place. She always wanted Jillian to come down and visit them, but they usually went away at the same time. And both of her kids had their own plans in August. Mark was going to Kenya with his girlfriend, and planning to do volunteer work in a village that needed help laying pipes to bring in water. And Alyssa was still undecided, but John Weston wanted to go somewhere with her.

When she talked to Alyssa that night, she

asked her how John was doing after the stress-ful week his father had had, and if John was very upset about it. The scandal had been quickly averted, but it nonetheless must have been unpleasant to have his father accused of having an affair and cheating on his mother.

"It was rough on him when it first came out. But it was over pretty quickly. He believed his father was innocent right from the beginning. Apparently, his older brother didn't think so, and thinks they just paid the woman off to shut her up." Fiona didn't say that her sister thought so too. She felt sorry for Marshall's children. It must have been upsetting for all of them, and his wife too, even if it wasn't true. And Jillian hadn't convinced her. Marshall had seemed in-nocent to Fiona. She wasn't as cynical as her sister. And she reminded Alyssa to bring John over soon, and Alyssa promised she would. Fiona was anxious to meet him and hadn't yet. Alyssa said the romance was going well and they were spending a lot of time with each other. And John would be coming to Malibu for a long weekend. Fiona was happy for her.

And for the rest of June, Fiona was busy at work, and trying to get assorted projects done before she took time off, to go to Malibu with her kids. She always had to pay her dues before she went on vacation, and even more so when she returned, but it was worth it to her.

And on the first of July, her bags were packed, and she flew to L.A. to get the house in Malibu ready for everyone. She could hardly wait to spend three whole weeks with them. They were arriving in time for the Fourth of July weekend. Mark's girlfriend couldn't get time off, but Mark and Alyssa would be there, and John Weston was coming the following weekend.

Jillian left for Italy the same day, and promised to return with two hot Italians in tow, one for each of them.

"I don't know what I'd do with that," Fiona said, laughing when Jillian called to say good-bye from the airport, while she was waiting for her flight.

"You'd figure out something," Jillian said with a grin. "Have fun with the kids. I'll call you."

"I'll miss you," Fiona said, feeling nostalgic for a minute. Jillian would always be the big sister who was the only adult family she had now, since their parents had died. She liked knowing that she was somewhere nearby, and they talked to each other often. "Take care," Fiona said, feeling like a kid again, and she blew her a kiss as they hung up. Fiona knew they were both going to have fun on vacation, doing what they each enjoyed most. Jillian was going to be meeting lots of new people, visiting old friends in Europe, and having new adventures. And Fiona was going to be with her kids, swimming in the ocean, and lying on the beach. It sounded like sheer heaven to her. And she was in great spirits and full of anticipation when she flew to L.A. that night.

Chapter 10

Both of Fiona's children arrived in Malibu on the same day, two days after she'd gotten to the house, and checked that everything was in good order for them. She had bought groceries and magazines and put fresh flowers around the house, and everything seemed to be working. They had been renting the same house for seven years, so it was familiar to all of them, and a little bit like coming home. Three weeks in Malibu always felt like real summer to them, no matter what they did later. And for Fiona, this was the best part, and the only vacation she took, except for a week at Christmas, when she went skiing with her kids the day after Christmas. She couldn't imagine spending vacations without them. Her sister's plans were always much more glamorous, but this was fun for her.

Mark arrived from New York by lunchtime, and Fiona was thrilled to see him. He hadn't been home since his spring break in March, and he looked thin and pale, like a real New Yorker, but he was happy and healthy. He was excited about his upcoming trip to Kenya, and told Fiona all about it, while they ate lunch on the deck, and waited for Alyssa to arrive. She arrived two hours later, with a suitcase full of bikinis and cut-off jeans. And whatever else she needed, she planned to borrow from her mother. Fiona lost half her wardrobe to her, with great frequency, except the clothes she wore to work, which Alyssa hated. She always told her mother she should dress "cuter" for work, which Fiona just laughed at. She didn't think "cute" was the right look for a CEO. She couldn't see herself arguing with Harding Williams at a board meeting in a miniskirt, although it certainly would have confirmed his opinion of her.

Fiona still hadn't had any definite conclusions from the investigative service about the boardroom leak. And finding the source was proving to be more difficult than they'd expected. But they were promising her definitive answers soon. And for the time in Malibu, she wasn't going to think about it. This was her time with her children, and it was sacred to her. And she was very grateful that at their ages they were still willing to spend time with her.

"So what do you two want to do for dinner tonight?" Fiona asked them, as they lay on the deck at the end of the afternoon. The three of them had gone swimming in the ocean, and taken a long walk on the beach. And Mark had used the surfboard that he borrowed there every year. He was a tall, handsome, dark-haired boy, who was a better-looking version of his father at the same age. The only thing he had inherited from his mother were her green eyes. And Alyssa was the image of her mother. "Do you want to go out, or should we cook dinner here?"

"Let's barbecue," Mark suggested, and offered to do chicken and vegetables, which sounded good to both women. And Alyssa offered to make the salad. They ate simple, healthy food, and none of them were enormous eaters. What they cared about most was being together. And what Fiona loved about their vacations was that she knew she would wake up every morning to the sounds of her children, and be with them all day. It was a real treat for her, and leaving them

at the end of the vacation was always wrench-
ing. But they had plenty of time ahead of them,
and after dinner on the deck that night, they
watched a movie on the enormous wide-screen
TV. The house had its own screening room,
with big comfortable leather chairs. There was
also an indoor pool in a separate building that
they seldom used. They preferred swimming in
the ocean and walking on the beach.

They were easy days and quiet evenings, and
they had been there for a week when Logan
Smith called Fiona on her cell phone, and she
was startled to hear him, and wondered how he
had gotten her number. She hadn't given it to
him, and the last time he had called her at her
office. His calling her while she was on vacation felt like an intrusion.

"Is something wrong?" she asked him, wondering if he had some hot tip about NTA, possibly about the boardroom leak before she heard
it herself. She was instantly wary, and worried
the moment he said his name. She hadn't recognized his voice.

"No," he said casually. "I told you I'd call you
again sometime. I just wanted to see if I could
talk you into that interview I asked you about
the last time we talked."

"That's why you called me?" She sounded shocked, and neither welcoming nor happy about it, although she had been pleasant to him the time before, but this was different. She was not at work.

"Yes. Why? Is this a bad time?" He sounded suddenly embarrassed at the tone of her voice. She was obviously annoyed that he had called her.

"I'm on vacation with my kids, and I'm not working. And I told you I don't want to do an interview. Now or later. I don't do interviews. And I don't talk business when I'm away with my kids." And from Fiona's standpoint, she didn't want to be a CEO when she was on vacation with them, just their mother.

"I'm sorry. I really am. I wouldn't like that either," he admitted. "I hope you're at least in the same time zone, so I didn't wake you up or something." He suddenly wondered if she was someplace exotic like Tahiti, Europe, or New Zealand. She could have been anywhere.

"No, it's fine," she said tersely. And then she thought of something. "How did you get this number?"

"Your office gave it to me." He was apologetic, and she made him feel as though he had committed a crime, calling her while she was on vacation with her children.

"My assistant is on vacation. The temp must have given it to you. I'm sorry, I don't mean to be rude. But I like focusing on my kids when I'm with them. My office knows not to call me unless something dire happens." She sounded slightly mellower as she explained it to him, but not much. "I'll be back in two weeks. You can call me then, but I'm not going to give you an interview," she reiterated, and he was beginning to believe her. She sounded definite about it, which blew all his hopes for a story about her. He was counting on her feeling differently about it when he called her again, and that was obviously not the case, and she made it clear to him. And in a way, he admired her for it, her total lack of interest in being in the limelight. She apparently had strong family values as well. She seemed like a nice person, and not what anyone would have expected of a woman in her position. It confirmed everything he thought about the difference between men and women in jobs like hers. Most men wouldn't have been annoyed if he called while they were with their kids. Fiona was serious about both her jobs, as mother and CEO.

"Look, maybe you'll let me take you to lunch when you get back, so I can apologize for intruding on you, and prove that I'm not as rude as you seem to think."

"I don't think you're rude, just pushy," she said, laughing and being honest with him. "You're hot after a story you're never going to get from me. I don't do PR for the company. I'm the CEO. I run the business, that's enough."

"That's what makes you so interesting, Fiona. All the male CEOs I meet are press whores. You aren't. And they bore me to extinction. They're dying to have me write about them. You won't give me a five-minute interview, and I won a Pulitzer, for chrissake. I'm good," he said, almost pleading with her, and she laughed again.

"I know you are. I've read your pieces, and my sister said so. She loved your series on Mandela. I just don't want to be in the press. I don't need it, I don't want it, and I don't like it. I'm not a movie star. I run a company. It's not sexy to read about, and how I do it is no one's business. And as long as my stockholders are happy, that's all I need. The general public doesn't need to know me. And I like being anonymous, and leading a quiet life with my kids, so you're barking up the wrong tree on that one. And I'm no

use to you as a source because I don't tell secrets, so you won't get anywhere with me." It
was as clear as she could be.

"I get it. I'm sorry. Really." He sounded both
discouraged and embarrassed. "I'll call you for
lunch sometime, although you'll probably tell
me you don't eat lunch and don't have time."

"Actually, that's true."

"Have a great vacation," he said, and meant
it, and hung up a minute later, and Fiona called
the temp in her office and told her not to give
out her cell number again, and the girl said she
wouldn't, and apologized for having given it to
Logan.

After that Fiona forgot about him, and con-
centrated on her kids. They were thoroughly
enjoying the house in Malibu, and Alyssa was
ecstatic when John came down and stayed
with them for four days, and Fiona was pleased
to discover that she really liked him. He was
bright, kind, polite, and wonderful to Alyssa,
and he and Mark got along like two brothers,
and even went fishing together. Mark was two
years older than John, but John was mature
for his age, and he was a wonderful addition
to the group. And Fiona had never seen her
daughter as happy. She got a chance to talk to

her about it when the two boys were out surf-
ing together.

"It's looking pretty serious between you two,"
Fiona commented. She had no objection to it,
but they were both young, and she didn't want
Alyssa thinking about marriage yet. She said
they weren't, but she readily admitted that they
were in love with each other, and Fiona was letting them share a room. He was a truly great
kid, with all the right values. And he had a profound respect for both his parents, which Fiona
was pleased to hear.

"We're just having fun, Mom," Alyssa said,
looking relaxed. "I don't want to get married
for another ten years, if then. And I still want
to go to business school, and I want to work for
a few years before I do. Johnny's going to apply
to Harvard too. It would be cool if we both get
in, or maybe Stanford, but that's a long way off.
We're not making any plans for the future,
we're just enjoying what we're doing now."

"That's the way it should be, sweetheart,"
Fiona said, and leaned over to hug her daughter. It was so nice being able to do that and be
together every day. "I really like him."

"He wants you to meet his parents. Maybe
we could all have dinner together sometime in

September. They're in Tahoe for the summer. Or at least his mom is, his dad is working and commutes on weekends. It sounds like his dad works as hard as you do." Fiona wasn't surprised to hear it. "His mom went to law school, and has a law degree, but she never practiced. She's a stay-at-home mom, which seems kind of too bad to me," Alyssa said, unable to understand a whole other generation of women who had gotten educations, and then married and never worked. "She helps his dad entertain clients. And took care of the kids. It sounds really boring," Alyssa said, and Fiona laughed.

"That's what corporate wives do, or used to. Nowadays most women work. Maybe she'll do something when John's younger sister goes to college."

"She does volunteer work, at a homeless shelter." It sounded noble to her, but Alyssa much preferred a life like her mother's, where she was working at her own career. It was exactly what Alyssa wanted to do when she finished school. And her mother had demonstrated to her that you could have kids and work, and even have an important career. And John had said he would prefer that too. She had talked about her parents' divorce with him, and how angry her father had been about her mother's career. She never wanted to be in a situation like that, and she knew her father's resentment of it had destroyed her parents' marriage. Her father and his mother were throwbacks to another time. And Alyssa was a modern young woman who wanted a big career like her mom's. And John was a modern young man, who expected his wife to work, and would be proud of her, if the relationship lasted and they got that far. And they secretly both hoped it would, but it was much too soon to tell.

Fiona liked everything she heard from her, and what she had seen of John in the past four days. And she was looking forward to meeting the Westons in the fall and getting to know them. She and Marshall would have much in common, although women like Liz Weston were less her style. Hers was a life that Fiona would have hated, but she liked their son a lot, which said a great deal about them, and both his parents were part of that equation, not just one.

On the last night of John's stay they went to an Italian restaurant in Malibu, and the four of them had a great time together, laughing and talking. John felt like one of the family, and Fiona said at dinner that she was going to miss him, and he said he hated to leave too. They had decided that Alyssa was going to visit him in Tahoe, after Malibu. And John invited Mark to come up for a weekend before he left for Kenya, and he was looking forward to it too.

John was teasing Alyssa about her pathetic fishing skills and disgust over taking the fish off the hook when two women walked into the restaurant and sat down at the table next to them. They had two little girls with them, and Fiona noticed immediately that they were identical twins. Alyssa glanced at them and smiled, and Fiona commented on what beautiful children they were, but so was their mother. She was a spectacular-looking young woman with a halo of soft blond hair, and the twins looked just like her. And the woman with them appeared to be a friend. The twins smiled shyly at Alyssa after she smiled at them, and their mother glanced over at the group at Fiona's table because they seemed to be having so much fun. Fiona noticed that the young woman's eyes were sad as she gazed at them. There was something wistful about her, as though she were unhappy about something, and she was very sweet to her children. John glanced over and smiled at the little girls too, and then went back to teasing Alyssa, until she couldn't take it anymore and threatened to throw food at him if he didn't stop.

"John Weston! You stop that right now, or I'm not coming to Lake Tahoe!" she threatened him, and he leaned over and kissed her and said he was only kidding. But as soon as Alyssa said his name, loud enough for the next table to hear her, Fiona saw the young blond woman's head turn instantly, and she stared at John intensely, as though studying everything about him. She was mesmerized by him. No one else at the table had noticed. The young people were all bantering with each other and talking about fishing, but Fiona saw the woman's eyes, and something about her wrenched at Fiona's heart. For the next hour, the woman stared at John and no one else, examining his every move and gesture, as though she were looking for someone she had lost. Fiona saw her whisper something to her friend, who then stared at John too. The two women couldn't keep their eyes away. And when Fiona's group left, the two women watched John until he left the restaurant. He never noticed, and Fiona didn't say anything. And once they were gone, Ashley looked at Bonnie with a devastated expression. Her own daughters' half brother had been only inches from them, and never knew who they were.

She had recognized Marshall's son instantly the moment she heard his name. He looked just like his father, and like he was having a great time, and he had smiled several times at her girls, who had been fascinated by the group at the next table and all the fun they were having. But it pained Ashley yet again to realize that she and her daughters didn't exist in Marshall's world. No one knew about them and maybe never would. Kezia and Kendall had two half brothers and a half sister they knew nothing about, and who knew nothing about them. They existed in another world, hidden by their father, and yet their paths had crossed that night anyway, by sheer chance.

Ashley was in tears when she dared to call Marshall that night and told him about it. He was on his way home from Tahoe, where he had spent the weekend with Liz and Lindsay and their friends. Ashley told him what a handsome boy John was, and how much he looked like him, and Marshall was shocked and frightened. Ashley seemed obsessed with him.

"Did you say anything to him?"

"No, I didn't. I couldn't," Ashley said sadly, and Marshall was relieved. "He and the girls are brother and sisters, and he has no idea they exist. That's not right," she said, sounding unhappy, but there was nothing he could do about it, and she knew that. He was just glad she hadn't lost her cool and said something to him, or introduced herself.

"One day they'll all meet," Marshall said to her, and for a long moment Ashley didn't answer. His double life was getting to her, and had been more acutely since the threatened sexual harassment suit. Ever since she'd learned that he had cheated on her, things were different—even if it had been a one-night stand, which she didn't believe. He had lied to Liz for eight years, and maybe now he was doing the same to her. "This isn't easy for me either," he reminded her, as though to elicit sympathy from her, but it didn't. He had the option to do it differently, but until now had chosen not to. He was still lying to Liz and keeping her and the twins in the closet. And now she had been inches away from one of his children, and they had passed like ships in the night, as though she and the girls didn't matter at all. And when they hung up, Ashley cried herself to sleep that night, realizing it might never be any different. She was beginning to lose hope that their situation would ever change.

Chapter 11

When Fiona went back to work, she was swamped, as she always was, for the first few days. But it was totally worth it, she had had a ball with her kids. And when they got back, Alyssa went up to Tahoe to visit John, and Mark went with her for a few days and then flew back to New York to meet up with his girl-friend and leave for Kenya. Fiona was working ten-hour days in the office, and several more hours at home every night, trying to catch up.

She was just beginning to get a grip on it when Logan Smith called her, this time in the office. He wouldn't have dared to use her cell phone again, although he had kept the number. She was about to tell her secretary to take a message when he called, and then decided to pick it up. She didn't want to add another call to return on her list, and she was aware that she had been curt with him the time before. She had been trying to return calls all week, and answer e-mails, along with everything else. There were problems in several plants, documents she had to sign, letters to answer, reports to read and analyze and respond to, and meetings she had to attend. When she took Logan's call, she was so busy she sounded vague.

"Yes?" For a minute, she'd forgotten who was calling as she looked for something in a stack of papers on her desk.

"Fiona? It's Logan. Logan Smith." How many people did he think she knew named Logan? she wondered.

"Yes, sorry. How are you?" She sounded as though she were going in ten directions and trying to be polite.

"I'm fine. How was your vacation?"

"Terrific," she said with a smile. "I hate it when my kids leave again. I love waking up in the same house with them every morning. It's miserable after they're gone, but I've been so busy since I got back I hardly have time to notice." She sounded warmer as soon as she mentioned her children. And he realized it was the way in with her. "So what can I do for you?" she asked, putting on her business voice again. "Not an interview, I hope." He could tell she meant it.

"I know you're busy, but I was wondering if you'd like to have lunch. I enjoyed talking to you when I called about Marshall Weston, and instead of harassing you for an interview, or disturbing you on vacation, I was hoping we could have lunch." He sounded a little nervous, and Fiona was confused.

"As a basis for an interview?" She was faintly suspicious, and she rarely stopped for lunch.

"No, just lunch. You can tell me about your sister's book." He had remembered what she said.

"I don't usually eat lunch." But she didn't want to be rude again. He had been nice every time he called, and she had enjoyed talking to him too. And she could hear her sister's voice in her head, telling her to go. It wasn't a date. Just a smart guy who might be nice to talk to over lunch. "Okay," she said, sounding hesitant. "Sure. Why not? As long as you promise not to print anything I say."

"I promise. And I won't ask you for any trade secrets, or about the sexual habits of the male

CEOs you know. That leaves weather and sports." She laughed at what he said.

"That could be a problem, I know nothing about sports."

"Okay. We can stick to weather. It looks like it might rain today."

And then she wondered if he would mind coming to Palo Alto to lunch. "I don't have time to come into the city," she said apologetically.

"I didn't think you did. I actually have an appointment out there this afternoon. Would today work for you?"

She thought about it for a minute and decided that it would. She didn't really have time, but as buried as she was, an hour off wouldn't make that much difference, as long as they were quick.

"I can get out of here for about an hour," she said, sounding slightly panicked, as she glanced at the stacks of files and folders piled up on her desk. She tried not to think about it and focused on lunch.

"That'll do." He could easily imagine how busy she was, and was happy she was willing to see him at all. He named a simple restaurant she liked where they could get a salad or a sandwich and eat outside, and she agreed to meet him there at one. He told her he was wearing a blue shirt, tweed jacket, and jeans. And he knew what she looked like.

She didn't have time to think about it. As she was driving to the restaurant, she realized that it was the first lunch break she'd taken, that wasn't for a meeting, in many months. She parked her car outside the restaurant and went in. She found Logan sitting at a table in the garden, reading e-mails on his phone. He looked up as soon as she approached the table and stood up. She was wearing one of her business suits, this one with a skirt, and had left her jacket in the car. She had on high heels, and a simple white silk blouse, and her hair in a bun. She looked very serious and businesslike in her work clothes, what she referred to as her "uniform," and she was surprised to see how attractive he was. He had dark hair with gray at the temples, and as Jillian had remembered, he was close to her age. And as she sat down at the table, she decided that he looked the way a journalist should look. Slightly intellectual, but interested and alert. He had lively brown eyes and a ready smile, and he looked very pleased to see her when she sat down. She was five minutes late.

"Sorry I'm late. I can never get out of my office without someone calling me right as I'm going through the door." She put her cell phone on vibrate as she said it, so they wouldn't be disturbed during lunch. And then she looked at him politely. "Thank you for inviting me to lunch." It was a first for her, without clients or associates.

"I felt like I owed you an apology, for calling you when you were on vacation and disturbing you with your kids."

"You couldn't know," she said pleasantly, and started to unwind. She had forgotten till then how good it felt to get out of the office in the middle of the day. "I try not to let my work interfere with my home life. When I'm with them, I belong to them. That's always been my rule."

"Your children are lucky. Both my parents were physicians, and I don't think I ever had a conversation with them, without one of them answering the phone or flying out the door. My father was an orthopedic surgeon, and my mother was a pediatrician, and still is. In a small town in Vermont. She's seventy-one years old, still practicing and going strong." It sounded good to Fiona, and an interesting way to grow up.

"How did you wind up here?"

"Like most people who come to the West Coast, by accident. I came out for a summer, fell in love with it, and stayed. But I travel a lot. Mostly to L.A. and New York. But I get a lot of work done here. I enjoy what I do." He was easy to talk to, and they only stopped long enough to order lunch. Caesar salad for both.

"So do I," Fiona said, about enjoying her work. "I always did, although I felt guilty about it when my kids were small. I stayed home for three years with my son, and I knew I couldn't do that anymore. I need to work. But I managed to be with them a lot too. It was a juggling act, but it worked. I was committed to the idea of having both, a family and a career. I still believe that, but it's not always as easy as it sounds." In fact, to him it sounded damn hard, with a career like hers, and he knew she had had big jobs for a long time. She'd been a major player in the business community for nearly twenty years, and by his standards she was still young. He didn't consider forty-nine old. He was four years younger.

"Did your husband help with the kids?" He was curious how marriages among the powerful worked, as a point of human interest, not just for his book.

She laughed before she answered his question. "No. He thought that was my job. So I did both. A lot of women do. But he was never happy about my career. He wanted me to help him with his family business, but I thought that would be a mistake, and an invitation to arguments and a bad situation. So I took jobs with other companies, and we fought about that instead. He really wanted a stay-at-home wife, and got it right on the second round."

"And you? No second round?" He was intrigued by her, and wanted to hear everything she was willing to say. He liked people and was always fascinated by them. She had been very open so far. And her divorce from David Carson was not a secret. It was even listed on the Internet, in her bio. It didn't mention the cause of their divorce, but she had told Logan the way it was.

"No time," she said in answer to his question, and she smiled again. "We've been divorced for six years. I've been busy with my work and kids. It doesn't leave me much time for anything else." And she didn't look deprived. She looked like a happy woman, who was doing what she wanted with her life. He liked that about her, and he was surprised by how attractive she was.

She was prettier than her pictures. And her hairdo, with her hair pulled back in a bun, and her simple white silk blouse and straight navy skirt reminded him of what corporate women were supposed to look like. He couldn't help wondering what she would look like with her hair down, in more casual clothes. But she could hardly go to work in a T-shirt and jeans.

"How old are your kids?" he asked, and she smiled at the question.

"My gut response is always two and five. Unfortunately, they're nineteen and twenty-two. My son is getting a master's in social work at Columbia, my daughter will be a junior at Stanford this fall. She's a business freak like me and wants to get an MBA. My son is the family saint. He's off to Kenya with his girlfriend this week to help lay pipes to bring water into a village."

"They sound like interesting kids," he said admiringly.

"They are, and nice people," she said proudly. "Do you have any?"

"Not that I know of. I've been divorced for twenty years."

"That's too bad," she said sympathetically, and then realized that not everyone felt about children as she did. Like Jillian, for instance, who was happy to have none at all.

"Yeah, I suppose it is," he said, sounding vague. He hadn't thought about having kids for years, and had decided long ago they weren't for him. It had actually broken up his marriage. His ex-wife had married someone else and had six. He was happy for her. "I'm not sure it even counts by now, it was so long ago. And I was only married for two years, fresh out of college. I married a gorgeous girl from Salt Lake, and after we got married, she told me she wanted to move back, have a million babies, and I was supposed to work for her father, in his printing plant. I tried it for a while, and I figured I would kill myself if I stayed another six months, so I ran. I came to San Francisco then, and I've been here ever since. I wanted to be kind of a journalist at large, freelancing from all over the world, or a sportswriter, and I wound up covering some interesting stories in Silicon Valley, and got pegged as an investigative reporter on business issues. I wound up discovering some criminal activities that fascinated me, and I got hooked. Maybe I'm a detective at heart and I'm good at that stuff. But I love the real human stories, like Mandela. Interviewing him was the high point of my life. Opportunities like that don't come up very often."

"My sister read those interviews and said they're fabulous."

Their salads arrived then, and they continued talking while they ate. They covered a variety of subjects, and he almost asked her about their boardroom leak and decided against it. He didn't want her to think that he'd had lunch with her to pump her for information, which he hadn't. He had taken her to lunch only because he admired what he knew of her, and wanted to get to know her better. He was fascinated by her, and how normal and modest she was, despite her very important job. Nothing about her suggested that she was one of the most important women in the country, running a mammoth corporation, and she was easy and unpretentious on top of it, and incredibly bright. But he liked how unassuming she was, and she made him laugh when she talked about her sister, who sounded like a character to him.

"I think you'd like her," Fiona assured him, and having gotten a good look at him now, she was sure that Jillian would be crazy about him. He was not only very smart and well educated, he was also very good looking, in a casual, easygoing way. "She's in Tuscany right now. She's a hell of a tennis player, if you like to play."

"Are you pimping for her?" he asked with a grin.

"She doesn't need my help." Fiona laughed at his question. "My sister always has a guy, when she wants one. She looked like a beanpole as a kid, she's just over six feet tall. And tall or short, young or old, guys drop at her feet. She has such a great personality, I've never met anyone who didn't like her." Even David, with all his complaints about Fiona, had thought Jillian was fun. And she always made him laugh.

"What about you? What were you like as a kid?" he asked her, and looked genuinely interested. He was asking her questions he normally wouldn't have asked at a first lunch, and she would have deflected them, but he was open with her, and she was so much more personable and warm than he'd expected, that they were surprisingly forthcoming with each other.

"I was shy. And I wore glasses and had buckteeth until I had braces," she said with a modest smile.

"And then you turned into a swan," he said, looking at her, and she blushed at what he said.

"Not exactly. I wear contacts, and a night

guard at night when I'm stressed, so I don't clench my jaw."

"Scary," he said, and they both laughed. "With all the stress you must have in your job, I'm surprised you don't wear a helmet and shin guards, and a protector for your teeth. I don't know how you do it. The responsibility for a hundred thousand employees would kill me. All I have to do is turn in my stories on deadline."

"That's stressful too," she said practically. "I don't know. I like what I do. I think that helps." She seemed totally focused on her job, in a very human way. She was completely different from the arrogant CEOs he met and interviewed every day, like the one he was meeting with that afternoon, whom he didn't like but was an important story. His subjects usually spent hours talking about themselves, telling him how great they were. And Fiona talked about having buckteeth as a kid, and wearing a night guard to bed. It was hardly a sexy image, despite her natural good looks, and she didn't seem to mind pointing out her own flaws. He thought there was something very touching about it. He found her astonishingly humble, particularly given how important and powerful she was.

"What's the one word you would use to describe your job?" he asked her, trying to get a sense of how she felt about it, but he already knew. And she was quick to answer.

"**Hard.** Second word: **fun.** What about you?"

He thought about it for a minute—he wasn't used to anyone asking him the questions. "**Fascinating. Surprising. Different every day. Exciting.** I'm never bored by the people I meet, even if I don't like them. And people never turn out to be what I expected." She wasn't either. She was even better than he had thought. He was only sorry that she wouldn't let him interview her. He could have done a great piece. But if they wound up friends, by some sheer stroke of good luck, that would be even better. And Fiona was happy she had had lunch with him too. She realized that Jillian was right, and it was interesting to meet new people. And she genuinely liked Logan, more than she thought she would. She had accepted lunch with him to be polite, and she was having a terrific time. She looked regretful when she finally glanced at her watch, saw that it was almost two o'clock, and knew that she had to go. She had a meeting in twenty minutes.

Logan paid for their lunch, and they walked out of the restaurant together.

"Thank you for meeting me for lunch today," he said sincerely as he walked her to her car. "It's nice to meet the woman who goes with the voice. You're nothing like I expected. Well, a little, but not a lot. You're just a regular person." He loved that about her.

"Yes, I am," she said simply. "Most people expect the Wizard of Oz, or the Wicked Witch of the West." She reminded him more of Dorothy than the witch the house had fallen on, although he had met plenty of those too. But not Fiona. She didn't take herself too seriously, and listened to what other people had to say. She had an innocent quality that he liked about her too, as though she were so clean and straightforward that she expected everybody else to be too, and they both knew they weren't. But she seemed like the kind of woman who gave people the benefit of the doubt and brought out the best in those around her.

"I hope your interview goes well this afternoon," she said as she unlocked her car and slid behind the wheel.

"You don't use a driver?" He looked surprised, and she shook her head.

"I'd rather drive myself. It's simpler. I only use one if I go to the airport."

"Yeah, me too," he said with a grin. "Well, take care, and thanks for joining me. Maybe we can do it again sometime. And I'd like to meet your sister."

"I'll e-mail you her number. You should call her." But even he wasn't brave enough to call her out of the blue, and he would have felt foolish calling her, just because Fiona said so. "Believe me, she's not shy. And she'd love to meet you and talk about her book."

"I'll let you make the introductions," he said.

"Thanks again for lunch," she said, and waved as she drove away, and Logan thought about her as he walked to his car, amazed at how easy and fun it had been. She hadn't disappointed him in any way, and the word that came to mind as he thought about her was **terrific**.

Fiona had had a good time at lunch too. When she got back to her spot in the parking lot and parked her car, she glanced at her BlackBerry and saw that she had a message from the investigation service they had used. She listened to it before she got out of her car. It was from the head of the company, and he said it was urgent.

She called him back as soon as she got to her office, and he told her he wanted to come in and see her that afternoon.

"That urgent?" Fiona asked him.

"I think so." They had taken long enough to get back to her on it, and now they were in a hurry. She knew she would be in meetings until six o'clock, and told him it was the best she could do, and he promised to be there then. And when she left her last meeting of the afternoon, he was waiting for her in her office. It had been a long day, and she was tired. And she was still paying her dues after her vacation.

She invited him to sit in a small meeting area with her, and he handed her a thick envelope with the initial results of their investigation in it, and she asked him to sum it up so she didn't have to read it while he waited.

"You may want to close the door before I do," he said carefully, and she smiled at the espionage aspect of it. Everyone else had left for the day, including her assistants.

"Do you know who the source of the leak was?" she asked as she followed his advice and closed the door to her office, although she felt silly when she did.

"Yes, I do," he said seriously. "I got final confirmation of it yesterday. And I checked it again this morning. Everything in the report has been verified, and we used no wiretaps or illegal sources. It's all been handled just as you requested, legally and cleanly." She nodded, satisfied by what he was saying.

"Why don't you tell me who it is? I'll read the report in detail tonight at home." She felt a ripple go down her spine as the head of the investigation looked at her. He was retired FBI, and had been highly recommended.

"Your leak on the board is Harding Williams," he said simply. Fiona stared at him in disbelief. It wasn't possible. They had to have made a mistake. He was pompous and disagreeable, and he hated her, but he was a man who followed the rules, and his integrity was above question.

"Are you sure?" Her voice was a squeak when she said it. "The chairman?" she asked, as though she needed to confirm who he was. It just couldn't be true.

"The chairman," he said with a somber look. "He's been having an affair with a very attractive young woman for the past year. She's a journalist, and it may have started innocently, but she's been bleeding him for information. I don't know if she's blackmailing him or not. I don't think so. But they meet once a week at a hotel, and whatever else they do, he shares information with her. Maybe he just thinks it's pillow talk, but she uses it. And he must have known it since the leak about the Larksberry plant. She actually told one of my operatives that she has a source straight from the boardroom at NTA. She's proud of it. And he's been hinting to his barber that he's having an affair with a much younger woman. She's thirty-two years old and a knockout." He reached for the envelope, took out a file, and extracted a photograph of a beautiful girl with a stunning figure. She had dark hair and light eyes, and in the photograph, she was exhibiting a fair amount of cleavage. Fiona stared at it for a long time and then handed it back to him, and he put it back in the envelope and sealed it.

"Are you sure he's having an affair with her?" Fiona said in disbelief, and he pointed at the envelope.

"It's all in there. I have photographs of them together, two of them kissing. He seems to be crazy about her." He was more than twice her age, and all Fiona could think of was the subdued woman he was married to, whom he bragged about being married to for forty-four years. And he had treated Fiona like a slut for twenty-five years, for a harmless affair she'd had at Harvard in her early twenties. And what Harding was doing was so much worse. He had violated his position of trust as chairman of the board, broken confidentiality, jeopardized their stock, and hurt the company. He had disregarded and disrespected the most important rules of the board, and made a lie of everything he claimed to believe in. He was a hypocrite and a liar, and he was sleeping with a thirty-two-year-old girl, a journalist, and sharing direly sensitive company secrets with her. Fiona felt as though she were ricocheting off the walls and could hardly believe what the investigator had told her. But she knew it had to be true. The investigator had photographs of him going in and out of the hotel to meet her and receipts for the hotel room, and the girl in the picture was the one who had first printed the leak, with her byline. There was no question. Fiona stood up with the envelope in her hand and thanked him. She was going to read it all carefully that night before making a decision, but if what he said was true, there could be only one outcome. Harding Williams would have to be fired from the board and as their chairman. She wanted to read the material, and then she would call an emergency meeting of the board. Even though she didn't like him, and he had tormented her for years, this was not the outcome she had hoped for, nor the one she expected. She would never in a million years have guessed that the leak on the board was Harding.

She left the building with the investigator and drove home to Portola Valley. She felt as though someone had shot her out of a cannon. It was all so hard to imagine. She couldn't understand how he could violate the ethics and morality he claimed to believe in and adhere to. It not only proved her sister's theory about men and power, and Logan's thoughts on the subject too, but it reminded her of the old adage, "There is no fool like an old fool." And without question, Harding Williams had been a fool. She didn't even have a sense of victory about it, of having discovered the source of the leak; she was just disgusted by it. She had thought he was better than that, but apparently he wasn't. He was as low as you could get, and what he had done was shockingly dishonest.

She didn't even bother to have dinner that night. She sat at her desk reading the report from beginning to end. And when she finished it, she knew what she had to do. She called Harding at home and asked him to meet with her in the morning.

"I have better things to do," he said irascibly. "I have appointments tomorrow. I'll come in the day after."

"I'm sorry, Harding," she said in an icy tone. "I need you there tomorrow. Ten A.M.?" She had an eight A.M. controller's meeting with the CFO, and expected it to last for two hours.

"What's so important that I need to come in tomorrow?" He didn't even sound worried, just pompous and unpleasant, as usual.

"I need you to sign off on some reports, and as the chairman of the board, I can only give them to you," she said, not wanting him to know the real reason she had asked him to come in. And he groused about it, but finally agreed.

"You shouldn't leave things like that till the last minute," he complained, but he could hardly refuse her as the CEO.

"You're quite right, Harding," she said clearly. "See you tomorrow." She tried to maintain a neutral tone and barely could.

After that she e-mailed the members of the board and asked them to come in the day after her meeting with Harding. She did not notify Harding of the board meeting, and planned to advise him of it when she met with him in the morning. She wanted an opportunity to speak to him first. But there was very little he could say. They had all the evidence they needed.

She walked around her house after that, thinking about him, and the lies he had told, the fraud he had been, the hypocrite he was. It made her feel sick to think about it. She wasn't looking forward to the confrontation, but she wasn't afraid of it either. Dealing with him now was part of her job as CEO. She had a responsibility to the board and the corporation she worked for, and their stockholders. Fiona never lost sight of what she owed them. And she loved the company and wanted to protect it.

Before she went to bed that night, she sent an e-mail to Logan, to thank him for lunch and tell him that she'd enjoyed it. It felt as though it had been months ago and not that afternoon, so much had happened since. She hit "send" and sent the e-mail off to him. And then she showered, brushed her teeth, and put her night guard in. And when she looked in the mirror and saw herself, she almost laughed, remembering what Logan had said at lunch when she mentioned it to him. "Scary." It was. And so was Harding Williams. Anyone that dishonest, who violated his ethics and responsibilities to the degree that he had, was truly scary. But now, after what she knew, he could no longer torture her. He had no power over her anymore. And she went to bed, and slept like a baby, feeling as though a thousand-pound weight had been lifted off her shoulders. He had condemned her as a young woman, and been rude to her for all the years she'd been at NTA. And now she knew the truth about him. He had abused his power as chairman, cheated on his wife, and lied to them all. But it was over now. The mighty chairman was about to fall.

Chapter 12

When Harding Williams showed up in Fiona's office the next day, he strode in without waiting for her assistant to announce him. Fiona was seated at her desk, going through some papers, and expecting him. He was twenty minutes late, and she didn't care. She had been thinking about him all morning, and had read the investigator's report again when she got up. She wanted to be sure she hadn't missed anything important, or even a small detail, but she hadn't. It was all there, along with the photographs of him with the young woman, even him kissing her in a dark doorway. It made Fiona feel sick when she saw it, and sorry for his wife of forty-four years.

"Good morning, Harding," she said quietly,

as he stood across her desk from her, glaring at her, annoyed that she had asked him to come in. She got up and closed her office door. "Please sit down." She gestured to the chairs in the sitting area, where she had met with the investigator the night before.

"I don't have time to waste," he said brusquely. "I have appointments in the city this afternoon. I can't run down to Palo Alto every five minutes to please you."

"That's fine," she said, as they sat down. "We can keep this short. I'd like you to resign," she said in a clear voice. "I think you know why. And I'd like to keep this simple for both of us, and the board." He looked stunned, by what she'd said and by how smoothly she'd said it. She didn't look angry or upset, just businesslike and cold. And she met his gaze without hesitating for an instant. "You violated your responsibilities as chairman of the board. You violated the confidentiality agreement you signed, which I'd like to point out to you is a legal document. You jeopardized this company. You gave information to a member of the press, whom you are apparently sleeping with, coincidentally. You're dishonest and hypocritical, and out of respect you no longer deserve, I'm giving you the opportunity to resign from the board today. And if you choose not to, you will be fired by the board tomorrow. I suggest you cite reasons of ill health. You were due to resign in December anyway, so no one will be surprised. It's only a matter of a few months' difference, and ill health is entirely plausible. I'm sure you'll agree." He had opened and closed his mouth several times but said nothing as Fiona went on, and he stared at her in outrage, and then stood up and paced around the room. He turned to her then with pure venom in his eyes.

"How dare you speak that way to me?!" He tried to intimidate her, but it didn't work. Fiona didn't look impressed by his posturing, and she spoke in a glacial tone.

"How dare you violate this board in the way you did, and give highly confidential information to the press, which affected thousands of lives, and could have caused our stock to plummet, just so you could sleep with some girl half your age, and impress her with what you knew. How dare **you**!" Her eyes bored into his, and this time the power was hers. Truth was a mighty sword.

"You don't know what you're talking about," he blustered, and without saying another word,

she stood up and handed him the photographs
of him and the young journalist that were in
the folder on her desk. He looked like he was
going to have a heart attack when he saw them.

"Her byline was on the first leak. That's
enough evidence for me, and it will be for the
board too. Who you sleep with is none of our
business, but when your lovers start publishing
confidential information about this company,
given to them by you, then it becomes my business, Harding. You're a danger to this corporation, and the board will undoubtedly agree. We
are bound by confidentiality not to disclose our
reasons for firing you, but if you force my hand,
I will. I don't think you'll want speculation on
why you were fired all over the newspapers and
the Internet. I wouldn't in your shoes." Her eyes
never left his, and they both knew she had the
winning hand.

"You little slut," he said in a voice filled with
fury, and he was literally shaking with rage.
"You whore!"

"That would be your girlfriend, not me," she
said coldly. "And you. I never was. I was an innocent young girl who was taken advantage of
by your friend Jed Ivory, and you've held it
against me ever since. I never liked you either,

but I respected you for your abilities, the integrity I thought you had, and your distinguished career. And it turns out that you're a sham. You're a fraud, while you brag about being married for forty-four years, and make speeches about morality. You have none. I want you off this board as fast as you can sign your name. You're a danger to us all."

"You had no right to have me followed," he shouted at her.

"That's not illegal. I assured all of you that no illegal means would be used to conduct the investigation, and they weren't. You're a damn fool to be kissing her in public and making a spectacle of yourself. If she were anyone else, I wouldn't care, although I think it's disgusting of you, and in poor taste. But the woman you're sleeping with is a reporter, you shared boardroom secrets with her, and she published them. That's where I draw the line."

"Closing Larksberry would have come out eventually anyway," he argued with her, but they both knew it would have been presented very differently at the right time. Instead, the information had been used to damage the company, turn the public against them, stir up their employees, and ultimately jeopardize their stock.

And Harding knew it too. His reporter friend hadn't used the information well or responsibly, and he was so besotted with her that he had put himself and the company at risk. "If you leak this to the press, I'll sue," he said menacingly, but Fiona wasn't frightened.

"This isn't slander, Harding. It's all true. You can't sue for libel against the truth. It's an iron-clad defense. And we won't leak anything to the press if you resign today. You can tender your resignation to the board tomorrow at nine A.M. I called an emergency meeting and I expect you to be there. It's all over after that." Fiona maintained a level tone, but he had been shouting at her almost since he walked in. "How you do this is entirely up to you. You can do it cleanly, or make a mess of it. It's your choice. Personally, I'd go quietly, if I were you."

"Women like you shouldn't be running corporations," he said viciously. "You don't know what you're doing." But the solidity of their stock even in a bad economy said otherwise, and he knew that too.

"I'm not under discussion here," Fiona said quietly, and handed him a resignation letter she'd had prepared for him that morning. He took a look at it, crumpled it into a ball, threw it at her feet, and walked out of the room. But she knew he would have to sign one like it the next day, or they would fire him. He was through, finished, over. He had been exposed as the dishonest person he was. She picked up the crumpled resignation letter and threw it in the wastebasket as her assistant came in with a worried look. She had seen Harding leave, and heard him shouting through the closed door.

"Do you need an Advil?" Fiona laughed at what she said. She had never felt better. She was only sorry she had let him torment her for six years, and make her feel guilty twenty-five years before.

"No, Angela, I don't," Fiona said, and went back to her desk.

She had a full day of meetings after that, and another finance committee meeting that night, but she wasn't even tired when she got home. And she looked fresh and alert the next morning at nine o'clock when she met with the board. They were already assembled when she got there, and they looked concerned and were anxious to know what the emergency meeting was about. And just as she arrived, Harding stormed into the room. His face was red with rage as he sat down and addressed them from the chairman's seat.

"I want you all to know what kind of person this woman is," he bellowed as they looked at him in astonishment. Fiona knew what was coming, but she didn't care. There were no more battles to be fought with him. He had lost the war, and the board members were about to find that out too. "She had an affair with a married professor when she was at Harvard. She seduced him, and lured him away from his wife. She caused him to divorce her. She's a home-wrecker and a slut. She's an immoral woman and has been all her life." The board members stared at him after his outburst. He looked deranged.

Fiona spoke up in a calm voice as they looked at Harding and then at her. "The man was separated when I met him. He was a friend of Harding's. And the professor in question had a habit of sleeping with his students. He divorced his wife to marry another student he got pregnant, which wasn't me, and broke my heart. I was twenty-four years old, and the girl he got pregnant was twenty-two. He took advantage of both of us, and a lot of other girls like us before and since. That's not why we're here today," she transitioned smoothly, as several of the board members squirmed in their seats. They didn't like what Harding had said, or the way he had tried to portray her. They respected Fiona, as a woman and as the CEO. "We're here because our investigators have discovered the source of our leak," she said calmly. "Unfortunately, Harding is our boardroom leak. He's involved with a journalist, and has been having an affair with her for the past year. She's the woman whose byline was on the story. There is no question of it, and I have a copy of the report for each of you." There was a stack of them on the conference table, marked confidential, with their names on them. She went on calmly from her seat. "I urged Harding to resign yesterday, for reasons of ill health, which would cause very little attention in the press, since he's due to resign in five months anyway. He refused. I would like to make the same suggestion today, or we can fire him. I don't care either way." She turned to Harding then, who was slumped in his chair. He had run out of steam, and every member of the board looked shocked by what they'd just heard. "Harding, do you have anything to say?" She asked the question without visible emotion and appeared to be in total control. There were whispered murmurs from the board members as they each took a copy of the report, and then he spoke up.

"I'll resign," he said as he stood up and looked at the faces around the conference table. "I want your assurance that none of this will be leaked to the press," he said with a terrified expression. Every board member nodded assent. He didn't deserve the loyalty he hadn't shown himself, but all Fiona wanted was for the matter to die a silent death. Exposing him would only harm NTA, which was her first concern and theirs, but not his, or he would never have done what he did.

"You have our assurance and our word," one of the board members spoke up. Harding nodded, and looked at Nathan Daniels, the most senior member of the board. He was a bank president, whom they all respected, and had been on the board longer than anyone else.

"I'll send it to you today. For reasons of ill health," Harding confirmed. And then he walked out without looking at any of them. He offered no apology, and never said goodbye. He didn't look at Fiona either as he left the room, and there was a long moment of silence as they all absorbed what had happened. He was the last person that any of them would have expected to betray them, or to have his head turned around by an affair with a young woman. He had risked his reputation and his honor for her, and she had betrayed him in turn by publishing what he said.

Fiona brought them to order then, and reminded them that they needed to appoint a new chairman before they left the room. NTA could not have a board without a leader at its helm. She suggested Nathan Daniels, who was respected by them all. Fiona's suggestion was adopted by the board and unanimously endorsed.

Twenty minutes later they all left the room with a copy of the report in their hands. They still looked shocked by everything that had occurred and by the proceedings that morning. Fiona went back to her office and asked the PR department to draft a press release, announcing Harding's resignation for reasons of ill health, and Nathan Daniels's appointment as chairman of the board. It was a benign announcement, and Nathan's long tenure made him a reasonable choice that would please their stockholders. The release was unlikely to cause comment in any quarter. And by one o'clock Fiona had Harding's resignation in her hands. It was over. The mystery had been solved. And Harding was gone. Fiona had handled it as she did everything else, with competence, dignity, and grace. She wanted to have a sense of victory about it, but she didn't. She felt nothing except relief, as she quietly went back to her duties of the day as CEO. But her mission had been accomplished; the board of the corporation she had been entrusted to run was safe at last.

Chapter 13

The first call Fiona got the morning after Harding Williams's resignation was from Logan Smith. She took the call and wondered if the timing was coincidental, or if he was going to comment on Harding leaving the board. She didn't have long to wait.

"Was he your leak?" was the first thing he said after hello. He was even smarter than she'd thought, and had figured it out. But she had no intention of telling him the truth. She liked him, but she wasn't about to divulge secrets to him, or anyone else.

"He's been sick," she answered calmly, as though nothing unusual had occurred. "He had to retire at the end of the year anyway. We have mandatory retirement, and he's turning seventy in December. It didn't make sense for him to hang on for another five months in bad health." She spoke in her most professional voice.

"He doesn't strike me as the kind of guy who would retire five minutes before he had to, even if he's half dead. I interviewed him two years ago, and he's a tough old bird."

"We all get old and sick. Even Harding. We were all worried about him. But it was the right thing to do." That much was true. But Logan was still suspicious. It didn't sound plausible to him.

"I can smell a party line when I hear one, Fiona." But he didn't insist. And then he thought of something else. "Did you know when we had lunch the other day? I'm just curious. I won't run it. You can tell me off the record."

"Actually, I didn't. I only discovered that he was leaving the board later that day." That was true too, when she met with the investigator in her office and discovered Harding was the source of their leak. But the decision hadn't been Harding's. It had been hers. "The board met yesterday to accept his resignation. He couldn't carry out his duties any longer." She was feeding him partial truths, and she didn't like it. She didn't want to lie to Logan, but she couldn't tell him the truth, nor would she. She wanted to get off the subject. But Logan wasn't ready to do that yet.

"It's no secret he disapproved of women in high corporate positions. He told me that him-self. And word on the street was always that he particularly hated you." It was a heavy state-ment for him to make and expect her to refute. And she was very careful what she answered.

"He was an outstanding chairman." Her voice was smooth as glass.

"I'm not going to get anything out of you on this, am I?" he said, sounding frustrated.

"Are you calling me for a story? Or as a friend?" She sounded sad as she asked. She didn't want to be used, by anyone.

"A little of both," he said honestly. "You're the best source I've got on this one, and something tells me there's more to the story. It was very sudden. You don't have to tell me what hap-pened if you don't want to, but don't lie to me at least."

"Then don't ask me questions I can't answer." She sounded tired as she said it. It had been a long few days since she'd had lunch with him.

"I'm not going to push you on this," he said

quietly. He respected her integrity, and knew how hard her job was. And she did it well. She wasn't the kind of woman who would have told him if Harding was the leak, and he knew it. He was wasting his time asking. "I was actually calling about something else," he said, changing the subject. "I have to do another interview in your neck of the woods tomorrow. I was wondering if you'd have dinner with me. I had a good time with you at lunch. I was going to suggest a bar I go to when I'm in Palo Alto. They serve beer and great burgers. Nothing fancy. And I promise I won't ask you about Harding Williams. You have my word. Just two pals for dinner and beer." She laughed at what he said. She hadn't had an invitation like that in years.

"In that case," she said, then hesitated for an instant. She'd been about to decline, but it sounded like fun, and she had no plans. And she was lonely at night after the vacation with her kids. "I'd like that. Can we make it early? I've had a long week."

"I'll bet you have," he sounded sympathetic. And he was sure that whatever had caused Harding Williams to resign hadn't been easy for her either. In the end, all the tough decisions rested on her, and were in her hands. "Actually, so have I. Is six o'clock too early?"

"That would be perfect." She could get home at a decent hour after dinner. It had been ages since she'd gone out for beer and burgers at a bar with a friend, but he was good to talk to. And she still wanted to get him together with her sister. He was perfect for her, even if he was ten years younger. She had a feeling that neither of them would care about the difference in their age.

He gave her the name and address of the bar, and told her he'd meet her at six o'clock the next day. And Fiona was pleased to see that any mention of Harding's resignation from the board, due to ill health, had been handled by the press in print and on the Internet as a non-event. There was some mild speculation, but no one could prove the link with their leak two months before. And they all emphasized that he'd been due to retire in a few months anyway. They were off the hook. She spent the rest of the day in meetings, dealing with the complicated business of running NTA.

And that night when she got home, she swam in the pool, which invigorated and revived her after a long day. And afterward she called Alyssa in Tahoe, where she was staying at the Westons'. Alyssa told her what they'd been doing and after a few minutes they hung up. Fiona was exhausted and wanted to go to bed.

But what Alyssa hadn't told her mother was that the atmosphere at John's parents' summer home was more stressful than she'd expected. They were very pleasant and polite, but there was a palpable tension between his parents that made everyone ill at ease. John admitted to her as they sat on the dock alone at the end of the day that it had been that way since his father was accused of sexual harassment, even though the woman who had done so had admitted that her claims were false. It didn't seem to make a difference, John told her. His parents had been upset anyway, ever since.

"The woman who accused him of it admitted she was lying, and my mom believed he was innocent all along," John explained to Alyssa, "but I think it freaked her out that anyone could make a claim like that. She's been really nervous since it happened. And my sister drives him insane. She's always looking for something to fight with them about. She told my dad she thinks he was cheating on my mom. And she still doesn't believe he didn't. So my dad is pissed at her, and my parents fight about that too. I guess it'll blow over eventually. But they haven't been the same in two months." And then he admitted his worst fear to her. "Most of the time they get along really well. But my dad is under a lot of pressure at work. Your mother must be too. I know it doesn't make sense, but I worry that they'll get divorced. None of my friends' parents are still together. Look at you," he pointed out. But Alyssa's parents had been divorced since she was thirteen. She was used to it by now, and Alyssa felt sorry for him. John said he couldn't wait to leave and go back to school. It was worse when his older brother was around. Tom and their father fought about everything, and he thought their father was a liar and a jerk, and he had pounced on the sexual harassment issue, and he believed his father was guilty of it too. John said that Tom never cut their father any slack.

"The perfect family, huh?" he said, looking like a little kid, as they sat on the dock and swung their feet in the icy water. Alyssa loved him and wanted to be there for him. He was very sweet to her.

"There are no perfect families," Alyssa said, leaning against him as he put an arm around her. "My parents used to fight all the time. My dad hated my mom's work. He thought she should stay home with us. I think that's why my mom doesn't even date anymore. All she wants now is peace. I worry about her being alone sometimes. It's lonely for her now that we're gone. But I think my father turned her off marriage and men forever. He picked on her about everything. He still does whenever he sees us. He always has something mean to say about her." Alyssa looked sad when she said it. Her parents' bad relationship had been painful for her all her life.

"Mine don't fight that much. But my mom's been really nervous since the harassment suit. She always wants everything to be perfect for all of us, and especially for him, and sometimes it just isn't. She wanted my dad to take a month off and stay up here with us, and he wouldn't. He's not even taking a vacation this year, just weekends. And he goes to L.A. every week. It's not easy being a CEO. I think I'd rather run my own business than a huge corporation, like your mom and my dad." He was becoming increasingly aware of the toll it took on everyone, not just his parents, but Alyssa disagreed.

"I'd love it," she said, smiling at him. "It's

really exciting. My mom loves what she does. I want to run a big corporation someday too." The apple didn't fall far from the tree. And her mother was her role model for everything in life. She admired what Fiona did.

"Yeah, but if she winds up alone because of it, what good is that? I'd rather have a solid marriage and a house full of kids," he said with a grin.

"I'd be happy with two, like my brother and me," Alyssa said demurely.

"I was thinking more like five or six," he teased her. "And imagine if all six of them were like my sister—I'd kill myself. I swear, she must spend all her spare time figuring out ways to piss them off. She told my father she's going to get a tattoo when she turns eighteen."

"I'll bet he loved that." Alyssa laughed. She thought Lindsay was funny, although a rebel to the core, but she was just a kid, and would probably outgrow it in a few years.

"My mom said she doesn't really mean it, but watch her get some ugly tattoo on her eighteenth birthday," John said with a rueful grin. And Lindsay had gotten considerably worse, and ruder to their father since the threatened harassment suit. John had been re-

lieved to get away from all of them and visit
the Carsons in Malibu. Alyssa's family seemed
like much happier people, and in spite of her
job, he thought her mother was more relaxed
than his father, and she obviously loved being
with her kids. His own mother was more uptight and under pressure to do everything
right and be perfect, and she worried about
everything, particularly lately. It just wasn't
fun at their house anymore, although it was
better when his father came up to the lake for
the weekend. He had bought them a Jet Ski,
which made his mother nervous. She was
afraid he'd have an accident on the lake. Once
his father arrived that weekend, Marshall let
John take Alyssa out on their boat, and they
sped around and went fishing and enjoyed it.
But the boat was a source of arguments between his parents too. The end result was that
they weren't having much fun, and they'd
been much more relaxed in Malibu. And the
lake was as cold as the atmosphere in the house
at times. That night Alyssa overheard John's
parents arguing about letting John take her
out in the boat.

"It's too dangerous. There are accidents on
the lake every day. People get killed. What if

she gets hurt while she's here?" Liz worried about everything these days.

"Oh, for chrissake, Liz. He's perfectly responsible. You can't treat him like a five-year-old. He plays football. That's a lot more dangerous than driving a boat around the lake."

"That's different." Liz tried to explain, but Marshall wouldn't listen, and when they went to bed that night, he turned to her and asked her what was wrong. As soon as he said it, she started to cry. She seemed to cry constantly now, and had for the past two months. It was like an aftershock of everything that had happened. She had been so solid and strong when he needed her to be, and now she was falling apart.

"Sweetheart, what is it?" he asked her gently as she clung to him and cried. She hated it when he went anywhere these days.

"I don't know," she said honestly. "I'm scared all the time that something bad will happen, to you, or the boys, or Lindsay." The accusation of harassment had rocked her world, and even though she believed him, the idea that he might have an affair was haunting her now. She had never believed he cheated on her, but suddenly she was worried that he would. She felt ugly and old. And the malice in the world, embodied by a woman like Megan Wheeler, had come too close to their peaceful life, and it had shaken Liz badly. Nothing felt safe to her anymore. She even worried that something would happen to him in L.A., or that the company jet would crash with him on it. She was suffering from a kind of nonspecific acute malaise.

"Maybe you should see a doctor," Marshall said, looking worried, and Liz nestled into his arms. He felt that she was upset all the time now, and he was helpless to calm her down. He wondered if she was sick.

"I'll see how I feel when we go home," she said quietly. He was worried about her, he didn't understand what had happened to her. She had always been his rock, and he could count on her, and suddenly she had gone weak at the knees. It was a relief for him every week when he went back to the city, and got away from her for a few days.

And things in Malibu were no better. Ashley was depressed too. The whole incident with Megan Wheeler had made her realize that Marshall might cheat on her again, even for a one-night stand. And she had become increasingly obsessed about Liz, ever since she'd seen them together on TV. She was fed up with his double life, between the two households, and she no longer wanted to wait for Lindsay to finish senior year. She wanted him to leave Liz now and move to Malibu to live with her and the girls. She harped on him about it every chance she got.

"I can't wait another year," she said, sobbing at breakfast, and Marshall felt like a Ping-Pong ball being batted back and forth between two crying women, both of whom were driving him insane. He tried to be patient with Liz, but Ashley was putting so much pressure on him that he expressed his anger more frequently with her, which only made things worse for them.

"I can't live like this!" he shouted at her one morning after the girls left for camp. He tried not to lose his temper around them, but he needed Ashley to be more understanding than she was being at the moment. Marshall pointed out that she was a grown woman, and his situation was not new to her. "I think Liz is having some sort of nervous breakdown, and I can't deal with you falling apart too." He ran his hands through his hair in desperation, and Ashley burst into tears and ran upstairs to their bedroom. She was sick and tired of hearing about Liz. He found Ashley sobbing in their bed half an hour later, and he didn't know what to do. Both women were driving him crazy. Neither of them felt sure of him anymore, and both of them were insecure. Their peaceful lives had been shattered, and whichever city he was in now, it felt like the wrong one to him. He was going from one unhappy woman to another. And Lindsay only made it worse when he was with Liz. She had barely spoken to her father since May. At least the twins still thought he was a hero, but no one else did. Ashley was accusing him of cheating on her, and Liz was afraid he would. He had no one to talk to about it, and he was barking at everyone wherever he went. He could hardly concentrate on his work, but at least going to the office was a relief.

"Ashley, you have to calm down," Marshall begged her. He wanted things to be better with her again, even more so than with Liz. Liz was his duty. Ashley was his dream. "You have to trust me. I swear to you, everything will be fine in a year. You'll have everything you want. But if I walk out on Liz now, my kids will never forgive me. Just let me get Lindsay through high school, and all your dreams will come true." But he knew she no longer believed him, and that everything Bonnie said to her when he wasn't around just made it worse. They were hardly making love. He could barely think straight anymore. All he wanted was for everything to be the way it had been for the past eight years. Ashley wanted more. She wanted everything, and a full life with him.

When he got back to Lake Tahoe on Friday, Lindsay had had a fight with her mother, and they weren't talking to each other. He poured himself a stiff drink and went out to sit on the dock, and a lone tear slid down his cheek. His life was a mess, and there was nothing he could do about it, and he didn't want to. He didn't want to rock Liz's world any more than it already had been. Megan Wheeler's claims had turned Liz's life upside down, worse after it was resolved than when it was happening, or so it seemed. And his admission of guilt to Ashley, even minimally for the sake of honesty with her, hadn't served him well. He was sorry he had told her what he did. He needed both of them to calm down so they could regain some kind of normalcy. And in a year, when Lindsay graduated, he could see where things were with Liz. But whichever way he turned, he knew he would destroy someone's life, or his own. That was the last thing he wanted. All he needed from both of them was peace, and their support, not their demands. He felt as though he had two boa constrictors around his neck, and they were squeezing him as hard as they could. It even made him nervous now when he went to L.A. Instead of being welcomed with open arms and jumping into bed with him, he had no idea what condition Ashley would be in, what she would accuse him of this time, and her demands had been strident ever since she'd seen him on TV with Liz.

He sat staring out at the lake, with his drink in his hand, thinking about all of it, wondering what to do. Everything seemed discordant in his life, and all it did was make him want to run away, from both of them. Ashley talked to him about his responsibility to her and the twins, which he knew came straight from Bonnie, who spent more time with her than he did, and had ample opportunity to poison her against him. And Liz was talking about spending more time together and even coming to L.A. with him in the fall if she could find someone to stay with Lindsay, which panicked him. He felt as though his whole world, and the women in it, were closing in on him. As he thought about it, he finished his drink, and dove into the icy water. Feeling his body tingle with the shock of it felt good to him. He swam out to the raft and then back to the dock and got out. And when he got back to the house, Liz and Lindsay were fighting again and both of them were in tears. It was more than he could deal with, and without saying a word to either of them, he walked past them and upstairs to his bedroom. He closed the door, and lay on the bed with his eyes closed, trying not to think about it. And as he lay there, he heard a text message come in. It was from Ashley. She knew she wasn't supposed to do that, but sometimes she did anyway. And lately she had been taking more and more chances, as a way of pushing him. He glanced at the text message and all it said was "I love you. We miss you." He erased it and closed his eyes again, and tried to go to sleep. But all he could think of was Ashley and the twins, and how good it felt to be in bed with her. He was going to L.A. on Tuesday, and all he could hope was that this would be a better week. And maybe by the end of summer they would all calm down again and get off his back. All he wanted now was peace.

Chapter 14

Fiona found the bar easily on Friday at six o'clock. It was exactly as Logan had described: kind of a dive, full of students from Stanford, and a few people who had stopped by after work for happy hour and a beer on the way home. It was dark inside when she walked in, and she saw him at a table in a back corner and smiled to herself. It wasn't the kind of place she went to usually, but it made her feel young and carefree, and not like a responsible CEO. She was wearing the trousers of her pantsuit, and had rolled up the sleeves of her silk shirt. And she had changed into flat shoes she had in her trunk, and just so as not to look like someone's mother among all the students, she let her hair out of the severe bun she normally wore to work, and her blond hair was cascading loosely to her shoulders. It was the best she could do to look more casual, given what she wore to work, and it felt better as she walked over to the table and Logan looked up from his newspaper with a grin.

"You found it." He looked happy to see her, and he was wearing a blue shirt and jeans, and his sleeves were rolled up too.

"No problem. How are you?" she asked as she slid into her seat. And although she hadn't planned it, or even been open to it at first, she felt as though they were becoming friends. It was exactly what her sister said she needed in her life, more people, less structure, to balance her enormous responsibilities. And as usual, Jillian was right. Fiona was beginning to like Logan and thought he would be a good friend, if he didn't press her for insider information about NTA, which remained to be seen. He had said he wouldn't, and she was going to hold him to his word, otherwise they couldn't be friends.

"I'm fine. Happy it's Friday," he said with a grin of relief. "How was your day?" It was refreshing and new for her to have someone ask. He actually looked interested when he asked her, and she hoped it wasn't a ploy to get her to talk about work, but she decided to be honest with him, as far as she could, like two ordinary friends meeting at a bar. This was new to her. Her social engagements were more formal, either dinner parties with old friends, which she rarely went to anymore since she wasn't a couple and was tired on the weekends, or evenings that were related to business, which were necessary but not much fun. This was very different.

"Actually, my day was a bitch," she answered him honestly. "I'm glad it's Friday. I need a couple of days off. How was yours?"

"Interesting. I just interviewed a fascinating young entrepreneur. Harvey Eckles. He's made a billion dollars on the Internet, and he's twenty-three years old. He looks like he couldn't find his way out of a men's room with a flashlight. But he's a genius, and talking to him was like meeting Einstein. I didn't understand a thing he said, which is why he made that kind of money and I didn't. But it was fun." He was smiling at Fiona and looked relaxed.

"What you do must be really fascinating. I had an internship at a newspaper when I was in college, but I discovered that I can't write anything interesting to save my life, just business reports. I got a C-minus in creative writing, which was the worst grade I ever got."

"I got a D in Journalism 101, which is why I decided to do that for a living. It's worked out really well for me. You probably had too much talent," he said, and they both laughed as the waitress came over and took their order. Logan ordered a cheeseburger with everything on it, while Fiona ordered a plain burger and fries. He ordered a Heineken, and she a Diet Coke. "So what do you do on the weekends for fun, Fiona?" He seemed interested.

"Work," she said, and they both laughed again. "Unfortunately, that's true. I take work home on weekends, otherwise I can't keep up. I have so many interruptions in the office, and scheduled meetings, it doesn't leave me much time to fill in the gaps. And I hang out with my kids, when they're home, which isn't often anymore. So I fill the void with work," she admitted, and he was watching her eyes as she talked. He saw a sadness there about her children and how much she missed them. And he didn't think she had a man in her life, or she wouldn't have had dinner with him, or filled her weekends with work. Those were the activities of a woman who had nothing else to do. He knew the symptoms well, and worked a lot on week-ends too. And he had no children to fill holi-days and vacations, just friends, which was enough for him.

"How did you manage to bring up kids and have a career like yours?" A lot of women he knew didn't, and wound up with screwed-up kids who resented them, or they regretted never having them at all. And from what she said, he got the feeling her kids were okay and he could tell that they were close and she enjoyed them.

"I'm a good juggler," she said confidently. "I returned calls when I took Alyssa to ballet, and I managed to get to almost all of Mark's soccer games, with my BlackBerry of course. And I worked at night when everyone went to bed. I didn't get a lot of sleep."

"Margaret Thatcher slept three hours a night," he informed her, "and she ran a country. I think people who don't need a lot of sleep have it made. They conquer the world while the rest of us are snoring for eight hours. I fall apart if I don't get seven hours myself, which is why I'll never be more than a lowly reporter, while you run one of the biggest corporations in the country."

"Yeah," she said, smiling as she shrugged off the compliment, "but there are other things I can't do. A lot of them in fact. I'm terrible at sports, except for tennis, which my sister made me play all my life and still does, and she's a fantastic player. I'm a lousy cook, according to my children. My son cooks better than I do. And according to my ex-husband, I was a terrible wife, and flunked seventeen years of it, so I guess you can't do everything. The woman he married after me makes her own Christmas decorations and is a fabulous cook and never worked. So I guess I got that one wrong from the beginning, but we have wonderful kids." She looked happy as she said it, and at peace.

"I'll be sure to call your successor when I decorate my tree. I'm not sure making your own Christmas decorations makes someone a good wife, Fiona. Who did he marry? Martha Stewart?" She laughed out loud and then looked serious for a minute.

"No, just a woman who hates the business world as much as he does. I think they have fun together. We never did. I was too busy trying to be the perfect wife and mother, and trying to do a good job at whatever company I worked for. It was pretty intense." And so were the arguments and the unhappy years, but she didn't say that to him.

"It doesn't sound like a match made in heaven to me. Like my wife. She would have buried me in Salt Lake, working at her father's printing business and having a baby every year. We make some pretty stupid choices when we're young. Some of us make stupid choices when we're older too. I lived with a woman for about four years, ten years ago. It was kind of a loose arrangement, looser than I thought I signed on for. I found out she was sleeping with at least three of my friends. She thought monogamy was 'unnatural' for humans. I still had a few illusions about that, which is admittedly limited of me. She's actually still living with my best friend. They have two kids but never married. And it seems to work for them. We all have our own crazy ideas about what makes relationships work. The trick seems to be finding someone with similar ideas, or compatible ones at least. I've never managed to pull that off. And like you, I work too hard. My last girlfriend said I was a workaholic, and she's right. And in my case, I travel too much, covering stories. I was in South Africa for six months when I worked on the Mandela pieces, and I wish I had stayed longer. I loved it. And I travel for stories whenever I get the chance. It keeps life exciting."

"I only travel for work," Fiona said with a look of regret. "The kids always want me to go to exotic places with them, and I never have time, or it seems too complicated, or I'm tired. I keep promising to take them to Japan, and I haven't yet. Maybe one of these days." But she didn't look as though it was going to happen anytime soon. "My sister is much better about that. She's in Tuscany this summer, visiting friends."

"Yeah, and from what you said, she doesn't run a major corporation, or have kids. That makes a difference. I don't know how you juggle what you do. And I'll bet you weren't a 'terrible wife,' no matter what your ex says. I have more faith in you than that." He could already sense that she was a perfectionist about everything she did, and tried her best, or she wouldn't have had the job she did, and healthy kids.

"Thanks for the vote of confidence. But he may be right. He's still pissed off about it, even now that he's married to 'Martha Stewart.' " She had a feeling the name was going to stick now that he'd come up with it.

"That's pretty pathetic if he's still carrying a grudge, after how long?"

"Six years."

"And what about you? Anyone important in

your life since?" He acted like a reporter even when he was out for dinner, and he wanted to know everything about her. She liked finding out about him too, and he was forthcoming about himself. He didn't seem like a man who had secrets, and he appeared to have good insights into himself. He wasn't unaware and knew who he was and how he related to other people.

"No," she answered his question honestly. "A lot of blind dates at first, set up by friends who felt sorry for me when David and I broke up. And they were unbelievably bad. Most men run screaming from the room when they find out you run a company and figure you're a bitch. The ones who stick around are deaf, dumb, or blind, or all three, or recently out of prison. Besides, I really don't have time. My life works the way it is."

"And how is it?" he asked with interest. He wondered how she perceived it. He saw her as a fabulous woman going to waste if she didn't have a man in her life at her age. He thought some lucky guy was missing out big-time if he hadn't realized how remarkable Fiona was, and her ex-husband sounded like a loser to him.

"My life is peaceful, busy, and sane. That

works for me," she said, and looked as though
she meant it. "No one is accusing me of what I
did wrong, hating me for my career, or telling
me how bad I am. I don't think you can have a
relationship, or a marriage, and a career like
mine. I tried and it doesn't work. No man, or
damn few, can put up with a woman who has a
bigger career than he does, or even one just as
big, and worse yet if she makes more money.
My ex-husband punished me for it for seventeen years. I have no desire to sign on for that.
It was miserable, although I tried to pretend it
wasn't. But it was. Why would I want to do
that again?"

"Not all men are as stupid as your ex-husband,"
he said bluntly, "or have such fragile egos. A
man who's comfortable with himself ought to
be able to respect you for your career, without
punishing you for it. And if you got in a new
relationship, what would you have to lose?" He
made it sound theoretical, and she hoped he
wasn't volunteering. She didn't want to get involved with him or anyone else. She really was
happy as she was, despite her sister urging her
to date again. It worked for Jillian, not for her.

"If I get involved again, I could lose my heart,
my sanity, and my time. I'd kind of like to hang

on to all three. And my self-esteem. I felt terrible about myself when my marriage failed. I
don't want to feel like that again. It's taken six
years for me to feel good about myself. I don't
want to give that up for anyone. Why should I?
I think with a career like mine, as a woman,
relationships just don't work. A man who's successful in business is a hero. For a woman, it's
entirely different. You become immediately
suspect, and besides, it's not sexy being the
CEO of a company. People act like you're a man
in disguise."

"If that's a disguise," Logan said, grinning at
her, and looking at her long blond hair, which
made her look much younger when she wore it
down, "it's not working for you. You still look
like a girl to me." But he also dealt with people
like her every day. He had interviewed hun-
dreds of successful, important women, and he
was neither fooled by the outer trappings that
went with it, nor impressed by them. What he
cared about was the person, male or female, not
the title on the door, or how important they
thought they were. And he liked Fiona as a
human being, which counted for a lot for him.
He was sure she would be a good friend if they
had the opportunity to spend time together.

And he thought she was shortchanging herself out of more. "I really don't agree with you, Fiona. Just like you thought you could have a family and a career, I think one can have a relationship and a big career too. I haven't found the right person, and I haven't really been looking, but I know she's out there. And you didn't give up being a woman the day you became a CEO. I don't think it's a choice you have to make."

"I don't have the time to find the right one," she said honestly, "and I really don't want to. I don't want all the headaches that go with it. At forty-nine, I feel too old."

"That's bullshit. What if you live to be ninety? Do you really want to spend the next forty years alone? That seems kind of sad to me." But the seventeen miserable years of her marriage to David seemed a lot sadder to her, and she didn't want to risk that again. She had never been as happy in her life as in the last six years.

"Maybe some people aren't meant to live in pairs. I think I'm one of them."

"You've just got war wounds. If you want to, you'll find the right guy one of these days."

"I don't want to," she said firmly. "Trust me, no one is lining up to date female CEOs. It's an occupational hazard. Our male counterparts seem to have all the fun, while all we do is work." Just like in real life, in her experience.

"Sounds like a bad division of labor and ratio of perks to downsides to me. Besides they may have all the fun, but look at the messes they get into. Bimbos, porn stars, blackmail, public apologies—they're always having to kiss someone's ass for the trouble they get into. It doesn't look like fun to me."

Fiona laughed. "Yeah, to me neither. Like Marshall Weston two months ago. He got out of that pretty quickly. It doesn't always work that way, with the woman recanting within a day, and cleaning it all up. He got off lucky."

"I'm sure it wasn't easy for him either," Logan said. "Who knows what contortions they went through to get him off the hook? I know there was a settlement, the terms of which were confidential. They must have paid her a fortune."

"He does a good job for UPI," she said fairly, hoping to change the subject. "He's a terrific CEO."

"Smooth guy. I've interviewed him too." But he hadn't liked him personally. Marshall was so slick that Logan had no idea who he was inside, and he hated subjects like that. It was like trying to look through a brick wall. By contrast, Fiona seemed open, honest, and transparent, and there was a human side to her that he liked. He liked her just as much as he admired her before, and possibly more now as he got to know her better. He really could conceive of being friends with her if she would ever let that happen, and of that he was not yet sure. She was very guarded about her private life and jealous of her time, of which she had very little.

"I met Marshall's wife when I interviewed him at his house in Ross," Logan volunteered. "She's one of those perfect corporate wives who do everything right, are never too much in evidence but just enough, and you have no idea who they really are. She was kind of like this perfect robot when I met her, built for his exclusive use, to meet his every need. Women like that make me nervous. I always figure that one day they'll lose it and go totally nuts and start shooting people from a church tower or something, after years of being treated like a machine and not a human being."

Thinking about it, she had to admit, Liz Weston had looked a little strung out when she stood next to Marshall at the press conference on TV.

She had met a lot of women like her in the course of her career and had nothing in common with them. Theirs was a life of service, designed to meet their husband's every need, and their only sense of achievement seemed to be measured by their husband's success. It looked like living vicariously to Fiona, instead of having an identity and accomplishments of their own. It wouldn't have been enough for her. The marriages of those women, and the status symbols that went with them, appeared to be all they had. It gave her the creeps. She had tried hard to make David happy, but she had never been willing to give up herself or her dreams, and she had taken a beating for it, which was why marriage didn't appeal to her anymore. And she didn't want a "corporate husband" to pay lip service to her, not that she had seen many in her lifetime. Those roles were almost always reserved for women. So many of the successful women she knew had wound up alone, just like her. It was the nature of the beast, and the price you had to be willing to pay. She had to carry her burdens and fight her battles alone; she couldn't imagine life otherwise anymore.

"Do you like baseball?" he asked then, changing the subject halfway through their burgers. He hadn't meant to get into a discussion about relationships with her, it had just happened, and she had been open to discussing the subject, which surprised him.

"Yes, I do. And football, although I never go to games."

"Let me guess," he teased her, "no time, and no one to go with. Well, if you're amenable, at least that can change. I'm a baseball fanatic, and I have season tickets. Do you want to go with me sometime?" She loved the idea of being pals with him, and she knew her sister would approve.

"That sounds like fun," Fiona said, smiling at him.

"Perfect. I'm going to hold you to it. How about next Saturday? There's a home game." She nodded agreement, and he told her who was playing, and reeled off a slew of statistics to dazzle her.

"You are a fanatic." She was impressed.

"I've loved baseball since I was a kid. I used to dream about playing professionally when I grew up. No such luck. But I'm an avid fan." And he was happy to have an excuse to see her in a week. It wasn't a date, just a baseball game. And it sounded great to both of them.

They talked longer than they planned that night. They eventually slid into politics, and from there to some of their favorite books. Fiona said she hated the fact that she had so little time to read current books, and he was extremely well read. But most of the reading she did was for work, which he understood. He was surprised that she read as much as she did, mostly nonfiction, and a novel once in a great while on vacation. She was always playing catch-up for work.

It was after nine o'clock when they finally left the bar. Fiona thanked him for dinner, and he told her he'd pick her up before the baseball game, and she said she'd drive in from Portola Valley and meet him in the city. It was too far for him to drive, and then have to drive her home again, and he said he'd call her and they'd make a plan. She wished him a good week until then, and they both drove off. She was pleased with herself for having had dinner with him. In her position, everything she did had to have a purpose and a goal. There were no random acts and associations, except for the time she spent with her children, which was entirely spontaneous and always enjoyable. But everything else she did was structured and planned. It had been nice having dinner with Logan at the last minute. And the bar in Palo Alto had been the perfect place for an easy dinner, where they could both relax.

And as Logan drove back to the city, he was thinking the same thing about her. It was hard to imagine any man feeling threatened by her, although he was sure that there were some who would, like her idiot ex-husband, who didn't sound like a good guy to him. And one thing was sure, as far as Logan was concerned, Fiona Carson deserved a good man. She was a lovely woman, and he was glad she'd come with him. And best of all, neither of them had talked about NTA all night. He had kept his word.

Chapter 15

Things went better in L.A. for Marshall the next week. And he had no idea why, but Ashley had calmed down. She didn't tell him that she had gone to see a shrink to discuss her anxiety over their relationship. She had followed Bonnie's earlier suggestion, and it had relieved some of the stress for Ashley. Their situation was no different, but she had set some goals for herself with the shrink. They had agreed that if Marshall didn't do something about his situation by the end of the year, Ashley would try to move on. Marshall would have been stunned if he had known. And knowing that she was going to do that, Ashley was more relaxed with him when he got to L.A., and she didn't complain as much this time. He felt as though he had come home to the "old" Ashley, the one who threw herself into his arms when he arrived. They were in bed ten minutes later, and Marshall felt as though he were floating on a cloud. It was sheer heaven being with her again. The girls were at day camp, and he had even managed to drive to Malibu at lunchtime, from the office, and spend an hour in bed with her before he went back to work. Just like old times.

"I feel like I've found you again, Ash," he said in a husky voice after they made love on his second night in town. "I felt as though I was losing you for a while." He was at far greater risk of losing her now, but he didn't know it. She was trying to make better decisions about her life, and not just let him string her along for another eight years. As the therapist had said to her, the situation he had with her was much too comfortable for him, and dangerous for her. She had given him eight years of her life, and he had given her the twins, who were the greatest joy in her life. But she had no security in the relationship, or proof that he would ever leave Liz, particularly if what he said now was true, that she was falling apart. Ashley wondered if part of Liz's supposed instability was due to fear of an empty nest in the next year, but she didn't want to ask. She didn't like asking Marshall about her, and she had never wanted to come to care about her. She didn't feel guilty about what she and Marshall had, and it was up to him to deal with Liz. All Ashley wanted was him, and a real life. And Liz still had that for now. It was all Ashley needed from him.

Marshall was so happy with Ashley that week, and so grateful that she didn't bring up any difficult subjects, and pressure him, that he stayed in L.A. for an extra day, and flew back to San Francisco on Saturday morning. He didn't get to Tahoe until late Saturday afternoon, and there was hell to pay when he did. Lindsay had had an accident on the Jet Ski, and escaped uninjured, but she had virtually destroyed it, and Liz blamed him for buying it in the first place. For the past two months, nearly three now, everything that happened was his fault, whether he was responsible for it or not. And he was tired of it. He and Liz had an argument over the Jet Ski again, and the boat, on Saturday night. And she wanted him to spend more time in Tahoe with her and the kids for the next month, like all the other husbands, according to her. At the end of the argument she wanted to know why he had been in L.A. for an extra night. She was suspicious of everything now, and he knew that Ashley was too. Megan Wheeler had had an enormous impact on his life, far more than during their affair.

"I stayed to have dinner with some of the guys in the office," he said innocently. "It's not a crime, Liz. And I drove up as soon as I got back."

"Why can't you take the month off like everyone else?" she lamented. She was trying to make him feel guilty for everything, and this time he didn't. The night he had spent with Ashley was worth even Liz's tears. And he had needed that. He felt as though at least he and Ashley were back on track again, which was more than he could say about Liz. He loved her, and she was a devoted wife, but lately she had turned into a woman he didn't recognize, who blamed him for everything that wasn't working in her life. He wondered if it was just her age. But Ashley was still on the sunny side of life, and looked and acted like a kid. When they were in harmony with each other, it made him feel like a boy again. And they had made love three times that night. They were making up for lost time in the past two months.

Liz reminded him again that all her friends' husbands commuted to the lake in July, and then spent the whole month of August there. She wanted him to do the same.

"They're not running the second-biggest corporation in the country, Liz. What are they? Doctors? Lawyers? Bankers? That's a lot different. You know that. Why is that an issue now? I never spend the whole month at the lake. Why don't you come to London with me in September? I have to go for three days." He tried to throw her a bone, but it didn't work. She knew what his business trips were like.

"You'll be in meetings all day, and have business dinners at night. I'll never see you. That's not the same as taking time off here. Besides, you'll never have a decent relationship with Lindsay if you don't make an effort and spend more time with her. She's angry all the time." And they had the unhappy example of their oldest son, who refused to make an effort with his father and just stayed away, and Liz felt that was partially Marshall's fault, for favoring John and spending more time with him because they got along better, and ignoring his problems with Tom. Liz didn't want that happening with another child. The only one

who truly got along with Marshall was John,
who adored his father and forgave him everything, even the time he didn't spend with
them. And Lindsay was a very different child.
Liz insisted that she needed more from him,
which Marshall felt was an excuse. It was Liz
who wanted more. Besides, he knew that Ashley would go crazy if he didn't come to L.A.
for a month, and spent all his time with Liz. It
was a delicate balance, and a tightrope he had
walked for eight years, and so far, from his
perspective it had gone well. And who knew
what would happen when Lindsay graduated
in a year? Despite his promises to Ashley, he
wasn't sure. He'd have to see how things were
going on both sides of his life then, and what
would make sense for him.

Marshall fell asleep before Liz that night, and
he got up early and went down to the lake for a
chill morning swim on Sunday. He had breakfast with Liz and Lindsay. John was away with
Alyssa again, visiting friends, and by lunchtime
Marshall said he had to leave. He had a heavy
week ahead, and was going to L.A. a day early
that week, which gave him less time in his Palo
Alto office. He offered no apology, and Liz was
chilly with him when he left. Lindsay didn't

even acknowledge that he was leaving and refused to say goodbye, and made a nasty comment to her mother after he had gone.

"He's probably cheating on you again," she
said, and Liz felt her comment like a slap that
took her breath away. It took every ounce of
self-restraint not to lash out at her for it.

"Go to your room," she said through clenched
teeth, with tears in her eyes, "and don't **EVER**
say anything like that to me again! What your
father does is between him and me. He's an
honest man, and a good father. And I expect
you to respect him as long as you live under our
roof." Lindsay could see that her mother was
beside herself over what she'd said, and near
tears over it. She went to her room without a
word, and stayed there for several hours, talking to friends on the phone and watching a
movie on her computer. She said it had been a
boring summer so far, except for when her
brother's girlfriend came to visit and was fun to
be around. But she reported that her mother
had been in a shit mood, and her father was
never around, which she claimed not to care
about, but in truth she did. It felt like ever since
he was accused of sexual harassment, their family had been falling apart. And she envied her

older brother Tom who almost never came home. She couldn't wait to get out.

When Marshall got to the office on Monday morning, he found the usual reports on his desk, and a few new ones. Things were always a little slow in the summer. And he found a message from Connie Feinberg. He hadn't spoken to her since the sexual harassment incident, and thought it was a good time to lie low. He had been very grateful for the way it had worked out, and for their support. He called her as soon as he saw the message, and she took his call immediately. He asked her how her summer was going, and she said she had spent July in Santa Barbara with her children and was now back at work.

"I'd like to come by to see you this afternoon, if you have time," she said casually, sounding as pleasant and easygoing as ever. He liked her, and they got on well.

"Anything special?" he asked, assuming it was just a friendly visit, but he liked getting a heads-up if there was something more. Things had been going well for them lately, and thanks to some strong decisions he had made in the last quarter, their stock was up significantly. It was why the board loved him and gave him their full support.

"I just wanted to catch up on some things with you." She complimented him on their stock increase, and said she'd be there at noon. It didn't sound ominous to him, just a standard visit from the chairman of the board, and he kept busy until then, answering letters and returning calls. He had just finished his to-do list when his assistant told him she had arrived.

Connie walked into his office wearing casual summer clothing. She was an athletic-looking older woman, with sharp blue eyes and neatly trimmed gray hair. And she was a brilliant businesswoman herself, despite the slightly grandmotherly look.

He complimented her on her tan, as she sat down on the other side of his desk, and had closed the door to his office as she walked in. They chatted for a few minutes about their families and nothing in particular, and then she looked into his eyes with a serious expression that told him the meeting wasn't going to be as easygoing as he'd thought.

"I'm here unofficially, Marshall, to discuss something with you privately. I've already discussed it with the board, and we'd like you to handle it this time **before** it becomes a problem. How you handle it is up to you, but we don't want this to become public knowledge, or an issue for UPI, or us as the board. We'd rather not be forced to take a position on it. So it's entirely up to you what you do.

"It has been brought to our attention, by several members of the L.A. office, that you've been involved with a woman there for many years, and in a fairly serious context. We've been told you have a second family there and several children with this woman. Apparently, one of the secretaries in the office is aware of it too, and says that this woman, your er . . . uh . . . mistress . . . other wife, however you view her, used to be an employee of the office. I realize that these things happen, and it's not the first time in the business community, that a man of your stature has a second, hidden family, for whatever reason. But it's a situation that could blow up in our faces, or yours. I have no idea if your wife is aware of it, but if she isn't and she finds out, it's going to be a mess for you, and she may not keep quiet about it. And far more likely, if the other woman, and mother of your other children, gets tired of the situation, she could create an enormous scandal that would make you look bad, and us by association. You know how sensitive people are about things like this, and hypocritical about moral issues. This is a very puritanical country, although personally I'm more realistic than that.

"But this isn't about my morals, or yours, or how I view them. This could turn into a major public scandal that would make you look bad to the public and the stockholders, and taint your reputation in an extremely negative way. I'm sure this is a heartbreaking situation for you. But the board wants you to clean this up as quickly as possible before someone goes to the press with it, or one of the women involved decides to make a public scandal of it. You're very important to us, Marshall, and we can't have you be this vulnerable to something that has all the makings of a gigantic mess. You're going to have to make hard choices here, for the sake of your career. If UPI is still your priority, then you're going to have to bring your personal situation into line with what's expected of you as our CEO. I've spoken to our lawyers about this, and we can't force you to get divorced, or marry another woman, but I can tell you that in the circumstance you're in now, should that become public, that's not the image we want for our CEO.

"The people we love are often more important to us, and should be, but this could jeopardize your career. And I thought it was only fair to warn you of that, to tell you that we've become aware of it, and give you the chance to clean it up as quickly as possible. At this point, if you do care about your job, you really have no other choice."

She looked at him with a serious expression, and if she had hit him with a two-by-four from across his desk, she couldn't have hit him any harder or taken his breath away more. It took him more than a minute to regain his composure after everything she'd said. He hadn't argued with her or asked her the details of how they'd found out. It no longer mattered. Over the years, some of his colleagues must have seen him and Ashley in various places, or with their daughters, and apparently his life with her was an open secret. And Connie had made it clear that if he didn't make a decision about it quickly, it was liable to cost him his career, something he couldn't allow to happen. But he nearly burst into tears at the idea of giving either of them up, and he had no idea which one. And he clearly couldn't continue to lead a double life after Connie's warning from the board.

She could see how undone he was, and she rapidly stood up. "I'll let you deal with this, Marshall. Please keep me informed of how you intend to proceed, and what you plan to do. No one is going to be shocked or upset if you decide to get divorced. And if you decide to end it with the other woman, I hope you handle it carefully, so this whole situation doesn't explode in your face and ours." He was sitting on a time bomb, and so were they. And the last thing they wanted was this kind of publicity for their CEO. They were a very traditional corporation, with a serious, respectable image, and he was thought to be a proper family man. And straightening out his current situation without shattering that image was going to be a major feat. People had to feel they could trust him, not that he was some kind of sleazy, dishonest two-timer, with two families in two cities. She just hoped that his mistress was a decent woman and wouldn't turn this into a circus. If the woman who had accused him of sexual harassment was any indication of the kind of women he favored, Connie was deeply concerned, and so was the rest of the board. And she didn't

envy what he had to do now. He was probably
very attached to both women, but if he wanted
to keep his job as CEO of UPI in the long run,
he would have to make a choice.

"I'm sorry, Marshall," she said quietly as she
left his office, and Marshall sat at his desk for a
long time, looking stunned. He had absolutely
no idea what to do now.

After sitting in his office with the door closed
for two hours, Marshall left at three o'clock,
without explanation to anyone. He told his
secretary he thought he was coming down with
something and just walked out. And she never
made the connection between his leaving and
the visit from the chairman of the board. It
wasn't the first time Connie had come to see
him, just for a friendly talk between chairman
and CEO. But this time had been entirely different, and only Marshall knew that. His whole
career was on the line, even more than it had
been with the threatened sexual harassment
suit, or maybe because of it. Maybe he had
used up his tickets with the board. But whatever the reason, Connie had made it clear, if he
wanted to remain the CEO of UPI, that they

didn't want him having a wife and family in Marin County, and a hidden mistress and two children in Malibu. He had gotten away with it for years and now he no longer could. The jig was up.

He couldn't call Liz to discuss it with her; nor could he tell Ashley. He knew that as quickly as possible, he had to choose one of them and clean up his life. Thinking about it made him feel sick, and as soon as he walked into the house in Ross at four-thirty, he walked upstairs to his bathroom and threw up. And he felt no better when he did. He was engaged in another nightmare, and this one wouldn't end as simply as Megan Wheeler's claims against him. There was no one to buy off, no compromise solution possible. If he wanted both women, he would eventually lose his job, and probably sooner rather than later, since the board was terrified of being involved in a scandal, and having it reflect on both him and UPI. And if it did, it could affect their stock. So he had to decide what to do now, or kiss his career goodbye. What he couldn't figure out was whether to stay married to Liz, with whom he had spent twenty-seven years, and who had always been the perfect wife, despite her recent emotional ups and downs, but whom he didn't love as he did Ashley. And it brought tears to his eyes when he thought of giving Ashley up, and he didn't think he could. But how could he do that to Liz? And his children, those he shared with Liz, would hate him for-ever if he abandoned their mother for the gor-geous girl who had shared his bed in L.A. for eight years, and given birth to his twins. He had no idea where to turn and no one to talk to. He had never been so terrified in his life, of making the wrong decision, but in this case, there was no right one, and he knew he would lose something and someone important either way, and a part of himself. Each of the women owned a part of him, and he would have to sever a limb to leave them, like an animal in a trap.

He sat in the dark in the house in Ross after nightfall, unable to move or clear his head. He just kept going around and around in his mind . . . Ashley . . . Liz . . . Liz . . . Ash-ley . . . Did he pick history or passion? Duty or desire? Youth or maturity? The perfect corpo-rate wife or the girl of his dreams? . . . He had loved them both for too long . . . He had been sitting there for several hours, alternately crying and unable to breathe, with a rising feel of panic that tasted like bile in his mouth, when he was suddenly aware of a sharp pain in his chest and a tingling down one arm, and he knew he was having a heart attack. And for a minute it seemed much simpler to die than to make the decision he had to make. And as he thought it, he was so breathless, he started to pass out, and instinctively reached for the phone and called 911. They answered immediately.

"I'm having . . . a . . . heart . . . attack . . . ," he said, in short sharp breaths. He had no idea what time it was and didn't care, and he still hoped he would die, but had called 911 anyway. He hadn't called Liz or Ashley and didn't want to. He wanted to die alone. It was another choice he couldn't make.

"What's your address?" the woman asked him in a calm clear voice, and he told her. "Are you close to your front door?" she asked him.

"No . . . can't get downstairs . . . I can't breathe . . . ," he said in gasps. "Pain in my chest . . . front door unlocked." He felt again like he was going to pass out, but he hadn't yet.

"Have you been drinking?"

"Two scotch . . . not drunk . . . I'm upstairs . . . in my bedroom."

"I'll send a unit out immediately. Keep talking to me. What's your name?"

"Marshall Weston," he said clearly, and it meant nothing to her.

"Marshall, are you alone? . . . Marshall?" she said sharply. He had gone silent for a minute, and then she heard him groan.

"Just threw up." It was consistent with symptoms for a heart attack. She had already dispatched the paramedic unit from the fire department, which should be at his house any minute. And then she heard voices in the room with him, and knew they were there.

"Marshall, are the paramedics with you?" She had to check to be sure.

"Yes," he said, and hung up the phone, as two burly paramedics knelt down next to him. He was lying on his bedroom floor in his own vomit. Marshall looked at them with eyes full of fear and despair. They checked his vital signs, and his heart was racing, but it sounded strong, as one of them listened with a stethoscope and nodded to his friend. There was a chance that they had gotten to him before the actual attack, but they had everything they needed to get his heart going again if it stopped on the way to Marin General.

"I can't breathe . . . my chest hurts . . . ," Marshall said as two firemen put him on a gurney and strapped him in.

"You're going to be fine, Marshall," the senior paramedic reassured him. He looked about the same age as Marshall and exuded confidence as he directed the others to get him into the ambulance. "We've already called the hospital, and they're waiting for you."

". . . can't breathe . . . ," he gasped again. He felt like he was choking, and he could feel his heart racing now, a thousand beats a minute, or so it seemed.

The paramedics talked to each other as they slid the gurney into the ambulance and closed the doors. They took off with lights flashing and siren screaming less than a minute later, as one of them sat next to Marshall and continued to take his vital signs. Marshall kept looking at him, with an oxygen mask on. He pointed to his chest and said "hurts," and as the paramedic nodded his understanding, Marshall lost consciousness into a sea of black.

Chapter 16

Lindsay was in her room, doing her nails and watching a movie while talking on her cell phone to a friend, and Liz was quietly reading on her bed, when the phone rang at the house in Lake Tahoe. It was late for anyone to call, and Liz assumed it was Marshall when she picked it up. Instead, she heard an unfamiliar voice that identified herself as an emergency-room nurse at Marin General, and she told Liz that Marshall had been brought in by the paramedics for a suspected heart attack, and they were checking him for coronary blockage. Liz sat bolt upright on her bed as soon as she heard the words. They had found her name and all their numbers in his wallet and called her as soon as they admitted him.

"How did that happen? Is he conscious? Is he all right?" She was already standing next to her bed, ready to bolt out the door. She was wearing jeans and a T-shirt, and she slipped her feet into sandals as she questioned the nurse.

"He just came in. He's having a cardiogram now. He lost consciousness in the ambulance on the way here, but he's alert now. You can call back in an hour."

"Thank you," Liz said, feeling breathless herself. "Tell him I love him." This was just what she'd been afraid of lately, and she wondered if she'd sensed it coming. She had a constant feeling of impending doom now, as though something terrible were about to happen. Maybe this was it. But she knew that people often survived heart attacks these days, and he was in good hands. As soon as she hung up, she grabbed her purse and keys and ran into Lindsay's room. "I'm going back to the city," she said with a look of panic, as Lindsay looked up at her in surprise.

"Why? What's wrong?"

For an instant, Liz wondered if she should tell her the truth. But she was sixteen and old enough to know, and he was her father.

"Dad had a heart attack. They just took him

to Marin General. I'm leaving right now." She knew that Lindsay could manage alone for the night, and the housekeeper would be there in the morning. And she could call the neighbor if she had a problem, or stay there.

Lindsay leaped off her bed immediately, closed the nail polish, and stepped into flip-flops on the floor next to her bed. "I'll go with you," she said, and followed her mother out of her room. Liz was already on the stairs. She didn't stop to argue with her, and was glad that Lindsay wanted to come.

Without thinking, they left the lights on, and Liz didn't want to lose any time. They were in the car two minutes later, and Liz drove as quickly as she dared. She knew that she could make it to Marin in three hours without traffic, and they could call on the way to see how he was. Liz had not been so frightened since Tom had a severe concussion when he fell off a horse at seven and Lindsay had a seizure from a high fever when she was two. And a heart attack was serious business. She prayed that Marshall would be all right.

Half an hour later, they were on the freeway, and Liz was quiet as she drove. Lindsay could see how terrified she was, and she knew how much her mother loved him. And even if she thought he was a jerk sometimes, she loved her father too.

"He'll be okay, Mom," she tried to reassure her, and Liz nodded with tears in her eyes. She was sure that the threatened sexual harassment suit had done it. It had been so stressful for all of them. She hated that woman for her lies. None of them had been the same since. Liz herself had been terrified of what terrible thing would happen next, and she felt guilty now for harassing Marshall about it and crying all the time. But she had been so upset for nearly three months, and he had been very patient with her. And now disaster had struck again. At least he didn't smoke, and drank very little, but he had so much stress at the office, and all the responsibility for running UPI rested on him. She wondered if he'd have to retire now. He was only fifty-one, but maybe he would be able to go back to work after this. She wondered if he'd have to have an angioplasty or bypass, or if they'd put in stents, like the husbands of some of her friends. Her mind was racing, but there was no traffic and they were making good time. She was flying.

They called the hospital after they'd been in

the car for an hour. The nurse who answered the phone in coronary urgent care said that his condition was stable and they were doing an angiogram. Liz thought of calling John and Tom, but she wanted to have a better idea of what was happening before she did.

Liz pulled into the parking lot at Marin General just after midnight. They had made it in just under three hours, and she rushed inside with Lindsay right behind her. They told her in the emergency room that they had moved him to coronary ICU by then. It didn't sound good to her, and she looked at Lindsay in panic. They were both fighting back tears, as they held hands, and got in the elevator to go upstairs. Liz rushed to the nurse's desk and gave them her name.

"He just got back from his angiogram," the nurse told her with a sympathetic smile. It sounded frightening to Liz and Lindsay, but at least he was still alive.

"How is he?" Liz whispered, terrified to hear the news.

"He's doing fine. Our resident on call is with him. We have him in a room by himself. You can go in, if you like." She was relieved that she didn't have to walk past all the little cubicles, with patients hooked up to monitors, and frightened relatives at their side. She was one of them now. Lindsay followed her to the room the nurse had indicated, and Liz cautiously opened the door, not sure what she'd find inside. The first thing Liz saw was her husband, looking pale underneath his suntan, and slightly gray, with a serious look as he spoke to the resident, a young dark-haired man in a white coat who looked like a boy to her. He was smiling at Marshall, who was surprised when he saw her.

"What are you doing here?" He hadn't called her, but he was vaguely aware that they told him someone had. There was a monitor in the room, next to his bed, and it was beeping softly, but the pattern on the screen looked regular as Liz glanced at it on the way to kiss him and take his hand.

"You thought maybe I'd sit in Tahoe waiting to hear how you were?" He smiled in answer. He knew her better than that.

"What took you so long?" he teased her. "I've been here for three hours." She squeezed his hand and looked at the doctor.

"How is he?" She wanted it straight from the horse's mouth, not played down by Marshall so she wouldn't worry.

"He's doing fine," the doctor said, glancing at Marshall, who looked sheepish in the bed, where he was lying flat with pressure on his groin from the angiogram.

"I didn't have a heart attack," Marshall told her before the doctor said it. He owed her that much at least.

"It sounds like a hell of a warning," Liz said, frowning, particularly if he'd lost consciousness in the ambulance on the way there. "That ought to tell you something. You need to slow down," she scolded him, and the doctor nodded. They had been discussing it when she walked in.

"It wasn't even a warning," Marshall admitted. "They went over me with a fine-tooth comb. Apparently it was an anxiety attack, which is nothing. Just me being neurotic and stressed out." Marshall looked embarrassed as the doctor confirmed it to Liz, and Lindsay sat down in the room's only chair. Marshall noticed her for the first time, and smiled and thanked her for coming. She didn't understand what was going on, and neither did Liz.

"An anxiety attack can mimic a heart attack pretty closely, at least in the superficial signs," the young doctor explained. "The big difference is that your heart is never at risk. Mr. Weston's heart is healthy, but he seems to be reacting to a considerable amount of stress. So you're not entirely wrong in saying he should slow down, or at least remove some of the stressors from his life. This kind of episode can be pretty unpleasant. And you don't want to be having an angiogram every week." That part of the evening's entertainment had been a lot more unpleasant than even Marshall had feared. And it wasn't an experience he wanted to go through again. They had passed a catheter into the artery in his groin to check his heart. And he had thought he really was having a heart attack while they did it. He knew that sometimes people did.

"So you're okay, Dad?" Lindsay asked from her seat, with a worried expression. She and her mother looked worse than he did, even with everything he had gone through.

"I'm okay, Lindsay. Thank you for coming with your mom," he said again.

"Of course." She smiled at him, relieved.

It was taking Liz a few minutes to absorb what the resident had said, and she wondered if he knew what he was doing, but as Marshall said, the angiogram didn't lie. He was fine. Just incredibly stressed. And he knew why, but he didn't share that information with Liz.

"I had a rough day at the office, and an emergency meeting with the board." He didn't say what it was about, and she didn't ask. She never pressed him about work, unless he volunteered. "It was no worse than any other day," he said—lying again, it had been considerably worse and rocked his world—"but I guess it just got to me." Liz felt guilty as he said it, knowing how shaky she had been lately, and how demanding of his time. Maybe it was her fault. But his anxiety attack had woken her up. They all needed to get over the aborted sexual harassment suit now. It was done, and time to move on.

"When can he go home?" Liz asked the doctor. It was one in the morning by then.

"Now, if he wants." And then he turned to Marshall. "You just need to keep ice on the entry site in your groin tonight. But there's no risk if you want to sleep in your own bed instead of ours." He smiled at Marshall and Liz. "Just take it easy. And try not to let things get to you this week." **Yeah, like which woman to choose to spend the rest of my life with, or destroy my career. Little things like that,** Marshall thought. No one had any idea of the mess he was in, or the risk to his career. His whole world was about to fall apart, whichever way he turned. He knew that, and they didn't. And as he thought of it, he realized that it was astounding he hadn't had a real heart attack. He thought it was. And Ashley knew none of what had happened. Only Liz. He hadn't wanted to upset either of them, and no one had called Ashley. Her name was nowhere on his papers, only his wife's.

They both thanked the doctor then, and he said he'd leave the discharge papers at the desk, and left the room. Marshall looked a little unsteady as he got out of bed. He'd been through a lot that night. Liz helped him dress, and treated him like a child. He always appreciated her motherly style, which made him feel better when he was sick. With Ashley, he was the adult and she the child. With Liz, it was the reverse. But she was a nurturing person and had been taking care of him for almost thirty years. That counted for a lot, and she felt safe and familiar to him as she helped him to the car, and Lindsay slid into the backseat with a yawn. All three of them were relieved as they drove home to Ross, with Liz at the wheel. And as soon as they got to the house, Liz put him to bed, and cleaned up the vomit on their bedroom floor. She brought him a cup of tea and some crackers to settle his stomach, which he said was upset, and an ice pack for his groin. And Liz kissed her daughter before she went to bed, and thanked her again for coming with her. At the root of it all, Lindsay was a good kid, just immature, and a little spoiled. Liz seemed in full control of the situation now. She was great in a crisis.

"Thanks, Liz," Marshall said, looking at her with a grateful smile as she sat down on the bed next to him. He knew it had been a terrifying night for her. "You always take such good care of me when I'm sick. But I'm not even sick, just stressed."

"Well, you will be sick if you don't take it easy. Next time it really could be a heart attack." Two of her friends had lost husbands who were younger than he was, one while he was jogging, and the other on the tennis court. And she didn't want that to happen to him. The doctor had offered to send him home with tranquilizers, but he had refused. "You need to slow down and relax," she said, and he nodded. And as he looked at her, he wondered how he could walk out on her now. The board was asking him to cut off his right arm . . . or his left . . . or his heart . . . head . . . or lose his job, which was the life force that pumped through his veins. It was a terrible choice. "Did anything special happen at the office today?" she asked him with a look of concern, and he shook his head, lying to her again, and he felt guilty for it this time, but he couldn't tell her the truth.

"The usual. Nothing special. We have some internal problems I have to work out. I had a meeting with Connie Feinberg about it."

Liz nodded, and felt guilty herself. "I'm sorry I've been such a pain in the ass lately. I think I just got shaken up with all the sexual harassment stuff. Even if it wasn't real, it felt like it for a while, and it made me realize that bad things can happen." And then her eyes filled with tears, "And I don't want anything bad to ever happen to you . . . or to us . . . ," she said, and he sat up and hugged her.

"Nothing will," he promised, and then wondered if he was lying again. How could he promise her that now? But what else could he say? That he wanted to leave her for a woman twenty years younger in L.A.? He had no idea how he would ever do it, or tell her. And he was sorry for a minute that he hadn't died that night. He'd thought he was dying. It would have been so much simpler. And he knew that

Liz didn't deserve what was coming, nor did his kids. Tears filled his eyes as he looked at her too, and Liz looked shocked. Marshall never cried, and it made her realize how scared and vulnerable he was too. She put her arms around him and held him, gently stroking his hair like a child.

She turned off the lights in the room then, and went to get undressed. Marshall was dozing when she got back, and he opened his eyes and looked at her as she got into bed. She was a familiar sight in his landscape, and he couldn't imagine what he would do without her, or how he would run his career.

"I love you, Liz," he said sleepily, as she snuggled up to him and rubbed his back. He smiled and closed his eyes, and she lay there watching him until he fell asleep.

When Marshall woke up in the morning, Liz was already downstairs cooking breakfast. He lay in bed for a few minutes, thinking. He wondered if the night before had happened for a reason, to show him what he had to do. He hated doing it, but it was clear in his mind now. He and Liz had been married for twenty-seven years. He couldn't leave her now. It wasn't fair to her. And he needed her too much. It would almost kill him to give up Ashley, but he knew he had no other choice. Liz was the mother of three of his kids, and the wife he needed for his career. It was the decision he had to make. And Ashley was young enough to move on and build another life, and even have more kids, with a man who was willing to marry her. It was just too complicated for him now at this point in his life. And it was going to be a scandal if he admitted to his involvement with Ashley now. They had two illegitimate children, and she was proof that he had cheated on Liz for eight years. It wasn't the side of him that he wanted to show the world. And he had a responsibility to UPI too, as their CEO. He had no desire to become the scandal of the century or even the year. It was clear to him now. And he knew he had to go to L.A. to tell Ashley. He was going there the next day anyway, for his usual stay.

He showered and shaved before he went downstairs, and he felt better having made the decision. Lindsay was still asleep, and he was dressed when he walked into the kitchen. Liz was wearing her nightgown, and she looked tired. She had gotten up early to make sure he was all right, and had gotten up several times during the night too. And he was sleeping peacefully every time. He looked as fresh as a daisy when he sat down at the table, and no one would have guessed he'd had an angiogram the night before.

"How do you feel?" Liz asked him with a worried look.

"Like a fool," he admitted to her with a sheepish grin. "I feel incredibly stupid. I thought I was dying, not having an anxiety attack. Isn't that something only girls have?" The doctor had told him otherwise the night before, but it was embarrassing anyway.

"Apparently not," Liz said, as she sat down across from him with a cup of tea. "I still want you to slow down. All that means is that you're stressed out of your mind, and you will have a heart attack one of these days. I'd like to avoid that. I don't want to be a widow."

"You won't be," he promised, as he ate the eggs she'd made him, and helped himself to a piece of toast just the way he liked it.

"Why don't you come back up to Tahoe with me and Lindsay, and take a couple of days off?" She was hoping he would, and she wanted to spend time with him. She felt like she had almost lost him the night before, and had been afraid she would before she and Lindsay could even get there.

"I can't," he said matter-of-factly in response to her suggestion. "I have to go to L.A. tomorrow. I have some things to take care of there too. Connie asked me to handle it yesterday." It was almost true, and had the ring of truth to Liz as he said it. "I'll try to come up to the lake early on Friday. That's the best I can do." He was back to being himself now. The CEO of UPI, with a thousand things to do and responsibilities that were always the priority to him. Liz sighed as she watched him, and wondered if he would ever slow down. Probably not, for a hell of a long time. He was only fifty-one years old, and he didn't even look it. She felt as though she did, and had aged another ten years the night before.

"Well, try to go a little easy today at least. And if you scare me like that again tonight, just because you stress yourself out today, I am coming down there to punch you in the nose." And then she thought of something. "Do you want me to stay until you leave for L.A. tomorrow? I don't have any plans at the lake. Lindsay and I could stick around and spend the night tonight." She looked hopeful. She hated to leave him so soon. But he was already looking at his watch and anxious to get to work.

"It's not worth it, but thanks, Liz. I'll probably have a long day today, be exhausted when I get home tonight, and leave at the crack of dawn in the morning. We'll spend some good time together this weekend," he said as he leaned over and kissed her, as Lindsay walked into the kitchen.

"How do you feel, Dad?" she asked, still looking worried. He had scared them both the night before.

"As good as new. We can all forget about what happened last night," he said, anxious to put it behind him.

"Good," Lindsay said with a grin as she sat down. "Then I can get that tattoo now, right, Dad?" she said, teasing him, and they all laughed.

"Great idea," her father quipped back. "I think I'll get one with you. Like a giant dragon on my ass, so I can moon the stockholders at the next meeting and have something to show them."

"I like that," Lindsay approved. He kissed them both goodbye then and left a minute later.

They could hear the Aston Martin roar off. "You okay, Mom?" her daughter asked her, concerned about her too, and Liz nodded. Lindsay had seen how scared her mother had been the night before and how much she loved him. "He'll be okay."

"Yeah, I guess," Liz said, and put his breakfast dishes in the dishwasher after she rinsed them. She suddenly felt a thousand years old. The night before had taken a toll. "He worries me though. He pushes so hard," she said sadly.

"That's who he is, Mom. He's never going to slow down. **That** would probably kill him."

"Maybe so," Liz said, smiling at her daughter. "Thank you for being so sweet last night," she said gratefully. It gave her hope that she and Lindsay might actually have a decent relationship one day. There was a good person in there.

"I love you, Mom," Lindsay said, and put her arms around her to hug her.

"I love you too," Liz said, and an hour later they left for the lake, and talked on the way. Lindsay explained why she wanted to take a gap year, and it didn't sound quite as crazy. She wanted to travel for a few months, and then come back and take serious photography classes to see if it was a career she wanted to pursue, and she said she didn't feel ready for college yet. And Liz wasn't sure she was wrong. She felt closer to her daughter than she had for a long time as they drove back to the lake, at far more reasonable speeds than they'd traveled the night before.

When Marshall got to his office, he didn't tell anyone what had happened the night before. Not even Ashley. He didn't call her at all, and knew he'd be seeing her the next day. He didn't want to mislead her by calling and telling her he loved her. He did, passionately. But he had made his decision. And he knew it was the right one. For him, his family, and his career, and for Ashley in the long run too. And he would always see his girls. They were his, forever. Ashley wasn't. He would have to tell Liz about the twins eventually, but not yet. Maybe when they were older. And if he'd been away from Ashley for long enough by then, maybe Liz wouldn't mind the girls so much. One day he would like to introduce them to their brothers and sister. They all had a right to know each other, they were siblings, and he loved them all. And as he walked into his office, as hard as it was, he was happy with the decision he had made. All he had to do now was tell Ashley the next day.

And once he did that, the worst would be over. And he could tell the board that the situation had been handled, and they had no cause for concern. That was all he wanted. And without knowing it, Liz would be the lucky winner. His relationship with Ashley was a sacrifice he'd have to make for his career. He was sure.

Chapter 17

On Monday night, while Marshall was having his anxiety attack, unbeknownst to Ashley, she was spending a quiet evening at home. After the twins went to sleep, she checked her website, to see if she'd received any e-mails from galleries. She had recently sent images of her work to several galleries on the East Coast, hoping to show her work with them. She needed to do something to get her career going, and her new therapist had suggested it, when she complained that nothing was happening or moving forward in her life, neither with Marshall, nor with her work. The therapist had pointed out that she couldn't force Marshall to act, but advancing her career was up to her. And Ashley realized she was right. It was still early to hear back from the galleries she'd approached, but she was hoping for an e-mail or two, if any of them were excited about her work.

There was one, as it turned out, from a gallery she wasn't very interested in, in Florida, telling her that they weren't taking new artists on at the moment, but they had liked her work very much. She was disappointed, but there were seven others she was more interested in anyway, and she hadn't heard from any of them yet, and knew she probably wouldn't for a while.

After she read the standard gallery response, she noticed another e-mail on her website. It was from an unfamiliar e-mail address, gmiles@gmail, which meant nothing to her, and the subject window said "Are you?" She opened it, and it was brief and to the point. It said, "Are you the Ashley Briggs who went to the Harvard Westlake School in L.A.?" and gave the year. "If so, my name is Geoffrey Miles. I moved to London when I was thirteen, and you were twelve. I just moved back this week, and would love to hear from you." He gave her his cell phone number. "The mention of a white horse we saw on the beach before I left may jog your memory. I hope this is you. If it is, I'd love to see you. Best, Geoff." The reference to the white horse made her burst out laughing. She knew exactly who he was. She had been madly in love with him when she was in seventh grade and he was in eighth. Geoffrey Miles. He had been a cute kid who looked like Alfalfa from **Our Gang**, down to the cowlick. They had gone walking on the beach in Santa Barbara when her parents took them there for the day. And as a rider on a white horse galloped past them, he had seized the moment to lean over and kiss her. He was the first boy she had ever kissed, and it had been clumsy and harmless, but at the time she thought he was the most exciting boy she'd ever met. His mother had been American, and his father was English, and a successful playwright, and a month or two after the kiss on the beach, they moved to England. She vaguely remembered that he had an older sister in high school. And she had heard from him once or twice after he left. It had been before e-mail, and his letters had taken forever to get to her, from a remote boarding school he hated in the wilds of Scotland. And after a few letters, they'd stopped writing, and she'd never heard from him again. She hadn't thought of him in years, but she remembered everything about him, and that ridiculous, awkward kiss that had seemed so exciting at the time, and seemed very sweet to her in memory, eighteen years later.

She was smiling when she answered his e-mail. She had nothing else to do, and the girls were sound asleep. And Bonnie was working again, till all hours, so they hadn't talked in days. They never did when she was working.

"Yes, I am that Ashley Briggs. And I remember the white horse perfectly, and what you did when we saw it. Where are you? How are you? Why are you back? And what have you been doing for the last eighteen years (in ten words or less)? I live in Malibu, by the way. Lots of beach. No white horses. Love, Ashley." She thought about using the word **love**, and decided it was okay for a childhood friend, although she wouldn't have signed herself that way to someone she just met. But they had been good friends.

He responded three minutes later, just enough time to read it, and she smiled when she saw it. This was fun. And livened up her evening.

"Dear Ash, sorry to hear there are no white horses in Malibu. I've been living in London and New York, writing screenplays. It's genetic. I just got hired by a TV show here. Got here

three days ago, looking for an apartment, pref-
erably somewhere around West Hollywood.
That's more than ten words. Best I could do.
What about you? Married? Single? Divorced?
A dozen kids? I see you're an artist. Nice work.
Love, Geoff."

To which she responded just as quickly. "Dear
Geoff, Santa Monica and Westwood are nice
too. So happy you're back. Congrats on the new
show. Thanks for the comment about my work.
I'm single, and have twin girls who are seven.
Would love to see you. Let's get together. Love,
Ashley." She included her cell phone number
that time.

He answered even faster. "Me too. How about
lunch tomorrow? The Ivy, 12:30? I don't start
work for another week or two. I came early to
look for an apartment. I'll call you in five minutes." She waited to see if he'd call before she
responded, and her phone rang three minutes
later. His voice was even the same as she remembered, although it was a deeper, more
grown-up version, and he had just a faint hint
of an English accent. He'd been gone for a long
time.

"Is that you?" he asked when she answered.
He sounded thrilled to hear her, and she was

delighted too. It was like a breath of the fresh air of her childhood, which had been a better time. Her parents had gotten divorced a few years later, her mother had died when she was in college, and her father had remarried and moved away, and died a few years after that. But when she'd known Geoff, everything was simple and happy, for both of them. And she knew his father had died too. She had read about it, since he was well known. "Is it really you?" he said again, laughing.

"No, it's the neighbor," she teased him, laughing too. "I can't believe you came back. That's so cool. And how great that you're working on a show here. You must be a good writer to get hired to come out here. There are lots of good writers in L.A."

"I just got lucky," he said modestly. "I was writing for a show in England, and I think my agent sent them a script. They probably wanted a little British humor on the show. What about you, with twin girls? That must keep you busy!"

"They're adorable," Ashley said proudly. "Do you have kids?" She had forgotten to ask him, she was so happy to hear from him. And she remembered perfectly the huge crush she'd had on him. He was a very cute boy. They had gone to school together for about five years, but only fell in love when she was in seventh grade. And then he left.

"No wife. No kids," he answered her question. "I had a girlfriend for four years, whom I lived with. A crazy French woman, an actress, who drove me insane. We broke up a few months before I got the offer to come here, and I was feeling sorry for myself. She dumped me," he said, but didn't sound upset about it. "So I decided to come to L.A. and close up shop in London. I'm glad I did. I love being back. I've been driving around for three days looking at landmarks from our childhood. I love this city. I always missed it. I lived in New York for a year, but I hated it. The weather is as bad as it is in London. I missed the sun. It's so great living in good weather. Everyone in London is depressed all the time, because it's either raining or freezing cold. I can't wait to see your girls. Do they look like you as a kid?" They had met when she was about that age, so he would be able to tell when he saw them. But she thought they looked more like Marshall except for their hair.

"A little. They look a lot like their father."

"Who is, or was? I notice you said you're single." He assumed that meant she was divorced, and she didn't explain.

"He's a fascinating man. A 'captain of industry,' as they say. He's twenty-one years older than I am. And it's a long story."

"Save it for lunch. How's tomorrow for you? The Ivy?"

"Perfect. Twelve-thirty," she confirmed. She couldn't wait to see him and wondered what he looked like now. Eighteen years later, it was like finding a long-lost brother, or best friend. She wasn't looking for romance, just old times. And she was sure that that was what he wanted too.

"Will I recognize you?" He sounded suddenly concerned.

"Easily. I weigh three hundred pounds. I have black hair, and I'll have a rose in my teeth."

"I'd know you anywhere." He laughed at her. She hadn't changed. She was as silly as she'd been as a kid, when he found her enchanting. He had spent his whole allowance on a box of Valentine chocolates for her the week after he kissed her. He had always been a really sweet boy, even when they were younger.

"What about you?" She hadn't thought about it before, and expected him to show up at the restaurant looking thirteen. And in his mind's eye, she was still twelve.

"I look the same, only a bit taller. Well, actually, a lot taller. I'm six-four." He had been a tall kid, but not that tall when she last saw him.

"I'll look up to find you."

"Don't you worry," he said happily. "I'll find you, Ashley Briggs." When they hung up, it made him wish he had stayed in touch with her. Talking to her now, he realized he had missed her, and he was happy he'd contacted her again. And so was she. She went to bed that night excited about seeing him. And she had an appointment with her therapist in the morning before lunch. She was looking forward to that too. It helped to talk to her about Marshall, although it was hard to explain the relationship to her, why she had been willing to remain hidden for so long, and had waited eight years for him to leave his wife, and why he still hadn't. The therapist was sympathetic and nonjudgmental about the relationship, and she acknowledged that Marshall must be an exciting and even fascinating man, but he also had a wife he couldn't seem to leave. She questioned Ashley about that at length. And Ashley had told her he didn't want to upset his kids. The therapist had just nodded, as though she understood, and Ashley felt foolish. After eight years, it sounded like a thin excuse to her too, when she said it to someone else. It seemed to make more sense when Marshall said it to her. But for once, she wasn't thinking about him. She was excited about seeing Geoffrey Miles.

When Ashley got to The Ivy the next day, she looked for a tall man who looked like Alfalfa, and didn't see one. All she saw were couples and groups sitting on the terrace and in the restaurant, and one well-known actor tanning in the sun, but no one who looked like Geoff. She felt a little lost for a minute as she stood on the terrace, waiting for the maître d', to ask him for Mr. Miles's table, and then she heard a familiar voice behind her. She would have known it even if she hadn't spoken to him the night before on the phone.

"Meeting someone for lunch?" he said softly, and she turned and looked up into the same handsome face and broad smile eighteen years later. He hadn't changed, he'd grown up, literally. He was a tall, very attractive man, and she wasn't short either. She was almost as tall as Marshall in heels, but not nearly as tall as Geoff. And he was slim with broad shoulders, but all she could see were the familiar eyes and smile, and he looked thrilled when he kissed her on the cheek and admired the woman she'd grown into. "Wow! You turned out to be a knockout!" he said, and she laughed. He thought she looked like an actress or a model, and she was much better looking than Martine, his French girl-friend in London, who had been very Gallic and a little nuts, smoked three packs of cigarettes a day in his tiny London apartment, and never did housework, in the hope that a maid would appear to clean up the mess she left everywhere. Geoff put up with it because he loved her, or thought so. She had left him for one of his friends, who was complaining about her now, and Geoff figured he'd gotten what he deserved. A giant pain in the neck, with subtitles. She hated speaking English, and his French had got-ten pretty good as a result, as he explained to Ashley once they sat down and ordered lunch. They both ordered salads, and he ordered a bowl of chili, which he said he had missed.

They had a lot of news to exchange, and he told her he was sorry about her parents once she told him.

"I miss them," Ashley said wistfully, "but I have the girls. They're my family now." He nod-ded, and envied her that.

He told her he was sorry he had wasted four years with Martine, and hadn't gotten around to marriage and kids yet. She hated kids, and thought marriage was redundant, although he'd asked her twice. "She said marriage is superfluous for intelligent people. I'm not sure what that had to do with it," he said to Ashley, and she laughed. "So when did you get divorced?" he asked her, as the waiter brought their salads and his chili. He looked blissful when he took a bite.

"I didn't," she said simply. She wasn't going to lie to him. They were old friends. She figured she could be honest with him, and if not, why bother? She wasn't proud of her situation, but she had made her peace with it, for now. Or she wasn't ashamed of it, at least. "I don't think marriage is 'redundant,' but I never married the girls' father. Or at least not yet."

"He's still around?" Geoff looked intrigued, and she nodded.

"Two days a week," she said, and he raised an eyebrow.

"This sounds mysterious. Tell me more." He wanted to know everything about her that he'd missed. They had a lot to catch up on. And her situation seemed odd to him.

"It's not mysterious. It's complicated. He's the CEO of a big company. He lives in San Francisco." It sounded normal to that point, and then she added the rest. "With his wife and three kids. One of whom is in college, the other in law school, and the third one is in high school. He didn't want to get divorced and upset his kids." She tried to make it sound normal, but it didn't to him.

"He's still married?" She nodded, and her eyes looked worried.

"For now. He says he's going to get divorced when his daughter graduates next year."

"And you believe him?" Geoff asked, wondering if she did. She hesitated and looked thoughtful.

"Sometimes. I want to believe him." And then she sighed, and looked her old friend in the eye. "After eight years, I wonder. It's been a long time. And he has a lot of reasons why he can't get divorced. Maybe he just doesn't want to. He spends two days a week with us. The girls are crazy about him," she said, as though to justify why she was with him. It sounded like a classic setup to him—married man with beautiful younger woman—but not a good situation for her. He was sorry to hear it.

"And you get two days a week, and no holidays or weekends. And you can't call him at night."

"Or in the office," she admitted. "He's very careful. He has a lot to lose if someone finds out."

"Like what? Alimony?" She could tell Geoff didn't approve of the arrangement. He approved of her, but not Marshall.

"Like his job. He can't afford to be involved in a scandal. He was for a minute this spring, and it was a mess."

"What kind of scandal?"

"A woman he had a one-night stand with, who basically blackmailed him, and got two million dollars to retract it. She went public."

"So he's married, and he cheated on you both. One-night stands count," he pointed out to her. "And you can't even call him in the office. Is that enough?" He wondered if her lover was supporting her royally in grand style and she needed the money, but Ashley wasn't the type for that, and she had worn a simple cotton sundress, and wasn't wearing diamonds. She was wearing the same gold cross on a chain around her neck that she'd worn as a child, and nothing she had on looked expensive. She was obviously in it for love, not for money.

"No, it's not enough," she said, looking off into the distance as she thought about it, and he was bowled over again by her beauty.

It was easy to see why her man wanted her, he thought. Who wouldn't? What wasn't clear to Geoff was why she was willing to accept so little, and to live on the thin hope that he'd leave his wife one day. But he agreed with Ashley, after eight years most men didn't leave their wives. They got away with it for as long as they could, and apparently Ashley had let him. He sounded like a powerful man, and he was calling all the shots. It made Geoff sad for her, and her children. She deserved so much more than she was getting.

"It's what it is," she finished the answer to his question. "I can't force him to get divorced."

"And you never wanted to leave him?"

"Maybe I would have by now without the girls," she said honestly, "but he's their father. I don't feel like I have the right to deprive them of him. And I love him. I keep hoping, and he always promises that after next year . . . next this . . . next that . . . after some major event happens, he'll leave her. But he hasn't yet. And I'm trying to come to terms with the idea that maybe he never will. That's new for me. It changed things for me when that woman came out of the woodwork in May, and he admitted to me that he'd slept with her. Once. But I wouldn't have done that to him. I think I've felt differently ever since."

"I'll bet his wife was thrilled too," Geoff commented.

"He didn't admit it to her, just to me. She doesn't know about me either. I sat next to his son in a restaurant recently, and it was a weird feeling, realizing that he had no idea who I was or that the girls are his sisters. It really hurt," she said, and the look in her eyes made him want to reach out and hug her, but he didn't want to scare her, or make her uncomfortable.

"It's amazing the compromises we all make just to hang on to someone we care about. I've finally come to believe it's not worth it. I knew Martine cheated on me the whole time we were together, but I pretended I didn't know, to her and myself. It costs you something to do that, and in the end it undermines the relationship, because it's not honest. A man who is living a lie, like your children's father, is not an honorable person. And if he lies to his wife, he's capable of lying to you."

"I know," she said softly. "I don't trust him

anymore. But I love him. I keep hoping I'll win in the end." Geoff didn't want to challenge her on it, but he couldn't help wondering what she'd "win." A dishonest man. It sounded like a bad deal to him. "Anyway, so that's my story. No husband, two kids. It's not what I had in mind when I was twelve, but I love my girls, and I'm lucky to have them." Geoff knew from looking at her and listening to her that there were a lot of men who would have been thrilled to give her two babies and a lot more than what she had. But he didn't say that to her. He didn't want to upset her. "I want you to meet them," she said, smiling at him, and he reached out and took her hand in his and held it while they looked at each other.

"Thank you for being honest with me. You could have told me you were married, or divorced, or to mind my own business." She had been so open with him and looked so vulnerable, it touched him deeply, and he would have liked to take a good swing at the married bastard who was breaking her heart, and had been for years. Geoff thought he should have gotten divorced and made an honest woman of her long since. She was decent, to her very core, which was more than he could say for the guy she was in love with. "So when can I meet your kids?" he asked with a warm smile. "How about tonight?" She looked surprised by the suggestion and then nodded. Marshall wasn't coming home till the next day, so it was fine. She didn't want to spend her brief time with him with anyone else, and never did, but tonight she was free.

"Sure. Why don't you come for dinner? The girls will love it. You can tell them what a brat I was as a kid."

"You weren't," he said, smiling at her. "You were a little angel."

"That's not how I remember it," she said, laughing at him. "We got in trouble in school together all the time."

"Well, you looked like an angel at least." And then he sat back and gazed at her with a nostalgic gleam in his eye. "You still do. You really haven't changed. You're just taller."

"You too. A **lot** taller." They both laughed at that.

And as they reminisced about their shared childhood, the time passed too quickly, and she had to leave to pick the girls up at day camp. And he had to see three apartments. He promised to be at her house at six. As she was driving to pick up the girls afterward, she felt as though a part of her history had been returned to her, and she was surprised by how good it felt. It was as though a piece of her that she didn't know was missing had slid back into place, like part of a puzzle, or her identity. She felt whole in a way that surprised her now that Geoff had found her. And it was nice to remember those carefree, happy days when they were children. And he had grown up to be a very sweet, gentle man. He had been sweet as a kid too, and she had liked his parents, although his father was very British and a little clipped, but his mother had been a warm, wonderful woman. Geoff said that she was still alive and living in England, and had remarried, to another writer, although this one was less famous than his father. Geoff said he went to visit them whenever he could. They lived in the country somewhere on a farm.

The twins were lively and excited when she picked them up, and she told them all about her friend that she had gone to school with when they were her age and older. She didn't tell them about the first kiss, she didn't think they needed that information and weren't old enough to know. But they liked the idea of her having a friend from school who had turned up. And they were very intrigued by Geoff when he arrived promptly at six o'clock with a big bouquet of flowers for Ashley, and a tiny one for each of the girls, and a bottle of wine for their dinner.

"We don't drink wine," Kendall explained, "but my mom does."

"That's good to know," he said seriously. "Do you drink beer?" he asked her, and she burst into gales of laughter.

"No!"

"What about Coke?"

"Sometimes," she explained. She was the more serious of the twins, and Kezia was more mischievous. He thought they were both gorgeous little girls, and looked just like their mother, soft blond hair and all. "But we're only allowed to have one Coke," Kendall explained to him, "and we have to share it, so it doesn't keep us awake."

"I see." He smiled over their heads at their mother, and he could see how much she loved them. Maybe it explained why she had stayed with Marshall for so long, in spite of the bad deal she was getting, and so much less than she deserved.

She made hamburgers, a big bowl of pasta,

and a salad. She poured the wine he had brought, and they had dinner on the deck. He had looked at the work in her studio while she was cooking, and the girls showed him their room and their favorite toys, and after dinner, they scampered off to play before bedtime, while he and Ashley talked.

"They're an amazing pair," he said with a look of admiration. "And you're a great mom."

"They're great kids. I was barely more than a kid myself when I had them. I was a temporary receptionist in his office for a month, to make money for art school, and then I got involved with Marshall, and life happened. He was going to leave Liz then, before I had them, but he didn't. And everything got complicated after that, and still is. We used to fight about it all the time, and lately I have been putting pressure on him. It just screws everything up when I do. He asked me to wait another year." She sounded sad as she said it.

"And you agreed?" Geoff asked with a look of regret. He was sorry for her.

"More or less. I started seeing a therapist recently, and I'm trying to take it day by day. Otherwise I just get worked up about it and upset myself. And there's no point screwing up

the little time we have together. It feels like real
life when he's here, and then I just kind of float
the other five days." And as she said it, it occurred to him that she was missing out on five-
sevenths of her life while she waited for Marshall
to return. It was a lot to miss. Seventy-five percent of her life was spent waiting for him, and a
real life. He wondered what she'd think if he
said it to her, or if she'd ever thought about it
like that.

They talked about other things then, the
writing he'd done, and the show he was going
to be working on. And after a while, she went
to put the girls to bed and let them skip their
bath. She read them a story and turned out the
light. Ashley and Geoff could hear giggles coming from the room for a while, and then they
stopped, as he and Ashley continued to sit on
the deck, and opened another bottle of wine. It
was a warm night, and they never went inside.
And they were both startled to realize that it
was after midnight when they got up, and he
said he had to leave. He had a meeting in the
morning, and she had to get the girls to camp.

"I had a wonderful evening, Ash," he said as
she walked him to his car. He said he was staying at a hotel that was full of rock stars who

partied all night and he couldn't wait to get his own place. He turned to look at her in the moonlight, and he had never seen anyone as beautiful in his life. She looked like a vision in the soft light, with her halo of hair around her face. And suddenly she didn't look like a child to him anymore, just an exquisite woman, and he took her face in his hands and bent down to kiss her on the mouth, and before he knew what had hit him, he had put more passion in it than he meant to, and they were kissing, he was holding her close to him, and she was kissing him back. All the longing and tenderness that had sprung from their childhood found its way into their kiss now, and it was a long time before they stopped, and when they did, they both looked stunned. Neither of them had expected to do that, it had just happened spontaneously.

"Oh," Ashley said to him in surprise. "What was that?"

"I'm not sure. But I think I just saw a white horse go by," he said, trying to lighten the moment, and she laughed. But they weren't twelve and thirteen anymore, and the kiss hadn't been as innocent as he'd intended. It had been a real one, for them both. And she suddenly realized that she hadn't kissed any man except for Marshall in eight years. And he could see that she felt guilty as she looked at Geoff. "I'm sorry, Ash . . . I don't know what happened." But he wasn't sorry, and she didn't look it either.

"I think I'm a little drunk," she said softly as an excuse. They had finished two bottles of wine, but over many hours.

"I think I may be too," he admitted, and then put his car keys in his pocket. "I think I'll call a cab."

They stood together, waiting for it to come, and he kissed her again, and neither of them used being drunk as an excuse. When the cab came, he hugged her and looked into her eyes.

"I'll call you tomorrow," he said, and kissed her again, lightly this time, and she waved as he drove away. And then she walked quietly into the house wondering if he was a gift from destiny, or a temptation that had been put in her path, or just a strange coincidence of fate. She had no idea, and before she could figure it out, she was in bed and fell asleep instantly.

Ashley woke up the next morning with a terrible headache, and she groaned as she got up.

The sun was too bright, the girls were too loud at breakfast, and her stomach was upset. And she remembered Geoff kissing her the night before with an acute pang of guilt. She was worried about Marshall cheating on her, and what she had done was almost as bad, or so it seemed to her. She had gotten carried away on their reminiscences and talking in the moonlight, and it was so easy being with Geoff. It had seemed so natural to kiss him, and she told herself it was the wine, but she wasn't sure that was true.

After she dropped the girls off, she called Geoff from the car. He had picked up his car and was on his way to a meeting, and he sounded happy to hear from her.

"Are you mad at me?" he asked her immediately, and she sighed.

"No, I'm mad at myself. I shouldn't have done that . . . but it was nice," she said, and giggled, and he laughed. She felt like a kid and so did he. Twelve and thirteen, on a beach.

"Yeah, it was. I'd be lying if I told you I was sorry we did it. Actually, I'm glad," he said honestly.

"Me too," she admitted. It seemed so simple and carefree, until she thought about Marshall, and then it seemed wrong. But when she had been kissing Geoff, she only thought of him. "I haven't kissed another man in eight years."

"Maybe you should have." He had to go into his meeting then. "Can I see you tonight?"

"No," she said sadly. "Marshall is coming home. It's Wednesday."

"When will he leave?" Geoff sounded hopeful. He wanted to see her again. Soon.

"Friday morning. But Geoff, I'm not going to do that again. I'm not going to see someone behind his back. That's no better than what he does, going back and forth between me and his wife, and lying to her."

"We can be friends, then," he conceded. "I promise I'll behave. We'll go easy on the wine." She laughed at what he said. "I'll call you Friday. Maybe we can do something with the kids this weekend. The beach, the zoo, whatever you do with kids that age."

"We can go to my beach club. They love to swim." It was fun having someone to do things with over the weekend. She never had anyone to spend weekends with, except Bonnie when she was free. Over the years, she had stopped seeing her friends, because her situation was so awkward and she didn't want to explain it.

"Good luck at your meeting." Her head was still throbbing from the night before.

"Are you kidding? I had three Tylenol for breakfast and I feel like my head is going to fall off."

"Yeah, me too," she laughed. "Talk to you soon." She drove home then, thinking about him, and when she got home, Marshall texted her. He had just gotten on the plane, and said he'd see her that night. He didn't add "I love you," which was unusual for him, and it made her feel guilty again. And worse when she thought of Geoff all day and the kiss the night before. She was wondering if she shouldn't see him on the weekend. It had been so wonderful to find him again, but now she was confused.

She felt as though she were on the spin cycle of a washing machine all day. Nothing felt right. She was impatient with the girls when she picked them up, and she had a headache until five o'clock, when she dropped them off at a babysitter. And at six, as she got out of the shower, Marshall walked through the door. He came upstairs to find her, and she was standing in her bathroom naked as he looked at her as though for the first time. And the moment she saw him, she knew how wrong she had been the night before. Marshall was staring at her, and he was seized by a tidal wave of passion. Knowing the girls weren't there, he strode across the bedroom, and a moment later she was in his arms, and they were taken by such a powerful force that they both lay breathless afterward, wondering what had happened. It had been like the very first time, only better. It was as though he had poured his heart and soul into her, and he couldn't pull away. He didn't want to let go of her ever again, and when she looked at him, there were tears in his eyes and rolling down his cheeks.

"Darling, what's wrong?" she asked him, and he just shook his head. He had come to end it with her, and the moment he saw her he knew he couldn't. He had to have her in his life. There was no way he could give her up. She owned him, he was addicted to her, and they couldn't stay as they were or he'd lose his job. If he wanted to keep his career intact, he had to give Liz up, but not Ash. Not now. He needed Liz for his career, but he needed Ashley for everything else. He sat up in bed then, and told her about the anxiety attack he had had on Monday, when he thought he was dying, and then she saw the bruise in his groin. She hadn't seen it before. They had started making love so quickly that she didn't have time to look.

"Why didn't you call me?" she said, sad that he hadn't.

"I didn't have time, it hit me so fast."

"You could have called me the day after. You didn't even text me. I just thought you were busy."

"I was. I figured I'd tell you when I was here," he said, but in truth he had already decided to end it with her, and didn't want any contact with her until he got to L.A. And then everything had changed again when he saw her naked and had to have her. And he wanted her desperately again. He felt as though he had lost her for the past two days, and it was already more than he could bear.

"Do you know what brought it on?" She looked worried about his panic attack.

He did, but he didn't want to tell her. "A combination of things. I had a meeting with the chairman of the board on Monday. Just the usual stress. I guess it got to me. I thought I was going to die," he said, and she shuddered. And then what would have happened? she wondered. Who would have called her, since no one knew about her? She would have seen it on the morn-

ing news or read it in the paper. It was a horrify-
ing thought that brought her situation into
instant focus. She had never thought of his
dying before. She didn't say anything, but she
looked upset when they went downstairs, and
he was particularly sweet with the girls that
night when the sitter dropped them off, and he
read them bedtime stories and played with them
for a while. The girls loved it when he came
home. And afterward he and Ashley went upstairs and made love again. After what he had
told her about Monday night, they were both
desperate for each other, as though clinging to
life. They were both exhausted when they slept
in each other's arms that night, and emotionally
drained.

And he lingered the next morning and waited
until she got back from taking the girls to camp.
She was surprised to see him still there.

"Are you feeling okay?" she asked him, concerned. Maybe he had overexerted himself, and
would have another attack, but he shook his
head.

"I have to talk to you," he said quietly, and
they went out on the deck.

"Is something wrong?" She had never seen
him look like that before.

"It was. Not now. For us. I had a visit from the chairman of the board on Monday. They know about us, Ash. And after the business of the sexual harassment accusation, they don't want another scandal. We got out of that one by the skin of our teeth, and they were very nice about it. But they don't want a CEO who is at the epicenter of a scandal every five minutes. My job is on the line," he said simply. This was serious business to him. As serious as it could get.

"They're going to fire you because of me?" She didn't understand and she looked shocked, but he shook his head.

"Not exactly. The chairman told me that they want me to clean up my act. They don't care who I stay with, you or Liz, but they know about my double life. Apparently people in the office here figured it out, and some secretary who knew you. I guess people have seen us over the years. No one said anything to me, but it got back to the board. They either want me to leave Liz, or you. I came down here to end it with you, Ash. That's why I didn't call you after the anxiety attack. I was going to tell you this morning that it was over for us. But now I can't."

"**After** you spent the night with me?" She looked horrified by what he'd just said, and the timing of it hadn't escaped her.

"I thought we could have one last night, and then say goodbye." He was being brutally honest with her, as he never had been before. He had wanted that last night before he told her, which was so unfair and so selfish.

"And what about our girls?" Ashley looked panicked at the reality of what he was saying. He'd been planning to leave her.

"I have a provision for the girls in my will, and for you," he explained. "I took care of that seven years ago."

"Would you see them if you left me?" Her eyes looked sad that she even had to ask him. She felt as though she didn't know him anymore.

"Of course. Eventually. I hadn't figured that out. I just knew that I had to end it with you, or my career at UPI is over. They made that clear. But when I saw you yesterday, I knew I couldn't do that. I can't live without you. So I'm going to tell Liz that I'm divorcing her. It's either that, or my job," he said miserably. He felt sorry for Liz, but there was nothing else he could do. He had to end it with one or the other.

He couldn't with Ashley, he had discovered, so it had to be Liz.

"And you're divorcing her?" He nodded. "Then why couldn't you do that for me? What about Lindsay's senior year, and your other kids, and all the reasons you gave me?"

"Lindsay's senior year is going to be a lot more unpleasant if her father is out of a job." Ashley knew he didn't need the money, but he needed the food for his ego, and the power, and everything that went with it. That was what this was all about, not his love for her, or Liz.

"And what if she changes your mind when you tell her? If she begs you, or threatens to kill herself?"

"She wouldn't do that. She's a sensible woman. And I hope you would never threaten me with that either." He didn't think she would, but you never knew.

"And what if they tell you to get rid of me one day, or they'll fire you? I guess then I'd be history too, wouldn't I?"

"Don't be ridiculous. They'd have no reason to do that, if I'm not leading a double life. This is what they're objecting to, not who you are. I could be married to a monkey for all they care, they just don't want me to cause a scandal,

which could drive stock prices down or infuri-
ate stockholders. This is business to them, it's
not about love and romance." He looked impatient as he said it. He didn't like the questions
she was asking, which he thought were unnecessary and superfluous. He was willing to give
her what she wanted now, and she was looking
a gift horse in the mouth and examining its
teeth. And he didn't like it. He didn't want to
be raked over the coals by her now, or interro-
gated about his decision.

"And what is this about to you?" she asked
him in a strained voice. "Love or your job? If
they hadn't forced your hand now, would you
ever have left Liz, or would you have left me
like this for the next twenty years, hidden away
in Malibu, while you live with Liz five days a
week?"

"That's irrelevant," he said harshly. "I told
you I'm divorcing her. I'm going to drive up to
the lake and tell her tomorrow. I'm going to fly
back tonight." He had it all worked out in his
mind. He had a plan. And by Monday he
wanted to tell the board the deed was done.

"What if she says no?" Ashley asked him.

"She has no choice in the matter. I'm going to
file for divorce immediately. I have to satisfy

the board." She could see the same thing happening to her one day, that was about to happen to Liz, and just as coldly. If her existence
ever put his career at risk, he would leave her
flat. And he was about to do that to Liz. After
all Ashley's begging and pleading for years, he
was leaving Liz for the board, not for her. She
felt an icy chill run down her spine as she looked
at him. He was the coldest man she had ever
met, and she realized now that all he cared
about was his career. She was just a body to
him, and a great piece of ass, which was why he
was choosing her, not Liz. But the real love of
his life was UPI. She knew that now. It was
clear. And even their daughters didn't matter to
him. They were in his will, but not his heart.
Nothing mattered to him except himself and
his career. It was frightening to think about,
and Ashley had never felt so alone in her entire
life. Winning him now was a hollow victory.
He had made the decision for all the wrong reasons, and if anything happened to change that,
she knew that he would turn around just as fast
and dump her too. She would never have a moment's security with him. As long as UPI owned
him, and whenever his career was at risk, her
life with him would be in jeopardy and could

be canceled at a moment's notice. She sat in silence watching him, and he had told her all he had to say.

"I'm flying back tonight, and I'll see her tomorrow. I'll call you this weekend and let you know how it went," Marshall said matter-of-factly, and she nodded. She didn't know what to say to him. "Thank you," "Good luck," "Have fun"? "I love you" seemed irrelevant now in his world. The board had told him to get rid of one of them, and it had almost been her, after he spent a night with her and made love to her while she had no idea that he was going to dump her. Instead it was happening to Liz. It made their lovemaking the night before seem like a travesty. He didn't love her. He needed her, in order to feel powerful and virile and alive. He didn't love anyone but himself. Ashley had suddenly seen that like lightning lighting up a night sky.

He put his arms around her before he left, and she felt wooden as he held her. She couldn't say anything to him. All she could think of now was that he had come there to break it off with her and had changed his mind, like a deal he had salvaged at the last minute. Mergers and acquisitions. He had traded one merger for another. She knew she should be grateful to him for picking her instead of Liz, but she wasn't. She just felt sick.

"I love you, Ash," he said quietly. "I always did." But she didn't believe him now when he said it, and she knew she never would again. The words meant nothing to him. He was going to be with her, thanks to the board, not to him. "We always knew that someone would get hurt in this, in the end. I'm glad it won't be you," he said generously, but she was hurting anyway, more than he would ever understand. And even if he got divorced now, she had lost in the end. She could no longer harbor illusions that he loved her, and wanted to be with her. He just didn't want to lose his job as CEO, and she was younger and sexier than Liz and made him feel more potent.

"I love you too, Marshall," she said, and kissed him. But they were just words now, and the kiss he returned wasn't a searing kiss like the night before when he had been overwhelmed with need and passion, or even a kiss like she'd had with Geoff the night their feelings had overwhelmed them. It was a small, cold kiss. It was the kiss of a powerful man who never did anything without a reason, or a benefit to be derived. On his profit and loss sheet, she had moved from loss to profit by a sheer stroke of luck, and nothing else. "Have a safe flight back."

"I'll call you before I leave," he said to her, and then left for the office. She stood on the deck for a long time, thinking about him, and wondering what life would be like with him. She had dreamed of it for eight years, and now she couldn't envision it. She couldn't imagine feeling as though he really loved her, ever again.

She couldn't help wondering too if he'd have the guts to tell Liz he was divorcing her once he got there. There was always the possibility that he'd change his mind again, or that Liz would convince him that she and their children needed him more. Nothing would have surprised Ashley anymore. He had rocked her world with what he'd told her, and all her illusions had come tumbling down.

Chapter 18

As Marshall had promised, he called Ashley from the car on the way to the airport on Thursday night. He sounded tired and subdued and told Ashley he loved her, but she no longer trusted him, and knew she never would again. He wasn't capable of the truth. They talked for a few minutes, and then they hung up, and she sat in her bedroom long into the night, thinking about everything that had happened. The sun had come up, and she could hear birds singing when she finally fell asleep.

The girls came upstairs the next morning to wake her, and she hurried downstairs and made them breakfast and then dropped them off at camp.

She was in her studio, staring at a blank canvas absent-mindedly, when Geoff called her later that morning. He had been thinking about her for two days, and said he had found an apartment in West Hollywood, right where he wanted, and he really liked it.

"You can give me decorating advice, if you want. I'm terrible at that kind of thing. Martine the Monstrous used to pick out all our art." She smiled at what he said, but she sounded distracted, and Geoff could hear it. "How did it go with him?" He had worried about her. It seemed like a terrible situation to him.

"Okay, I guess. He said he's going to divorce his wife now." But she didn't sound happy about it, which surprised him. Geoff wondered if he had promised to before, and failed to do it, and now she didn't believe him.

"Well, that should be good news if you've been waiting for eight years." Maybe Marshall did love her after all. Geoff hoped so for her sake, but had his doubts. He didn't like married men stories for his women friends.

"The board made him do it," she said flatly.

"The board is making him divorce his wife? Is that any of their business?" It seemed strange to him.

"They found out about us, and the girls. And

they told him he had to get rid of one of us, and clean up his act. They don't want him involved in a scandal. It was either that or lose his job."

"So he's divorcing her to save his career?"

"That's about it. He said he was going to dump me, but he changed his mind," she said to Geoff, and felt ill when she did.

"He told you **that**?" Geoff was as shocked as she still felt after hearing it the day before.

"Yesterday, before he left."

"And how do you feel about it?"

"Actually, kind of sick. I haven't figured it out yet. He would do just about anything not to lose his job as CEO." He had proved that now.

"Apparently. So now you move to San Francisco and live happily ever after?" He sounded sad as he asked her. He had just found her and was about to lose her again. But he had no right to interfere. She had waited eight years for this and had two children with the man. Geoff didn't want to mess it up for her. He cared about her too much to do that.

"Maybe," she said in answer to his question. "I need to think about this. It hit me like a freight train yesterday when he told me. It's not exactly what I consider romantic. It's just business, which is the real love of his life. He made that pretty clear. If they hadn't given him an ultimatum, he'd be staying with her. For another year anyway. He may still change his mind before he tells her, just like he did with me. I don't know what he's going to do." She didn't trust him anymore, and Geoff could hear that too. He thought Marshall was a truly bad guy.

"Can I interest you in dinner tonight?" Geoff asked her cautiously. She seemed like she had a lot on her mind.

"I don't know if I should," she said, sounding confused. "I don't want to make a bigger mess than I'm already in, and I don't want to screw you up too."

"You won't. I'm a big boy. It's just dinner, and I promise to behave." She smiled when he said it, and remembered their kisses. She wasn't sorry now that she'd kissed him, but she didn't want to do it again. She was confused enough as it was. "Why don't I take you and the girls out to dinner? I saw a cute place yesterday they might like. It's a pizza parlor with a jukebox and arcade games with a little merry-go-round outside. What do you think?"

"They'd love it. Thanks, Geoff." It sounded like a nice way to spend the evening, and fun for the girls.

"I'll pick you up at six. Is that good for you?"

"Perfect."

And when he arrived they were dressed and ready to go. She hadn't heard from Marshall all day, and wondered if he'd gone to Lake Tahoe. But at least when they were out with Geoff, she wouldn't think about it.

The girls rode the merry-go-round before they ate dinner, and she and Geoff tried to talk over the jukebox. He could see that she was upset, and the strain in her eyes. It had been a rough two days with Marshall, and Geoff felt sorry for her. She looked as though all her illusions had been shattered.

And after the pizza, they danced for a few minutes and the girls played the arcade games. They were already half asleep in the back of his car by the time they got home. It had been a perfect evening, and he helped her carry them inside and waited on the deck while she put the girls to bed. They were asleep before she turned off the light.

"Thank you. That was fun for them," she said as she sat down in a deck chair next to where he was sitting.

"I enjoyed it more than they did," he said, smiling at her. "You're lucky you have them.

One of these days, if I ever find the right woman, I'd like to have some kids too." He looked wistful as he said it.

"They're the best thing in my life," Ashley said, looking tired, and she closed her eyes for a minute as he watched her, wishing he could make things easier for her. But there was nothing he could do. And when she opened her eyes again, she smiled at him. "I wonder what would have happened if you hadn't moved to England?"

"I'd have married you at fourteen and we'd have fifteen children by now," he teased her, and then he reached over and held her hand. They sat there quietly for a long time, in the moonlight, lost in their own thoughts. She was thinking about Marshall and wondering what was happening in Tahoe, and Geoff was thinking about her and what she was going to do if he really divorced his wife now. He hated to see her wind up with him. And she didn't look happy about it either.

He stayed for a little while longer, and then he got up to leave. She looked tired and distracted, and he had work to do. He had some scripts to work on for the new show.

"Do you still want to go to your beach club tomorrow?" he asked her, and she nodded. She knew it wasn't right spending time with him, but it was all she wanted to do now. She felt safe with him, as though he were a refuge from everything that was happening to her.

"We can have lunch there, and the girls play in the pool all day."

"Sounds good to me," he said, and this time when he bent to kiss her chastely, she melted into his arms and clung to him. He held her for a long time and stroked her hair. He didn't want to do anything to upset her, and then she kissed him, and everything about it was simple and pure and felt right to both of them.

"I don't know what I'm doing," Ashley whispered.

"It's okay," he said gently, "you don't need to know right now. We'll figure it out later. And whatever you end up doing will be fine with me. I showed up a little late on the scene. You don't owe me anything." And he meant it.

"Thank you," she said softly, and he left a few minutes later after promising to pick them up at noon the next day. Ashley didn't know what was happening, but it felt right to be with him for now, and he wasn't asking for anything. At the moment, she had nothing to give anyone, not even Marshall. After what Marshall had said to her the day before, she felt empty inside, and she couldn't imagine ever feeling anything again. She was numb.

When Marshall landed in San Francisco on Thursday night, he went to the house in Ross to spend the night. He felt strangely peaceful now that he had made his decision, and he didn't feel anxious anymore. He knew he was doing the right thing. It would be a shock for Liz, but it was time to be honest with her. He had lied to her for too long. And he felt lighter now knowing that it was almost over.

As he walked into their bedroom, he wondered if she would sell the house or continue to live in it. He had to start looking for a house to live in with Ashley now. He was going to call a Realtor on Monday, and his lawyer, after he called Connie Feinberg. But first he had to talk to Liz.

He drove up to Lake Tahoe on Friday morning. It took him four hours, and when he got there she was out, getting a manicure, the housekeeper said. And Lindsay was at a friend's. He put on his bathing suit and went down to the lake to take a swim. It was a beautiful day.

He was still sitting on the dock when Liz got home and found him. She was surprised to see him there so early, and wondered if he was feeling sick again, but he seemed fine to her, and she was pleased he had come.

"When did you get back from L.A.?" She smiled at him.

"Last night," he said, looking at her, but he wasn't smiling. She felt like a stranger to him now. He had already left her in his mind. He hadn't texted her when he got back, which was unusual for him. He always told her where he was. "I took the day off today." She could see that, and he noticed that her nails were bright red. She looked more rested and relaxed than she had when he left for L.A. "I came up to talk to you," he said finally with a serious expression.

"Did something happen? Did you have another attack in L.A.?" She was instantly worried, and he shook his head, as she sat down on the dock near him.

"Something happened on Monday," he said, as they sat on the dock looking at each other. She had a strange feeling that something was about to happen, but she didn't know what. He was staring at her oddly, while she waited for him to explain. "Connie Feinberg came to see me in my office. And she basically forced me to do something I haven't had the guts to do in eight years."

"And what's that?" Liz didn't understand.

"Be honest with you. I've been living a lie for eight years."

"What about?" It sounded odd to her.

"There's another woman in L.A.," he said, as though it were the most natural thing in the world. She stared at him in disbelief. Her mind refused to accept what he had just said, as though someone had pressed a button that said "delete." The information wouldn't process.

"What do you mean?"

"I've been involved with a woman in L.A. for eight years," he said coldly. "I never wanted to leave you or tell you, so I spent two days a week with her. We have two little girls who are seven years old, twins. They live in Malibu." Liz looked at him as he said it and thought she was going to faint. "Someone told the board, and they want me to clean up my situation, or they're going to fire me." He said it as though he expected her to understand, but she didn't. She didn't understand anything he had just said or how it had happened, and why she had never known about it, or even suspected. She had trusted him completely. She stood up and almost fell over. She was shaking like a leaf. He reached out to steady her, and she pulled away, as though his hand would burn through her flesh, the way his words had just ripped through her heart.

"You have two children with her?" Her voice was a high-pitched squeak that neither of them recognized. And Marshall was frighteningly calm as he watched her. All he wanted now was to tell her the truth, for the first time in years. "And you made love to me during that time? And lied to me? And to our children? How could you do that to me?" She choked on a sob and burst into tears as they both stood there next to the lake. She looked as though she was going to hit him, and he wouldn't have blamed her if she did. This was hard for him too. It wasn't easy admitting it to her, but he wanted to now, to make things clear and explain his decision.

"I was in love with her. Crazily, passionately, unreasonably. I thought it would blow over, but it didn't. It just kept going, year after year. And she got pregnant right in the beginning. She wanted to have the babies, especially once we knew it was twins. Maybe she thought it was the only way she'd keep me. She was very young at the time."

"How young?" Liz asked in a strangled voice. She wanted to know everything now. He had ripped her wide open, and she thought it couldn't get any worse than it was.

"She was twenty-two when we started. She's thirty now. It's not about her age, Liz," he said quietly. "You're a beautiful woman, and I love you. When Connie told me I had to make a decision, I was going to stay with you. I went down to L.A. to tell her, but I couldn't. If I left her, I'd sneak back to her in a week. It's just something I need. I don't even know what it is, or why. It's beyond reason. You and I have had almost thirty years. Maybe we've just played it out and there's nothing left except respect and duty and something familiar. But I know I'm not done in L.A. And she's waited a long time for this. I'm divorcing you, Liz," he said as though he expected her to step down gracefully and wish him well.

And instead she let out a terrifying scream that reverberated across the lake, as he stared at her, not sure what to do to calm her down. She just kept on screaming until the housekeeper came running out of the house, and he waved her away. He tried to put his arms around Liz then to calm her down, and she hit him, hard. She was flailing at him wildly, screaming at him about how he could do that to her. She had always been there for him, and gave him her life and three children, and he had made her whole life into a lie. "It wasn't a lie," he insisted. "I loved you. I still do. I just can't be with you anymore." She looked at him then like an ax murderer and ran back to the house. He followed her, but he left her alone when she ran into their bedroom and slammed the door. He went to the door an hour later, and he could hear her sobbing and didn't go in. The housekeeper knew that something terrible had happened and stayed away. She was afraid that something had happened to one of the boys, but she didn't dare ask, and sat crying in the kitchen, without even knowing what was going on.

Lindsay came home while Liz was still in the bedroom crying, but she couldn't hear her, and was surprised to see her father there so early on Friday afternoon, when she passed him in the hall.

"Where's Mom? Are you feeling okay, Dad?"

she asked with a look of concern. He was touched, and wondered how long it would last, given what he had just told her mother. He knew he was about to become persona non grata to them all, if Liz decided to tell them the truth.

"She's not feeling well. She's in her . . . our room. I don't think you should go in right now."

Lindsay went downstairs to get something to eat then, and found the housekeeper crying, and wondered what was going on.

"What's wrong?" she asked her, looking scared. She thought of her brothers too.

"I don't know. Your mother is very upset. I think they had a fight."

"Oh," Lindsay said, and left the kitchen, and decided to check on her mother. She found her facedown on her bed, sobbing incoherently, and when she glanced up at Lindsay, her face was ravaged by grief. Lindsay looked terrified when she saw her, and the condition she was in. She had never seen her mother that way before. "Mom, what happened?" All Liz could do was sob as Lindsay took her in her arms and tried to console her, but all her mother did was cry. "Did you and Dad have a fight?" she asked, after what the housekeeper had told her, and Liz answered in a shaking voice.

"We're getting a divorce," she said bluntly, as her daughter stared at her with wide eyes. "Your father is in love with someone else. He's leaving me for her." She didn't tell her it had been going on for eight years, nor that they had twin daughters. It was all she could bring herself to say for now.

"With who?" Lindsay almost didn't believe her, but it was obviously true.

"A young girl in L.A."

"How young?" Lindsay looked at her, horrified.

"She's thirty," Liz said, and tried to regain her composure, as Lindsay sat down on the bed next to her and started to cry too. They held each other for a long time, unable to believe what had happened. It was dark when they finally went downstairs. Marshall was sitting in the living room, and he was visibly distressed when they walked into the room. Liz's face was red and swollen, and their daughter looked even worse. They had been crying for hours.

"I'm sorry," he said in a grim voice. "I know this is hard for everyone. It is for me too. But I had no choice but to tell you," he said to Liz, as she stared at him with broken eyes.

"How could you lie to me for all these years?"

"I didn't want to hurt you. And I didn't know what to do. I didn't want to leave either one of you. And I'm not sure I would have, if the board hadn't forced my hand." He was being honest with her now, and what he said wasn't lost on her.

"So you're divorcing me to save your job?"

"It's not going to help if my career goes down the tubes too. Our marriage is already over, Liz. It has been for years." It was what he had always told Ashley, but they both knew it wasn't true. He had acted like her husband and had still wanted her to act as his wife for all those years, even in bed.

"It wasn't over, and you know it," Liz shot back at him as Lindsay listened to them in horror and then ran upstairs to her room. "It wasn't over. You made love to me last week. Or was that just out of duty too?" Marshall didn't tell her that for the last many years it had been out of affection and respect, and what he thought he owed her, but he was enough of a gentleman not to say it to her now. "And what kind of girl is she to spend eight years with a married man, and have children out of wedlock? What kind of little whore is she?" Liz was screaming at him again, and Lindsay could hear them from her room, although she couldn't distinguish the words.

"She's suffered more from this than you have," Marshall told her harshly. "She's known about you for eight years. At least you had the benefit of what you thought was a real marriage."

"And you didn't?" She looked outraged.

"I knew the truth."

Liz realized then that she was the only one who hadn't. He had played at marriage with her five days a week, and spent two days a week in L.A. with the girl he really loved, and their children.

Liz went back upstairs then to talk to Lindsay, and Marshall slipped quietly into one of the guest rooms and went to bed. Nothing more of any use was going to be said that night, or possibly all weekend. All that was left were insults and recriminations as Liz looked back over the last eight years, now that she knew the truth. And as she got into bed, she remembered that John was coming home for the weekend and bringing Alyssa, and she couldn't let them come. She texted him that they needed a family weekend, and he couldn't bring Alyssa to the lake, and he called his mother as soon as he saw the message. He sounded angry and embarrassed.

"Why not? I invited her weeks ago. You can't cancel on her now, Mom. That's rude." And he thought his mother sounded strange. "Are you sick?" She didn't know what to say, and she didn't want to tell him the news on the phone.

"I have a cold. It's just not a good weekend to bring her. Tell her I'm sorry and she can come another time."

"That's not fair. Then I won't come home either."

"You have to," Liz said, sounding desperate. "Just this one weekend." Her voice wavered then. "I need you here."

"Why?" He sounded belligerent and unhappy, which was unusual for him.

"I just do."

He hesitated for a long time and then capitulated. His mother sounded really sick.

"All right. But it's really rude, Mom," he scolded her, and she apologized to him, and said she'd apologize to Alyssa herself the next time she saw her. And after that, Liz lay in bed, remembering everything Marshall had said to her, and she knew she'd remember it for the rest of her life. Twenty-seven years, gone in the blink of an eye. And he had a mistress with twins. The whole thing was beyond belief and right out of a bad movie. But the bad movie had turned out to be her life.

When John arrived the next afternoon, his parents were waiting for him, and Lindsay was sulking in her room. She had refused to speak to her father since the day before. And Liz had called Tom that morning and asked him to come to Tahoe, but he refused. He said he had other plans. So Liz knew she'd have to call and tell him after she spoke to John. She would have preferred to tell Tom in person, but he had no desire to see his father. And Liz knew he'd have even less once he heard what he was doing and why. Tom would never forgive him. Everything Tom had said about his father for years had turned out to be true.

When John walked into the house, he saw the serious look on their faces and knew instantly that something terrible had happened. He could see now that his mother wasn't sick, she was crying. And his father looked uncomfortable and stressed.

"What's going on?" John asked them both. "Is Tom okay?" He had had the same thought as everyone else. Only a death in the family could have justified how they looked. And there had been a death, their marriage. But Liz was quick to reassure her younger son.

"Tom's fine. I talked to him this morning. I asked him to come up, but he couldn't."

"So what is it?" John asked with a look of panic.

"It's Dad and I," Liz said quietly, trying not to cry. "We're getting a divorce." She burst into tears again as John stared at them in horror. It had been his worst fear, especially lately. He'd had the feeling something was wrong.

"Why?" John asked them, starting to cry too, and his father didn't answer. Marshall couldn't. It hurt him more to see his son look so devastated than it did to see Liz. He knew how much his son loved and respected him, and he didn't want to lose that too. He was afraid that John would hate him now. Lindsay had declared war on him the day before and called him a liar and a monster, and he was used to that from her. And his older son had hated him for years. Tom had seen right through him, and said he was a fraud. And Marshall wondered if he was right. Maybe Tom instinctively knew. They had never seen eye to eye since he was a little boy. And it would only get worse now. He had lost an entire family in one fell swoop, but he had expected that. And it was a choice he had made when he had decided to save his career, leave Liz, and stay with Ashley.

"Your father is involved with another woman," Liz explained to John, through her tears. "They've been together for a long time." She looked at Marshall before she said the rest, but she had to tell him and Marshall didn't try to stop her. "They have two children, twin girls." She delivered the coup de grace, and John's eyes flew open wide.

"You **what**?" he said, turning to his father. "Somebody please tell me this isn't true!" he shouted.

"It is," his father confirmed to him. "I brought pictures with me, if you'd like to see them. They're your sisters." John stared at him as though he were insane.

"Are you crazy? You're going to show me pictures of my **sisters**? How old are they? Fifteen? How long has this been going on?"

"Eight years," Marshall answered him in a somber tone. "They're seven, and they're beautiful little girls. You would love them."

"I am never going to meet them," John said in an anguished tone. He felt he owed his mother at least that. And he didn't want to see them anyway. They were living proof of his father's betrayal. "Did you bring pictures of your girlfriend too?" he asked, looking shocked, but his father only shook his head. He had actually thought they would all want to see pictures of the girls, out of curiosity if nothing else, but he had been wrong. None of them wanted anything to do with his twins, or Ashley. Marshall left the room then, and sent her a text from the guest room. All he said was that he was in Tahoe, taking care of things, and he loved her. He didn't tell her that his entire family was devastated, and they all hated him now, and her even more. He thought he could at least spare her that. And he didn't want to make her feel guilty for their pain. He was doing this for her, but for himself as well, and he was willing to take responsibility for that.

It was an agonizing weekend with endless tears. No one would speak to him except to make accusations, or hurl insults at him. But he stuck through it, and when he left on Sunday afternoon, no one would say goodbye. He had told Liz he was calling a lawyer on Monday morning, which made it even more real, and she told him she wanted him moved out of the house in Ross by the time she got back. He said he was moving out in the next week, and he would stay at a hotel.

As he drove away from the house in Tahoe,

he felt as though he had been beaten all weekend, and he had been. And he knew he deserved
it. What hurt him more was the sight of all of
them miserable. And in some ways, Liz's fury at
him by Sunday was a relief. He could deal with
rage better than tears. And the sight of John
sobbing had nearly broken his heart, and worst
of all was when his son had looked at him and
said, "I am so disappointed in you, Dad." He
thought it would kill him.

Liz called Tom to tell him, and he said he
wasn't surprised. His father had just proven everything he'd thought of him for years.

And John had called Alyssa on Saturday night
and told her everything he knew, even about
the twins and Ashley. It had been his worst fear
all his life, and now it had happened. Alyssa
kept telling him that he'd be okay, that they'd
get used to it, and in some ways it would be
better later. But he didn't believe her. Their
family as he had known it had been destroyed,
and his father had turned out to be a liar and a
cheat, and he didn't see how any of them would
recover, especially his mother, who suddenly
seemed a hundred years old and hadn't stopped
crying all weekend. None of them had. And as
they sat around the dinner table on Sunday

night, after Marshall left, they looked and felt like the survivors of a shipwreck. But at least they had survived, and as they started to eat dinner, Liz glanced up in surprise as her older son walked in, and for the first time in two days, John smiled.

"I figured you guys needed a hand here," he said gruffly. He was a tall, handsome boy who looked like his father in his youth, but the resemblance ended there. Tom sat down and ate dinner with them, and afterward the two boys talked late into the night, and John felt better to be able to share his thoughts. At least Tom had come home. It was the only good thing about the weekend. And Liz kissed them all goodnight when she went to bed. It was the worst weekend of her life, but all her children were there, and they seemed closer than ever, as they joined forces against their father, and took sides with their mother.

The two boys drank a little too much beer that night, and they handed two to Lindsay. She had been talking to all her friends on the phone and telling them what had happened. All of them were shocked, although most of them had divorced parents too. But they thought the Westons had seemed so happy.

Marshall sent Ashley a text that night when he got back to Ross, and told her he loved her. But Ashley didn't respond. And Marshall was too tired to think about it or call her, and went to bed. He was emotionally drained after a nightmarish weekend. As he fell asleep, he reminded himself to call Connie Feinberg in the morning and tell her everything had been taken care of. And he drifted off knowing that his job at UPI was safe. He couldn't think of anything else.

Chapter 19

That Saturday, Ashley and the twins had spent the day at the beach club with Geoff. They all swam for an hour, and then had lunch by the side of the pool. Kezia and Kendall went back in the water almost as soon as they finished eating, and Ashley and Geoff lay on deck chairs in the sun, while she watched them dive in and play with their friends. As she looked at Geoff, it seemed amazing that he had only reappeared in her life days ago, and now he seemed like part of the family. It had all happened so quickly, and seemed so comfortable to be with him. He was working on his scripts, but he had made time to be with her and the girls. It was as though they had been waiting for him to arrive and hadn't known it, and now it seemed like the most normal thing in the world to have him around, and even the twins acted as though they had known him all their lives. He had that kind of easygoing quality about him. He could already tell the girls apart, which most people couldn't, and even Marshall made a mistake sometimes. Geoff seemed completely at ease with them, and he and Ashley with each other, as though he'd never left and they'd been friends for the past eighteen years.

And the romantic undertones between them seemed strangely natural too. Ashley had to keep reminding herself that Marshall was coming back, and he was finally divorcing Liz to marry her. She didn't feel like someone who was going to get married, and it didn't seem celebratory now, only sad, understanding the real reason why he had finally agreed to leave Liz. She knew the catalyst had been the board of UPI that had made him choose, and he did it not for his love for her, but for the love of his job.

Geoff was dozing in the sun as she watched Kendall and Kezia, and once in a while one of them hopped out of the pool and came over to say something to Ashley. And after a while, Geoff opened one eye, smiled, and looked at her.

"I've died and gone to heaven, right? I'm just checking, not complaining by the way. Ten days ago, I was living in a miserable flat in London, where I'd been alone for four months after my cheating girlfriend left me, and I'd been feeling sorry for myself. Presto magic, turn the dial, great new job, terrific apartment in West Hollywood for half the price, find childhood friend again, lying in sun at beach club, playing with her gorgeous kids, and trying to forget she's probably going to marry someone else, but falling for her anyway. Come to think of it, already have." He summed it up in a few words, and she looked over at him and smiled.

"The flip side of that coin is me crying over my married boyfriend for eight years with no one to do anything with on weekends." Bonnie was still working straight through on her current film, without a day off. "And now you're here, and I'm lying here like a lizard in the sun with you as though I always have, while we watch the girls." And she reached for his hand. She didn't add, "And yeah, falling for you too, and trying not to think about it so I don't freak out." She was still feeling confused. Marshall was breaking Liz's heart that weekend so he could deliver the good news of it to the UPI board on Monday morning, and to her. Or maybe he had changed his mind again, and was having fun with them in Tahoe, and planning to dump her, which knowing him was possible too.

What she didn't know now was what to do herself. Should she just be grateful that he was willing to have a life with her, and would probably marry her to satisfy the board? Or should she look at the fact that he'd come to Malibu three days before and slept with her one last time before he was going to end it with her, but didn't? And that he could dump her anyway, anytime it suited him? She had never felt so insecure with any man, or had so much at stake as she did with him. She had been hanging by a thread with him for eight years. And now she could no longer kid herself that he loved her and that his promises were true. He had shown her that he did and said what worked for him in the moment, and he could fire her whenever he wanted, without ever looking back. She knew he was capable of that.

And she wasn't looking to Geoff to solve the problem, and didn't want to. They didn't know each other well enough anymore, and he'd been gone for a long time. But it was odd how he had turned up at just this moment, and they were so comfortable. And she couldn't help wondering what would have happened if he had come back before she met Marshall. Would it have worked with them? Could it ever? Or were his kisses and willingness to spend time with her just a distraction or a temptation to throw her off course in her real life? She had absolutely no idea, and knew Geoff didn't either. It was much too soon, or too late. And she couldn't risk everything she had waited for, for him. He wasn't even asking her to do that. He wasn't asking her for anything. They were just taking it day by day. But being with him felt frighteningly right, more than it ever had with Marshall.

"What were you thinking just then?" Geoff asked, as he looked at her. She was wearing a tiny pink bikini, hardly bigger than the ones her daughters were wearing, and it looked great on her. She had been frowning as she stared into space.

"I was just thinking how confused I am and how crazy I feel sometimes, and how weird life is. You wait eight years for something until it almost kills you, and then it falls into your lap looking like this big, gorgeous gift, until you see there's a worm in the apple, or a snake's handing it to you, and you don't know whether to eat it and risk dying, or walk away. I don't know what to believe anymore, or what to think." He wasn't sure either, but he thought it was interesting that she was comparing Marshall to a snake. Geoff was in total agreement without ever having met him. Trusting Marshall again sounded like a bad idea to him. But he also knew she loved him, had waited a long time, and had two kids with him. And sometimes it was hard to walk away from what you had wanted so badly, even if you knew it was dangerous, or bad for you. It was easy to tell yourself everything would be okay, even when you knew it wouldn't.

And Ashley was no longer blind to what and who Marshall was. She had seen it clearly that week. He was a man who always served his own needs first, at everyone else's expense. Marshall wasn't the husband Geoff, as a friend, would have liked to see her with. As a man, he wanted her for himself, but he knew that was self-serving too, and he knew he was no better than Marshall on that score. As someone who loved Ashley, he wanted what was best for her, and he wanted to protect her, not put her at risk, and he would never have lied to her.

Ashley could sense Geoff's feelings about her. Why did a good man have to cross her path now, just when the one she wanted was within reach? And to make matters worse, the kisses with Geoff unnerved her. She hadn't even looked at another man in eight years, and now she wasn't sure who the snake was, Marshall, Geoff, or herself.

"Life is just too weird," she commented as they lay there side by side. If she pretended for a minute, she could imagine being married to him, while he wrote for TV and she painted, and they brought up the girls, just as though he'd always been there. But he hadn't. And who knew what paths their lives would take? She knew now that you couldn't trust anything or anyone, because in the blink of an eye everything you'd ever dreamed of could disappear, or your dreams would change. "Maybe I'm too old to change course now, and I just have to stay on the path I've been on."

"Not if it's heading off a cliff," he reminded her. "And if you're too old at thirty, I guess we'd better both throw in the towel, and I should be sitting here crying over Martine because I invested four years with her. I'm not. I'm counting my lucky stars that she left. And I was doing

that before I found you again. You can't just
stick with something because you've been doing
it for a long time. Maybe life is giving you a
message here, and I don't mean me. I mean you.
Something opened your eyes this week, Ash.
Don't just close them again without taking a
good look. At least know where you're headed
and if it's safe for you or not."

"Is that you sitting there, or my shrink? She
said the same thing when I called her yesterday.
She said to go into this with my eyes wide open
and be sure it's what I want. And that history
repeats itself, and people don't change. What
people did to you before, they'll do again."

"She's a smart woman. I kept going back to
Martine every time we broke up, or she cheated
on me, and I'd try to work it out with her again.
And I couldn't. She did the same damn thing
all over again every time, and I kept acting surprised. And the last time, I just let her go and
wished her well." And then he thought of something else. "But then again, we didn't have kids.
I guess that's different. You have to do what's
right for them too. I only had to think of myself, and I didn't want her to throw me under
the bus again, and she would have. She's already
cheating on my friend, and he doesn't know it.

I figure he'll get it eventually, and if he doesn't, it's his problem now, not mine. And he was willing to screw me over too. They deserve each other, so maybe it will work for them." Martine was an entirely different woman from Ashley, and he'd never really respected her, he had just been besotted with her. Everything he felt for Ashley was different. "This isn't about you and me, you know," he reminded her, "it's about you and him. Maybe I just showed up to give you a breather, kind of like a life preserver so you didn't drown. But you won't drown even without me. And maybe the right answer for you is some other guy you don't even know yet who'd be perfect for you. Maybe I'm just a space saver for you until he comes along. Or maybe the right answer for you is no guy for now, and just you and the girls for a while. Or Marshall. You'll figure it out, Ash. You're a smart girl. You always were." He had faith in her, even if she thought she was confused.

"Thank you. Now I'm totally mixed up." Everything he said made sense. "Thanks for the vote of confidence I don't deserve. I haven't been smart for all these years while he bullshitted and lied to me and stalled me. He told me he was going to leave her as soon as I got pregnant, and we'd be married before the girls were born. And then with one thing and another, he always had some excuse that made sense at the time. I don't think he was ever going to do it, he just didn't want to lose me, so he said whatever it took to keep me around. The board lowering the boom on him now is the only thing that ever forced him to make a move. My friend Bonnie is right, and my shrink— this has been comfortable for him, and I made it that way. I just sat here waiting for him to show up two days a week, if he wasn't on vacation with them, and didn't have something better to do. I was always the dessert, and they were the main meal. And his wife is probably much better for his career than I am. I don't know how to do that stuff, I've never even seen it. I just love him. And suddenly he's willing to give her up, but until now he kept her in the job, and all I was to him was a piece of ass," she said harshly. She felt like it now, his whore on the side, which was how his family would view her too, especially his kids. She had stayed in the shadows for too long, and now she looked as bad as he did.

"I'm sure you were more than that," Geoff said quietly. "You're not that kind of woman."

He couldn't see her that way, and never would. She was too decent a person to categorize her that way, but it was the role she'd been assigned.

"Don't be so sure," Ashley said sadly. She was being hard on herself these days, but she thought she deserved it. And her therapist was making her look at herself, and why she had stayed with Marshall for so long, not getting what she wanted or deserved. It happened in affairs with married men—you just kept sitting and hoping and pretty soon you were someone you never wanted to be and never thought you could be. Ashley had always been a very moral, good woman, and suddenly she'd become The Other Woman, and a disgrace in her own mind. "I'm sure it just started as sex for him," Ashley commented, and Geoff suspected it was true. "I was like a drug for him. He couldn't get enough of me in the beginning. Then he got hooked. He still is. But the bitch of it is, I did too. He got hooked on my body, and I got hooked on wanting to be his wife. Maybe it was an ego trip, wanting to be married to someone that big and powerful. It's exciting being with a man like that, until you realize all that goes with it, and guys like him don't get there by playing fair. He never does. He doesn't have to. He owns the world."

"He doesn't own you, Ash," Geoff said quietly.

"He has till now," she said honestly. "I don't know who owns me now." She looked at Geoff.

"The only one who should own you, is you," he said with a serious expression. He didn't want to own her, just be with her, if it was right for both of them. And that wasn't clear yet. All they both knew was that they liked each other, had a powerful childhood bond, and they were attracted to each other. It wasn't enough to build a future on, nor to end an eight-year affair over. But it was a good start if they were both free. She wasn't. She was still completely enmeshed in her feelings for Marshall, however badly he had behaved. That didn't seem to change how she felt. So she was still hooked. Just like Marshall. And Geoff wondered if she'd ever get free. He wasn't asking her that question now. He knew she didn't know the answer, and was desperately looking for it herself, like a lost shoe in a closet. She knew it was in there somewhere, but damned if she could find it. And Geoff was a patient man.

They got back in the pool with the girls, and

stayed at the beach club with them all afternoon. He dropped them off at Ashley's place in Malibu at dinnertime, but he didn't stay. He said he had work to do on scripts, and he thought she needed time alone, which wasn't wrong. He didn't want to distract her. And he worked on Sunday too, while Ashley tidied up the house, played with the girls, and did some laundry, and all the while she was trying not to think of Geoff, and concentrating on Marshall. There was no question that seeing Geoff again, and discovering that she had feelings for him, or could have, was heavy on her mind, while Marshall weighed on her heart like a stone now.

Before Geoff left her on Saturday, he kissed her after the girls went into the house, and he knew they wouldn't see them. He didn't want to confuse them too. They loved their father, and their relationship with him was a lot simpler and cleaner than Ashley's. The kiss she and Geoff shared was searing.

"I don't want to make this harder for you, Ash," he said with a worried look, but every time she was close to him, he couldn't resist her. It was why he wasn't staying for dinner or seeing her on Sunday. It was turning his world upside down too. He didn't want to fall like a ton of bricks for a woman he couldn't have and who belonged to someone else, but it seemed to be happening anyway, and all he could do was try to put the brakes on and slow it down if he couldn't stop it. "I don't want to upset you," he said as he kissed her again, and he felt like he was talking to himself, because he didn't want to confuse himself either.

"It's okay," she whispered as she kissed him again. "Confuse me. I think I love it." He laughed and shoved her gently out of his car.

"Go home. Why do you have to be so gorgeous and sexy? Why couldn't you have at least grown up to be ugly?" She laughed as she got out of the car, and waved as he drove away. She'd been thinking the same thing about him. Why had he grown up to be so wonderful and loving and handsome? And he was twenty years younger than Marshall. It wasn't about the difference in their bodies, which was obvious, but in their lives. Ashley and Geoff had similar points of reference and history, and the same interests. Marshall was at a different place in his life, surrounded by successful people and grown children. Ashley was just beginning. And Marshall was a man of power, who wielded it like a flaming torch that lit up the night. It was heady stuff, and Ashley realized that that was part of the magic for her too. His appeal to her was not that he had been unavailable, but that he was, and enticing. It was like conquering Everest every time she was with him, and knew how much he wanted her. And that was going to be hard to give up, **if** she ever did, or could. She had never wanted to till now.

Chapter 20

Logan and Fiona had exchanged e-mails on Friday afternoon and agreed to a meeting point in the city the next day. She was going to leave her car in a garage and wait for him outside AT&T Park. He told her exactly which entrance, fifteen minutes before the game. Alyssa called her right before she left the house and wanted to have lunch with her, and she couldn't believe her mother was going to a ball game.

"Why are you doing that, Mom?" It didn't sound anything like her mother, who spent all her spare time working or with them and knew nothing about sports.

"I got invited by a friend, and it sounded like fun. You need to do something different once in a while. At least that's what your aunt Jillian tells me. I thought you were in Tahoe," Fiona suddenly remembered, and she was sorry she couldn't meet her for lunch and felt slightly guilty about it. She never had plans on the weekend, and was always available for her daughter. Today was a rare exception.

"I was supposed to. But John's mom is sick or something so she canceled. She wanted him to come anyway, but she wasn't up to having a houseguest. He was all upset about it, but I'm fine. I guess I'll go to the house and do my laundry." She sounded a little mournful about it, which made Fiona feel even worse that she was going to the city to meet Logan.

"I'm sorry, sweetheart. I shouldn't have accepted. I just figured you'd be busy."

"That's fine, Mom." She laughed. "You get to have a life too. So who's the friend?" She couldn't imagine who her mother was going to a ball game with, and she knew Jillian wasn't back from Europe.

"A reporter I met a while back. Interesting person. Pulitzer Prize winner." She sounded casual about it.

"A **date**?" Alyssa was surprised. Her mother hadn't had a date in several years. And in some ways it was convenient. It meant she was always around for them, when she wasn't working. Their father was much less available with his new wife, and now that he was retired, they traveled all the time. They loved taking cruises, and had taken a four-month cruise around the world the previous winter, which Fiona would have hated.

"No, just a friend," Fiona corrected her quickly. "He's a business reporter, mostly for **The Wall Street Journal** and **The New York Times.** He won the Pulitzer for a series of interviews with Nelson Mandela. Interesting person, and apparently a baseball fanatic, so he offered to take me. He probably couldn't get anyone else to go with him." She knew that wasn't entirely true, but she didn't want to make her daughter nervous, and she didn't consider Logan a romance. But she was enjoying getting to know him and their growing friendship.

"Well, have fun. Maybe I'll come by tomorrow before John comes down from Tahoe. It won't be a lot of fun up there this weekend with his mom sick."

"I'll be home," Fiona assured her, and took off for the city. She was thinking about her daughter as she stood outside the ballpark, waiting for Logan. She was wearing jeans and a red sweater and Nikes, and she'd brought a jacket in case the fog rolled in, which was more than likely in San Francisco in the summer. But it was a nice day so far, and the sun was shining when she got there, and two minutes later she saw him approaching, and he waved at her. He was wearing a Windbreaker and jeans too, and a Giants cap, and he was smiling when he reached her.

"I forgot to tell you to bring a jacket, in case it gets chilly. I'm glad you brought one. I could have given you mine," he said as they headed toward the ticket taker, and the atmosphere was so festive, she was happy she had come. There were families and young people, and couples, and groups of men, and people trying to sell tickets right outside, and everybody looked happy and as though they were expecting to have a good time. The Giants were doing well, and Logan said he was expecting them to make the World Series. And he was right about the jacket. It had been eighty-five degrees when she left Portola Valley, and twenty degrees less in the city, and cool and breezy in the ballpark. She would have been cold without her sweater, and probably freezing by the end of the day if she hadn't had the jacket with her. Most of the time it was foggy all summer, but not today. It was one of the reasons why she liked living on the peninsula south of the city. The weather was always warm, and it was convenient for her for work. She didn't want to commute.

His seats were excellent, and as soon as they sat down, he offered to get her a hot dog and a beer, and she went with him, and they chatted along the way.

"Do you come to the games a lot?" she asked, smiling at him as they lined up at one of the concessions with dozens of other people. She didn't know why, but she felt like a kid at a birthday party, and was glad she had come. And he looked like he was enjoying it too, especially with her. He had a way of making her feel welcome and at ease, and as though they knew each other better than they did. He was comfortable to be with, probably more so because it wasn't a date and they only wanted to be friends.

"I try not to miss a game," he told her, and then ordered their hot dogs, french fries, and beer, and stuffed a wad of paper napkins in his pocket and asked if she liked mustard, ketchup, or relish and pickles. And she said ketchup and mustard, and then he stopped at the next concession booth on the way back to their seats, and he bought her a Giants hat and handed it to her with a grin. "Now you look like a fan," he said as he put it on her head, and she settled it into place. She had worn her long blond hair in a ponytail and not in a bun, and he smiled when he saw her in the hat. "Very cute, Fiona. I like it. You should wear it to work." She laughed, and as soon as they got to his seats, they dug into the food, and were chatting happily as the fans streamed into the stadium, milled around, and eventually sat down. There was music blaring, and people laughing and blowing horns around them. The crowd was a mixed bag as it always was at baseball games, with fancy-looking people in expensive season seats, families with kids, people of all races and nationalities, and some who looked like they had had to beg, borrow, and steal to get there. But Logan's seats were well placed, right behind home plate, and had a perfect view of the field in the still relatively new stadium.

"I love football too," he told her, already halfway through his hot dog, and he grinned when he saw ketchup on her chin and wiped it off with one of the napkins. "You're a messy eater," he teased her, "but you look good in the hat. I really wanted to be a sportswriter," he confessed, "if I couldn't be a ballplayer. I broke my pitching arm when I was fourteen, so that was the end of my career in the major leagues. I used to play soccer, but I got too old. It damn near killed me. I tore my Achilles two years ago, and that did it for me. I quit after that."

"Do you play tennis?"

"Sometimes. I was a better soccer player."

"My sister is a terrific player," she said, putting in a plug for Jillian, and he looked at her oddly, as he started in on his second hot dog. Fiona had only ordered one, and it had been great. She ate a french fry and took a sip of her beer, smiling at him.

"Why do I get the feeling you're trying to fix me up with your sister?" He looked surprised. It was about the tenth time she had mentioned her, and the references seemed consistent and purposeful, particularly the last one. And he didn't look thrilled about it. He was enjoying her. He was more than willing to meet her very interesting-sounding sister, but not for a date. He could already tell she wouldn't be his style, and he didn't want to go out with a shrink, who might spend her time analyzing him and why he did what he did, and how they were going to fix it, or more specifically **him.**

"Maybe because I am trying to set you up with her," Fiona said honestly. "I think you two would like each other."

"I didn't know being friends with you gave you license to play matchmaker," he said with a meaningful look, and she laughed.

"Of course it does. I didn't know being friends with you meant I'd get to go to baseball games, and I'm having a ball. Try to keep an open mind."

"I am. But dating your sister is not what I had in mind."

"You don't know her yet," Fiona said confidently. "Men fall at her feet. She's tall," Fiona admitted, so he wouldn't be surprised when he met her, "but she's great. Everybody loves Jillian."

"Then I'm sure I will too," he said cryptically, and changed the subject.

"She's coming back sometime this week. Maybe we can play tennis together next weekend, if we can find a fourth for doubles."

He raised an eyebrow and gave her a look that was meant to be menacing and wasn't. "Don't push!" Fiona didn't answer and just laughed, and then the game started, and the Giants scored two runs in the first inning, and everyone went wild. Logan was cheering loudly, and bought ice cream for him and Fiona when they finished their beer.

The score was four to nothing, with the Giants winning, halfway through the game. Logan was ecstatic, and they were that much closer to the play-offs and eventually the World Series, which he was hoping they'd get to. And when they won six to one, he considered the day a success, and they filed out of the stadium with all the happy Giants fans. Fiona had had a ball, and it had been great being with him.

"Thank you so much, I had a terrific time," she said, smiling at Logan, and she was going to go back to the garage, get her car, and drive home.

"I loved it too," he said happily. "Do you have time for dinner, or do you have to get back?" He didn't know if she had plans, or needed to work, which he knew she did on weekends.

"No, I'm fine. I don't have too much work this weekend, for once. I got pretty well caught up this week." Work always came first for her, she was a woman of responsibility and duty, and he felt the same way about his work.

"I don't have any deadlines this weekend either, which is rare for me," he said with a look of relief, as they walked to his car, and left hers in the garage.

She wasn't hungry after all they'd eaten, but he suggested a Greek restaurant near the Embarcadero where he said they could get some small plates of food if they wanted, or hummus, or just a bowl of avgolemono soup, which Fiona actually loved. It sounded good to her.

The restaurant was busy and noisy when they got there, with brick walls and fireplaces in several rooms, and lots of good-looking young people at the bar. It was a busy Saturday in San Francisco, and everyone looked lively and in a good mood, as Logan and Fiona slid into a quiet booth in one of the back rooms. She'd never been there before. Everything she'd done with him so far had been a new experience for her.

They talked a lot about his work at dinner, and the pieces he was currently writing. He had several interviews scheduled that sounded interesting to her.

"I think it would be exciting to meet different people all the time. I work with the same ones year after year. It's hard to keep things fresh, and get everyone motivated," she said, and he nodded.

"Your job is a lot more challenging than mine, Fiona, and harder," he said with a look of admiration, "but I enjoy what I do. My father always said 'do something you love.' I took it seriously. He was a smart guy. He loved practicing medicine, and so did my mother. And I love writing and journalism. One of these days I'm going to write a book, when I have time, which isn't now." He was busy as an investigative reporter, juggling all his assignments. "I'm kind of a rabble-rouser with the pieces I write. I'm always looking for the seamy underbelly, or the hidden dishonesty of what people don't tell you. Even if you don't see it, you know it's there."

"Did you think that about me?" she asked, looking a little shocked. His eyes had lit up when he talked about digging up the truth.

"No," he said immediately. "I've been a fan of yours for years. You're a straight shooter, about everything. And it shows. You shine like a beacon in the midst of some damn dishonest people in the corporate world," Logan said as their dinner arrived. His blunt opinions reminded her of her sister again, although her delivery was more diplomatic. But she loved analyzing people too, and she said as much to him. He smiled when she said it, and she laughed.

"Okay, so why is it that you don't want to go out with my sister? I take it you don't trust my matchmaking abilities." Fiona smiled at him. She could see that he had no interest in meeting Jillian for a date, which seemed too bad to her. She was sure they would have fun together. It was hard not to with Jillian, and she had a wicked sense of humor, much like his, which was razor sharp. But his tongue was not. He was a kind person, with a good mind. Not unlike Jillian either.

"I don't trust anyone's matchmaking abilities after some of the blind dates I went on arranged by friends. I got smart about that a long time ago," he said, and Fiona didn't disagree after her own experiences with fix-ups by friends when she first got divorced. Alone was always better than the blind dates she'd been on. "But I don't want to go out with her for another reason, although I'd like to meet her," he said simply. "She sounds like a lot of fun. And smart, like her younger sister," he said, paying her a left-handed compliment that made Fiona smile.

"So? You're not up for dating at the moment?" Fiona inquired. It seemed like a waste to her, if that was the case. He was a great guy, and she thought any woman would be lucky to go out with him, and he was right up her sister's alley.

"Actually, I am up for dating," he corrected her. "I just don't want to go out with her." Fiona looked disappointed, and he lowered his voice so the people in the next booth wouldn't hear, in case someone had recognized her. "I want to go out with you," he said, looking her straight in the eye.

"With me?" She was shocked as he nodded. He was making it perfectly clear and had realized that she wouldn't get it otherwise. She didn't consider herself dating material anymore and had put it out of her mind. She considered him a friend. And he had something else in mind. He could tell she wasn't getting the message, so he said it again: "I want to go out with **you.** On a date."

"Why?" she asked with a puzzled look, and he laughed out loud at her question.

"Because you're beautiful, honest, nice to be with, extremely intelligent, a good person, have integrity, and I have a great time with you. Do you want more?" He hadn't listed **successful, powerful,** or **a CEO,** none of which he cared about, although others would. "And that's just a start. I admire you. I like you. I think you're a terrific person. And I think you're shortchanging yourself if you give up on men. You've had some bad experiences, but that's no reason to quit. I think one can have a relationship **and** a big job. The two are not mutually exclusive, if you're with the right person and do it right. Maybe you never have before. And I realize that I'm not a CEO, or chairman of the board of a large corporation, or a 'captain of industry,' but I like what I do, and I'm good at it. I'm comfortable in my own skin and with who I am. I'm not threatened by you, or angry because you make more money than I do or have a bigger job. I like you. I have fun with you. I'd like to go out with you. More, I'd like to date you, not your fantastic older sister who is six feet tall and smart as a whip and a fabulous tennis player. You. Her little sister. That would really work for me. What about you?" He knew it wasn't what she had in mind initially, but he hoped she'd be open to it now.

"I never thought . . . I didn't realize. . . ." She stumbled over her words and lowered her eyes as she chased crumbs around the table and didn't know what to say. And before she could say anything, he reached across the table and held her hand in his. He didn't want to scare her, but he also didn't want her to run away, and she looked as though she might.

"It doesn't have to be complicated. Just give it a chance and see what happens. Lives won't be lost if we decide we're not made to go out with each other. The worst that can happen is we'll wind up friends. I've got room for a new friend in my life. What about you? Are you willing to give it a try?" He was direct and not afraid to say or go after what he wanted. Fiona was the same way in business, but not in her personal life. She had given up on that years before, maybe even before she and David broke up. He had beaten her down for years, and she didn't want to go through that again.

Her eyes were sad as she looked at him, and he could see the hurt there. And she seemed so vulnerable and so scared that he wanted to take her in his arms, not talk to her across a dinner table.

"What if we hurt or disappoint each other? If we do, you'll hate me."

"No, I won't." He looked her in the eye fearlessly and seemed confident, in her and himself. "I'll be disappointed. But you're not going to screw me over or do something dishonest. I already know that about you. Neither am I. You don't know that about me yet, but it's true. And who knows, maybe we'd have a great time and it would work. It's worth a shot." He smiled then. "People like you and me don't come along every day. In fact, we're pretty damn rare. We're both honest, honorable people. And maybe we'd be happy. If nothing else, we can go to dinner and ball games and have some fun. You need some fun in your life, Fiona. You can't work all the time, and neither can I. And I'm a workaholic too. I'm not going to bitch at you about your job. I'm willing to take whatever time you have left over, or work when you do. There are plenty of weekends when I have deadlines and can't go out, and eat three meals a day at my desk. You don't have to make any big commitment to me. Just leave the door open, and see where it goes." He was very convincing.

She opened her mouth to say something and then closed it again. She looked at him for a long time, and her hand was still in his. She hadn't pulled it away, which he considered a good sign. And she was surprised by everything he had said. It had never even occurred to her that he'd want to date her, or be involved with her. At first, she thought he was using her as a source for information, and then she thought he just liked her as a pal, like another guy. She had no concept of herself as a woman anymore, nor any idea how beautiful he thought she was. And he didn't give a damn that she was four years older, she didn't look it. In fact, she looked ten years younger than he did. And age seemed irrelevant to him. He liked everything about her. He felt her squeeze his hand gently before she finally spoke.

"Yes," she said so softly he almost didn't hear it, but he saw her lips move.

"Yes? As in yes, you'll go out with me?" He looked as shocked as she had when he told her he wanted to date her.

"Yes." Her voice was stronger this time, and she laughed. "I think you're crazy and I don't know why you want to date me. My life is nuts. I work crazy hours, and almost all the time. And I need to spend time with my kids when they can see me. But if you can put up with everything that comes with it, then yes, maybe you're right, and you have to leave the door open in life, and it's worth a shot, as you put it. But one thing I want us to agree on." He was waiting for her to come up with some terrible condition that would screw the deal. He knew just how tough she was in business, and wondered if she was in her personal life too, although she didn't look it. No one who didn't know her would have guessed she was the CEO of a major corporation. She wasn't tough as a person, she was gentle and feminine and kind, which was part of what he loved about her. She was no ballbuster. He waited to hear the deal breaker for her. "I don't ever want you to use me as a source. I'm not going to leak anything to you, Logan. Don't ever ask me to, or try to pump me for information, or use me." He could see that she meant it, and he wouldn't have done that anyway. He knew it would have blown everything to smithereens and he didn't want that to happen, now or later. Especially later, if things were going well. He wouldn't jeopardize that for anything in the world.

"Of course not," he said, surprised she even felt she needed to say it. "You have my word." He stuck his right hand across the table. He was holding hers in his left. And she reached up and shook his. "I promise." And she could see that he was being honest with her, and she trusted him to keep his word.

"Then we have a deal," she said, smiling at him, and she looked carefree and young, and suddenly laughed at him. "But I still want you to meet my sister. You're going to love her. You really missed a great opportunity with her." She looked like a kid when she giggled.

"I'll just have to live with the deal I just made," he said, smiling back, and meaning her. "I think on the whole I did okay." Their dinner arrived and they started talking animatedly and the evening flew by.

He drove her to the garage after dinner, and walked her to her car. She invited him to come to the house in Portola Valley the next day to hang out at the pool. It sounded good to him, and just before he left her, he kissed her on the cheek and then ever so gently on the lips. He didn't want to scare her, or rush her, and he had a feeling it had been a long time since she had been with a man, and he was right. And they had time.

"See you tomorrow," he said, smiling, as she got in her car.

"I had a wonderful time," she said, thanking him, and then with a wave she drove away and he got back in his car, looking pleased. It had gone better than he'd ever dreamed. It had been a very, very good day.

Chapter 21

On Sunday morning Fiona slept in later than usual, and was drinking a cup of coffee and reading the Sunday **New York Times**, when Alyssa walked into the kitchen, looking upset. She had been on the phone with John most of the night. She slipped into a chair at the kitchen table and looked at her mother with wide eyes. Fiona could tell that something was up. She wondered if she and John had had a fight.

"Everything okay?" Fiona asked her with a frown. "Do you want breakfast? Good morning, by the way." She leaned over and kissed her daughter, who looked as though she had been crying. "Something happen with you and John?" It was the only explanation she could think of for the look on Alyssa's face, and she wondered if the canceled weekend was for some other reason than that his mother was sick.

"No, it's not okay. It's John, but not what you think. We're fine. It's his parents, Mom." She looked at her mother and made her promise not to tell a soul.

"Who am I going to tell, for heaven's sake? Of course I won't tell. What's wrong?" After the sexual harassment incident, she wondered if Marshall was in some kind of trouble again.

"His parents are getting a divorce," she cut to the chase. "His dad came up to Tahoe on Friday and told his mom he's divorcing her, and John says she's falling apart. But it gets worse. He told her he's had a girlfriend in L.A. for eight years. She's a lot younger than his mom, I don't know, twenty-five or thirty or something. But he's been with her all this time, and that's why he goes to L.A. every week, to be with her, and I guess he has to work there too. But they even have a house together in Malibu. And Mom, you won't believe this, they have two little girls together, twins! Can you believe that? He wanted to show John and Lindsay pictures of them, because they're their sisters. Lindsay had a fit. John was on the phone with me all night. I didn't even know what to say to him. Anyway, his dad is filing for divorce, and he's going to marry the girlfriend with the twins."

"Holy shit," Fiona said with a look of astonishment. She had heard stories like it before. People had second hidden families, and mistresses, but this was very close to home, and Marshall had appeared to be such a model husband and father. You just never knew what went on in people's lives. She felt sorry for John and the other children, and especially for his mother. So the poster boy CEO wasn't such a good guy after all. Logan's instincts about him had been right. And he probably was guilty of the affair in the harassment suit too.

Above all, Fiona felt sorry for his wife. She had stuck by him through the threatened harassment suit. And maybe there were others, who knew. Marshall wasn't nearly as respectable as he seemed, far from it. Fiona wondered why he had decided to marry the younger woman now, after so many years. Fiona felt sorry for them all, except the mistress with the twins. She should have known better than to get involved with a married man and have babies with him. Fiona assumed she was some gold digger who was after what she could get and had hung on long enough to win the jackpot, or maybe blackmailed Marshall into it. But she surely wasn't a decent girl, sleeping with a married man, and breaking up his family for her own. Fiona did not approve, and all her sympathies were with Liz and her children, and her heart went out to John.

"He says that was always his worst fear," Alyssa told her, "that his parents would get divorced. Especially after that woman accused his father of sexual harassment and said she had an affair with him. Maybe she really did, and he paid her off to lie about it." Anything seemed possible now. Marshall had lost all credibility with his family and those who knew him, once they heard the story of his mistress with the twins. "John says his mom's been a nervous wreck ever since that woman came forward and accused him of having an affair with her. John says his mom believed his dad, but she was upset anyway. I guess it scared her. And now John says the whole family is in an uproar. His older brother says he'll never speak to him again. He thinks their dad is a sociopath. And Lindsay hasn't spoken to him all weekend. John doesn't know what to think. He's always respected him so much. He idolized him." Alyssa spilled out the whole story to her mother's astonished ears.

"Mom, what can I do?" Alyssa asked her with a worried look. "John's so upset. And he says he's ashamed for his father too. And he's sure it'll be all over the press."

"It probably will," Fiona confirmed to her. "These things come out eventually, especially if he's going to marry her now." Several public figures had been in similar situations, and the tabloid press always had a heyday with it. "There's nothing you can do, sweetheart, except be there for John, and comfort him. He didn't do anything wrong. None of this is his fault."

"He loves his father so much, and now he says he'll never forgive him."

"Maybe he won't. Or he might one day. It'll all take time."

"He said he'll never meet those girls, or accept them as his sisters."

"That's sad for them too. They're automatically outcasts because of what their parents did, which isn't fair to them. All the children are paying the price for the sins of the father. And so is his wife. I can only imagine how John feels." And it suddenly occurred to her that it

supported all of Jillian's theories about the out-
rageous sexual behavior of men in power, and
that power was an aphrodisiac to them. This
was a perfect example of just that.

Fiona looked at her watch then and realized
that Logan was about to arrive any minute, and
she still had to shower and dress. She cleared
the table and Alyssa helped her. They had been
talking for two hours. And Fiona told her she
had to dress.

"Are you going somewhere, Mom?" Alyssa
looked surprised. Her mother never went out
on Sundays. She stayed home and worked, or
spent time with Alyssa or Mark.

"I'm having a guest," Fiona said, avoiding her
eyes as she folded the newspaper and put it
away.

"Like who?"

"A friend," Fiona said vaguely, and Alyssa
looked at her with wary eyes.

"What kind of friend?"

"The one who took me to the baseball game
yesterday."

"You mean you're seeing him again?" Alyssa
looked shocked as her mother nodded.

"It's not a big deal, I've had dinner with him
a couple of times, and he's good company. I was

going to introduce him to Aunt Jill, but I guess we had too much fun and she's been away for too long." Fiona smiled at her daughter, who still looked concerned. She was not used to her mother dating and wasn't sure it was a good idea. What if he turned out to be a jerk? Or mean? Fiona had had the same concerns, but she didn't now. She was almost certain Logan was a good guy, whether they turned out to be compatible or not. Time would tell.

"Isn't he an investigative reporter?"

"Yes. Why?"

"For God's sake, don't tell him about John's dad, Mom." She looked panicked.

"Of course not." He had given her his word the night before, but she wouldn't have told him a story like that. It would come out soon enough without her adding to it. And out of respect for John, she wouldn't have told anyone. "I would never do that," she assured her daughter, who looked relieved. "Why don't you stay and meet him? You can have lunch with us at the pool. I think you'll like him."

Alyssa didn't comment and looked at her mother with concern. "Why are you dating him, Mom? You have us. You don't need a guy."

"That's probably true," Fiona said matter-of-factly, knowing instantly what her daughter was worried about. They were jealous of her time, and didn't want to share her with anyone else. Her solitude and availability suited them, and there was no one for them to compete with. "But you and your brother are both in college. He's in New York and only comes home for school vacations, and you're busy and now you have John. It's nice for me to have a little fun too. I'm not going anywhere, and you're always going to be my first priority," she reassured her. "But this might be nice for me. If it isn't, I'll stop. We're not serious about this, and we're going to keep it light. Okay?" She smiled at her, and Alyssa nodded, but now she wanted to take a look at the guy. Her mother hadn't had a date in years, and she couldn't understand why that had changed. She had no idea that her aunt had been urging her mother to get out and date. And she wasn't at all sure she liked it. It was different for her dad, they hardly ever saw him, but their mother was always around in the evenings and on weekends and free for them, and she didn't want anything to be different now. But her mother seemed sensible about it, and not all romantic and wound up.

Alyssa lay by the pool until her mother was

ready. Fiona had put on shorts and a T-shirt, and she hadn't gotten all dressed up. She wasn't wearing makeup, and her hair was down. She was wearing flip-flops and looked totally relaxed and like herself when the doorbell rang. Alyssa liked the fact that she hadn't gotten all dolled up for her date, which she would have considered a sign that her mother was now out of her mind, like John's father. And she was pleasantly surprised when Logan walked in. He was wearing jeans and a T-shirt, was clean shaven, and had dark hair. He looked intelligent, attractive, and relaxed, and he was wearing flip-flops too, and he had brought French bread, cheese, and wine for them. He seemed happy to see Fiona, and treated Alyssa like an interesting adult and talked to her about more than school. And when they all sat down at the table by the pool, he treated her mother more like a casual friend than a date, although it was obvious that he liked and respected her. Alyssa couldn't find anything she didn't like about him, and when she helped her mother clear the table, she whispered to her in the kitchen.

"He's cool, Mom . . . he's hot!" She giggled.

"Which is he?" Fiona laughed at her. "Cool or hot? Don't confuse me."

"Both. He's nice, and I think he likes you." And this time she seemed pleased. She approved.

"I thought he'd be perfect for Aunt Jill," she said with a tinge of regret.

"He's too young for her. She'd look silly with him. He's just right for you."

"So you like him?" Fiona checked the polls again, and Alyssa laughed.

"A lot." She left a little while later, and Logan complimented her on her daughter, as they lay in bathing suits by the pool.

"She's a really bright kid, just like you." He smiled at her and then looked worried for a minute. "Did I pass muster?" He knew how important her children were to her, and he could see how protective Alyssa was of her mother.

"With flying colors. You are both 'hot' and 'cool.' I think that's high praise from that age group." He looked relieved, and then turned on his side to look at her.

"I really like you, Fiona. I feel so comfortable with you."

And she was enjoying being with him too. Nothing exciting happened that afternoon. They just lay in the sun and talked. They ate the rest of the cheese and wine for an early dinner, and then he drove back to the city. And he kissed her before he left, on the lips this time, with more fervor than the day before, but not too much. She didn't feel as though he was crawling all over her, or desperate to get her into bed. Everything was happening at a comfortable pace for her. She had only just agreed to date him, so he wasn't rushing anything, and they were savoring each moment together. And they had agreed to go out the following weekend, which worked well for her, she had a busy week ahead.

He sent her a text when he got home, thanking her for a great day. And she did the same when she answered him. And so far it was an even exchange, which was exactly what she wanted. She wanted a partner and a friend, not someone who would push her around, and she didn't want to push him around either. Logan seemed like an even match. She was very pleased. And she couldn't wait to tell Jillian about it when she got home.

On Monday morning, Marshall did all he planned to, in order of importance, as soon as he got to the office. It had been a long, unpleasant, stressful weekend, and he was happy to take refuge at work. He hadn't heard from Liz or his children since he left Tahoe, but he didn't expect to. He had told Liz to find a lawyer. He wanted to get the divorce moving soon, and she needed to decide what she wanted to do about the house, if she wanted to keep it or sell it. He was amenable either way, and he was going to buy a new house for him and Ashley, possibly in the city, which might be fun for her, or maybe in Hillsborough, where the girls could have horses. The peninsula would be easier for him. And he was going to leave Marin County to Liz, so they didn't run into her. He had already thought of everything.

His first call of the day was to Connie Feinberg to tell her he had "taken care of business" over the weekend, just as she had wanted.

"Liz and I are getting a divorce," he told her simply.

"I'm sorry to hear it, Marshall." She sounded sad, far more than he did. She was a little shocked at his callous tone when he made the announcement. "And I'm sorry if the board pressed that decision. We would have been fine either way. We just didn't want you vulnerable to another scandal, which would eventually involve UPI. But I'm sure this is a heartbreak for all of you, if this is how it worked out."

"The kids will get over it," he said matter-of-factly, "and Liz and I need to move on. The other situation would never have happened if our marriage was still viable. And I stuck with it much too long. It was time to clean this up. The board was right. I'm calling my attorney this morning. I'd like to file as soon as possible, which means that Ashley and I could get married by February. If there's any stall on the money issues, we can bifurcate that from the divorce so nothing gets slowed down." He was moving ahead at full speed. Connie had scared him.

"We're not asking you to rush this," Connie said, feeling responsible, and sorry for his soon-to-be-ex-wife. "Once you tell people you're separated and getting divorced, the rest is up to you, and you can be seen with or involved with anyone you want. I'm sure there will be some comment at some point about your young daughters, but these things happen in today's world. The order of how people do things seems to have changed, and it's not nearly as shocking as it would have been twenty or thirty years ago. As soon as people hear about it, they'll forget. At least we hope so. And thank you for dealing with this so quickly." She had spoken to him exactly a week ago, and she hadn't expected him to move so fast, but she was glad he had. "Is Liz okay?" She sounded worried, but Marshall seemed very relaxed. Once he had made the decision, particularly after he saw Ashley, it was done. After years of indecision and inertia, when Connie lowered the boom on him, he had moved faster than the speed of sound.

"She'll be fine," he said about Liz. "I'm planning to take good care of her." He meant financially, which Connie instantly understood. But Connie knew that there was more than that involved. A fifty-year-old woman had just lost a twenty-seven-year marriage, her status, her job, her purpose in life, and the man she loved. Connie was sure that Liz felt she had lost everything, and couldn't imagine a life without Marshall. She hoped he was aware of it too. It didn't sound like he was, but it was none of Connie's business now. He had done as she had asked. Her involvement stopped there. She thanked him again before they hung up.

His next call was to his attorney, to tell him he

was getting divorced. He told him he wanted to move quickly, and to bifurcate the financial matters if necessary, and he was prepared to be generous with Liz, within reason. He wanted to give Liz their houses, both Ross and Lake Tahoe, and a handsome settlement, commensurate with his fortune and his income. His attorney told him that there were charts to calculate that, but Marshall said he was prepared to go beyond that. He wanted Liz comfortable and secure for life, so his children would have nothing to reproach him for. And he told the attorney that he wanted to get married in six months, as soon as the ink was dry on the divorce, so he wanted it filed immediately, if possible that week. They could serve Liz the papers through her attorney. And when he said he wanted to get married quickly, his lawyer wondered if there was an impending baby involved. That was usually the case when men were as definite and moved as fast as Marshall was doing now.

"Is there a baby on the way here?" the lawyer asked him cautiously, not wanting to offend him, but he thought he should know.

"Yes, two," Marshall admitted with a grin. "They're seven years old." He had had a lawyer in L.A. draft his last will, so his local lawyer didn't know about the provisions for Ashley and the girls, which would have stunned everyone at the reading of his will if he had died.

The attorney promised to take care of everything as quickly as possible. And Marshall called a real estate agent after that. He told her he was looking for a large house and property in Hillsborough, or possibly in the city. He described what he wanted, and the amount he had in mind to spend. The agent said she had several possibilities and would be in touch with him in a few days.

And then he called Ashley, in the same businesslike tone. He told her he'd been busy.

"I told Liz this weekend," he said, and there was silence at the other end. She hadn't spoken to him since he left L.A., and she'd been wrestling with her own thoughts for days. She had decided not to see Geoff the day before, or until she knew what she wanted. It didn't feel right to be spending time with him right now. They couldn't seem to just do it as a friendship, without being attracted to each other, and she had too much on her mind. She wasn't comparing the two men, she was trying to search her heart. And she only wanted to think about Marshall right now. Geoff was much too appealing, and after not seeing him for eighteen years, too much about him was unknown, and would take time to find out. All he could be right now was distracting, and when she talked to him the night before, he said he understood. He was willing to do whatever she wanted. They knew they cared about each other. For now, that was enough.

"How did she take it?" Ashley asked him finally about Liz. She had waited eight years for that moment, and now she felt sorry for her, and guilty.

"Badly," Marshall said matter-of-factly. "I expected that. She never suspected, although maybe she should have." But he had been careful not to leave a trail for all these years. "I told her about you and the girls. I was totally honest with her, and the children."

"How were they?" Ashley asked, sounding far more devastated than he seemed to be. She really felt like a homewrecker now. She was responsible for destroying four lives, and he was her partner in crime.

"They're taking their cues from their mother. I'm being treated like Public Enemy Number One. I think they'll all calm down in time. Except maybe Liz. I'm not sure she'll get over it." Ashley wondered if she would have, and what kind of condition she'd be in now, if he had broken up with her the previous Wednesday as he intended. He had known someone was going to get hurt. Either Ashley or Liz. And he had decided it would be Liz. But it could just as easily have been her, at the flip of a coin. If it hadn't been so fabulous in bed the week before, she might have been the one crying now. And it could still happen to her, if she ever became a risk to his career. She had no illusions about it now.

"I spoke to my attorney this morning. We'll be filing the divorce this week. And I called a real estate agent about a house for us. Hillsborough would work well for me, but I think it would be nice for you and the girls too, and I told her we'd look at some things in the city. We're going to need a rental house too, until the house we buy is ready. As soon as the divorce is filed, I think you should move up here, so the girls can start the school year here. I'll get you some names of schools to call, and I'm going to put the house in Malibu on the market." He had made all the decisions without her, and Ashley felt as though she were being swept away on a torrent of river rapids with no control over her own life. That was how it worked with men like Marshall. They made decisions and they moved fast once the decisions were made. She felt as though she were part of a business deal, and she was shocked about her Malibu house.

"Can't we keep my house down here? I love it," she said sadly.

"You don't need it anymore. You'll be living with me," he said calmly.

"We could spend a weekend here once in a while, for old times' sake." She had had some of the happiest times of her life there, and the saddest. And she had been living there when the twins were born. It was full of memories for her. But she had him now, and a whole new life. She tried to feel happy and excited about it, but all she felt was scared. This was how he did business and lived his life. She had never seen it that clearly before. And he hadn't told her once that he loved her since he called. She didn't dare complain about it. He had just left his wife for her, finally, after eight years, and maybe in his mind that was proof enough. And she suddenly found herself wondering what he'd be doing now in L.A. without her when she was in San Francisco as his wife. She wondered if one day she'd be in the same situation as Liz.

They talked for a few more minutes, but he had told her everything he had to say, and he told her he'd see her on Wednesday night.

"Marshall . . . ," she said hesitantly before they hung up. "Thank you . . . for everything you're doing." It seemed too little to say for four lives he had turned upside down for her, and the wife he had given up. "I hope I'll make you happy," she said with tears in her eyes.

"You will," he said coolly. He seemed to have no doubt and no regrets. Once he knew what was at stake, he had made his move. Ashley knew that it was just the way he was. Everything was a business decision for him in the end, and she had never been that for him before, till now. The board of UPI putting his job on the line had put her on his radar screen in a real way. Her heart, and their two little girls, had never been enough to do that. But she had nothing to reproach him for now. He was all about making decisions. And suddenly it was all moving very quickly. Almost too quickly for her.

"I love you," she said softly, wishing he were there so she could look into his eyes and better understand who he was and what he felt for her. She needed to know now.

"So do I," he answered, and was in a hurry to hang up. He was late for a meeting. And Ashley sat on the deck afterward for a long time, still holding her cell phone in her hand, wishing she could reach out and touch him. She felt as though she had lost him in the last few days, even though she finally had him. Everything was moving so fast, her head was spinning, and she longed for the days when she was sure he loved her. She wasn't sure he loved anyone right now. He loved his job. And anyone who interfered with that would be destroyed. She felt lost when she walked into the house, and was glad she was seeing her therapist that afternoon.

Bonnie called her that night, and Ashley didn't pick up. Geoff called the next day, and his message said he was worried about her, but she didn't return his call. It was Tuesday, and on Wednesday night Marshall would be there, to talk and make plans, and make love to her. A real estate company had already e-mailed her about putting her house on the market. Marshall had had his secretary e-mail her the names of schools for Kezia and Kendall, but she hadn't contacted them yet. Ashley felt like she was swimming underwater. She was awake all Tuesday night, and Geoff called her three times, but she couldn't talk to him now. She realized how wrong she had been to see him and then to kiss him. She had to abandon everything now, for Marshall. He had left his wife for her, and she owed him her loyalty, her life, and her future. She was going to be his wife, just as she had wanted to be. And maybe it didn't matter how she'd won the prize, whether the board of UPI had handed it to her, or he did. She had waited eight years for this moment. And as the sun came up on Wednesday morning, she lay on the deck thinking about the man she was going to marry. She had climbed Everest and survived it. The air at the summit was so thin she could hardly breathe, but Marshall was there with her. They had done it. Finally.

Chapter 22

Ashley took Kendall and Kezia to day camp on Wednesday morning as she always did. And she felt different this time. She was one of them now, all the mothers who had husbands and children. She was going to be married to an important man who had loved her enough to leave his wife and make her respectable at last. No one was going to feel sorry for her now, or be shocked by her, or whisper behind her back and say she was the girlfriend of a married man who only spent two nights a week with her. She had lived through all that for him and survived it. It was worth it now. When she got back to the house after she dropped the girls off, Marshall texted her that he was in town, and she started to shake violently. She wondered if something was seriously wrong with her. She sat down on the deck and put her head between her legs. And when she stood up again, she was still dizzy. And all she knew suddenly was that she had to see him. She needed to see him, and look into his eyes and know he loved her. She couldn't guess at it anymore, or hope he did, or wonder if it was true, or trust anyone else's judgment or even her own. She needed to see it.

She felt like she was in a trance as she got in her car and drove downtown to the building where his offices were. She left her car parked on the street in front of a hydrant. And she rode up to the offices where she hadn't been in the eight years since she'd worked there. She was wearing a flowered summer dress and sandals, and she walked into the reception area of the UPI offices with a dazed look. She remembered where his office had been, and wondered if it was still in the same place, and she walked down the hall feeling like a ghost until she found it. No one noticed or paid attention to her, and then she saw him through an open door, sitting at his desk. He was on the phone leaning back in his chair in his enormous corner office. It was the same one he'd had when she was a receptionist there.

And now she was the mother of his children and going to be his wife.

Marshall stared at her when he saw her and instantly hung up. He stood up and walked around his desk to meet her. She had a strange, vacant look in her eyes.

"Ashley, are you all right? What are you doing here?" She wanted to tell him she wasn't sure, and didn't know, but she didn't say anything, and stopped to catch her breath.

"I had to see you," she said, searching his eyes for the answers she had been looking for for days, months, years. All she saw was the CEO of UPI in his corner office. She wondered if that was all that had ever been there and she had imagined the rest, or if at first it had been different. And even now, when he made love to her, his eyes were full of desire and passion. He wanted her, but she was never sure he loved her, and she wasn't now.

"I'll see you tonight," he said with a worried expression and walked over to close the door while she watched him. "You can't come here, Ashley, I'm busy. Go home." She looked out of control, and he could see that she was shaking. But suddenly she felt more lucid than she had in years.

"Do you love me?"

"Of course I love you. What's this all about? Why did you come here? I just left my wife for you. I think that's ample proof that I love you." But she looked at him and shook her head.

"You left your wife to save your job, not because you love me. If you loved me, you'd have left her years ago, and you never did till they put your job on the line, and your ass," she said bluntly.

"What difference does it make? You got what you wanted. Isn't that enough?" He was starting to look angry. He didn't like her question, or her attitude, and he wanted her to leave. She was out of line. And he didn't want her making a scene in his office.

"No, it's not enough," she said quietly as she stopped shaking. "Because you almost got rid of me last week instead of her. And next time it might be me."

"Not if you behave," he said just as bluntly, with anger smoldering in his eyes. She was supposed to be grateful to him, and she wasn't. She wanted more. She wanted his heart.

"And what does that mean? What am I supposed to do for you? What are the ground rules? I had your babies. I stuck by you. I loved you for eight years. That wasn't enough to make you leave her. And Liz did everything you wanted for almost thirty years. And what did she get? You cheated on her and lied to her and came down here to sleep with me. You had two children behind her back. And now you fired her, to save your job."

"Is this about money? Do you want some kind of financial guarantee?" It didn't surprise him. Nothing did. But he didn't like it from her. And she just shook her head.

"No, it's not about money. It's about love," she said, and she could see the answer to her question in his eyes. "You don't love me, Marshall. You never did. You don't love Liz. You don't love our kids, hers or mine. You love you, and your career. And you know what? That's not enough. I don't need a house in Hillsborough, or even the one in Malibu. I don't need your money. I only needed you. And all you'll ever give me is all the stuff that goes with it, for as long as it's convenient for you. As long as I don't cost you your precious career in some way. But you don't love me." She had the answer that she needed now. It was crystal clear to her, and she knew it might nearly kill her, but she had to get away from him, whatever it took. "I can't do this. I gave you everything I had for eight years. There's nothing left. You killed it. When you came down here to dump me last week and told me about it after you changed your mind, it was over for me. I know that one day you'll do the same thing to me you just did to Liz. I don't trust you, Marshall. I love you. But I could never trust you again. And I can't live with a man I don't respect." She was calmer as she said it than she'd ever been. And as she said the words to him, he crossed the room and grabbed her arm. He had a viselike grip on it as he looked into her eyes.

"I don't care if you trust me, Ashley. Or respect me. You'll do what I say. I just left my wife for you, which you've been torturing me to do for eight years. Now you have what you wanted. You can't go back on it. We have children. We're going to get married, and you're not going to catapult me into some kind of scandal because I left Liz for you. I'll pay you whatever you want."

"I don't want anything from you," she said, "except for you to be responsible for your daughters. Beyond that, I want nothing for myself. And I'm sorry if you left Liz and it causes a scandal for you. You should have thought of that a long time ago when I got pregnant and you told me you'd marry me and never did. You should have left her then, not now for UPI. That's between you and them. I'm not going to be the solution to your problem if you don't love me, Marshall. I'm not going to spend the rest of my life with a man who doesn't love me and never did. I deserve better than that."

"Is there someone else?" he asked, letting go of her arm. He had frightened himself for a minute at how hard he was holding her. "Is that what this is about? Another man?"

"No, there isn't." She knew she wasn't leaving him for Geoff, so she was honest when she said it. She had no idea what would happen with Geoff, if anything. This was only about Marshall.

"You'll pay for this forever, Ashley, if you leave me now," he said, with murder in his eyes. He would never forgive her if she walked out on him, and she could see it on his face. But staying with him would be worse.

"I already paid for it, for eight years, with everything I had. I can't do it, Marshall, I'm sorry." She walked to the door, and he watched her go. She turned to look at him as she opened the door. "I love you. I always did,"

she said, and walked out of his office as he
stared after her with a look of rage. He strode
to the door and saw her disappear down the
hall, then slammed it with his entire force.
But he didn't run after her. He didn't try to
stop her. He knew what he had to do now, if
it wasn't too late.

Ashley left the building with tears streaming
down her face. She knew that she still loved
him, but she couldn't be with him, and now she
knew all the reasons why. There was no one
inside those eyes. She had never let herself see
that before. She hadn't wanted to. She had listened to his words and promises and forgiven
all he never did. But she no longer could.

She drove home to Malibu, blinded by her
tears, and walked into her house. She wondered
if she'd have to move now, but it didn't matter
if she did. He could have the house back, in
exchange for her life. She had all she needed,
the memories of how much she loved him, and
her girls.

With shaking hands, she looked up the number of one of the mothers from day camp and
asked her to take Kendall and Kezia home with

her. She said she had a fever and a terrible flu, and the other woman very kindly offered to keep them for the night, which Ashley said would be great. And she sounded as sick as she claimed.

And then she went upstairs and went to bed. She curled up in a fetal position, and she wondered if Marshall would show up and try to convince her to stay with him. It might have meant something if he did, but she knew it wouldn't change her mind. But he never came or called that day. He had let her walk out of his life like a business deal that had gone sour. And she knew she would never forget the fury in his eyes. He wasn't heartbroken or afraid of losing her. He was livid that she wasn't doing what he wanted her to, and that he had ended his marriage for nothing, for her, after all this time. She couldn't blame him for being angry. She knew he would be. But she had to save herself.

Geoff called her several times that night. She didn't answer, or listen to his messages. She didn't want to hear his voice. She needed time to mourn. And Marshall never called her at all. She lay in bed and cried all night. The truth had been exposed, and no matter how much it hurt, she knew she had done the right thing. She was free.

Marshall left Los Angeles at six o'clock that night, the same day he had arrived. It was a slow week in L.A., and he had nothing more to say to Ashley. He wasn't going to play those games with her and "prove" to her that he loved her. He had done enough. He called Tahoe on the way to the airport, and the housekeeper told him that Liz had gone to Ross for the night and would be back the next day. That was easier for him anyway.

They touched down in San Francisco just before seven o'clock. And he reached the house in Ross at eight. There had been traffic on the bridge.

He let himself into the house, and Liz was in the living room and looked at him when he walked in. She was going through stacks of books and there were cartons on the floor. She had already called a Realtor, and they were having an open house the following week, and she was starting to get rid of things.

"What are you doing here? I thought you were in L.A." It was why she had come down, and she had left Lindsay at the lake. They were alone in the house. She had spoken in an icy tone.

"I came back," he said in a subdued tone. "I want to talk to you."

"I have nothing to say. I want you to leave now. I'm going back up to the lake tomorrow. You can come here then. And I want you out before we move back. They're starting to show the house next week."

"You're selling it?" he asked her, and made no move to leave. Her face looked ravaged and her eyes were bleak. She was wearing torn jeans and an old T-shirt and sneakers to pack up the books. And she looked as though she didn't care how she looked. He could see that she had lost weight just in a few days.

"Yes, I'm selling the house," she said in a flat voice. She didn't tell him, but she had decided to move to the city, and Lindsay liked the idea. So did she. She wanted a whole new life and to forget everything about her life with Marshall. She wanted to get out of the house in Ross as fast as she could and never see it again. Their whole existence there had been a lie, and she wanted no sign of it in her life. She was selling everything, even their furniture and the art.

She wanted a fresh start, with no evidence of him. "I asked you to leave," she said again. This was harder than he thought. He sat down instead and watched her work while she ignored him.

"Look," he began in a gentle tone, "what I said to you the other day needed to come out. I couldn't live with the lies anymore. I should have told you years ago, Liz, but I didn't. I was wrong," he said, standing up again and slowly approaching where she stood, like an animal he was afraid to frighten away. A wounded animal he had shot and injured and was now looking for in the woods. She was hiding from him. "I got myself in a tough situation, and I didn't know how to get out of it. I felt obligated to her. She was young, she had no money, she wanted to have the babies, but my allegiance was always to you, which was why I never left you for her." He wondered as he said it if it was actually true, if he had loved Liz more than he thought, and that was why he hadn't left her. Or had he wanted to avoid the scandal of leaving his wife for another woman who had had two children by him? He was no longer sure. All he knew was that he didn't want the scandal it would create now. It would be better for all of them if they just put it behind them and went on as they were. Better for him anyway, and for Liz, rather than facing a whole new life alone at her age, although he didn't say that to her.

As he spoke, Liz stopped what she was doing and turned to look at him with eyes so full of contempt and hatred that it shook him to his core. Ashley had looked agonized when she came to his office, and he knew she loved him even if she didn't want to be with him anymore. But Liz was ice cold. And her voice was venomous when she spoke. He was dirt under her feet.

"Let me make this clear to you," she said to the man who had been her husband and whom she hated now. "I don't care what you think, or what you said, or how you did it, or what you want to explain to me. I don't care about any of it, Marshall, nor about you. You did it. It's over. And you did it for a lot of years. You made a lie out of our life, and you made a fool out of me and a joke out of everything I felt for you and tried to do for you. I actually cared about your career, and about you. I loved you. I don't know why, but I did, while you were living with that woman and having babies with her. As far as I'm concerned, you're dead. It's over. I feel nothing for you. I don't care what happens to your career or to you. I don't give a damn if you're sorry or thought I should know the truth, or why. Now I know. You're history, and I want to forget everything I ever knew about you or that I know you at all. I don't. I had no idea who you really were then, and I don't want to know now. Now get out of my house, or I'll call the police." She stood staring at him, and he knew she meant it from the look in her eyes.

He started to say something to her but knew he couldn't. He had lost them both. He had miscalculated and made the wrong move. He should have gotten rid of Ashley in the first place, and never told Liz the truth. He had played it wrong.

"Liz, will you reconsider?" He was pleading with her. He needed her. He knew that now. He didn't need Ashley, he had wanted her, which was different, but he needed Liz.

"I hope you're joking. No, I won't reconsider. I told you, I'm calling the police." She reached for the phone as she said it with a wicked look in her eye. He was a stranger to her now.

"I'm leaving," he said quietly, to calm her down. She watched him pick up his jacket and walk to the door. "Liz?"

"No," she said, and watched him close the

door behind him. And as he walked to his car, there were tears streaming down his cheeks. He had lost everything with one fell swoop. And as she heard him drive away, Liz went back to boxing up the books, and hoped she'd never see him again.

Chapter 23

It took Ashley three days to come out of her shell. She lay in bed until then, barely able to move or talk. Kendall and Kezia stayed with their friends for two days, and they came back to Ashley at bedtime on Friday night. When she saw them, she couldn't help wondering when Marshall would ever see them again. She had had an e-mail from his attorney, offering her a settlement she didn't want, and explaining to her about the trusts Marshall had set up for the girls when they were born. And he was giving her the house and putting it in her name. But the attorney had said nothing about visitation, school holidays, vacations, or wanting time with the girls. He said that Marshall would address those issues later when everything else was settled. He wanted to see the girls, but not Ashley. And she didn't want to see him either. But their girls needed a father. She knew it shouldn't have surprised her that he was in no rush to visit them, given everything she knew about him now, but it did anyway. And all she could hope was that he would spend time with the girls in the future. They adored him, and not being with him even for a while would be hard on them.

The twins were happy to see her, she told them she'd been sick, and she put them to bed that night, and took a long hot bath. She'd had a dozen messages from Geoff, and she knew he was worried sick about her, but she wasn't ready to talk to him yet. She texted him to stay away.

The first call she took was from Bonnie on Saturday morning. She had just finished work on her latest movie, and wanted to check in. They hadn't talked in weeks, and she had no idea what had been happening in Ashley's life.

"So what's new?" she asked Ashley, sounding bright and cheerful. She had missed her, and wanted to see her and the girls. She suggested dinner that night. Ashley felt like she was convalescing from a long illness or a serious accident and wasn't sure she was up to going out. It had only been three days, but she felt like she was detoxing from eight years of hard drugs. Marshall had been the hardest drug of all.

"Nothing much," she said to Bonnie. She was still tired but better than she had been.

"That was some picture," Bonnie told her. "You wouldn't believe the special effects. I thought they were going to blow us all up on the last day. They used real dynamite."

"I left Marshall." There was silence at the other end.

"You what? Rewind that for a minute. Did I miss something? You were madly in love with him the last time I talked to you, and wanted him to leave his wife."

"He finally did. For all the wrong reasons. The board found out about us, and they told him he had to clean up his act. Liz or me. He was going to get rid of me, and told me about it. But he got rid of Liz instead. And then I went crazy for a few days and realized that it had nothing to do with me, just his career, which is really all he cares about. So I went to his office and went a little nuts, and walked out on him. That's the short version, but it tells you enough."

"Holy shit, Ash. He left Liz and you left him after that?"

"Yeah."

"He must have been ready to kill you."

"He looked like it. He was ready to file for divorce. I never thought that, when I got what I wanted, it would be so meaningless. I don't think he ever loved me, or the girls. He must have tried to go back to Liz the same day." She knew him well.

"If she took him back. It sounds like he blew it with both of you. Pretty stupid for a smart guy."

"Yeah, maybe so."

Ashley invited her to come over later, and then she called Geoff and apologized for not calling him sooner.

"Are you okay?" He had sounded frantic on his messages, but calmer now that he could hear her. He had been worried sick about her, and wondering what was happening with Marshall. He thought she might be in San Francisco with him, but she said she wasn't.

"I was right here," she said softly. "But I couldn't talk to you. I needed to mourn it."

"Mourn what?" he said sadly. He thought she meant him.

"I left him. Finally. Long overdue."

"You left him?" He sounded even more astonished than Bonnie, but he didn't want to let
on how happy he was. She sounded so sad.

"I didn't leave him for you," she made clear to
him. "I didn't want to do that. That's why I
didn't want to see you or talk to you. I didn't
want you in my head. I left him for me."

"That's the right way to do it," he said, and
admired her for it. "How do you feel now?"

"Like shit," she said honestly, and then laughed.
"I guess I will for a while."

"Maybe not as long as you think. I admire
you for what you did. Have you talked to your
shrink about it?"

"Every day." She was the only person she had
talked to, other than her kids. "I know it was
right, it just hurts a lot." She still loved Marshall, no matter how bad he was, or how wrong
for her, and she knew she would for a long time.
But she'd left anyway, which was very brave.

"Can I see you?" he asked hopefully.

"Not yet. I'm not ready. Maybe soon." She was
vague about it and asked him how the show was
going. He was very excited about it, and loved
writing the scripts. And he didn't press her about
seeing him. He knew she needed time.

"You know where I am if you need me, Ash. I'm not going anywhere."

"Me neither," she said, and promised to call soon, and then hung up.

Bonnie came over that night with a pizza, and they had dinner with the kids. Ashley didn't want to talk about Marshall, so they didn't. And the girls asked for him a couple of times. Ashley told them he was working. And they accepted that for now, but she knew they wouldn't forever.

And little by little, she returned to the land of the living, day by day. Marshall had never called her after she had gone to his office, and she knew he wouldn't. She wondered if he was back with Liz, but there was no one she could ask, and she didn't want to know. Whatever he did was his business now, and no longer hers.

When Jillian came back from Italy that week, she called Fiona, and they made a date to play tennis on Saturday. She said she'd had a fabulous trip.

"What about playing doubles this time?" Fiona asked her, and Jillian sounded suspicious immediately.

"Why would we do that? I can beat you all by myself. I don't need help," she said and laughed.

"You wish," her younger sister called her on it. "I just thought it might be fun," she said innocently.

"I smell a rat. Are you trying to fix me up with someone? Some boring corporate creep that no one else would want?"

"No, I was. And he's not a creep. I met someone I thought you'd like."

"Let me tell you, after the Italians I went out with, one in Venice, and two in Positano, and one in Rome, you're going to have to come up with Brad Pitt to impress me." She had the busiest love life of any fifty-five-year-old woman Fiona had ever known. "We wound up traveling all over Italy." She sounded happy and relaxed.

"Well, you missed out here. You stayed away too long," Fiona told her.

"How's that? He met someone else?" Jillian sounded intrigued.

"Kind of. Actually, I've sort of gone out with him a few times. I know that sounds crazy, but he's nice."

"It doesn't sound crazy to me at all." Jillian was delighted for her. "Welcome to the human race, I can't wait to meet the guy who seduced the virgin queen."

"Don't get too excited. I haven't slept with him yet."

"That's too bad," Jillian said, sounding disappointed. "I don't know how one of us wound up so virtuous and the other one a middle-aged slut." But she was having a good time and Fiona laughed. "Any chance you'll get laid in this century, or this lifetime? I should have lit candles for you in Rome."

"Don't worry about it. We're having a nice time. I'm taking it slow, no need to rush."

"Of course. Getting laid once every five years is enough for anyone. Fiona, dead people have sex more often than you do. You should drink more or something. So who is this guy?" She was curious about him.

"I told you. Logan Smith, the reporter. Remember? He called me trying to get information, and we wound up making friends instead. He took me to a baseball game. So can he play tennis with us on Saturday?"

"Of course. I want to meet him. Do I have to let him win?" She sounded worried.

"No, just don't hit him with your racket if you lose. It might make a bad impression, and I've been telling him how fabulous you are."

"I'll be on my best behavior," she promised, chuckling.

"I'll see if Alyssa wants to be our fourth," Fiona said, and sent her an e-mail, and Alyssa said she'd be happy to. The four of them were planning to have lunch afterward. Fiona told Logan about it when he called her that night. He was calling every night now.

"Something tells me I should be scared of your sister," he said, laughing about it.

"Honestly, she's terrific. She's just very outspoken, has an insatiable appetite for men, and is a jock."

"Ohmigod, now I'm scared shitless. And you wanted to set me up with her?" He pretended to be terrified.

"It's not too late," Fiona offered.

"Yes, it is," he said in a serious tone. He was crazy about her, and things were going well. "So when are we having dinner this week?" He never pushed her, but they were both organized, which worked well for them. They agreed on Thursday and Saturday night, tennis on Saturday, and Sunday at her pool, if they were both in the mood. It sounded perfect to them both.

And Jillian didn't let Fiona down on Saturday when they played doubles with Logan and

Alyssa. Jillian beat him, but she didn't humiliate him totally on the court, and she was extremely funny over lunch when she told them about some of the men she'd gone out with on her trip. And she and Logan eventually got on the subject of her latest book, and her theories about men in power, versus women, and the different ways it affected both, and how the opposite sex perceived them.

"Take my sister, the vestal virgin here," she said about Fiona, who looked like she was ready to hit her. "She's a classic example of what happens to female CEOs. They take their jobs too seriously, become major workaholics, and no one wants to go out with them, until . . . ," she said, as though she expected a drum roll, ". . . a handsome prince comes along . . . or investigative reporter. He kisses the CEO, and she turns into a normal woman again, presto magic, and everyone is happy. As opposed to her counterpart, the male CEO, who is so taken with himself that he runs around like a sex maniac, overworking his libido and screwing every woman he can lay hands on. He spends his life apologizing to people on TV, and makes a total ass of himself, and everyone realizes he's a complete jerk, and in some cases, his wife sues him for a lot of alimony, or his girlfriend," she said, and they all laughed. But they all knew there was a certain truth to it, and Alyssa thought her description sounded like Marshall Weston.

After that, Logan and Jillian got into a serious discussion about their theories, and made a lunch date the following week to go over some of her research. And they were talking about writing an article on the subject together. She wasn't his cup of tea as a woman, she was too outspoken and aggressive and too much of a jock, but he liked her a lot as a friend.

"Now that's the kind of woman I can be friends with," he said to Fiona at dinner that night. He had taken her to a very good restaurant in Palo Alto and insisted he didn't mind driving home to the city that night. She felt bad expecting him to do that, but she wasn't ready to sleep with him yet, and he didn't push. He said he'd rather wait and have it be right.

"I have a proposition to make to you," he said, smiling at her at the end of dinner. They'd had a lovely evening and a very good meal. They hadn't had a bad time together yet. "I have to go to New York next weekend. I have to do an interview on Friday afternoon, but it won't take very long. I could do it on the phone, but I get more spark out of it if I do it in person, and he's an important subject. I thought I'd go to the theater on Friday night, stay at a terrific hotel, take in a Yankees game on Saturday, a good dinner Saturday night, and come home on Sunday. Would you like to go with me?" He looked hopeful as he asked her, and she looked touched, but hesitated. And she felt she knew him well enough to ask the fateful question.

"One room or two?" He laughed at how simply she put it.

"Your call, princess. Whichever you like. The offer stands either way." It sounded like a mini-honeymoon to Fiona, and she appreciated that he wanted to make it so much fun for her. They'd been out a number of times now and it was clear that they were crazy about each other.

"I'd like that a lot," she said, smiling warmly, and then she surprised him. "One room, please. I think I can handle that."

He beamed at her, and took her hand in his own, and kissed it. "Yeah. I think I can too. And I'd like to try. You're on."

Chapter 24

Fiona took Friday off, something she almost never did, so that she could fly with Logan, and he had insisted on treating her to the tickets, and had bought seats for them in first class, which really touched her. He told her how much he appreciated her coming with him. And they talked almost all the way, then watched a movie, and she slept for the last hour before they landed, and he dropped her off at the hotel, and left immediately to do his interview, so he could get it behind him. He was interviewing one of her male counterparts, a well-known CEO, who had been involved in a recent scandal about insider information, and the interview was a big deal. He promised to be back by dinnertime, and they had decided not to go to the theater, in case the interview went longer than planned.

They were staying at the Four Seasons on Fifty-seventh Street, where Fiona got a big discount because she always stayed there, so after some arguing about it on the plane, he let her take care of the hotel. She said it was only fair since he had paid their airfare and was paying for everything else. It seemed like an equitable arrangement to both of them, and Fiona was pleased to see they had given them a big suite on the forty-eighth floor, and she had already changed for dinner by the time Logan got back to the hotel at eight-thirty. Their dinner reservations were for nine. He was taking her to 21, and she was wearing a black cocktail dress that looked very elegant but was short enough to show off her legs. She looked sexier than he'd ever seen her, and he rushed off to take a shower and get dressed himself, while she watched CNN in the living room of the suite.

He showered, shaved, and changed quickly, and came back wearing a dark suit, white shirt, and dark blue tie at five to nine.

"Wow!" she said, looking at him. "You look fabulous!" He looked better than she'd ever seen him, and they were already having a good time.

"We look very grown up, don't we?" Fiona said as they sat down at their table at 21. It was one of her favorite restaurants in New York, and his too, they'd discovered, so they had decided to have dinner there the first night. And he was planning to surprise her on the second with dinner at La Grenouille, which was about as elegant as it got in New York. But this was a special trip, and he didn't plan to take her slumming, and he could afford it. He'd never been as excited about a trip, and she was the most terrific woman he'd ever been out with. He was proud to be at her side. "So how did the interview go?" she asked, and he told her all about it, and knew he could trust her with some of the information that he had learned, without violating confidentiality. Much about the subject and his situation was already public. He had narrowly escaped going to prison and might still wind up there. And it had been Logan's hot story from the first. "Sounds like it's going to be a good one." She was impressed by what he did, and how well he did it, as much as he was with what she did. So far their relationship had been based on mutual respect and admiration.

They walked up Fifth Avenue after dinner, and went to the Sherry Netherland for a nightcap, and then they walked the three blocks back to their hotel. And as they walked into their suite, it suddenly hit her. She was spending the night with a man, and he could see the panic in her eyes.

"Take it easy, Fiona," he whispered to her as he kissed her. "Nothing bad or scary is going to happen. We don't have to do anything tonight." He felt like he really was on a honeymoon with a virgin bride.

"Why not?" she whispered, and he laughed. He was dying to rip her clothes off in response, but he forced himself to go slow, and no further than she wanted. They sat in the living room of the suite for a long time, kissing, and looking at the view from their windows in the dark. It was a very romantic scene, and he couldn't keep his hands off her as they lay making out on the couch. Fiona felt about sixteen, and he eighteen, and then finally he unzipped her dress and unhooked her bra, and she was taking his clothes off, and the next thing he knew they were both naked on the couch. He could see in the moonlight that she had a beautiful body. All the swimming she did, and the careful diet had paid off. She had the body of a young girl. And he looked just as athletic, as she ran her hands over his body, and suddenly she wasn't frightened or shy anymore, she was as comfortable with him as she was with him now everywhere else. She took him by the hand and led him into the bedroom, and his desire for her was plainly obvious as they fell onto the bed. And a moment later, they were making love as though they had known each other forever. It was perfect and just what each of them had hoped for, but he hadn't dared expect. He had been afraid that it would be awkward and she would be painfully shy. Instead, she turned out to be a lustful woman and not hesitant with him at all. They came together, and afterward, he lay panting and out of breath next to her with a broad grin.

"Fiona, you're fantastic! I think you're going to kill me. What do you mean, you're shy?"

"I haven't done this in a long time," she whispered, and then kissed him again.

"Mercy! Mercy!" he teased her, and she laughed, and then as they fooled around with each other, they wound up making love again, and it was even better. "Ohmigod," he said afterward, "when we go home, I'm never going to

let you out of bed. Maybe we should both retire." They laughed and talked late into the
night, and finally fell asleep with him cuddled
up behind her holding her in his arms. And
when he woke up the next morning, she was a
vision standing next to the bed, naked, with
her long lean body, smiling down at him, and
pleased by what she saw. He opened one eye,
saw her, and was instantly overwhelmed with
desire, and pulled her back into bed, made love
to her again, and then they went back to sleep
for another hour. And the next time, he woke
her up. He had promised her she could go shopping for at least an hour or two before the Yankees game. She wanted to go to Bergdorf's, and
he ordered room service while she showered
and dressed.

She came out wearing a white cotton dress
and flat shoes. She looked young and pretty
and fresh. It was a whole different look from
her business suits, and hair in a bun. She was
wearing her hair down the way he loved it, and
lipstick and blush.

"My God, how did I get so lucky?" he said,
looking at her. "You're beautiful, Fiona." He
leaned over to kiss her, and then he rushed off
to dress himself before he gave in to his desire

for her again. He could hardly keep his hands off her.

They walked to Bergdorf's, and he kept her company while she shopped. She bought two pairs of sexy shoes, a silk shirt for work, and a soft pink cashmere shawl, which was all they had time for, and then they walked back to the hotel to get their car and go to the game. The Yankees lost, but they had a great time anyway, and he bought her another hat, as a souvenir.

"I think I'm starting a collection," she said, looking happy, eating a hot dog, in her pretty white dress. It took twelve innings for the Yankees to lose, and they had a terrific time. And they kissed in the car on the way back.

"I'm going to have to straighten out your sister," he commented, as they watched the skyline of New York slide past the limousine. "She called you a vestal virgin, and is she wrong on that one." He looked at Fiona like a besotted young man.

"I'm just not a slut like she is." Fiona laughed. "She always got all the boys when we were kids, but she's older than I am, so she had more experience. And she's been working on it ever since." She had just slept with half of Italy, but she seemed to make friends wherever she went, men loved her, and she stayed friends with them forever. Fiona had always admired that about her. She had always been much more reserved.

"I definitely got the right sister," Logan told her, "but I'd love to work on that book with her. I think we'll try an article first."

"She's great to work with, very methodical and organized and always on time. I've written a couple of articles with her myself. They always turn out well." He could see that might be true.

They lay down on the bed when they got back to the hotel, and watched the news on TV. Fiona started to doze off after their long day and night, and he woke her in time to dress for dinner. And this time she stunned him with a sexy red dress that was even shorter, and black stiletto heels, and he was even more impressed by how she looked than the night before.

"Why don't you wear stuff like that more often?" he asked as they left the suite to go to the restaurant.

"Where?" She laughed at him. "To work? Or our favorite bar in Palo Alto? AT&T Park? Where am I going to wear something like this in San Francisco? I've been saving it for two years." And it was perfect for that night. Every man in the room looked at her when she walked into La Grenouille and not because they recognized her as the CEO of NTA. They had no idea who she was, she just looked elegant and sexy, and Logan whispered to her as they started dinner, "You look hot. I'm going to bring you to New York a lot if this is the way you dress here."

They had a fabulous meal at La Grenouille, and went back to the hotel and made love. They watched a movie on TV that they had both wanted to see but hadn't had time for, and then they made love again and finally fell asleep.

They had breakfast the next morning and went for a long walk in Central Park, around the model boat pond. They were both wearing jeans for the trip home. All of Fiona's pretty clothes were back in her suitcase, and when she looked at Logan as they sat on a park bench and watched the passersby, she saw something different about him.

"And what's that?" he asked when she told him, as he kissed her neck and put an arm around her.

"You look like you're mine," she whispered, and he smiled.

"I am. You own me forever after this weekend."

"Me too," she said with a long slow smile, and then they went back to the hotel, picked up their bags, went to the airport, and flew home. Fiona slept most of the way back, with her head on Logan's shoulder. She was tired and relaxed and totally at ease with him now. It had been the best weekend of her life. And when he dropped her off at home that night, he looked into the eyes of a woman, not a CEO.

"Why don't you stay?" she asked him, and he hesitated. He didn't want to push his luck or intrude on her real life, the night before she had to go to work.

"Are you sure?"

"Yes, I am." She showed him where everything was, and he kept her company while she unpacked. And she grinned when she saw him in her bed. "Now there's a gorgeous sight," she said, and they both laughed. They brought their New York romance home to Portola Valley, and afterward they swam naked in her pool. She liked that he had stayed with her. She would have been lonely if he hadn't, after being with him in New York.

"You're not sick of me yet?" he asked her as they dried off and walked back into the house, and stopped in the kitchen for a snack, discussing the news and stock market trends and what they meant to the economy. "I like this," he said, as they went back to bed, and this time slept until her alarm went off at six o'clock.

He made her a breakfast of scrambled eggs, toast, and coffee, and he smiled broadly when she appeared in the kitchen, in a dark gray pantsuit with a pale gray silk blouse and her hair in the tight bun she wore to work. She looked very different than the private side of her he knew now. But he loved her this way too.

"I love you," he said, as he leaned over and kissed her, and she grinned as she took a sip of the coffee and grabbed **The Wall Street Journal.** She liked getting to her office early, so she could get a head start on her day, and he did too.

"I love you too," she said, smiling over the paper at him. She handed him **The New York Times,** and half an hour later, they both left for work.

Chapter 25

On Labor Day weekend, Mark flew out from New York to see his mother. He had just gotten back from Africa, and Fiona wanted to see him before he started school. His girlfriend was on duty at the hospital, so as usual he came alone. And he was startled when he discovered that his mother had a man staying there for the weekend.

"When did that happen?" he asked his sister when he saw her in the kitchen.

"This summer," Alyssa said, with a knowing look. "Don't get all uptight about it, he's nice. And he's crazy about her." It was obvious that Alyssa approved.

"I never thought we'd see that around here." Mark wasn't sure how he felt about it yet, and he wanted to reserve judgment till he talked to him for a while. He was very protective of their mother.

"Neither did I, but it seems to work. And he kind of disappears when Mom and I want to spend time together." Mark listened and nodded, and sat down next to Logan when he went out to the pool. They talked about Africa for a while, and Logan told him about his time with Mandela. Mark was visibly impressed, particularly that Logan didn't brag about it, he just said that it had been the most interesting, humbling experience of his life. And it was Fiona who casually mentioned that he had gotten the Pulitzer for the series of interviews. He immediately rose in her son's esteem.

And Jillian joined them on Saturday for lunch. She brought a stack of papers with her, spread them out on the table at the pool, and told Logan she had brought him the research she promised, and they spent an hour going over it together.

They all had dinner together that night, and they laughed a lot, which seemed to be the hallmark of Logan's relationship with Fiona. And the next day he took Fiona and her children to the baseball game. He had gotten two extra seats, and Logan sat with Mark, since they both knew what was going on, and the two women didn't. The Giants won again, and much to Logan's delight, the World Series was almost a sure thing. He was happy to discover that Mark was a fan too. And on Monday, Logan left them alone so they could spend time as a family together. He didn't want to intrude, and he wanted to go back to his place in the city to work on the material Jillian had shared with him.

"I like your new friend, Mom," Mark conceded over breakfast after Logan left.

"Yeah, me too." Alyssa seconded the motion.

"So is it serious?" Mark asked with a look of mild concern.

"I'm not sure what 'serious' means at my age." She smiled at her children. "Do I like him? Yes, a lot. Do I love him? I think I do. It seems to work, and I think that's all we need to know for now. I'm not going to get married and have more children. You guys are it." They both looked pleased. "How's John doing, by the way?" she asked Alyssa. He had been spending all his time in Tahoe with his mother since his father's big announcement, and Fiona hadn't seen him since. Alyssa hadn't seen him much

either, although they talked and texted constantly. He said everyone was still very upset.

"They're moving to the city, to an apartment,"
Alyssa filled her in. "They haven't seen their
dad since it happened. No one wants to. They're
all pretty pissed." It was easy to see why, and
Fiona felt sorry for them. "Apparently, he isn't
going to marry the other woman now, but their
mom doesn't want him back."

"I don't blame her," Fiona said quietly. "Send
him my love when you talk to him," Fiona said.
"Tell him he's always welcome here."

Mark left for New York that night, on the
red-eye, and Alyssa was starting classes at Stanford that week. The Westons were moving
down from Tahoe after that weekend too, and
Lindsay had to start school.

The weekend in Tahoe went better than Liz
had expected. Tom had come up for the weekend, and her other two children were there too.
She told John that she missed Alyssa, and he
said that she was in Portola Valley with her
mom and brother that weekend.

"I'm sorry this has been such a screwed-up
summer," she said to all of them. But now that

the worst had happened, she felt strangely calm again. She had nothing more to fear. It had been the worst summer of her life, but they had survived it, and it was nice seeing her older son back in the fold again and at home more frequently. She had no idea when any of them were going to see their father, but that was between him and them, and she didn't want to be involved either way.

She had heard from John that Marshall and Ashley weren't getting married. Marshall had told him. And she wasn't surprised, since he had tried to get her back when he saw her at the house in Ross. She wondered if Ashley didn't want him either. She felt sorry for their children.

"When are you moving to the city, Mom?" Tom asked her over dinner.

"I don't know yet. I'm looking at a few places next week. I want to find something big enough so all of you can visit," she said, smiling at them. She still looked sad, but she was getting better, and Lindsay had been very sweet and helpful to her mother. They had been getting along better since Marshall had dropped the bomb on them. Lindsay had been surprisingly mature and supportive and had grown up overnight.

They knew, but didn't discuss, the fact that their father was moving out of the house in Ross that weekend, and no one seemed to know where he'd be staying. John thought maybe the Four Seasons in Palo Alto, but he wasn't sure, and Marshall had said he was putting whatever he was taking into storage. And he had submitted a list of what he wanted to keep for her approval.

The kids went waterskiing several times over the weekend, and Liz made an effort not to complain about it or act too worried. She was just glad that they were home, and she knew Tom was responsible, and she trusted both boys with the boat, as long as they didn't let Lindsay drive it.

Liz still felt tired all the time, and as though she had been in a terrible accident, but slowly, day by day, she was getting better. She tried not to think of Marshall, and she never mentioned his name. He had become a taboo subject.

She stood on the dock, on the last day of the summer, before they drove back to the city, and she looked out at the lake. It was already chilly, and she knew that she would always remember that this was where Marshall had told her about the girl in L.A., their two children, and that he was divorcing her. She was going to sell the house in Tahoe too, but she hadn't told the children yet. She thought maybe they'd rent a house somewhere else next summer. She never wanted to come back here again.

"Ready, Mom?" Tom called out to her. He had loaded up the car, and was driving her back to Ross with Lindsay, with all the things they had brought up over the summer. John had brought his own car to drive back to the city. He and Lindsay had a few weeks before they had to start school.

"We look like gypsies," she commented, as she got in, and realized she was smiling. It felt unfamiliar, and Tom smiled at her, and at his sister in the rearview mirror. He hadn't thought so for a while, but it looked like they were going to make it. Liz closed her eyes and put her head back against the seat as they drove away.

Geoff had driven Ashley and the twins to the Coral Casino in Santa Barbara for the day over the Labor Day weekend, and he was explaining to Kendall and Kezia that he and their mom had come here when they were kids, which made them giggle. Ashley had finally told him that week that she was ready to see him. It hadn't taken her long, but it had seemed like forever, to both of them. He rushed right over after they spoke.

"I was beginning to worry that I wasn't going to see you for another eighteen years," he teased her. She looked the same as when he'd first gotten back to L.A., but she was quiet, and he noticed that she was thinner, but she was in good spirits. And he'd been fiercely busy working on the scripts he was writing for the TV show.

He didn't say anything to her about what had happened, he was just happy to see her, and he was surprised as they walked along the beach when he felt her slip her hand into his. He turned to look at her, and she smiled at him, and he suddenly knew that all was right with the world. He had been terrified that he'd blown it with her by kissing her when she was trying to figure things out with Marshall. And he felt guilty for confusing her. But she seemed to have figured it out anyway, and now she looked at peace. He could still see the pain in her eyes, and he knew she'd been grieving the loss, and mourning Marshall, but he could see that she was a lot better. He held her hand in his, and then they ran into the water, still holding hands, to play with the girls. He splashed them, and they splashed him back, and then Ashley splashed him, and he doused her, and everyone was squealing and laughing and splashing, and Ashley's halo of blond curls was soaking wet, and then suddenly he bumped into her and looked into her eyes as they stood close to each other.

"I missed you," he said to her.

"Yeah, me too," she admitted with a grin, and then she pulled him into the surf with her, and he was soaking wet, as Kendall and Kezia laughed at them from the beach.

And when they drove back to L.A. that night, they all agreed it had been a very good Labor Day. Geoff looked at Ashley when she said it, and she smiled a long, slow smile at him.

Chapter 26

The meeting got under way as soon as Marshall walked into the room. He looked dignified and serious, and he was wearing a dark suit. There were three men at the conference table, across from him, from a company in Boston that was not quite as large as UPI, but very close, and its growth rate had been remarkable in the past two years. It was well on its way to becoming the largest corporation in the country and outstripping all its competitors. And all it needed now was a powerful leader at its helm. And everyone at its base in Boston had agreed that Marshall Weston was the one. They had no idea if he would consider leaving UPI, and they doubted it after fifteen years, but they had come to California to try and convince him to do it. And he was listening raptly to what they said. It was their second meeting in two days, and they were going back to Boston that night.

Marshall hadn't committed to anything yet, but he was interested in what they had to say. In order for him to make the move, they would have to make it worth his while in every possible way—stock options, signing bonus, shares in the company, and every possible advantage and perk he could get. He had a sweet deal at UPI, and loyalty to the company, but like anyone else in his position, he could be bought, and Boston Technology was doing everything it could.

"Well, gentlemen, it's an interesting proposal," he said noncommittally, but they could tell they hadn't hit the high note for him yet. They were disappointed, but they had a few more aces up their sleeve, which they had saved for last. Just before the meeting ended, the head of their search committee who was a member of their board slipped a piece of paper across the table with a neatly typed list. He had been authorized to make the final offer. A private plane for Marshall's use at all times. An additional ten million a year, and two hundred million dollars of stock that he could sell at any time. An additional three hundred million in five years, from the day he signed on, regardless of their profits. They were that sure of what he could do. It amounted to half a billion dollars if he stayed with them for five years. Marshall read the piece of paper, smiled, stood up, and stuck his hand across the table. "You have a deal." He was beaming, and so were they. It was the best offer he had ever seen, and it was going to make history in the field. They agreed to keep the terms and conditions of it confidential, and no announcement was to be made until he resigned from UPI and notified the board, out of courtesy to them. Everyone concurred, and the deal was struck.

Marshall left the conference room of the neutral location they had chosen, soon to be a very, very rich man, and he was no pauper now.

He strode out of the building to the waiting limousine he had hired for the occasion, not wanting to use his own driver, and went back to his office at UPI. It was a perfect end to what had been an unpleasant summer, and just the way he wanted to leave UPI. Ever since the threatened sexual harassment suit, and their blackmail over Ashley, he had wanted to leave. He might have felt differently if things had worked out with her, or if it had been salvage-able with Liz, but he had no ties here now. His children were grown and almost on their own now. His family had been shattered by the di-vorce. He was sure the kids would calm down eventually and come to their senses. He had gone to Malibu to see the twins once, and he was going to see them at Christmas for a few days, and take them to Hawaii. It would be eas-ier for him to see more of them when they were older, but right now he knew they were in good hands with Ashley, and he had important things to do. And he wanted no contact with their mother, nor with Liz. He had burned his bridges behind him, and he was a free man. Free to take the best offer, and go wherever he chose. And Boston Technology was one of the most exciting young companies in the country. He was ready for a change and new frontiers. And they had suitably acknowledged what he had to offer them and were willing to reward him commensurately, according to his worth. Half a billion dollars within five years suited him just fine. In addition, they had offered him an astronomical salary, which they had just in-creased, and bonuses from profits, which he could multiply exponentially every year. He was sure that in five years, or at worst ten, he'd have a billion in the bank. It more than compensated him for the headaches he had had in recent months. They wanted him in Boston by October 15, which worked well for him too. It wasn't a long notice for UPI, but it was reasonable enough, and all he felt they deserved. And his loyalty was no longer theirs. Boston Technology had won his heart, at the right price.

As the car drove him back to his office, he was a happy man.

Five days after Marshall's meeting with Boston Technology, Fiona spoke to Nathan Daniels after their board meeting. He was abuzz with the gossip he'd just heard that Marshall Weston was leaving UPI and had been lured away by BT for an astronomical price. The story had been confirmed by a friend of his at UPI. Apparently it was true. Nathan Daniels said that rumors were running rampant about the amount, which no one knew for sure. It was the hottest piece of news in the industry in years, maybe ever. And rare for Nathan to gossip, but he couldn't resist.

And Fiona could hardly contain herself when

Logan walked in that night. He'd been spending several nights a week with her in Portola
Valley, and she loved coming home to him at
the end of her day. They cooked dinner together, and often took a swim in the pool before they went to bed. She liked his apartment
in the city too, in the Upper Haight, but it only
worked for her to go there on weekends. During the week, she needed to be close to work,
which Logan understood, so he drove from the
city several times a week to make life easier for
her, which he seemed to do on every front.

"You won't believe what I heard today," she
said excitedly the minute he came through the
door.

"Should I guess?" He looked interested and
amused. He loved coming home to her too.
Their sex life was fabulous, and everything
about their relationship seemed to work, even
better than he'd hoped.

"It's pure gossip I heard after our board meeting today, and I don't want to be your source,"
she reminded him. "But Marshall Weston is
leaving UPI, he's going to Boston Technology,
and they are paying him a fortune to do it, and
incredible perks. Possibly stock options he can
sell at any time without penalty, a plane, you

name it, they threw in everything but the kitchen sink and a sex change."

"Now that might do him some good! I can't think of a better candidate for that!" Logan laughed. By then everyone had heard about his antics with the woman in L.A., the two illegitimate children, and he had just filed for divorce. Someone at UPI had talked, and they were doing it again about his new job at BT. Logan had heard the rumors too, but hadn't said anything to her. His information came from a reliable source in the company, not just gossip.

"The plane is a seven fifty-seven, **of his own**." Her eyes were lit up with excitement, and Logan was amused. She was in the big leagues too. But all the CEOs in Silicon Valley seemed to keep track of each other and loved to gossip about the latest deals, some of which were astronomical.

"Baby, you should get a raise," he teased her.

"Damn right." She pretended to be outraged, but she was enjoying the gossip about Marshall. And she had a pretty sweet deal with NTA. She and her children were set for life, and Logan was pleased for her. It was all way out of his league, and just sounded like Monopoly money to him. Fiona never talked about what she made, and he didn't ask, nor did he care. She led a very modest life, with all the creature comforts she wanted and no desire for more. She was a sensible woman. "So what do you think?"

"I think he's a lucky guy. He's an asshole, but he seems to constantly fall up. It sounds like he screwed everyone over this summer, including his kids, both of the women in his life, caused a scandal for UPI with some bimbo, and nearly got himself into another one with the girl in L.A., and now BT is buying him for a gazillion dollars, and he comes out looking like a hero. You've got to hand it to the guy, he knows how to play the teams. He always comes out on top. With the big bucks anyway. As a human being, he's at the bottom of the food chain as far as I'm concerned." Fiona didn't think much of him now either, but it was fascinating to watch him manipulate his way to an even better situation. "And on top of it, he's getting out of Dodge because he screwed over everyone here, including his family. What a guy!"

"Are you going to write about it?" she asked with interest. "You can't use anything I said, although the gossip is everywhere that he's leaving and going to BT. I called a friend, and she's guessing he's getting close to two hundred million." Fiona didn't look jealous. She looked intrigued.

"Baby, I have a source I use for these kinds of stories. I've been talking to him all week, but I want to make sure my information is accurate before I run with the story." Logan didn't deal in gossip, he was a responsible journalist, and he wrote news.

They talked about Marshall Weston for the rest of the evening, and on a more human note, Fiona wondered how John was going to feel about his father moving to Boston. From what she'd heard, it was a done deal. But Alyssa said the children weren't seeing him anyway and didn't want to, in support of their mother. Fiona was curious, but she couldn't ask Alyssa, in case John knew nothing about it. The deal hadn't been announced yet, and supposedly wouldn't be for several weeks, until right before he left, so it didn't destabilize UPI before they found a replacement. But when it got out, it was going to be big news.

And then finally Logan and Fiona ran out of comments on the subject, relaxed in bed, and talked about other things, and they ended the evening as they almost always did, making love. Fiona hadn't been this happy in years, if ever.

Fiona heard nothing more concrete about Marshall at work for the next few days, and the hot news was another scandal where a well-known young entrepreneur was found to have stolen a hundred million dollars from a hedge fund, which was small potatoes these days, but a good story, and Logan wrote a big piece about that.

He spent Thursday night in the city, and said he was working on a deadline, but he was due back at her house in Portola Valley on Friday night. And on Friday morning, she opened **The Wall Street Journal,** alone over breakfast, and found herself staring at a photograph of Marshall Weston on the front page, with every detail she had told Logan the other night. It mentioned an undisclosed source at a high corporate level, and quoted everything she'd said, and more. She was livid. And his byline was on it. There was no denying what he'd done. He had used her as a source and broken his word to her. She would never trust him again. She didn't give a damn how wonderful he was in bed, he was a liar. She was the source at "a high corporate level." She wanted to kill him. He texted her before she left for work, and she didn't answer. She was steaming at her desk all day.

He called her at lunchtime, and she didn't take the call. She didn't tell him not to come that night, because she wanted to rip his head off personally, and tell him to get out. She had no intention of seeing him again after that. He was dangerous for her career and a dishonorable person who didn't keep his word. Trust was the most important thing in her life, and should have been in his. And if anyone traced his "undisclosed source" to her, she would look like a fool. And she couldn't afford anyone screwing with her reputation. He just had.

She was angry all day and waiting for him in her living room that night when he walked in. She had left work early to be there, and as soon as he arrived, and saw the look on her face, he knew instantly that something was very wrong. As he came through the door, she threw the paper at him.

"What's that about?" he said, with a look of surprise. "I tried to call you all day, and you wouldn't take my calls." Now he understood why.

"I wanted to tell you to your face what a lowlife I think you are. And what a little worm. You made a promise to me, you gave me your word that you would never use me to get infor-

mation, as a source, and you just did!" She
pointed to the copy of **The Wall Street Journal**
on the floor that she had thrown at him, with
Marshall Weston on the front page.

Logan's face grew hard, and he was shocked.
"You told me your 'gossip,' but I didn't run anything on it. I waited until I got it from the
source I always use. They told me everything
you did and more. I didn't use a word of what
you told me, Fiona. I wouldn't do that. I always
keep my word. I got everything you told me,
from my source, and more. I don't take information from amateurs, Fiona. I use pros." He
looked both angry and hurt, and both their
voices were raised. Fiona was at fever pitch.

"You told me less than half of what I got from
my usual source. I don't deal in backstairs gossip, I use the real deal. And as a source, you're
not it. You're smart and you're discreet, and I
wouldn't screw you over like that. I happen to
love you, and what's more, I respect you. Or at
least I did until now. So don't go accusing me
of what you don't know about. I have only one
interest in you, and that's as the woman I love,
whom I make love to, and care about. I may
gossip with you. But believe me, baby, you're no
source for a guy like me." And with that, he

slammed the door and walked out, and she wanted to throw something at him, but she had nothing at hand. And she didn't believe what he'd said. He had used her every word. She read the article again, and there was a lot more in it, but he had used everything she had told him, every word. And her eyes nearly fell out of her head when she saw that Marshall Weston was due to get half a billion dollars within five years. That was sick. And the guy was a prick. And so was Logan Smith, as far as she was concerned.

She stormed around her house that night, slamming doors and opening closets. She was happy that she'd never let him move in, although they'd discussed it as an eventual possibility, but she would have thrown him out now. She did laundry that night and did it too hot and fried it. She put dinner in the microwave and burned it. She got in the bath and ran it too hot. She thought of sending him an e-mail to confirm what an asshole he was, and she didn't, and she didn't hear from him either, not a word of apology or even a text, and she didn't care. She would never forgive him for breaking his word, and violating her trust. She suddenly realized that she was no better than Harding Williams, who'd been sleeping with a journalist and told her confidential information. Now she had done almost the same thing. The only difference was that she wasn't married and cheating, and she hadn't divulged the secrets of her own company, but she passed along gossip, and in her opinion, what Logan had done was worse. He had used her as an "undisclosed source," no matter how hotly he denied it, and broken his word to her.

She lay awake thinking about it all night and was even angrier in the morning, at him and herself. She was sorry she'd ever gotten involved with him at all. She had a tennis date with Jillian, and she wanted to cancel it, but decided to go after all. She got out of her car at the tennis courts looking like a storm cloud, and her sister winced.

"Oh dear, it doesn't look like a good day. Something wrong?"

"I'm fine," Fiona said, and headed for the court. She opened with a serve that nearly took her sister's head off, and Jillian jumped back.

"Jesus Christ! What happened to you? Are we at war?"

"No, I'm just pissed," Fiona admitted, and served again, almost as hard.

"Lovers' quarrel?" Jillian asked her.

"It's over. I don't want to talk about it. He's an asshole."

"I'm sorry to hear it. Anything I can do to help?" Jillian liked Logan, and she hoped the rift would only be temporary. But Fiona looked homicidal. Jillian hadn't seen her sister in a temper like that in years. She won the tennis game, but at what price glory.

They stopped to talk for a few minutes afterward. "He used me as a source," Fiona finally told her. "He gave me his word in the beginning that he never would, and he did."

"Are you sure?" Jillian looked surprised. "With all due respect, the guy is a pro. He probably has better snitches in his pocket than you."

"No, it was me," Fiona said, and suddenly looked depressed. "And I like him too. I even love him, that's the bitch of it. But I won't go back to him. It's over. I won't be with a guy I can't trust. Besides, it's too dangerous for me if he's going to quote me over breakfast."

"I'm really sorry," Jillian said. She felt bad for her. Beneath the rage, Fiona looked so disappointed. It broke Jillian's heart to see it, and Logan seemed like such a great guy, but a reporter was a reporter, and, in her experience, they weren't people you could trust. Occupational hazard.

Fiona left a few minutes later and went back to her house. She found Logan sitting outside, although she had given him a key. He handed it to her as she walked by him.

"I came to give you back the key," he said tersely. And he looked as grim as she did. "And this," he said, handing her an envelope. "I want you to know that I've never divulged a source in my life. Ever. I don't do that. I protect my sources, but I wanted to show you something, because I'm not going to have you think I break my word. I don't. The material I got from my source is in there. I wanted you to see it. I gave you what he sent me, and I blacked out his name because I won't betray a source even to you. But you can see what he sent me, and how thorough it is. I pay him a bundle to leak information to me, and it's worth every penny I pay him."

"Isn't that illegal?" she asked him coldly.

"Maybe. But that's how it works. It's how I make my living, and how he beefs up his. It's a system that works. So thanks anyway," he said, turned on his heel, and left. She watched him drive away, and she was still holding the envelope when she walked inside and sat down at the kitchen table. She opened it and found an e-mail Logan had printed up, from someone at UPI. The name was blacked out, but it was from corporate offices, which was shocking in itself. She read the e-mail, and everything he had used in the article was in there, almost verbatim. The source at UPI had spilled his guts and told Logan everything he knew. Everything she had said to him was there too, and infinitely more. What she could see from reading it was that Logan had told her the truth. He hadn't lied or broken his word. He hadn't used her as a source. He had waited and gotten the whole story from the very indiscreet executive of UPI. And as she read it, Fiona felt sick. She didn't know what to do as she sat there. She tore the printed e-mail into tiny pieces and threw it in the garbage. She thought of sending him an e-mail or a text, but she felt stupid. She had been wrong, and had accused him of something he didn't do. She owed him an apology. Even if they never saw each other again after that, she had to at least tell him she was sorry for accusing him of betraying her. He hadn't.

She picked up her purse, and went out to her car, and drove to the city. She got to his apartment and rang the bell, and he wasn't there, so she sat down on the stoop and waited. Two hours later she saw him coming down the street, carrying groceries, and he saw her before he got there. When he got to her, he could see that she wasn't angry anymore. She looked deeply apologetic, and was near tears.

"I'm sorry. I shouldn't have said those terrible things to you. I thought you used me." Her eyes were full of the sorrow she felt for having accused him, and he looked very hurt.

"I wouldn't do that to you, Fiona. I gave you my word. That's sacred to me. And so are you." He looked sad as he said it and put the groceries down on the front step. "I would never break my word to you." And as he said it, he held his arms out to her, ready to forgive her. And she flew into them, ready to do the same. It was their first big fight, and they had come through it battered and bloodied, but still loving each other. And then he pulled away and looked down at her. "You called me a lowlife and a worm," he said, and he was laughing.

"I'm sorry. I shouldn't have said that." She looked sheepish and embarrassed.

"I've been called a lot worse. That's pretty tame. Do you want to come up? I was going to cook dinner." She followed him upstairs, and they made dinner together and talked about his source at UPI. She was still shocked at what was written to Logan in the e-mail.

"How could he do something like that? He completely violated his position!"

"People do. That's how I do what I do. People talk. Some of my best sources are people in high positions."

"We fired Harding Williams for that. Well, we let him resign. He was our boardroom leak."

"I knew you fired him, or squeezed him out! I never believed that bullshit about 'ill health.' " He was grinning. But the story wasn't interesting enough to pursue. That had been way at the beginning, after the first time she had lunch with him, and he had called her the day after Harding had resigned as chairman. "You lied to me." He laughed. "You're a lousy source, Fiona. I'd never use you," he said seriously.

"I know that now. I'm sorry."

They slept in his bed that night, and went back to Portola in the morning. Jillian called her that night to see how she was, and she said that she was fine, and she and Logan were cooking dinner.

"Ahh . . . so you two made up?" She sounded pleased to hear it.

"Yeah. I was wrong. He didn't use me as a source. He had a much better one."

"I'm glad to hear it. And don't ever play with

me again after you have a fight with him. You damn near killed me. One of your serves nearly took my head off."

"I'm sorry." Fiona laughed. They hung up, and Fiona went back to the kitchen to help Logan with dinner. "That was Jillian. I was so mad, I beat her at tennis yesterday." He smiled and handed her a glass of wine. "What's for dinner?" He had brought his groceries from the city, and had been busy at the stove without her.

"Crow," he said. "I made you an extra big serving." She laughed, set down the glass of wine, and put her arms around him, and he kissed her. "I love you, Fiona, even if you called me a worm and a lowlife. I'll have to think of a suitable punishment for that. But I have another idea first." He turned off the stove, and she had the same idea as she followed him to her bedroom. The fight was over. They both won, particularly in bed.

Chapter 27

Marshall went through security at the San Francisco airport and thought that it was the last time he would ever have to do that. His new plane was being delivered to him as soon as he got to Boston. This was the last commercial flight he'd have to take, and he knew he wouldn't miss it. He boarded the plane with the rest of the first-class passengers on the flight to Boston. He was wearing a suit and carrying an overcoat, and the flight crew had already been advised of who he was, and greeted him accordingly, as soon as he stepped on the plane.

There was a young woman in the seat next to him, and she noticed immediately the flight attendants making a fuss over him. They offered him a glass of champagne, which he declined, and hung up his coat for him, and he settled into the seat next to her and discreetly looked her over. She looked to be in her mid-twenties, and she was wearing a Balenciaga jacket and jeans and high heels with red soles. She was a pretty girl, and he commented lightly when they took off that he usually sat next to the air marshal, and this must be his lucky day to be sitting next to her instead. She laughed and put down the magazine she'd been reading. She said she was going to Boston to visit her mother, who lived there.

"So do I. Or I will be." He smiled at her again. "I'm moving there for a new job," he said modestly, but she already knew he was someone important. His suit was impeccably cut, and his shoes looked expensive and were perfectly shined. His haircut was flawless, and he was wearing a gold watch. She didn't know who he was, but everything about him exuded power and success. "How long will you be in Boston?" he asked her, as they settled into their seats for the flight, and he was suddenly a little less unhappy to be flying commercial. It had given him the chance to meet her.

"I don't know yet. A few weeks. Maybe longer. I might look for a job there." She was vague and a little shy, and she realized that he was about the age of her father. But everything about Marshall was exciting. He had the vitality of a young man, enhanced by his self-assurance and charm.

"What kind of work do you do?" he asked her.

"I used to model. I've been a personal assistant for the last year. I've been thinking about going to art school." She was all over the map, but Marshall didn't care. She had long dark hair that framed her face and hung down her back. She was a very pretty girl, and she looked at him with wide eyes. "What do you do?" she asked innocently.

"I run a company," he said, smiling at her, as she moved a little closer to him, without even realizing that she had. He could see the delicate sweep of her white throat, and the shadow of a breast and a lacy bra inside the Balenciaga jacket she had left partially unbuttoned.

"That must be exciting," she said, smiling at him.

"Sometimes," he acknowledged, wondering what it would be like to kiss her. It was more exciting knowing that he could have her if he wanted, or any woman on the plane once they knew who he was, what he did for a living, and how much they paid him to do it. It was like shooting fish in a barrel. It was so easy.

He talked to her for a while, and then he closed his eyes and slept, and when he woke up, she was watching a movie. He gazed at her for a while, and then with the slightest gesture, as though by accident, he touched her hand, and she turned and smiled at him, and took her earphones off.

"I'd love to see you in Boston," he said softly. "Maybe we could have dinner sometime."

"I'd like that very much," she said, feeling breathless. And a few minutes later she handed him her mother's number on a slip of paper, and her cell phone number. He nodded and slipped it in his pocket.

"I'll call you tomorrow," he promised. "Would you like a ride into town?" he asked her as an afterthought, and she nodded, wide-eyed again. "I have a car and driver waiting."

"I was going to take a cab."

"You don't have to do that. I'll drop you off on my way. I'm staying at the Ritz Carlton." He gave her his card then with his cell phone number on it. And she put it in her purse and went back to watching the movie.

They talked while they were having dinner,

and when they landed, she followed him off the plane. It happened just the way he had expected. He helped her with her bags at the baggage claim, and his driver took them from her. And moments later they sped away, and she had stars in her eyes as she looked at him. He was the most exciting man she'd ever met. And to Marshall, she was just another pretty girl, easy prey, and a nice way to begin his life in Boston.

She thanked him profusely when he dropped her off at a nice house in Beacon Hill. She was a girl from a good family with a little money. She would be just right for the beginning, and maybe for a while. He would call her, and take her to dinner. He called her on her cell phone before he got to the hotel.

"I miss you already, Sandy," he said into the phone, and he could hear the catch in her voice when she answered.

"Thank you, Marshall." She sounded as though she had won the lottery, and she thought she had, for a man as impressive looking as he was to even notice her and want to take her out.

"See you tomorrow night?"

"I'd love that." She sounded as though she meant it.

"I'll pick you up at seven-thirty," he promised. And after dinner, they would go to his
hotel. And when she woke up in the morning,
she wouldn't believe that it had happened, that
a man like him wanted her. It was so easy to
begin it, and much harder to end it, but he
didn't have to worry about that now. It was all
a new beginning. Boston, the job, the girl, his
new plane. He smiled to himself as they arrived
at the hotel. The manager was waiting outside,
and he was treated like royalty. Boston Technology had reserved the penthouse suite for
him, and when he looked around, he knew it
was exactly what he deserved. And he could already imagine the girl from the plane in it.
Sandy. It was perfect. And all he needed for
now. His new life had just begun.

Liz had reserved the freight elevator for four
hours on Saturday, so she and Lindsay and the
boys could bring the rest of her boxes into the
apartment in the city. The movers had been
there for two days with her new furniture, and
everything looked just the way she wanted. She
had used a decorator to help her, and there were
rooms for Lindsay and both boys, for whenever

they came home. The building was on Nob Hill with a view of Huntington Park, the Fairmont, and Grace Cathedral, and from her bedroom, there was a view of Alcatraz and the bay. And as she and the boys carried in the last of her clothes from the house in Ross, they set them down in her large, sunny new bedroom. And Liz smiled as she looked around her.

Her children were there, and everything in the apartment was new. She had sold everything else at auction.

"Wow, it looks great, Mom," John said as he looked around. It was the first time he had seen the new apartment. And they were there in time for the holidays. It was a fresh start for his mom and Lindsay. She had been on good behavior since the summer, and she and her mother were actually getting along. She loved her new school in the city and was getting decent grades. She had been commuting since September. And Lindsay loved the idea of living in the city, and so did Liz. Liz had gotten a new haircut and looked better than ever. And she was talking about volunteering at a legal project for the homeless. She had done everything she could to embark on a fresh start.

John finished unpacking in his new room and told his mother that Alyssa was coming over that afternoon to see them. And Lindsay groaned as he said it.

"Crap. I promised Mom I'd do my Berkeley application today. I'd rather hang out with you two."

"Berkeley application?" he teased her. "What happened to your gap year?"

"I guess I'll just settle for getting a tattoo." She didn't have the heart to upset her mother after everything their father had done. And they were all relieved to know that he had moved to Boston the month before. None of them had seen him before he left, and had no plans to anytime soon. He had already told them he wouldn't be there for Christmas, he was going to Aspen. And if they wanted to see him, they'd have to come to Boston, which they didn't intend to do. They didn't want to leave their mother alone over the holidays, and had even less desire to see him.

Tom liked his new room too, although he wouldn't be there often. He had his own apartment in Berkeley, but it was nice to feel welcome. And he brought in the last boxes and released the elevator when he was through.

"Thanks, guys, for helping me," Liz said with a broad smile. "It looks good, doesn't it? What do you all want for dinner?" There was a restaurant across the street at the Huntington Hotel, which she and Lindsay had already tried, and an assortment of places at the Fairmont, a block away. And they'd been ordering takeout on most nights since they had started moving in two weeks before. Lindsay had given up being a vegan, which was a lot simpler. And Liz hadn't cooked dinner since the summer, and wasn't sure she would again. Her days of slavery were over, waiting for Marshall to come home every night, and waiting on him hand and foot. She didn't miss it. Or him. It was as though he had been erased from her life. And she was doing all she could to wipe Marshall out of her mind and heart.

While Liz was unpacking boxes, Alyssa dropped by as she had promised, and she loved everything she saw. She thought it was prettier than their house in Ross, and she was happy to see John's mother looking better. There was a spark in her eyes again.

In the end, they ordered pizza and Chinese takeout, and sat in the kitchen. Everyone was talking and laughing, as Liz watched them. She was smiling, life felt good again, they had landed safely, and she was home.

The same weekend that Alyssa visited John at the Westons' new apartment on Nob Hill in the city, Logan was doing a reverse commute, and brought a car full of his belongings from his apartment in the Upper Haight to Fiona's house in Portola Valley. Fiona had assigned him half of one closet, and he was trying to fit everything into the allotted space, without success.

"That's it? That's all I get?" he asked her with a disgruntled look. "You can't do better than that, in this whole house?"

"That's it!" she said, not budging an inch, and suddenly he burst out laughing. He had just remembered what she had said in the beginning. She had warned him, and he had forgotten.

"Now, I remember," he said, sitting on the floor, surrounded by his running shoes, of which he had brought too many, but he thought he'd use them here. "You told me you had all the closets and you liked it that way. As I recall, that was one of your main reasons for not wanting a relationship. I got your body. Now I want your closets."

"You can't have both," she said, laughing with him, as she sat down on the floor next to him with all his shoes.

"You should have fallen in love with a nudist. Can we negotiate this? We need closet counseling," he said as he pulled her down on the floor with him and lay beside her. He still wondered how he'd gotten so lucky, to find a woman like her. She was a real woman, and had become his best friend as well as his lover, even if she was a closet hog.

"Why don't you give away your clothes," she suggested, "and we can stay in bed all the time? We never get out of bed anyway. You don't need running shoes."

"Good point." The honeymoon feeling that had started in New York hadn't worn off yet, for either of them. They were happy together, and everything in their lives seemed to work better now that they were a couple. He had been thinking about marriage lately, but Fiona didn't seem to care either way, and he didn't want to spoil what they had. But he was glad they'd be living together now, if only she would give him someplace to put his clothes.

She finally agreed to give him a few more feet of floor space, and to put some of her older business suits downstairs.

"If you were a stripper or a cocktail waitress, your work clothes wouldn't take up so much room," he pointed out to her. "Maybe you should stop wearing suits to work." He liked her better in the clothes she wore at home or when they went out, but she had an image to maintain at work, and she was strict about it. He had finally gotten her to wear the red dress he loved, that she had worn in New York, to dinner in the city, but she had complained all night about feeling overdressed. And they were planning another trip to New York. She had a meeting there, and had invited Logan to come along. "Does that make me a corporate boyfriend?" he asked her. "Like a corporate wife. Is that what I am?" He didn't have a title. What they were to each other didn't seem to have a name, but the one thing that was clear to both of them was what he had hoped in the beginning. Whatever it was, it worked.

Geoff took Ashley and the girls to the Biltmore in Santa Barbara for one of the last warm weekends in October. The weather was perfect, they went to the Coral Casino and built sandcastles on the beach. It reminded Geoff and Ashley of their childhood, when they had done the same things. And now they were doing them with Kendall and Kezia. It was hard to believe that their own childhood was nearly twenty years ago.

Ashley was painting again, furiously, for a gallery show in the spring and Geoff's TV show was going well. The ratings were great, and his scripts were being well received. It was a huge amount of work, but he enjoyed it. He was spending more time in Malibu than West Hollywood. And he loved taking them away on weekends whenever he could.

"Why don't we move here?" he asked her as they walked down the beach, with the twins running far ahead, and she looked surprised at the idea. "I don't have to go to the office every day. I could work here, and so could you. Why don't we rent a house here and try it for six months?" Ashley liked the suggestion, she had never thought of it before.

"I like the thought of something new," she said, smiling up at him. The house in Malibu felt haunted to her. She had too many memories of Marshall there. And she wanted a new life with Geoff, and a new place, and they had happy memories here.

"Why don't we look at some houses tomorrow before we go back?" he suggested, and she nodded, as she heard the sound of hoofbeats in the sand behind them, and they both turned to see a rider on a white horse gallop by. And they both thought of the same thing at the same time. "You know what that means, don't you?" he asked her with a look of mischief in his eye.

"No. What?" she asked innocently.

"It's good luck. Remember what happened the last time we saw a white horse on the beach?" And before she could answer, he kissed her, just as he had the first time, when she was twelve. "I love you, Ash," he said after the kiss.

"I love you too," she whispered. He kissed her again then, as the girls doubled back to find them. Ashley and Geoff had lagged too far behind.

"I want to be with you and the girls forever," he said quietly. "Will you marry me?" he asked, before the twins could reach them, and she smiled at him, and looked just the way she had as a girl.

"Yes." He wanted to have more children with

her, and adopt the ones she had, if Marshall would let him. And if not, he was their father now in all the ways that mattered. Marshall was making no effort to stay in regular contact with them and was only interested in his own life and work. She couldn't imagine him seeing them more than once or twice a year for a vacation now that he'd moved to Boston. And Ashley's only contact with him was through attorneys, on practical matters, which suited her just fine. Geoff and the girls were all she needed, and whatever other blessings came along later. She was grateful for what she had, and that Geoff had come back. He had come at the right time. She wouldn't have been ready for him before.

They looked at houses the next day, and found one that was perfect for them, within walking distance of the beach. They rented it for a year, and as they drove back to Malibu on Sunday afternoon, he thought of the question he had asked her on the beach, and her answer, and he smiled at her, as the girls chattered in the backseat.

"Don't forget that you said yes," he reminded her in case she had forgotten, or hadn't really meant it. But she had. And she remembered it as well as he did.

"What was that question again?" She teased him.

"I'll ask you again later, just so you don't forget. On bended knee if you like."

"That would be very nice," she said, and leaned over and kissed him. She had gotten her "happily ever after," after all.

About the Author

DANIELLE STEEL has been hailed as one of the world's most popular authors, with over 600 million copies of her novels sold. Her many international best sellers include **Winners, First Sight, Until the End of Time, The Sins of the Mother, Friends Forever, Betrayal, Hotel Vendôme,** and other highly acclaimed novels. She is also the author of **His Bright Light,** the story of her son Nick Traina's life and death; **A Gift of Hope,** a memoir of her work with the homeless; and **Pure Joy,** about the dogs she and her family have loved.

Visit the Danielle Steel website at
daniellesteel.com.

LIKE WHAT YOU'VE READ?

If you enjoyed this large print edition of
POWER PLAY,
here are a few of Danielle Steel's latest bestsellers
also available in large print.

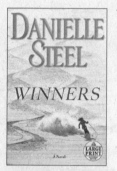

Winners
(paperback)
978-0-8041-2105-7
($28.00/$31.00C)

First Sight
(paperback)
978-0-385-36325-9
($28.00/30.00C)

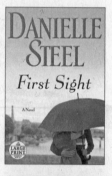

Until the End of Time
(paperback)
978-0-307-99091-4
($28.00/$30.00C)

The Sins of the Mother
(paperback)
978-0-307-99084-6
($28.00/29.95C)

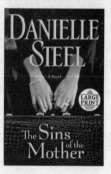

Large print books are available wherever books
are sold and at many local libraries.

All prices are subject to change. Check with your
local retailer for current pricing and availability.
For more information on these and other large print titles,
visit www.randomhouse.com/largeprint.